Praise for Laura Purcell

"There are ghosts, ghouls, and ghastly goings on aplenty in the tale of Agnes Darken. . . . There are some spine-chilling moments in this twisty tale, and fans of murder mystery and Gothic fiction will love getting lost in Agnes's and Pearl's spooky world."

—*Daily Mirror* (London)

"[*The Shape of Darkness* is] dripping with atmosphere with a corkscrew plot, Laura Purcell just gets better and better."
—Stacey Halls, author of *The Familiars* and *The Foundling*

"Purcell paints a colorful portrait of her tale's distant time and place and immerses the reader in an era when superstition was a tenacious thread in the social fabric that bound its people. Her tale of secret guilt and atoning for it through ancient customs will please fans of classic Gothic melodrama."

—*Publishers Weekly*

"Purcell excels at creating a spooky Gothic ambience . . . [*The House of Whispers* is] a dark and unsettling novel for lovers of *Rebecca* and *Jane Eyre*."

—*Kirkus Reviews*

"[*The Poison Thread*] is a well-wrought chiller."
—*The Wall Street Journal*

PENGUIN BOOKS

THE SHAPE OF DARKNESS

Laura Purcell worked in local government, the financial industry, and a Waterstones bookshop before becoming a full-time writer. She lives in Colchester, the oldest recorded town in England, with her husband, and is the author of *The Silent Companions*, *The Poison Thread*, and *The House of Whispers*.

THE
SHAPE OF
DARKNESS

—

LAURA PURCELL

PENGUIN BOOKS

PENGUIN BOOKS
An imprint of Penguin Random House LLC
penguinrandomhouse.com

First published in Great Britain by Raven Books,
an imprint of Bloomsbury Publishing Plc, 2021
Published in Penguin Books 2021

LIBRARY OF CONGRESS CATALOGING-IN-PUBLICATION DATA
Names: Purcell, Laura, author.
Title: The shape of darkness / Laura Purcell.
Description: First edition. | [New York] : Penguin Books, 2021.
Identifiers: LCCN 2021002147 (print) | LCCN 2021002148 (ebook) |
ISBN 9780143135548 (paperback) | ISBN 9780525507208 (ebook)
Subjects: LCSH: Paranormal fiction. | GSAFD: Suspense fiction.
Classification: LCC PR6116.U73 S53 2021 (print) |
LCC PR6116.U73 (ebook) | DDC 823/.92—dc23
LC record available at https://lccn.loc.gov/2021002147
LC ebook record available at https://lccn.loc.gov/2021002148

Printed in the United States of America
1st Printing

Set in Stempel Garamond LT Pro

'. . . we together called into being, a weird shadow which was neither of us, only an unshapen, un-formed thing . . . the ideas crossed each other as the lines of two wet drawings laid face to face become crossed, blotted, effaced and unrecognisable.'

Elizabeth d'Espérance, *Shadow Land or,*
Light from the Other Side

THE
SHAPE OF
DARKNESS

Chapter 1

It is the cocked hat that draws her to him: the way it arches above the barricade of toppers. Its golden edges end low to the brow and gild the face beneath.

He stands talking with half a dozen other gentlemen under the dying bonfire of Sydney Gardens's autumn foliage, impeding the passage of walkers like a clot in the blood. As he extends a hand, emphasising a point to his nearest companion, Agnes sees it: the perfect pose for a full-length silhouette.

She reaches for the scissors in her reticule but her fingers are cold, fumbling. By the time she has hold of the handles and the sable paper gripped, ready to walk through her hand, the man has already turned and replaced his arm at his side.

She will have to cut him from memory.

There is the familiar slip in her stomach, the tangle of breath within her breast. Hope refuses to die. Never will she see the dark blue coat of the Royal Navy without a wild belief that somehow, *somehow* . . .

But this man is not Montague. Even through her cataracts, Agnes can see enough of his features to dismiss that fantasy. If John Montague is still alive – and she has no guarantee of that – he will not be a slim, active man engaged in debate, but a seasoned sailor, even older than herself. Decades on deck will have weathered his skin and aged him beyond his years. There may be a paunch beneath his waistcoat, or a limp from a bullet wound. Her dashing lieutenant belongs only to the past.

She cuts the outline of his face in smooth, bold waves, sliding the paper between the pad of her thumb and the finger that still bears his ring.

The breeze picks up. Her paper flutters, objecting. It has grown damp on the walk and does not hold its form as it should, but Agnes persists.

Once she passes the neck, her work becomes easier. Bodies are a different language. Shoulders with epaulettes, the coattails, moving down to the breeches and the lead foot, always cut dead flat. This naval officer must be fresh home. He is not supposed to wear his uniform on furlough. It is a rare sighting, a gift; a glimpse, however tenuous, of a happier time.

Wind gusts. The trees cast their treasuries of gold and bronze down upon the men and an oak leaf, crisp and brown, sticks upright in the rim of the cocked hat. It would be a beautiful detail to include, if Agnes had not cut that shape already.

She moves on to the final curve, the one she must not rush, even though her knuckles are beginning to cramp and . . . there. The shade emerges from its background, triumphant. Another puff of wind snatches the waste sable paper and sends it, spiralling, into the leaden sky above.

Agnes frowns at her work, dissatisfied. She has overdone the nose and underplayed the chin. This is a nuance people rarely understand about her art: a shadow, an exact replica of the shade a person casts, possesses next to no likeness at all. It must be honed and exaggerated before they will recognise the profile as their own. But she does not have time to make changes. The group of gentlemen are taking their leave. Clouds pillow fast behind the limestone of the old Sydney Hotel.

For all her talent, Agnes cannot work in the rain. It is time to return home.

She plods these days, a legacy of the Accident. Or perhaps she is just getting old. Bath's streets seem harder to navigate, and the soles of her half-boots slip whenever there are cobbles underfoot. Umbrellas sprout, making the crossing at Pulteney

Bridge an ordeal of twice its usual bustle. Damp woollen coats press against her. The kennels run fast in the rain, carrying the odours of horse muck and sewage.

Surely it never used to be like this?

The Bath of Agnes's childhood was a city of palaces. People came for the cure, of course, but they were not all invalids in Merlin chairs back then; the fashionable paraded in the Pump Room by day and danced in the Assembly Rooms by night. There was always a play or a concert in some white stone mansion.

Now carbon deposits have stained the buildings, giving them a funeral aspect. Dirt bleeds into the river, into the sky. The soul of Bath has left and its body is decaying. Only the Somerset hills glow in the distance, preternaturally vivid.

A horsewhip cracks the air. Agnes pulls up short on the edge of the pavement, just in time. A great cart lumbers past, its wheels squeaking, and splashes her skirts.

By the time she has reached the abbey churchyard, the breath is grating painfully in her lungs. Really, it was foolish to wander as far as Sydney Gardens. Barely two years have passed since pneumonia nearly claimed her life. She had not been strong even before the fever, but when she became lucid again she noticed a profound physical change: her body felt like a stranger's, unwilling to obey her like it used to.

Take it slowly, Simon counsels her. But it seems, at times, that she has taken her whole life slowly: at the sedate pace of a minuet dance. A spell in the wing chair by the fire, reading *Varney the Vampire* with her nephew Cedric, will fix her. Illness might have left her frail, but she is not beaten yet.

The rain spits with malice. Mustering all of her energy, she launches herself across the churchyard and round the bulk of the abbey.

Her home cowers in the abbey's shadow, its walls discoloured by time and soot. Ivy-choked pillars support a portico above the front door. Magpies have taken to nesting here, although there is no sign of them at present. All day long they chitter and cackle, disturbing her work; mocking it, as others do, dismissing it as the vestige of a bygone age.

But to Agnes the black paper shapes in her windows still look as beautiful as ever. The conversation pieces she designed to lure the browsing customer: a group of ladies at tea, horses riding to hounds. Then there are the brighter ovals, painted in Etruscan red; spots of vivid colour on this dreary day.

She is not the only one to view her work with admiration. As she draws closer, she notices two men standing by her parlour window. One consults his pocket watch and then knocks at the front door. From his manner, it appears that he is not knocking for the first time.

Cannot Mamma hear? And where is Cedric – can he really be out playing, in weather like this? Shaking her head, she scurries forward, determined to reach the visitors before they turn away. A fine artist she will look – panting and half-drowned – but she cannot afford to lose even a whiff of business.

It is only as the clouds part, letting slip the tiniest ray of light, that she discerns the man rapping on her door is no usual visitor. Raindrops drip from the portico onto his tall, beaver hat.

The stovepipe hat of a policeman.

'Miss Darken! You see, Sergeant, I am a man of my word. I told you she would not venture far on a day like today.'

Before Agnes can gather her wits, she recognises Simon's voice; sees Simon's watery blue eyes reproaching her beneath the sodden brim of his hat.

Simon and a police officer, waiting on her.

'I . . . needed some air,' she explains. 'I turned back as soon as it started to rain.' She sounds guilty, like a child caught.

'Miss Darken, I'm Sergeant Redmayne.' The policeman possesses a granite slab of a face, unmarked by any trace of a smile. He tips his head forward and water cascades from his hat, wetting her feet.

Agnes represses a sigh. Manners seem to be declining faster than the city itself. 'And how may I help you, Sergeant?'

'It's a tad delicate, miss. Might I come inside?'

Simon clears his throat and fidgets with his collar. No doubt he is thinking the same as Agnes: that the sight of a policeman might set Mamma off on another of her strange turns.

The sergeant's eyes sharpen at their hesitation.

'If you must,' she says begrudgingly. 'Please excuse the mess. I have been working this morning. I did not expect . . .' she gestures at him, 'you.'

Fishing in her reticule, she produces a set of keys and clunks one awkwardly into the lock. She hopes the sergeant does not notice the tarnished brass of the letterbox, or the magpie droppings plastered on the door panels. Perhaps it is just as well he is not a customer, after all.

Agnes leads them in. No call answers the sound of her footsteps, or the slam of the door behind Simon, who enters last. Cautiously, she peers into the parlour – a small chamber dominated by the fireplace and an old, oaken grandfather clock that wheezes as it ticks. Captain Darken maintained vehemently, until his dying day, that the clock was made with wood from HMS *Victory*, but Agnes entertains her doubts.

A teacup remains on the side table where she left it, the dregs leaching into the white bone china. Nothing but ash lies in the throat of the fireplace.

Thankfully, Mamma is nowhere to be seen.

'Here you are.' She ushers the visitors in, ashamed of the dust and the paintbrushes dotted about the room. Even the profiles framed on the wall seem to avert their faces, refusing to look upon her clutter. 'Will this take long? Shall I boil water for tea?'

'That won't be necessary, Miss Darken.' Sergeant Redmayne sits heavily in the wing chair.

Agnes would rather change her clothes, stoke up the fire and take some refreshment before he relates whatever he has to tell, but the sergeant's manner is so grave, so dampening, she can do nothing but take a seat and remove her bonnet, waiting dumbly for his words.

'I called earlier, but you were out. Instead I met your physician, here.' He throws Simon a look that would fell a slighter man. 'Strange enough, he turned up again, just as I came back for a second try.'

'Fortuitous.' Simon smiles, but Agnes senses he is not altogether easy. He has not yet sat down.

'If you say so, Doctor. Look miss, I won't beat about the bush. You had a Mr Boyle come here for his portrait last Saturday, the twenty-third?'

'Not quite a portrait, Sergeant. I did some preliminary sketches. He wants the shade painted onto glass and bronzed with detail for his wife. A remembrance for the anniversary of their wedding day, if I recall.' Agnes twists the limp ribbons on her bonnet. 'But . . . how do you know of this?'

'Mr Boyle wrote the appointment in his engagement diary. *Darken, two o'clock.*'

'Yes, that was about the time . . .'

She is at a loss. What has a police officer to do with her work? She tries to remember this Mr Boyle. An unassuming man, old-fashioned. Not much in the way of a profile, except for his plump lips. The kind of man her sister Constance would have scorned as a *fogram*.

'Is Mr Boyle in some kind of trouble?'

'You could say that, miss. He's dead.'

'*Dead!*'

Simon steps forward. 'Really, Sergeant, that is not the way to break news to a lady—'

But Sergeant Redmayne carries on regardless, his voice as devoid of emotion as his face. 'Murdered, in fact. Found the body in the Gravel Walk with the head smashed in. Looks like they did it with a mallet. No doubt the villain wanted to delay the identification of his victim for as long as possible.'

'Now look here . . .' Simon objects.

Agnes is grateful for his bulky presence, and the salts he waves beneath her nose. Their tang acts as a lash, keeping her upright.

'How hideous,' she gasps. 'Who would want to—'

'That's what we're trying to establish. Boyle had a dinner engagement after he saw you, at seven o'clock. Didn't keep it. But you can confirm he was here?'

Simon finally seats himself at her side. The sofa sags with his weight. Helplessly, her body topples in his direction, leaving her propped against him, shoulder to shoulder, like a house of cards. She rights herself.

'Yes,' she replies tentatively. 'Our business did not take long. One can sketch very quickly, you know . . .' To think that her eyes would have been amongst the last to see Mr Boyle alive! It is some consolation to think that she chronicled the lines of his face before they vanished. Or collapsed. A *mallet*, did the policeman say? 'We spent longer discussing the final product. I suppose he left me at . . . a quarter to three?'

Sergeant Redmayne nods. Not once, in the duration of their interview, has Agnes seen him blink. 'And how did he seem? Agitated? Preoccupied?'

Agnes tries to cast her mind back. Truth be told, Mr Boyle was a forgettable sort of man. Had she been overrun with sitters, as in the old days, she would scarcely have remembered him. As it is, she has an image of his face, turned to the left, captured for the last time on paper. No features, just pencil outlines. Already fading from memory. She had cut him a shade on black paper, to show him how it would look, before he opted for the paint.

'Oh,' she breathes on a downward note. 'Oh, no. He did not pay me.'

'What?'

'Mr Boyle was to pay upon collection of the glass painting. It is practically finished. All that work!'

The sergeant clicks his tongue, irritated. 'I can't see *that* as the greater of the two evils, miss. Some would say he has paid the ultimate price.'

'I do not mean to sound unfeeling. But one cannot eat pity, I cannot heat a house through the winter on pity. I daresay if the police station failed to pay your weekly salary—'

Simon's elbow nudges her. Perhaps she *is* being unreasonable. It is the shock. She is not herself.

'If we might return to how Mr Boyle appeared on the afternoon in question?'

The magpies shuffle in their nest, their feet going tack-tack on the roof.

'He was . . . ordinary. So far as a person unacquainted with him can judge. We spoke of his wife and the commission, I believe. Nothing more . . . He seemed perfectly in spirits. Oh, yes! He made a jest, about a silhouette of my sister. So I did not think him troubled in the least.'

Sergeant Redmayne nods again. 'I see. Well, perhaps if you do think of anything else, Miss Darken, you'll wait upon me? I'll leave my name and direction.'

He produces a calling card from his pocket and pushes it across the side table with his finger.

'Yes, yes I will.'

'You may have been the last person to see Mr Boyle alive. Except for the killer, of course. You'd oblige me by remaining in the city.'

She gasps a laugh. 'Wherever would I go?'

He shrugs and rises to his feet, leaving a watery mark on the wing chair. 'People go all sorts of places when the police start asking questions.'

It is Simon's turn to stand. 'I will answer for Miss Darken staying in Bath. Her health is not currently strong enough to permit travel in any case. Now,' he gestures to the door, 'we have distressed the lady enough for one day.' The grandfather clock whirrs, preparing to strike the hour. 'I would be happy to show you out, Sergeant.'

They are finally moving, finally shuffling through the door to the hallway, taking their hard voices and awful tidings with them.

Agnes lets herself fall full-length upon the sofa. Only now does she realise how cold she is, her teeth chattering uncontrollably. She should change out of these wretched, damp clothes, but she has no energy. Every part of her feels heavy.

By and by, Simon's hand lightly touches the back of her head. 'Forgive me, Miss Darken. I told that blasted fellow all this would make you ill again. Not that he heeded me. These newfangled police give false consequence to upstarts like him.'

'I would forgive his impertinence if he had not brought me such dreadful news.' She coughs. 'Poor Mr Boyle! My first customer in months!'

'Hush, now. Hush. You lie there. I will fix you something to drink.'

'Where is Cedric? Mamma? She must not hear of this—'

'No.' He pauses. 'All is . . . quiet upstairs.'

'Thank you, Simon.'

Exhausted, Agnes closes her eyes, but the lack of vision only heightens her aches and her pains. That burning in her chest. A drum pounding, deep in the sockets of her eyes. The sight of that policeman has brought the Accident back with a clarity she would not have supposed possible, after all these years.

The house stretches and pops. She sinks her face into a cushion, ignoring its demands.

When she returns to herself, there is a shawl draped over her. Flames caper in the fireplace. On the side table, a fresh cup of tea steams beside a slice of cake.

Simon sits watching her. He has removed his coat and rolled his shirtsleeves up his broad arms. His right hand nurses a glass containing a whisky-coloured liquid. Opiates, possibly.

'Tea first,' he instructs. 'Then a dose of this to help you sleep.'

Dear Simon. He has waited upon her like a hired hand – and she cannot even afford to pay him for the medicine.

'How is Mamma? Cedric will be expecting his supper, we always try to eat that together and read a story . . .'

Simon takes a deep breath. 'They are asleep.'

No light shines through the paper silhouettes tacked to the window panes; their shapes blend into the black of the night outside. It is far later than she had reckoned.

'I have kept you too long, Simon. You have better things to do. Other patients . . . and who will have fed your little dog?'

A thin smile. 'Morpheus will manage well enough without me. Come, drink your tea. I want to see you settled before I take my leave.'

Obediently, she reaches for the cup. The liquid is too hot, but she forces it down.

'Simon, if news of this murder gets out . . . and no doubt it will . . .' She takes another gulp. 'I worry it might lend a certain *notoriety* to my business.'

'There will be time enough to discuss that later.'

This is hardly comforting. Her mind teems with questions and worries – it would be a relief to talk them over with Simon, but she has known him for long enough to recognise the pro-fessional closure in his face. This man is no longer her ally but 'Dr Carfax,' who absolutely forbids excitement.

Instead she swallows the last of the tea, tasting nothing but heat, and takes a bite of dry cake. Simon hands her the opiates and she drinks them down as a bitter final course.

'Now you must go straight to bed.' He looks as if he could use a long sleep himself. In the firelight, his eyes are bloodshot. 'Promise me.'

'I will. But first let me see you out.'

She lights a candle and they leave the parlour together.

A chill breeze rushes in the moment she opens the front door, forcing her to cup a hand around the flame of the candle. The rain has stopped, but its metallic scent lingers. The street lamps cast sulphur pools on the pavements.

It is horrible to think of Simon venturing out there alone, with a murderer on the loose.

'Be careful, Simon. Walk quickly.'

He bows – a proper bow, one leg slightly behind the other. Even with his girth, he has more grace than the police sergeant.

'Until tomorrow, Miss Darken.'

Placing his hat upon his head, he turns. Agnes watches him walk away, his shape articulated against the light of the street lamp.

Always 'Miss Darken.' They have known each other since childhood; he is practically a brother to her, yet still there is this constraint between them.

Damp air sneaks around the abbey and touches her cheek. As the sound of Simon's footsteps die out, she shuts the door and bolts it.

The walls exhale.

Quietly, she begins to climb the stairs. *Straight to bed*, Simon said, but practice has taught her she has ten minutes, at least, before the opiates begin to drag.

She must look. Just once.

The doors to Mamma's and Cedric's bedchambers are closed. Neither of them makes a sound in their sleep. Avoiding the creaky floorboard, Agnes creeps past the threshold leading to her own cold bed and enters her studio.

It is the only place in the house where the air feels alive. Even at night, lit by the wavering flame of her candle, her workplace emits a sort of radiance. Perhaps it is the brass glow of the various machines and apparatus she has acquired over the course of her labour: a physiognotrace with its long pole and a camera obscura amongst them. They were necessary purchases. The modern public want machines, not people: something more like a daguerreotype.

Agnes does not see the appeal. A copper plate, a bit of mercury and they call it *art*. She is one of a dying breed who would rather have something drawn with soft pencils, or painted lovingly with the stroke of a brush.

So was Mr Boyle. But he will have had his image immortalised by now. Policemen always seem to be photographing crime scenes these days. She swallows against an ache in her throat, tries not to imagine Mr Boyle translated into chemical shades of silver and grey, his blood a vast, inky pool.

She places the candle on her battered desk. Pushing aside bladders of paint, moving stacks of paper, she finally locates the item she seeks: a great leather-bound book, as big as the family Bible. Her album of duplicates: a copy of all the shadows she has captured.

She does not begin at the start, where her early work resides. It embarrasses her to look upon those blunt cuts of Constance and acknowledge them as her own. Instead, she flips far to the back. On and on she turns. The little black figures flash before her eyes, seem to move. At last she finds a piece of paper pushed inside the album hurriedly, unstuck: the head and shoulders of Mr Boyle.

She holds the profile to the light.

She did not take enough care placing it inside the book. The weight of pages has squashed her work. Mr Boyle is creased. Crumpled. The outline of his face is bent, almost as if . . .

Her hand begins to shake.

It is too cruel. A barbarous coincidence. The lines of Mr Boyle, his forehead and his nose, are not preserved at all. His shade has suffered the fate of his mortal physiognomy.

It looks exactly as if it has been hit with a mallet.

Chapter 2

It's Pearl's first time.

She sits in the cabinet as usual, behind its black damask curtain, but already she feels like someone else. Tonight she hasn't got the floor-length veil over her face and there aren't any ashes smeared on her skin. She isn't playing a spirit guide now: she's the Main Event.

She worries about how it will feel when the ghosts take possession of her. Myrtle used to screw up her face and roll her eyes – but that was all for show. Myrtle freely admits it.

'I'm a Sensitive,' she told Pearl. 'I hear the voices. But that ain't enough for ladies and gents. They want a thrill. Tables rocking. Materialisation.'

The spirits have since whispered to Myrtle that her real power lies in manipulating auras and controlling the universal force: Myrtle is a mesmerist.

It's Pearl who possesses the Gift of Mediumship: she's the Genuine Article.

She closes her eyes and inhales the familiar scent of lilies – waxy, like the black candles that stand beside them in the parlour. It doesn't calm her nerves.

Myrtle's voice echoes in the hallway, tuned to the pitch of sympathy. A woman answers her. Pearl gleans what she can – she's in the habit of professional eavesdropping – and gathers that there are two women coming in: Mrs Boyle and Mrs Parker. They've both lost a man.

Was he their husband and father? Son and brother? Either way, the bonds seem close. She hopes she can satisfy them. It would be dreadful to let the mourners down. But if she succeeds . . .

A man will possess her. Speak through her mouth, see through her eyes. What if he doesn't go away again? He might occupy her for the rest of her life, use her like some sort of devilish puppet.

Pearl swallows her bile.

She shouldn't fear the dead. She's tasted death, as Myrtle's fond of reminding her. 'You did the dying part, before you were even born,' she says. But Pearl doesn't remember that, any more than she remembers the mother who lost her life bringing her into this world.

Footsteps sound in the parlour, followed by the movement of chair legs. Pearl ventures to open her eyes. Myrtle's turned down the lamps. She doesn't need to squint from the pain of their light any longer.

'Mrs Boyle, Mrs Parker. I must ask you to take your seats and remain in perfect silence. She will come to us presently.'

It's that breathy way of speaking that Myrtle has perfected. She ought to have been on the stage.

'But how—'

'She'll know. Leave the glove upon the table. If she requires anything further of you, she'll ask.'

Upholstery squeaks as they sit down. A little shuffling, settling in. The candles will be lit by now, their fiery eyes reflected in the crystal ball.

Still, it's not time to go out there yet.

Pearl takes a deep breath, longs to run from the cabinet and never come back. But she's eleven now, no longer a child. She has to work for the family like everyone else. She clenches her hands into fists. Waits until the silence begins to crackle.

Now.

She rings the bell. It cuts through the hush like lightning.

'Ladies!' Myrtle announces, 'The White Sylph arrives.'

Slowly, slowly, Pearl eases the curtain aside and steps out into the darkness.

There's always that little shock, the intake of breath when the mourners see her. But today, respect mingles with their awe. She has the Power – they can see it flowing from her in waves. Beside her they're desolate things: pinched and tear-stained, their clothes blending into the false night of the parlour.

She takes her seat. No one can see how her knees tremble beneath the tablecloth.

'Please, join hands.' Pearl uses the gentle, fluting voice Myrtle made her practise. Already, she's given up a part of herself. She swallows some more, tries not to think of what will happen next.

Gingerly, the women stretch out their fingers and clasp hers.

'We'll begin with a hymn.' Myrtle sighs softly, like a girl in love.

Myrtle insists upon this, says hymns help convince people they aren't taking part in something sacrilegious. She opens her bow-shaped mouth and begins:

> Behold, a Stranger at the door!
> He gently knocks, has knocked before,

Mrs Boyle and Mrs Parker join her in a feeble contralto:

> Has waited long, is waiting still:
> You treat no other friend so ill.

Pearl doesn't take part but instead sits, staring into the crystal ball. She's always thought it's cruel to make mourners sing. If there's one thing she understands about grief, it's how it chokes: the fingers of death, squeezing the throats of the living.

At last, the hymn ends. The air grows taut.

What now?

Remembering Myrtle's instructions, Pearl releases the mourners' hands and takes up the gentleman's glove that's been left for her upon the table. It's made of kidskin; warm from the candlelight, slightly stained on the palm. Is that a rip, by the ring finger? Hard to see. Her vision is clouding, as if she's gazing through fog.

She opens her mouth, exhales. A luminous ribbon flows out of it, drawing gasps. Her pulse goes wild. This has never happened before.

The ghosts are coming. Her arms are glowing, her breath is glowing. She's being swallowed.

Myrtle says, 'He's here.'

Something whispers, soft in her ear. Then cool, feathery hands touch her: dozens of them stroking her hair, patting her arms. She wants to scream but there's a buzzing sensation in her jaw, holding it shut.

A figure rises up from the mist. He's trailing garments and has candle flames for eyes. Can Myrtle see him too? She doesn't know; the others are invisible to her and she's alone in the dark with this . . . thing.

The spirit parts his lips, revealing a great void.

Pearl can't take any more. Her mind pulls the shutters down.

When she wakes up, the lamps are back on. Two black candlesticks stand before her on the table, smoking.

The younger mourner has her arm about the shoulders of the elder. Both are sobbing.

'He remembered!' the old lady cries. 'H-he always remembered.'

Myrtle practically hums with delight. 'Hmm. The message has significance for you?'

'Yes! Today is the anniversary of our marriage.'

A fresh burst of grief.

Pearl feels bruised, hollow, as if the spirits have taken her up and dropped her from a great height. She folds her arms on the table, rests her head upon them.

What happened? What did she say?

'But if that was Papa,' the younger woman reasons, furrowing her brow, 'if it truly *was* him . . . He would have told us, would he not? That is the reason we *came* here.'

Myrtle soothes them. 'Ladies, please, speak softly. There's no cause for quarrel. The language of the spirits is no more under our control than another mortal's voice. Why, you might be in the same room as a person, but you can't force them to talk to you. And if they do, you can't compel them to tell the truth. The spirits keep their own secrets.'

'Do not doubt, Harriet,' the older lady chides her companion. 'How can you question it? Look at the Sylph, how she glows!'

'It's the ectoplasm,' Myrtle says wisely. 'Spirit matter.'

'A miracle. Truly a miracle.'

Softly, the door shuts.

Coins chink. Pearl hears the farewells; hears Mrs Boyle and Mrs Parker speaking through the window when they gain Walcot Street.

'She could have looked up the marriage,' Mrs Parker insists from the pavement. 'And the murder was in the papers.'

'I know you do not believe, Harriet, but it gives me comfort. I *felt* him, I am sure I did. Please do not pooh-pooh it.'

'All I am saying is that she could not solve the crime, could she? Is that not rather convenient? Papa would not omit to tell us who killed him. He would be calling out for justice.'

The footsteps peter out.

Only one word remains with Pearl. *Murder*.

Her mouth is dry. It feels sullied, unclean, like it's been used without her consent.

Myrtle returns and lowers the lamps back to a comfortable level. 'All right, then. Bit of supper?' The genteel accent assumed for customers slides away as easily as a cloak shrugged aside. 'Got to keep your strength up, you know. Them spirits take it out of you.'

A tumbler of whisky and water is thrust before her, followed by a slice of bread coated in blackcurrant jam. The objects flicker, double. Pearl blinks.

'Thanks,' she manages. 'What . . . what happened?'

Myrtle sits down and plucks at a lily in its vase. 'You did it. Told you so. Genuine medium. Channelled the spirit of one Mr Boyle.'

Pearl's stomach cramps. 'He was here? He spoke through *me*?'

'Of course he did.'

It would be less disturbing if she remembered this Mr Boyle, if she felt like she'd met him. But now she's left with the sensation that something appalling has happened, and she's the only person who didn't see it.

'D'you think it's true, what the ladies were saying, Myrtle? That the man who spoke through me was murdered?'

'I know it's true. Read it in the paper.'

'But you didn't tell *me* that!'

Myrtle shrugs. 'Didn't think I needed to. The dead talk to you, don't they?'

'Through me,' Pearl mutters. 'Not *to* me. I never heard a sound.'

'You will. Now you've started to bleed each month, the power will grow. You'll harness it.'

Pearl takes a steadying breath. Her ears tingle, the only parts of her left untouched.

'Will I hear *her*?' she asks quietly.

Myrtle doesn't like to speak of Mother. A spasm of pain crosses her face and she purses her lips. 'I haven't. But you might.'

It would be worth it. Worth this awful, dirty feeling to hear Mother just the once.

She forces herself to sit up and nibble on the bread. 'And so no one's been scragged? For killing this Mr Boyle?'

'No. The bluebottles don't even have a suspect yet.'

She shivers. 'Then that means . . . There's a murderer on the loose. Here, in Bath.'

'Yes.' Myrtle pats her hand, gives a wink. 'That's good for business, ain't it?'

Chapter 3

For a sleepless night and half the next morning, Agnes debates taking Mr Boyle's silhouette to the police station. Absurd as it sounds, she feels guilty keeping the discovery to herself, as though she is concealing evidence. When she looks in the mirror to fasten her hair, it is the haunted face of a criminal she sees: an accessory to murder.

Of course they will tell her it is a coincidence. She could not have *caused* Mr Boyle's death by scrunching up his silhouette. But is it not uncanny? Something beyond the realms of an everyday occurrence. She has never squashed a piece of work before; she has never had a client die before. The two hang together with an ominous weight.

If not the police, then maybe she should seek out Mrs Boyle. Present her with the finished painting and include the ruined paper shade as an afterthought. Let the widow make the connection, determine some significance, if she can. Yes, perhaps that is the best course of action.

She puts on a lace collar and fastens it with a brooch. It has been so long since she paid a social call that she has forgotten the correct hours, and the form. Well, Mrs Boyle will probably be too deep in grief to notice if Agnes does not observe the niceties. All the clocks in her house will be stopped.

In the studio, Agnes wraps the glass oval and squashed silhouette in brown paper and string.

She checks the address in her ledger one last time before descending the stairs.

The grandfather clock ticks. Mamma dozes in the parlour with a rug spread across her knees. She has added fuel to the fire, again, wasting their scant resources while Agnes was upstairs. Cinders drop in the grate as if they are setting out to vex her, to show her how quickly it all turns to ash.

But there is another noise rising above that of the flames. A pathetic *peep*. It is so forlorn that it makes her heart clench.

Warily, she cracks open the front door.

'Cedric? There you are! I missed you at breakfast.'

Her nephew kneels beneath the portico, his breath misting the air. In his hand is the stick that he uses to propel his toy hoop. That hoop, however, is nowhere in sight. Instead he pokes tentatively at a magpie.

'Whatever are you doing? Be a good boy and leave that nasty thing alone.'

He carries on, regardless. 'Aunt Aggie, it's got a baby! Look!'

She bends down to his height and instantly recoils.

A pink, downy lump squirms on the ground, the stubs of its wings circling frantically. The eyes are sealed, bluish bumps; only the beak gapes wide.

Agnes glances at the magpie and realises it cannot be the chick's mother. It has plundered the nest of a wood pigeon.

'Oh! Well, you had better let it be. Do come inside, Cedric dear.'

'But I want—'

'This instant, young man.' Her upbraids never sound convincing. No wonder he often ignores them.

A couple strolling gaze in their direction. Agnes smiles tightly at them, attempting to appear in control of the situation.

'Do as you are told, there's a good boy.'

It is the magpie that moves, kicking the chick, making it scream.

'Why is it doing that?'

She seizes his arm. 'I must show you something, Cedric.'

'No, don't!'

Before he can fend her off, she pulls him inside the house. The stick clasped in his hand leaves a dirty scrape along the hallway wall.

She elbows the front door shut just in time. The next sound from outside is a terrible squelch.

Of course she has seen it before: the cannibalism of magpies. It never ceases to appal her. Cedric may love his stories of monsters, but she does not want him to really see a bird turn on its own kind, picking off the young and weak with no compunction for its atrocity.

'Auntie Aggie, you're hurting me.'

She drops his arm at once. 'Do forgive me, Ced. But I would not have to pull you about if you heeded me when I speak to you. Those birds can spread all manner of disease and I want you far away from them. It is for your own good, dear.'

He cocks his fair head to consider this. Or perhaps he is listening to the disturbing, wet noises creeping through the door.

'Is the baby bird eating his breakfast?' he asks.

'Yes,' she says hurriedly. 'Yes, he is eating. Now you must go along to the kitchen and eat too. I have made your favourite: egg fritters. Chop-chop.' She shoos him with her hands.

Sighing, Cedric trudges towards the back of the house, dragging his stick on the floor behind him, as if she has denied him some unparalleled treat. A great knot of love and frustration tightens inside her chest.

Much as she enjoys seeing him play, he should be above games by now. They take boys into the navy at the age of twelve and can you *imagine* one of those little midshipmen disobeying an order or running around with a hoop and stick? It is partly her own fault. She has indulged him, bought him Penny Dread-fuls instead of sending him out to work as other families would do. But she thought his father would have made plans for him by now.

Cedric should have an education. An apprenticeship. He is likely to get neither unless the widowed Mrs Boyle coughs up some coins.

She picks up her parcel, unfastens the front door and squeezes herself through the smallest opening, taking care to snap it shut behind her so Cedric does not see the magpie's gruesome work.

Yesterday's shower has left puddles on the streets. No rain yet this morning, but filthy rags of cloud strewn across the sky pose the threat. The abbey clock chimes ten. Already nurses are wheeling the crippled and infirm to the Pump Room. One man with a bald pate slides his vacant eyes in Agnes's direction and she feels a jolt of his confinement. To be trapped, in that manner. Unable to walk where you will. She remembers the days lying sick with pneumonia and quickens her pace, just to prove that she still can.

By Union Street she regrets it. Her lungs protest with a spasm and her heart gives that great swoop that often precedes a fainting fit. Chastened, she relapses into her habitual dawdle and turns away from the shops of Milsom Street and Bond Street. A cart has spilled some of its vegetables into the road, where they lie, rotting; a heap of bulbous shapes so dirty that Agnes cannot identify them. The same might be said for all around her. Dull, hopelessly dull. Gritty ash in the air. Birds wheeling like charred scraps from a fire.

How can bright young Cedric find his future in a place like this?

Beneath her glove, she twists the ring on her finger. It is the only way she can believe that Montague ever walked these streets. Montague, that man of vivid and impossible colours. He carried something of the places he had seen: a certain spice that spoke of the West Indies, even Africa. He told her of an ocean like aquamarine, so clear you could see the fish swimming in its depths. Rocks where the coral grew orange and pink at the waterline. Miraculous things she would scarcely credit from another mouth, but they *are* real and they are still out there, somewhere. Beyond her reach, because Montague has left her; left her with nothing but black and white.

Queen Square is quiet. A few tortured-looking oaks occupy the garden at the centre. Wind has already stripped them, burying their roots in the brown compost of their own leaves. A squirrel watches her from a naked branch, so still it might be a taxidermy model.

Agnes finds the Boyles' residence almost at once. There is the telltale straw laid out before it to deaden the sound of wheels and the windows are shuttered fast. She adjusts her grip on the package. Perhaps this was not a wise notion, after all.

Black material swaddles the brass knocker. It makes a muted, pathetic sound as she lets it fall. Some moments later, the door opens like a tender wound. Behind it is a squat woman dressed in mourning, but the expression upon her face is one of harassment, not grief. Her hands show coarse and red – evidently, Mrs Boyle is comfortable enough to keep a servant.

'I am here to offer my condolences to your mistress.' Agnes inserts her calling card through the narrow opening before the domestic has a chance to demur. 'She will not recognise my name, but I was acquainted with her late husband.'

The woman frowns at it, as if the letters mean nothing to her, but the thick quality of the card must make some impression, for she bids Agnes step inside.

'Don't know if she's up to receiving,' she warns. 'I'll check.'

Still staring at Agnes's card, she walks through an inner door and shuts it behind her. Agnes can hear the servant's clomping footsteps and the rumble of voices in conversation.

She had forgotten all of this: the stale, oppressive atmosphere that follows a death. Unaired rooms, mirrors covered in black fabric. A clock hangs on the wall, but its hands are stopped at ten and she wonders where this time has come from. Mrs Boyle cannot know the minute her husband breathed his last. Is this the hour they discovered the body, or when she received the news?

It was a mad, half-baked scheme to come. What is she doing here, uninvited, trespassing on a stranger's grief? She is tempted to slip back outside when the domestic returns, this time without the card.

'She'll see you. This way.'

Queen Square has not been a fashionable address for many a year. No one would suspect the Boyles of being wealthy, but they exude respectability. Agnes eyes the covered shapes of paintings and the nap on the drawn curtains, feeling the contrast with her own home forcibly. It was not always so. When her father was alive . . . But perhaps Mrs Boyle will find herself overcome by a similar onslaught of retrenchments and economies. Perhaps her days of keeping this dumpy servant are numbered.

The widow sits by the light of a spermaceti candle. What a profile she would make, with her aquiline nose and double chin! However, she is quick to cover it, flicking down her veil before standing and exchanging a formal curtsey with Agnes.

'Miss Darken. How kind of you to call.' Red cheeks burn beneath the netting of the veil; Mrs Boyle has evidently been crying.

'Forgive my intrusion, I . . .' Agnes gazes helplessly at the maid, whose eyes are pinned to the floor.

'Leave us, Mary.'

Mary bobs a curtsey and trots away.

The forced darkness is unnerving. Mrs Boyle extends a black-gloved hand to gesture at a chair on the other side of the table, and for a moment she looks like one of Agnes's full-length shades come to life.

Warily, Agnes perches on the edge of the seat. Her parcel fills her lap and she worries at the string with her fingers. 'Thank you, Mrs Boyle. I shall not detain you for long. I simply heard what had happened and I . . .' She wets her lips. What can she say? What can anyone say to atone for this? 'I am so terribly sorry,' she supplies feebly.

The widow sits opposite her with slow, heavy movements. 'Thank you. You are in mourning yourself?'

Agnes glances down at her own black dress, momentarily bewildered. She has not worn a coloured garment in so long that she forgets how it must appear to others. But Mrs Boyle is unlikely to comprehend the general, lingering melancholy that causes her to prefer dark clothing. 'A distant relation,' she embellishes. 'God rest them.'

The veil wafts as Mrs Boyle nods. She has certainly gone all out on her weeds – she must have emptied Corbould's mourning establishment. Tassels, jet buttons, a ring already mounted with her husband's grey hair. But then, who would not do the same? This is not simply a bereavement: the affliction of murder calls for shades deeper than a warehouse can supply.

'I have not been receiving visitors,' Mrs Boyle admits. 'I have an abhorrence of their pity and their . . . questions.' She places a hand on her chest, as if to put her emotions in order before continuing. 'But I recognised your name. From the engagement diary. You . . . you saw him that day, didn't you?'

The string pings from Agnes's fingertips. She knows. Naturally, she knows. What a simpleton Agnes was not to think of it before. The policemen would hardly requisition the engagement diary without keeping Mrs Boyle abreast of their investigations.

Rather than answering, she pushes the package across the table.

Mrs Boyle unfolds the paper with painful exactness. This low candlelight is the perfect illumination for Agnes's art. Little bronzed details glint – hair, a coat collar, the shell of an ear. Mrs Boyle draws in a breath.

'There was to be a second appointment. A collection. Alas . . .'

The crumpled papercut is there too, on the widow's lap. She does not heed it. Instead she strokes at the glass, leaving smudges.

In paint, the line of the face is softer. There is something angelic about this black and gold rendition of Mr Boyle. He is a mate for the shadow bride behind her veil.

'Thank you,' Mrs Boyle croons. 'Thank you, Miss Darken. What a blessing. He said there was to be a surprise. That was his way.'

'For the anniversary of—'

'Yes.'

Without the package, Agnes's hands feel obtrusive, too large. She could let matters rest here; retreat and leave the poor widow with her memories.

But that squashed papercut is like a rotten tooth: she cannot help worrying at it, glancing out of the corner of her eye to see its black curl. Someone else needs to share the horror of this coincidence.

'I included my preliminary cut in paper, madam. You will find it there, loose in the package. I am afraid it became rather damaged, but . . .' She trails off as Mrs Boyle picks up the shade and smooths it out.

Agnes watches intently, unable to close her mouth or breathe until the widow speaks.

'Yes. Thank you.'

That is all.

The anticlimax is so great that her shoulders drop. Can Mrs Boyle not see it?

'He told me to expect a surprise,' Mrs Boyle repeats. 'He must have known that you would come.'

'I do not understand.'

The widow's expression is opaque through her veil. 'I spoke to him, Miss Darken. Across the divide. The things that are possible, these days. When I think back to my youth, I would not have credited such discoveries. Railways, telegraph, spirit mediums like the White Sylph . . . Why, the Abolition of the Trade was thought radical enough!'

Agnes shivers. This is not the first time she has heard of spiritualists, although she usually keeps such talk at a distance by saying she does not believe. A more honest statement would be that she does not *want* to believe. She wants the dead safely caged in Heaven or Hell, not wandering, watching her through the cloudy eyes of a corpse. But a small part of her acknowledges it could be true. It feels true, when Mrs Boyle speaks it.

'And the . . . spirit . . .' Agnes gulps. 'He did not give any hint as to who ended his earthly life?'

Mrs Boyle shakes her head. 'He has moved beyond such concerns. He does not call for justice or vengeance. He is at peace, and I suppose I should be also. I shall endeavour to be. But it is very difficult. How can I forgive those brutes?' Sudden as a gust of wind, Mrs Boyle's composure blows apart. The paper on her lap begins to rustle. 'Heaven help me! Was it not enough to cut his throat and take his precious life? Why must they be so cruel as to obliterate his dear face too?'

Agnes cannot stop her ears pricking at this new intelligence. The sergeant never mentioned a cut to the throat. If that was the injury that killed Mr Boyle . . . well, it puts her artwork in a less sinister light. There is no incision *there*. Footpads slit Mr Boyle's throat and smashed his face for spite. Or, as the sergeant proposed, to delay identification of the body. She must have been beside herself to think otherwise. This was a fool's errand.

'I have trespassed on your grief long enough,' she begins.

Mrs Boyle bids her remain seated with a motion of her hand. 'No. No, I beg your pardon. I should not have become agitated.'

Agnes would rather leave this suffocating room, but perhaps the widow is lonely.

'You shall not want for anything, Mrs Boyle?' she asks gently. 'You have family?'

'Our daughter is married to an excellent man. My grandchildren will keep me occupied, no doubt. I shall be as comfortable as one can be, once the joy of her life is gone.'

Agnes swallows. 'I am glad to hear it. You are fortunate. When my own father died . . .' She nods at the silhouette on Mrs Boyle's lap. 'Well, you can see. My pastime was obliged to become a trade.'

Mrs Boyle shuffles uncomfortably beneath the paper wrapping. She glances from the profile to Agnes and back again, as if it had not occurred to her that women of her class might fall into penury. It had not occurred to Mamma either. If Agnes had not risen to the occasion, and Simon was not so kind, all three of the Darken women could have ended up in the workhouse.

Clearing her throat, Mrs Boyle reaches into the folds of her skirt. When she speaks again, the tone is more formal. 'And you are most competent, Miss Darken. Permit me to contribute a little something for your trouble.'

Agnes holds out her hand and a silver shilling drops into it. The Queen's profile, grimed in dirt, stares indifferently. One shilling for all this heartache. The charge for bronzing would usually be more, but Agnes would not dream of saying so.

'Thank you, madam.'

Mrs Boyle sniffs. 'I shall call for Mary to see you out.'

She closes her fingers over the coin. Was her hint so tactless? Surely she has done no wrong. She *does* care, she has not come purely for the money, but she needs it. She wants to be independent, not reliant on Simon for charity.

Of course, she will never be able to explain this to a woman like Mrs Boyle, who has coin to spare on frivolities such as spirit mediums. Patiently, she waits in silence for Mary to answer the bell and lead her through the gloom to the door.

'Good day,' she says with a curtsey.

Mrs Boyle nods.

Compared to the twilight of the widow's parlour, the autumn day in Queen Square now seems perfectly bright. Agnes dawdles homewards, glad to have put Mr Boyle's death to rest. Her art is innocent. She has done nothing amiss – although she has been made to feel like an impertinent beggar woman.

She pulls the brim of her bonnet low to shield her face from passers-by. After Mrs Boyle's cold look, she does not want to meet the eyes of the square's other haughty residents.

It is not often she misses Constance, but she feels as if she would take comfort in speaking to her sister now. Constance would tell Agnes how little store she should set by the opinion of such dullards as the Boyles. She might even claim that the murderers had done a public service by putting an end to Mr Boyle.

Horrible, unforgivable things like that.

Still, they would make Agnes feel better.

Chapter 4

Pearl doesn't remember living in London, and she doesn't see a lot of Bath either. There's the parlour, the kitchen and the hallway, plus three other small rooms, which they use as bed-chambers.

Sometimes, lodgers arrive and live in the rooms upstairs, but they never stay for long. The landlord won't let Pearl and Myrtle up there. They've only paid to rent the ground floor of the house. He might be hiding treasure or caged tigers above them for all she knows. She ought to check, but she's too afraid.

Today is market day, when she ventures to the front door to get some air. Her chair rests just inside the threshold and an old coal-scuttle bonnet screens her eyes from the worst glare of the daylight.

Her glimpses of the world outside are slight, like a tongue darting between the lips and slipping back in again. She sees cows shambling over the cobbles, their tails swishing at flies. A mass of black bricks and chimney stacks. Wafts of steam from Ladymead Penitentiary, where Myrtle sends their washing.

It's the smells Pearl enjoys the most. Even the straw and the dung. There's something alive about the scents in the street. They make her sit up and take notice.

Myrtle's already been out into the throng and returned with a punnet of blackberries for their favourite jam. Now she stands in the kitchen, behind Pearl, pulling them apart and pulping them.

Pearl turns and watches her sister. It's at times like these she tries to imagine Myrtle's father, Private West. He'd be a tall man, definitely. Probably handsome too, because he was Mother's first husband, and she married him at sixteen. You wouldn't marry that young if it weren't for the wildest romance.

Pearl always wonders what would have happened if Private West hadn't been killed in action. With a different father, she might have been born with Myrtle's lustrous eyes and widow's peak. Or maybe not. Maybe Mother wouldn't have birthed a second child at all. She'd still be on this side of the veil and it would be Pearl's soul wandering in that mist, without a home.

'I'm not saying the séance weren't good.' Myrtle wipes her forehead with the back of her hand. She's rolled her sleeves to the elbow and there are purple splotches all down her forearm. 'She was pleased as you like, that Mrs Boyle. But we can make it better for when the Society come. Can't we?'

'I don't know,' Pearl mumbles.

'Well, we can. People want a show. Don't matter to them you've got a genuine gift. They won't believe us unless we dress it up in tinsel.'

'But I can't control it! How am I meant to make it better? I don't even know what's happening to me.'

Sighing, Myrtle drops a blackberry into a bowl and crushes it beneath her spoon. 'I'll rig something up, won't I? I've been reading *Missives from Summerland*. Some places in London have these things they called *apports*.'

A cow lows from the street. Pearl turns to look. It's a dun-coloured beast, objecting to a man running his fingers down her legs. Does he want her for milk, or food? She's surely too pretty to be made into beefsteak.

'Pearl? Are you listening?'

She blinks, draws her eyes away from Walcot Street. 'Yes. What's an apport?'

'You drop them from the ceiling. Fruit, feathers, petals. Like a gift from the spirits. I could make that happen.'

'You don't think . . .' Pearl wobbles on her chair, struck by a terrible thought. 'It won't just *happen*, will it? They won't just start giving presents through *me*?'

Myrtle considers this while she inspects a blackberry. 'I dunno, Pearl. Don't think so. Seems to me real ghosts are more subtle than that.'

Pearl recalls the way the spirit matter flowed from her mouth and it makes her stomach cramp in panic. What else might come on that luminous tide? She might vomit forth objects. Manifest limbs. Anything could spew from between her lips and she wouldn't be able to stop it. She wouldn't even know it had happened.

'What about the fire?' Myrtle pounds into the bowl again. 'I could toss some coloured dust into it. That would go down well.'

'I hate it when you do that! It hurts my eyes.'

A sound of irritation escapes her sister, a harsh *tssssk*. 'Well, work with me, then! Think up something you *can* stand.' She's pummelling the berries so hard that the bowl shifts. 'I've got enough on my plate trying to work on *my* gift. Mesmerism ain't easy, you know. Don't you want to help me? Don't you want your father to get better?'

This stings sharper than the firelight, and Myrtle knows it. Pearl grits her teeth. 'Yes.'

'Then act like it. Cudgel your brains.'

'I'm trying, but it's hard. Lifting the veil makes me feel sick. Did it make you sick at the start?'

''Course it did,' Myrtle says, more kindly, putting her spoon down. 'But you don't see me whining, do you? Buck up, my love.'

She envies Myrtle's strength. The spirits are right: her sister is vital, magnetic. Even in their shabby kitchen, wearing an apron, she vibrates.

'Can't the almshouse help Father?' Pearl pleads. 'While you're learning to heal with Mesmerism?'

Myrtle looks as if she's bitten into rotten fruit. 'Told you, they're stuck up. Either you ain't destitute enough for their help, or you don't deserve it. Them do-gooders don't consider "spirit medium" a good trade. They think we're all atheists, hysterical women and lecherous men.'

Pearl watches the smoke drifting from the chimney stacks outside, dark and free. How must she appear to those charitable workers? She didn't choose this gift, any more than she chose her albinism, yet she's punished for both.

'The Dispensary, then. Don't they help no matter what your religion?'

Myrtle's face shuts. 'Blinkered ignoramuses. Poisoners. Do you want them touching him?'

These fancy words are straight from the penny spiritualist paper, *Missives from Summerland*. The Society of Bath Spiritual Adventurers echo them in other forms. Drugs alter the natural flow of energy, Pearl is told. It's the one topic she dares to nurse a different opinion on – but she keeps that to herself.

The sun peeks out from behind a cloud. Even its watery autumn rays cause pain. Pressure masses beneath her forehead. She's a terrible thirst upon her.

'Too much light.' Pushing up off her chair, she wobbles to the kitchen where a jug of water sits waiting. She drinks one glass, two. She'd gladly drink the whole thing.

But that would be selfish. She's being selfish, even now: not helping her sister make the jam, getting in the way of her father's recovery. She gazes around the damp room and up to the sooty ceiling. Is Mother here somewhere, watching her disapprovingly?

Myrtle goes on smashing the berries.

Prodded by guilt, Pearl fills a fresh glass and totters down the narrow corridor to the sickroom. She can't recall it ever being anything else. Father has always been ill.

Not *this* ill, though. As she pushes the door ajar, a rotten stench twines out to greet her: bad milk, fly-blown ham. It takes studied effort to place one foot in front of the other and creep inside.

Father lies on his back, fever-bitten. His head doesn't rest on the pillow but twitches this way and that. Does he see her? She's never certain these days. Whether he's alone or in company, he produces the same jerky movements, the same liquid-choked moans.

The curtains are drawn and the light is kind. Pearl edges closer. He's thrown the sheet partially off his body, exposing his shoulders, chest and one atrophied leg. How thin he's grown. A tortured shape, slowly disappearing into the mattress. He can't take solid food any more. Instead, the disease feeds upon him.

'D'you want some water, Father?' she asks softly.

He flings his head in her direction. *Yes.* She hears his voice clear as a bell, even though he can't speak. Maybe this is part of the Gift. Maybe her spirit can commune with Father's and they'll have no need for words between them.

With an unsteady hand, she reaches for the funnel. Father attempts to open what's left of his lips for her, but he can't control that black jaw. She wedges the spout in as best she can.

Few teeth remain. They jut at impossible angles. The actual jawbone is dark and decaying. When he could talk, Father said he needed a surgeon to cut it out.

Myrtle called them all butchers.

Pearl tries to imagine how Father would look after such an operation: he'd be a strange, broken doll of a man. She shudders at the thought. Maybe Myrtle's right about the surgeons.

Carefully, she tips the glass. Water trickles slowly down the funnel. She sees it slide over his gums, and the flick of his poor tongue. Of course there are drops that run to wet the pillow, but she's practised at this. She knows how to administer the liquid without choking him.

Her own mouth is still dry, despite her earlier drink. Maybe it's because of the nausea. Pearl listens to the soft flow of the water in the funnel and it becomes all she can think about.

At last the glass is done, and she can remove the funnel. The end that sat in Father's mouth is coated in something phlegmy. Pearl closes her eyes momentarily, sways on her feet. If only she was strong like Myrtle. Myrtle wouldn't even flinch.

Father looks exhausted by the short ordeal too. She watches his eyelids droop, whispers, 'Rest, now.'

Pity wars with revulsion. She tries to focus on the parts of him that still look normal. His hair. It's a sweaty tangle, turned grey from all his pain, but at least it still resembles hair.

As she stares at him, something seems to shift and lighten. Pearl tilts her head. There. Behind him. It looks like an aureole of light. A glow disturbingly familiar . . .

Spirit matter.

Spirit matter teasing at his edges, seeking to claim him.

With a muffled sob she turns and runs from the room, leaving the glass and funnel behind.

Myrtle was right; she's always right in the end, no matter how harsh she seems. Time is running out. Father's mortal life will end if they don't find a way to treat him.

She leans against the wall and slumps into it, letting her head rest on the faded paper. *Help me. Help me, Mother. Tell me what to do.* She closes her eyes, wills and strains with all her might.

But Mother keeps her silence. The only image that fills Pearl's mind is colourless, shifting water.

Chapter 5

'Agnes! Agnes!'

Her stockinged feet slide across the floorboards. Dread clamps her chest in place of the corset she has left off fastening to hurry to her mother's aid.

But although Mrs Darken's wail suggested fire or murder, the lady herself sits composed in the wing chair, a newspaper spread over her lap.

'What is it, Mamma? Are you ill?'

Mamma turns her face up to the firelight. Dropsy has made it rotund and ruddy-skinned, rather like the characters in the Gillray prints Papa used to collect. 'They've put your advertisement in the paper, dear.'

Agnes pants, out of breath from her dash. 'I do not understand you. What advertisement?' Now that she stops to consider, Mamma should not have a *Gazette* in her grasp at all. Only last Wednesday, she told the boy to end their subscriptions because she could not pay the bill. 'Where did you get that from? We cannot afford . . .'

Her voice disappears. As she draws closer, the print becomes less blurred. *Murder in Gravel Walk*.

'If you can pay for an advertisement, you cannot begrudge me my papers,' Mamma huffs.

Agnes snatches the newspaper so fast that a corner rips off in Mamma's fingertips.

She holds it close to her face. It is just as she feared. Those insidious journalists have crept in like so many lice.

> *The victim, last seen alive at Darken's Silhouette Parlour, Orange Grove, was ostensibly killed by an incision at the throat, although he endured multiple injuries after death.*

What need had they to mention her premises? As if her little business were not struggling enough! It is as though they are *trying* to take away the one employment that gives her satisfaction.

'Did you *read* this, Mamma?'

Mamma fidgets her shoulders. 'You did not give me the chance. I only saw our name and thought you would like to know . . .'

While Mamma subsides into grumbles, Agnes tears the paper up, tossing the shreds onto the fire, where they twist and writhe.

'Well, I never did! Whatever has got into you, Agnes? I might have expected this behaviour from *Constance*, but not you.'

She closes her eyes, tries to fetch enough air into her lungs. It is not Mamma's fault.

'Forgive me, Mamma, but they really do print such trash these days. I will see if I can stretch to a magazine. *The World of Fashion* . . . But first you should eat. Where' – she casts a quick, unhopeful look about the parlour – 'where is Cedric? I thought we were to play backgammon. He is not out and about this early, surely?'

Mamma plaits her fingers. 'Ah, little Cedric. He'll be begging ginger lemonade from the soda manufactory or spying on the girls in Mrs Box's seminary. A wandering spirit, that boy. Just like his father – aye, and his grandfather before him.'

Agnes flinches. Her mother does not observe it, for she is gazing into the past now, her eyes filmed over.

'Lord, how he did drag me about, that papa of yours! If it wasn't Gibraltar it was the West Indies, or some other godforsaken place at the ends of the earth. You are lucky he took his half pay after Constance was born. Who knows where we should have ended up otherwise?'

A burn at the core of her chest, which has nothing to do with her bad lungs. 'I should have liked to see the West Indies,' Agnes replies softly.

'Oh no you would not! That life would not suit *you* at all. The heat is like the bowels of Hell. It took all morning just to get a *hint* of curl in my hair. Then I could barely eat. I lost so much weight, I had to take in every one of my gowns, I remember.'

Strange how Mamma can recall details like this, but not the pain her daughter has endured; how all Agnes's hopes of happiness were once centred on a ship cutting through the surf and ports in foreign climes.

'Speaking of gowns, I had better put mine on. I shall be back presently.'

The stair treads yawn beneath her feet. Agnes echoes them, rubbing the grit from her eyes. As she stumbles onto the landing, her shoulder knocks against a frame hanging on the wall. There is a crash followed by the dreaded tinkle of broken glass.

'Agnes?'

'It is nothing, Mamma.'

Stooping down, she turns the oval frame face up. Shards of glass fall to the floor. Behind them, unmarked, rests the profile of Constance.

This is the only shade of her they keep on display in the house. It is blind, without the eyelash Agnes now cuts in as a matter of course, but it remains one of her best pieces. There is a depth to it that conjures up the woman herself.

Indeed, time has softened the memory of Constance's face to such an extent that these lines now seem to represent her entirely. A dark hole that you might stare into and accidentally fall down.

In her bedchamber Agnes rests the broken frame upon the dresser and takes a gown from the press. Its dark shade calms her. Black: always ordered and neutral.

Reliable.

She notices something misshapen lying at the base of the cupboard. Her reticule. She chucked it hastily aside after the policeman's visit, but it had rained that day; she ought to have turned the bag out in front of the fire. Bending, she tuts to see the material is pocked with water marks. When she untangles the strings and opens it, it is even worse; a mouldy smell assails her nostrils.

'No, no, no.' Flames of rust lick the blades of her scissors, still nestled inside. She owns another pair, but these ones are special instruments – they do not come cheap. As for the silhouette she cut of the naval officer in the park, it is utterly ruined: limp and turning to pulp at the bottom of the bag. She blows out her breath. At least it was not a good likeness to begin with.

Frustrated, she throws the bag to one side and continues to dress. Her old governess always accused her of being easily distracted, and here is the proof: a smashed frame, rusting scissors and a ruined silhouette – all in one morning. She never means to abandon tasks. But there is so much pressing upon her mind. More than it can possibly contain. It is only natural that certain things should . . . slip out. Since her spell of illness it has only become worse: sometimes a whole hour will pass by without her even noticing.

She fastens her hair. It is an unpleasant surprise to see the woman in the looking glass. The fine bone structure that Montague praised as 'delicate' now only serves to make her look drawn. And then there is that grey streak in her hair; a vivid shock down one side like the blue band in a magpie's wing. That came after the pneumonia too. She has still not grown accustomed to it.

Her eyes dart to the broken frame and to Constance's shade. Her dead sister has smooth, unwrinkled skin and her hair colour is without variation. All the spikes and bristles of her character are concealed safely behind black lines. She looks almost *amenable* in this form. It goes to prove that the silhouette really is the kindest form of art.

Back down the staircase to the accompaniment of another mournful, weary sound from the treads. Mamma remains just as she left her, peering through her spectacles at the fire.

'I am afraid you will have to take your breakfast tea without milk, Mamma,' Agnes sighs. Her mother raises an ear trumpet to catch her words. 'I shall have to go and fetch some more later . . .'

'Oh, Agnes. Do you never keep your wits about you, dear?'

'I did not *forget*,' she explains irritably. 'I used it all making Cedric—'

'We won't be able to afford milk or anything else, will we, if you carry on ignoring customers like that?'

'Ignoring . . . ?'

Mamma jerks her head in the direction of the window.

Peering through the thicket of silhouettes tacked to the glass are the startlingly bright eyes of a young man.

'He's been there for at least five minutes, knocking.'

Agnes is aghast. Today is market day. The sound of his banging must have been swallowed by the general bustle from outside. 'Why did you not call me?' she demands as she dashes to the door.

Mamma does not reply, but drops her ear trumpet and picks up last week's newspaper.

———

Agnes is old enough to be this young man's mother.

She feels antiquated, foolish, sat before him in her studio with her spare pair of scissors. Will he go to a coffee house with his friends after this, and joke about the old maid in Orange Grove?

She can almost picture them: their checked waistcoats and greased hair. Laughing. Laughing like the magpies outside.

But she is spoiling the experience for herself. This is her first chance to do a real piece of work since Mr Boyle's appointment, and she should relish it. The youth has an attractive profile, worthy of a place in her duplicate book. She glances from the paper to his face, enjoying as she always does the crisp sound of that first cut.

'You seem rather a young man, to be having your shade cut,' she ventures. 'I thought it was all daguerreotypes with your generation.'

'Well—' He turns to face her. Remembers, too late, that he isn't meant to move. 'Oh. Sorry.'

'Never mind. Just look to the side again if you would, sir.'

'Ned, please. No need to stand upon ceremony with me.'

How strangely the young conduct themselves nowadays! He is asking her, a woman he has just met, to call him by his Christian name. Not even that, an abbreviation of the name. She pulls the paper towards the jaws of her scissors and works on his lips. It is a shame that she cannot capture the tentative beginnings of a moustache that sprout beneath his nose.

'Ned, then. What prompted you to come to me for a shade?'

'It's my gran. She has a whole wall full of silhouettes. Every family member you can think of. I *did* give her my photograph, but the old dear wasn't pleased with it.' He laughs. 'Bit of a blow to my pride, eh? She said it looked odd amongst all those shadows.'

Agnes pauses as she repositions her scissors and begins to tackle the chin. 'Well, your grandmother is correct,' she says proudly. 'The shade is the purest of all portraits. Beside it, a photograph would appear too . . .'

'Too alive?' he supplies. 'Too *real*, perhaps. I don't know why, but when I see her wall of silhouettes . . . To me, it looks like a display of death masks.'

'Oh, no, surely not?' This judgement dismays her. She has

always managed to find beauty and purpose in the clear lines of a silhouette, no matter what else is going on in her life.

'Yes, I'm afraid they look that way to me. Like shells of things with the souls snuffed out.'

The blade slips. Only a little way, a quarter of an inch at most, but with this nick under the chin, she will struggle to cut the throat and shoulders. Damn these second-rate scissors.

'A good profile *exposes* the soul of the sitter,' she explains, frowning at her work.

'Well, a photograph is a good deal quicker. I thought you had machines to do this silhouette business?'

It stings, but he is correct. At the height of her powers, she had been able to cut a shade freehand in – what – two minutes? Sometimes less. The memory is like a small death. Skill is forsaking her too, contrary as any lover.

'There *are* machines, but I favour the personal touch . . .' Outside the window, the magpies beat their wings, squabbling. Agnes sighs and lays down her scissors. Here is a way out of her present difficulty with the nick, at least. 'I would be happy to show you my physiognotrace, if you prefer?'

Ned turns again, his brown eyes sparkling. 'Really? Could I see it? I wouldn't want to be a bother.'

Despite herself, Agnes smiles. His enthusiasm is infectious. In a few years, Cedric will be like this: fancying himself an engineer and championing progress. An odd turn of events, considering the workers of Mamma's generation did all they could to smash the machines that stole their livelihood. But such is humankind: hopelessly fickle.

'It is no trouble at all. I will clean the contraption and we will use it to take your profile. You will enjoy the experience. It's very clever, in its way.'

Bustling to the corner, she moves various pads and paint palettes off the machine. It is so webbed in dust that she coughs.

'Here,' says Ned, rising to his feet. 'Let me help.'

Piece by piece, they reveal a chipped wooden box with a hatch on the side. Agnes is startled to think how long it's been since she last used the instrument. What appeared then as the cutting edge of innovation now looks poor and dejected, its quaintness the only virtue left.

Without asking for permission, Ned reaches and opens the hatch. A small brass cylinder, topped with a metal hoop, protrudes from the bottom of the box. Opposite it, on the far 'wall' a piece of yellow paper is tacked.

'Smells a bit musty!' he laughs. 'Well, how does it work?'

'Let me change the paper first, and then we will fit the pole.'

The holders are a little corroded, but Agnes manages to work the old paper free. It is powdery in her hands, as insubstantial as the past. Casting it aside, she reloads the machine with something crisp and white. She is quite looking forward to trying this again.

The other lengthy pole belonging to the machine is propped in the corner beside a bookcase. One end still holds a pencil, miraculously hard and sharp after all this time, while the other tapers into a rod.

Ned guffaws. 'Bless me! You could take someone's eye out with that pole.'

He means it innocently. He is not to know that his words bring Mr Boyle bobbing to the surface of her mind. Smashed, broken . . .

But she must put that behind her.

'I promise to be careful. If you would fetch the chair and position it . . . yes, that will suffice.' She threads the pole through the metal hoop.

Ned sits, keen as a puppy. 'And what – the rod passes over my face, does it?'

'Yes.' She smiles at him. His zest seems to be infusing into her. 'You must remain very still, even if it tickles.'

'And the pencil on the other end draws it there, in the little box?'

'Indeed. The image will be small, and upside down. That is of no matter. I will use a pantograph to make it larger, and we will turn it into an artwork worthy of your grandmother.'

'Well, fancy that! Let's get underway, shall we?'

She starts the rod at the nape of his neck. Feels the heat of his body rise to her trembling hands. He smells of bergamot pomade.

It is all rather enchanting. She cannot remember the last time she stood this close to a man. Other than Simon. And there is nothing thrilling about Simon's clammy fingers at her wrist, feeling her pulse.

She holds the rod steady with both hands and softly traces the top of Ned's crown. His greased locks ruffle out of place. One or two strands cling to the pole with static. She senses him tense, trying not to laugh.

He closes his eyes as the rod comes sweeping over his forehead and down his nose. It kisses his lips, dipping between them and departing with the slightest gleam of moisture.

She is disappointed when it ends.

'Is it done? Can I see?'

'Just a moment.' She opens the contraption and reveals his double, inverted and ever so faint.

'How clever! That is me, isn't it? You can see, even though it's so small. It's unmistakably me.'

Agnes glances from the drawing to Ned and back again. It hardly does him justice.

'Remarkable accuracy,' he enthuses. 'Just from a rod! The things they invent. So you'll make it bigger and then it's done?'

She can imagine him presenting this paltry shade to his grandmother with aplomb, singing the praises of the blasted physiognotrace. *See, Grandmamma, you don't even need a person to draw these now!* Is she really going to let a machine best her?

'The head is too wide and flat,' she decrees. 'It needs an artist's touch.'

Taking a piece of black foolscap, she makes a single vertical incision and begins to cut Ned's profile as a hole in the centre of it. A hollow-cut – she has not used the technique in years.

For a moment she worries she has outstretched herself. The twists and turns of his face are tight. Slivers of paper peel away as she works on the detail of his cravat, her tongue clamped between her teeth in concentration.

But at last it emerges. Stunning. Her best piece in a long time.

She mounts it on white stock card. A shade reversed. Ned's profile is a light in the darkness, glowing with the purity of fresh snow.

'Do you call that soulless, Ned?'

He snatches it up, delight written all over his face. 'Why, that's remarkable! You did it in white, just for me?'

She glows with pride. 'Now you can cut a figure on your grandmother's wall. It is enough like the others to fit in her collection, but you have your own flair.'

He shakes her hand. Does not notice that she retains his a little longer than necessary.

'I'm so pleased,' Ned rattles on as he gathers his coat. 'I hadn't planned to do this today. I was just passing and saw your display. Isn't it lucky I knocked?'

So he has not seen the *Gazette*.

'It is very fortunate for me.'

Coins exchange hands. Although she is glad of the money, she is sorry they must part. Soon the shilling will be spent and she will have precious little to remember him by, this sunny boy who has brightened her day.

He is too young for her, of course, but there is something about him that reminds her of Montague. That easy manner, the ability to make her smile.

'Good day,' says Ned.

'I hope we will see you here again.'

He grins but does not reply.

It was a silly thing for her to say. Ned has no reason to come back to this forlorn house: he is young and free. But there is comfort in the thought that she will go with him. Her name, signed in pencil, will never part from his profile.

In some small way, she has claimed him.

Chapter 6

The gas lamps are up. Not high, but enough to taunt her. By their light, the parlour looks shabbier: the wallpaper a weak and faded lilac chintz that depresses the spirits. Pearl's spirits, that is. She doesn't know about the ghosts. They haven't complained about the decoration as yet.

Myrtle's been buzzing around like a honeybee all day. It's tiring just to watch her buffing the chipped wooden furniture, arranging the doilies in a thousand different positions before settling on the right ones. She's managed to get a tea service, good stuff but not matching. The seedcake she baked earlier still flavours the air.

Pearl can only watch her sister in admiration, wondering if they're really related. It's not just Myrtle's energy that amazes her, it's her dogged patience.

That hairstyle alone must have taken hours. Fat, sausage ringlets fall over one shoulder. Pomade makes them look like meadow hay. It's a big improvement on their usual dirty blonde colour. Myrtle can't afford to dress in a crinoline, but the deep maroon gown – which she sewed herself – has enough pleats in the skirt to swing full and fashionable.

Pearl has been decked out in dove grey, but she doesn't care what she looks like. The whole point of girls like her is to *not* be there; to subtract herself from the room.

'I'll introduce you to Mr Stadler and Mr Collins – he's the chap who takes the photographs,' Myrtle calls over her shoulder as she plumps cushions. 'Just a few of them tonight.' She smiles artificially and adopts her posh accent. 'A *private* gathering. Can't have them thinking we're putting on a show.'

'But you said the other day—'

'I know, but you can't have them *think* it, Pearl. The minute they see you actually want to get paid for your work, they'll call you vulgar. Who else? Oh, Mrs Lynch—'

'I've already met them,' Pearl points out. 'You don't need to introduce me to Mr Stadler. I've sat on his lap as Florence King.'

Myrtle releases a sound of exasperation. For a minute, Pearl fears she'll throw the cushion at her. 'For God's sake, don't act like it! Don't let on. You've been an invalid, confined to your bed, remember?'

Pearl shuffles in her seat. She's going to say something bad. It tickles in her chest, then bubbles in her mouth. Usually good sense would press it down again, but the gas lights make her peevish.

'Don't you feel guilty, lying to them?'

Myrtle's cheeks turn the colour of her gown. 'I never lied. I did hear a spirit called Florence King. I just got you to play her. There had to be *some* use in you being pale as a ghost.'

Pearl shrinks back into her seat. Why does she say things like that to Myrtle? It's always a mistake. Each time she questions her sister she's filled with this painful, searing shame.

There's a rap at the door.

In a second Myrtle's over, straightening Pearl's posture in the chair, wiping a smear of jam away from her cheek with spit and a threadbare handkerchief.

'You'll be fine,' she whispers. 'Just dandy.'

Pearl thinks she might be sick.

She remains frozen in place while Myrtle goes to the hallway and opens the door. The voices of the Society enter before their bodies do. A full bass, another with cut-glass vowels and one at a higher, chirpier octave.

For people intent on peering into the grave, they sound unusually jolly.

'A dusting of snow,' Mrs Lynch announces from the hallway. 'It caught me quite by surprise. Look at my cloak!'

'Do permit me to brush down your shoulders.' Pearl is not surprised to hear it's Mr Stadler saying these words. When she acted the part of Myrtle's spirit guide, she was forced to endure this man's caresses. Having summoned a ghost, all he wanted to do was dandle it upon his lap. She remembers him displaying her to Mr Collins for the first time. 'She is quite real, Walter. Just feel these hip bones . . .'

Pearl can't blame the spirits for wanting to talk through her, rather than showing up themselves and letting people manhandle them. The indignity of it all is breathtaking.

There's a thump as Mr Collins struggles inside with what must be his photographic equipment. 'Is she here?' he demands. 'Is she ready for our experiments?'

Myrtle laughs gaily. 'You're very eager, Mr Collins. Won't you let us drink some tea first?'

Pearl sighs inwardly, knowing the version of Myrtle that comes back into the parlour won't be the sister who raised her, but the theatrical counterfeit. And she's right. Myrtle marches at the head of the pack, her eyes sparkling. She waves her hand with a flourish and says, 'Ladies and gentlemen, may I present Miss Pearl Meers? Or, as those who have seen her powers have come to call her, the White Sylph.'

The four visitors, two men and two women, stare. Pearl opens her mouth and closes it. Ought she to stand? She's left it too late.

'Hello,' she offers.

No one says a word.

The clock ticks. It makes the visitors' silence seem even more profound. Pearl registers their blank, shocked expressions, and feels a stab of foreboding. Do they recognise her as

Florence King? Myrtle took so much care to make her look different tonight, and they both presumed that no one had seen her face clearly behind Florence King's long veil. It would destroy Myrtle if the Society found out . . .

But at last, Mrs Lynch finds her voice. 'How extraordinary! You did not tell me, my dear Miss West, that she was an albino child.'

A blush stings Pearl's cheeks.

'Didn't I? I must have forgotten,' shrugs Myrtle, who forgets nothing. 'But I did tell you she was always upstairs, ill, when we performed our previous séances here.' She flicks a curl over her shoulder and raises Pearl to her feet. 'Pearl's been delicate since birth. I thought it was because her body's different, but—'

'But now we know better,' Mrs Lynch finishes sagely. 'How often it has been remarked that the Gift manifests itself after a period of severe illness!'

'Indeed, indeed,' Mr Collins cuts in. 'The Power always follows sickness and frequently comes to the gentler sex. The lower in status they are, the stronger they seem to grow. Deprivation, frustration and discontent: these are the grounds in which mediumship breeds.'

Pearl sees the rictus set into Myrtle's cheeks. This prig insults them openly, in their own home. If she was braver, she would spark back. But she's saving her strength for more important things.

At the last séance, she knew the name of the person she was summoning: Mr Boyle. This time, any ghost might come through. She shivers, feeling like the skin is shrinking on her bones.

The other woman, who looks like a facsimile of Mrs Lynch, pushes forward and lifts a lock of Pearl's hair from the shoulder of her gown. 'Look! Pure white! Even paler than Florence's. She might have come from the spirit realm itself, Mamma.'

'Well,' Myrtle considers, 'maybe she did. She was born with

the cord wrapped around her neck, you know. Not a whiff of breath in her. It were me what brought her back to life.'

They all gasp.

Myrtle's eagerness to share the tale breaks through her false voice. No one seems to care.

She tells them the story, but there's one part she leaves out: she doesn't mention how their mother slipped away while Myrtle was busy reviving Pearl. None of the Society will know that it was all Pearl's fault; that if she hadn't been a distraction, someone might have saved Mother.

But Pearl remembers. She's heard it enough times.

Myrtle pats her on the shoulder. 'Come on,' she says. 'Let's sit down and have some tea.'

She guides Pearl to the table, her hand in the small of her back. When they sit down, she's careful to perform the introductions again, more thoroughly, giving Pearl the names of Mr Stadler, Mr Collins, Mrs Lynch and Miss Lynch.

Although they've all come to consult Pearl, they don't seem to want her. Myrtle pulls their gaze like a giant magnet.

'Such a pity, Miss West, that Florence King had to leave us,' Mrs Lynch laments. 'I cannot step foot inside this house without recalling your dear spirit guide. That farewell séance! I will never forget how tenderly she clasped me. But my loss is nothing compared to yours. You must miss her most of all.'

Myrtle concentrates on pouring the tea, avoiding Mrs Lynch's eye. 'Of course I regret that dear Florence had to go,' she sighs. 'But I knew her guidance would only be given to me for a short time. She's happy in Summerland now, and I'm living out her message here on Earth. It was Florence, you recall, who told me what would happen to my sister, and that I should study Mesmerism.'

'I myself possess a great interest in the mesmeric force,' Mr Collins announces pompously. 'A magnetic fluid that flows through all creatures, ready to be manipulated and controlled, it is like a chemical, dear ladies. As a photographer, I have a vast knowledge of chemicals, and it is my opinion that spirit matter is just another such substance. I have high hopes of being able to photograph its fumes tonight.'

'Do *you* consider the mesmeric force to be like spirit matter?' Mr Stadler asks Myrtle, pointedly turning away from Mr Collins. 'Is it composed of the same material?'

'That's what I'm going to find out,' says Myrtle, flashing a confident smile.

Pearl listens with bemused interest. She only knows bits and bobs about this. All her knowledge comes from the parts of *Missives from Summerland* that Myrtle decides to read out loud to her.

Myrtle learnt to read when she worked at the match factory with Father, but she hasn't taught Pearl.

'I have heard the drollest anecdotes about Mesmerism,' Mr Stadler says. 'Accounts of nice young ladies suddenly swearing and kicking up their skirts whilst in a trance! One mesmerist even made his patient think that the water she drank was sherry instead. They willed it with the power of their mind, and she actually tasted sherry!' He tips a wink. 'Makes you think twice about the Miracle at Cana, eh?'

Pearl doesn't like to hear him talk that way. The contributors to *Missives from Summerland* sound like good-hearted people, committed to the cause of truth, who want to use their supernatural learning to make the world a better place. They're as devout in their faith as any Jew or Methodist. But the Society of Bath Spiritual Adventurers seek phenomena, and nothing more. All Mr Stadler wants the sisters to do with their precious gifts is to make ladies dance!

'Myrtle's going to heal my father,' Pearl stammers. 'She's – she's going to help people with *her* Mesmerism.' All eyes turn towards her. Her palms sweat and she wipes them on her lap. 'He thought he needed a – a doctor, but—'

'Pshaw, my dear!' Mrs Lynch cries. 'You cannot trust a physician. These medical men seek to impose their control on our bodies and souls with their drugs. They think to steer the course of our destiny.'

But why is that a problem? Pearl has never been in control of her own destiny.

She focuses on the centrepiece of the table, wishing she hadn't spoken.

Tonight, the crystal ball's been replaced with a large glass fishbowl, half full of water. On the surface, purple flower heads float.

She'd like to drink that water. The tea hasn't quenched her thirst at all. Ever since market day, she keeps thinking of water. Does it mean something? It feels like there might be water building inside of her: this heaviness across the chest and at the back of her neck. It's like the pressure of a river behind a dam, desperate to break through.

'Must we delay any longer?' Mr Collins gulps the remains of his tea and surges to his feet. 'I am eager to begin.'

Mr Stadler cocks an eyebrow. 'We had not guessed.'

Everyone except Pearl puts their napkins aside.

She doesn't know what to do with herself. The others seem to have tasks: Myrtle turns down the gas lamps; Mrs Lynch and her daughter unpack notebooks from their bags; the men begin to assemble some monstrous contraption with a single glass eye.

Pearl looks at the machine, unnerved. Can it . . . *see* her? Maybe the glass part is just like the crystal ball: something for her to stare into and glimpse the Other Side through. But whereas Pearl's crystal ball is a bubble of soft light, this shape is blind. She squints, trying to see into the big wooden box behind it. Only darkness lies within.

'Careful with that, careful!' Mr Collins scolds his companion.

She's so intent upon the men that she loses sight of the ladies. Pearl almost forgets that they're in the room – until one screams beside her ear.

She whips round to see what accident has happened, but Miss Lynch is standing still, unharmed, gaping at Pearl.

'Look,' she gasps. 'I can see it. I can see the spirit matter flowing from her.'

A reverent silence falls.

Pearl looks down at her pale hands. Gentle wisps rise from them like breath on a cold day. They are coming, then. Ready to claim her.

Her shoulders turn solid with fear.

'The plate,' Mr Collins urges. 'Quickly, man.'

Before Pearl can draw another breath, a flash of white-hot pain scorches across her vision. Stunned, she claps her hands over her eyes, but that burst of light keeps repeating and repeating.

'Myrtle!' she cries.

Myrtle runs to her, buries Pearl's face safely inside the folds of her new gown. It radiates her familiar scent of berries and violets.

'What d'you think you're doing?' she demands.

'The – the magnesium powder.' Mr Collins holds up a tray that smokes. 'Friends of mine have used it to great effect. Through spirit agency, the—'

'If you've read so much, why don't you know better? Mediumship takes a toll upon the Sensitive. She's fragile.'

Pearl feels it. But it soothes her to hear the rumble of Myrtle's voice through her bodice and sense her hand moving over her hair. Much as they squabble, Myrtle is the only mother she's ever known.

'Poor dear,' frets Mrs Lynch. 'Pass her this tea.' Pearl drinks it greedily, her eyes squeezed shut. 'I remember, Miss West, how Florence King weakened *you*. Those bad nights you spent with your nerves in tatters.' She sighs. 'Such is the price of great power.'

'But if we can *capture* this,' Mr Collins enthuses, undeterred, 'if we could prove with an image what we witness here with the naked eye, it would alter everything! You must understand that? Our enemies will be forced to eat their words!'

'No more flash powder tonight,' Myrtle rules. When Mr Collins puffs with frustration, she adds, 'Patience and care, sir. You don't catch spirits with stomping feet.'

Gradually, Pearl can sit upright again. When she opens her eyes they feel raw, as if she's peeled a layer of skin from the lids.

Mr Stadler crosses the room to take her hand. 'Tell us what you feel equal to, Miss Meers. We all wait upon your convenience. But surely you will not send us home so early in the evening?'

She wants to snatch her hand away from him, but she doesn't dare.

'Last time,' Myrtle tells them, 'some friends and I sat in a circle and a spirit spoke through Pearl. Actually possessed her and used her mouth! I never heard her talk in such a deep voice before.'

'What power,' he marvels. 'Most spirits, even the materialised ones, have no utterance.'

'*Can* she materialise a ghost?' Mrs Lynch pushes forward, brimming with excitement. 'We might get Florence King back, or someone else entirely. What is your guide's name, dear?'

Myrtle snaps upright. 'The White Sylph has no need of a spirit guide.'

'Do you remember, dear Miss West, how we used to blindfold you and tie you in the cabinet while you made Florence appear?' Myrtle's face says she remembers only too well. 'We proved, beyond a doubt, that your gift was real.'

'Are you proposing that we tie Miss Meers up also?' Mr Stadler's fingers tighten around Pearl's hand. They are damp, as if the idea excites him. 'In the name of experiment?'

'What do you think might happen?'

The Society remind Pearl of dogs about to fall upon a bone. It's too much; the volley of voices, the wide, eager eyes. She flings Myrtle a terrified glance.

'I won't have my sister bound like a criminal. She isn't in the penitentiary.' Myrtle pats her hair back into shape. 'But let her try the cabinet by all means. We might get a surprise.'

It's a reprieve, of sorts. Pearl should probably be grateful.

Standing up, she edges reluctantly towards the cabinet. It gapes at her like a giant mouth. She thought this would be like the last séance. Why aren't they sticking to what she knows?

At least it's dark inside. She pulls the black damask curtain across the rail, free for a blissful minute from the Society's scrutiny. A sigh escapes her as she sits down.

Now what?

Her spine presses hard against the loose panel in the back of the cabinet. That's where she used to wait, dressed up as Florence King, quiet as a mouse, while the others tied Myrtle with silk scarves and sealed the knots with wax.

One time, she remembers she felt a sneeze coming, and nearly bit through her lip trying to stifle it. But even that was easier than what's being asked of her tonight.

She hears the fizz of a match lighting a candle. The gas lamps go out. Chair legs shuffle, Mr Collins clears his throat.

There is an ominous, charged silence.

Then they begin to sing:

> When the hours of day are numbered,
> And the voices of the night
> Wake the better soul, that slumbered,
> To a holy, calm delight.

The table is just on the other side of the curtain, but the distance between Pearl and the others feels huge.

> Ere the evening lamps are lighted,
> And, like phantoms grim and tall,
> Shadows from the fitful firelight
> Dance upon the parlour wall;

It's horrible to be trapped here, cut off from flesh and blood. The Society all get to sit with another person's warm hand in their own, but Pearl . . . She trembles, realising anew how small and thin she is.

> Then the forms of the departed
> Enter at the open door;
> The beloved, the true-hearted,
> Come to visit me once more;

Tears form. It never used to feel like this in the cabinet. Myrtle was always there. There's something different in the air behind the curtain tonight. It's . . . agitated.

> He, the young and strong, who cherished
> Noble longings for the strife,
> By the roadside fell and perished,
> Weary with the march of life!

She looks from the left to the right. There's nothing there, just black, but it feels, it *feels* . . .

> They, the holy ones and weakly,
> Who the cross of suffering bore,
> Folded their pale hands so meekly
> Spake with us on earth no more!

A current of cool air lifts the hair from her neck.

What is it? A trapped bird, fluttering around her, stirring up the atmosphere? She can't move, she can't speak, but she knows there's something alive inside the cabinet.

> And with them the Being Beauteous,
> Who unto my youth was given,

> More than all things else to love me,
> And is now a saint in heaven.

Cobwebs. Itchy, sticky *cobwebs* are passing over her face. Frantically, she tries to bat them away.

It's only when she lowers her hands that she sees the cloud of downy white, floating before her.

> With a slow and noiseless footstep
> Comes that messenger divine,
> Takes the vacant chair beside me,
> Lays her gentle hand in mine.

The cloud expands.

The others keep on singing as something rises up from the middle like a head beneath a bridal veil.

> And she sits and gazes at me
> With those deep and tender eyes,
> Like the stars, so still and saint-like,
> Looking downward from the skies.

Shoulders emerge but it has no arms, no body, no legs.

> Uttered not, yet comprehended,
> Is the spirit's voiceless prayer
> Soft rebukes, in blessings ended,
> Breathing from her lips of air.

From behind, a freezing hand falls heavy on her shoulder.

Pearl screams.

The singing stops. Chairs scrape but Pearl is faster than them, flinging the curtain back on its rail so hard that it makes the rings clatter.

She runs.

'Pearl!'

Commotion erupts around the table. She can't stop to explain herself to the Society; she can barely breathe for sobs. Hands – mortal, this time – try to restrain her.

'No!' she cries, flinging them off. 'No, I won't do it!'

She darts for Father's room.

There's a shout behind her. A sudden *bang* and *splash*.

Pearl doesn't stop until she reaches the door, where she risks a quick glance back.

The fishbowl of flowers has exploded outwards, drenching the spiritualists in water and glass.

Mrs Lynch stands spluttering, her arms held out at her sides. The ends of Myrtle's curls drip.

Water, again.

Pearl races inside Father's room and locks the door.

Chapter 7

Every year it's the same. Agnes does not wait for the almanac to tell her that winter is approaching; she feels it in her knuckles and her wrists. They become burning, swollen lumps: the price she must pay for her decades spent cutting shades.

With difficulty, she coaxes her gloves from their stretchers and pulls them on to keep her hands warm. The cold season seems to be starting earlier and earlier – either that, or she is getting old. Perpetually chilly, like Mamma with her thin blood and eroded defences. Agnes shoves the thought away. *Not yet*.

As she goes to leave her bedroom, her skirt sweeps against something on the dressing table and sends it floating to the floor. Constance's silhouette. She forgot she had left it there.

She resents having to bend and pick it up, having to pack her sister tidily away yet again. Without looking at the shade, she marches to her studio and opens the book of duplicates. A musty perfume rises from the pages. It always falls open at the same place, but she will *not* put Constance's shadow on this page beside *him*. If that is petty of her – well, she does not care.

Agnes flips to the very back of the book, pushes Constance in and slams it shut.

It all started with her birthday: that was the first thing Constance took. She arrived exactly five years from the day Agnes entered the world, and she did not even soften the blow by being the little boy Mamma had promised.

Constance was not a winsome infant; she was born with the colic. In those first weeks she was not so much a baby as a pink, shrieking ball of rage.

Agnes remembers sitting on the stairs with her hands pressed over her ears, hoping Papa would take Constance away when he boarded his next ship.

The grandfather clock pings the quarter hour. Agnes swallows down her memories. She will be late for morning prayers at the abbey.

Downstairs, Mamma is reading an old *Herald* before a fire that scratches and ticks. More coal is gone, but Agnes cannot really blame her mother for using it today. The temperature has shifted palpably; it is as if the air has whetted its teeth overnight.

Cedric crouches by the side table, idly spinning the top Agnes bought him from the toyshop in Morford Street.

She smiles at him. 'Would you care to accompany me, dear?'

'Where?'

'Church.'

He pulls a face.

Cedric means no harm, but it hurts her to be spurned like this. Everything is much more cheerful when he is with her.

'Do come,' she wheedles. 'Say a prayer, for your Mamma in Heaven?'

The top falls over. Cedric's green eyes meet hers.

'Is *that* where she is?'

Agnes bites her tongue. She is reminded of the phrase the pawnbroker used, when she tried to get a better price for Captain Darken's medals. *Not bloody likely.*

'Yes, of course it is. We have discussed this, Cedric. Listen, dear, if you come along to church with me, perhaps I will take you for a bun at Sally Lunn's afterwards. What do you say to that?'

'I'd rather stay here and read.'

'But we can read together *after—*'

'Let the boy alone.' Mamma wets her finger and turns the page of her newspaper. 'He's well enough here with me.'

Sighing, Agnes puts on her bonnet and makes for the door. Before she steps onto the mat, she is forced to pull up short. A torn piece of paper lies at her feet. It looks like it has been pushed underneath the door, rather than through the letterbox. She is forced to bend yet again, to the protestation of her knees.

The paper is of a good quality. Suitable for sketching, and indeed someone has used a pencil to write four faint words upon it.

Agnes peers, pulls it closer.

Did you miss me.

She frowns and turns the paper over. Just that. Not even a question mark.

Who on earth would write such a thing? She cannot imagine anyone sending her notes except Simon, and he called only the other day, after young Ned had left with his white silhouette. Besides, Simon's correspondence is always a template of formal elegance.

She takes a few steps back to the parlour. 'Cedric, have you been playing with my sketchbooks again?'

'No.' He has pulled *The String of Pearls* onto his lap and is already engrossed.

Perhaps the writing is too developed for his young hand. But it does look familiar . . .

'Did you happen to see who delivered this note?'

The boy shrugs, still reading his book.

Well. How perplexing. She reads the words again, and they touch a chord deep inside her. For the answer is *yes*: she misses so many people.

One in particular.

He would write her notes. Play games. But it cannot be, not after all these years . . .

She tucks the note inside her newly dried reticule and leaves the house.

The sharp air cools her flaming cheeks. Frosty cobbles skid beneath her feet, and she forces herself to walk carefully, head down, concentrating on not slipping.

But her mind is running wild.

The man in the naval coat. She had been sure, at the time, that he was *not* Montague, but she was at a distance, struggling against her encroaching cataracts. It *is* possible . . .

She begs herself to stay calm. This is not the first time hope has surfaced. She should not trust it, but it is intoxicating; she can almost taste it in her mouth, like a rich wine.

Maybe Montague read of the Accident abroad. News from home might have been delayed, and perhaps this is the first chance he has had to return since. She must find a way to check the Navy Lists. She must know where he is.

The anticipation is almost more than she can take.

The abbey is always beautiful, but today it is especially so. Inside, the colours he promised her spill in a cascade from the stained-glass windows, right across the floor. Walking over them feels akin to passing through a cleansing stream. She takes a pew in sight of the golden cross. Usually she views it not only as an emblem of Christ, but the crucifixion of her own dreams.

It does not appear so this morning.

A few of her acquaintances nod to her from their seats – other impecunious spinsters, with which the city is swelling to capacity. Agnes does not count many friends amongst the pale, tired faces peering out from beneath dark bonnets. Even her own kind brand her as rather *odd*. They use the word as a sort of armour; in truth they are shying away from the scandal, the poverty and, most of all, the legacy of the Accident. It saddens her, but she does partly understand. She would not know what to say to a woman like herself either.

The bells toll eleven o'clock.

The Honourable Reverend Brodrick acquits himself admirably during the service. It is not his fault that Agnes cannot lose herself in the sweet unity of prayer. She blames the engagement ring, which today feels enormous and insistent when she clasps her hands together. She wants to settle, to give thanks, but her thoughts are ungovernable. They fly around the abbey like a flock of doves let loose.

Did you miss me.

What if it *is* him?

She remembers her father coming back to shore. How she would pitch into his arms and sob, overcome with the relief that she was no longer alone. It sounds foolish, because of course she had Mamma while he was away, but it was not the same, just as having Simon around is not the same as having Montague.

She has missed Montague more than anyone.

When she was so ill with pneumonia, Simon said it was a miracle that she survived, and maybe it was, maybe *this* is why: she has been granted a second chance to live the life that was stolen from her.

Montague will be different now. Older, wiser, less susceptible to temptation. She can forgive his past errors. In all honesty, she never fully blamed *him*, but he left before she had the opportunity to explain that. She imagines the joy of introducing him to Cedric and their future taking a different course, away from Bath. She sees them being able to afford holidays together. How she would love for the three of them to visit the Isle of Wight!

Left to her own devices, Agnes would have passed from the abbey and back home caught in her dreamy cloud. But half a dozen women are clustered in the aisle, blocking her way, their cloaks pulled high on their hunched shoulders. Although they lean forward and show all the indications of whispering, their voices echo.

'Drowned, they told me. Humane Society couldn't revive him.'

'Oh, how sad.'

'That's nonsense. He would have been able to swim.'

'Look, I'm just telling you what I heard.'

'Does anyone know who he is?'

She pretends not to heed their chatter, but she can feel herself growing cold. They seem to be talking of the River Avon, which always sends her into a panic. Whenever she thinks of it, her mind fills with black water, her mouth with a brackish taste.

Agnes clears her throat. 'Excuse me, please,' she requests loudly.

They draw aside to let her past.

Before she opens the door, a hand reaches out and touches her arm. She stops and sees Miss Grayson: a small, sweet-looking woman; a portrait painter by trade, almost as short on work as Agnes herself.

'Pardon me, Miss Darken,' she says, drawing her aside from the group. 'I wanted to tell you the news, in case you had not heard.'

'News?'

Miss Grayson offers a wistful smile. 'I felt for you so awfully when that man was killed, right after your appointment. It was all anyone talked about.' Her hand squeezes Agnes's arm gently. 'But that's done now.' She nods at a wide, red-faced woman holding forth to her companions. 'Miss Betts has something new to gossip about.'

Agnes knows the reassurance is kindly meant, but she feels belittled by it. 'How fortunate for Miss Betts,' she says tartly. 'Pray, what is the latest scandal the crows are feasting on?'

Miss Grayson shoots a glance over at her companions. They really do resemble carrion birds, and perhaps she sees this, for her mouth puckers.

'A dreadful tragedy, Miss Darken. I swear it does not bring anyone pleasure to hear of it, but for your sake. A body has been pulled from the river at Weston Lock.'

Although Agnes prickles with sweat to hear of it, the event

itself is not uncommon, particularly amongst the poor wretches living down in the Avon Street slums. 'Another drunk,' she guesses. 'Or perhaps *felo de se*?'

'No, Miss Darken. That's just it.' Miss Grayson shakes her head sadly. 'The man was a naval officer. He drowned wearing his uniform.'

Chapter 8

There's an airless silence in the chamber as Myrtle stands over the bed. She looks at Father as if he offends her sense of order. Beside him she appears more vital than ever, her skin peaches and cream.

She takes a breath. Then she begins.

Crouched in the corner, Pearl watches, fascinated. Myrtle's hands move with a careful intensity. Up and down, side to side, in fluid motions. It's like hearing poetry.

Sometimes Myrtle's palms face downwards, magnetising the body. As she makes a pass from shoulder to shoulder, she flips her wrist, so that the backs of her hands are closer to Father's skin.

How does she know when to do that?

Myrtle says a good mesmerist can see inside their patient, like they're made of glass. Pearl wishes she could see too. She'd rather that cold, clean image than the one actually before her eyes: the discharge and the wasted skin.

Between each pass, Myrtle shakes her hands, ridding herself of the diseased magnetism. Pearl studies the air for a hint of the force but it's invisible to her.

Why can't she get a glimpse of it? Myrtle says it has colours, a different one for each person. It sounds pretty.

Pearl shivers and wraps her shawl tighter around her shoulders. She's been freezing all day. She turns even colder when she remembers that the shivering started just after Myrtle came home, yesterday afternoon. Almost the exact minute her visions of water abruptly stopped.

She shakes her head like Myrtle shakes her hands; ridding herself, casting it off. No good. Bad energy might drip from Myrtle's fingers, but it remains firmly lodged in Pearl's mind.

The ceremony reaches its conclusion. Myrtle dips into her apron and produces a clean handkerchief.

'What's that for?' Pearl whispers.

She doesn't receive an answer.

Myrtle opens the handkerchief and lays it gently over Father's face, like a shroud. It sticks to the ooze around his jaw. Myrtle leans over him. Then Pearl hears her breathe.

A heavy inhalation through the nose and out through the mouth, onto the handkerchief. Four, five times. The sound of air puffing through her sister's lips. She's reviving him. Trying to pass some of her own vigour to Father.

Pearl hunches into her shawl and closes her eyes. It's so cold. But only she can feel the chill, and that means . . . After yesterday's discovery, she daren't think what it means.

Myrtle's hand latches on her shoulder. 'Come on. Let him rest now.'

Her sister bundles her out of the room, back into the darkened parlour. Pearl climbs into an easy chair and curls her feet up beneath her for warmth. The crystal ball is back in pride of place on the table opposite her. It took them ages to clean up the shattered fishbowl. All that glass and water, everywhere . . .

The kettle whistles.

When the teacup finally arrives, it's so hot that it burns. Pearl cradles it in both hands, nonetheless.

'Don't spill it,' Myrtle warns.

Pearl thinks she wouldn't mind being scalded by hot liquid today.

Myrtle sits down, takes a bite of the toast she's made them.

She's given all the jam to Pearl. 'That went well, I think,' she says through her mouthful. 'I'll keep at it. Phew! Mesmerism don't half take it out of me.'

But she doesn't look depleted in any way. Her eyes still dazzle beneath the frame of her widow's peak.

'How can you be so calm?' Pearl marvels.

'What d'you mean? He weren't no worse than usual . . .'

'No! Not about Father. I mean after yesterday.'

'Oh.' Myrtle picks at the crust of her toast. 'That. It's sad, Pearl. But these things happen. And we both know death ain't the end.'

'But you found the body in the river! Touched him . . .' A tremor runs through her as she thinks of the cold, clammy skin.

'I don't know what you're getting so upset about. You were here, you didn't see nothing.'

'Yes I *did*!' Pearl insists. Tea slops from her cup onto her shawl. 'I kept seeing water in my head . . . And then the fish-bowl exploded . . . Don't you follow? I predicted the death. All I could think about was water, and then you found a drowned man.'

Myrtle shrugs and takes a vicious bite of toast.

'You don't think that's weird?' Pearl prompts.

'You're a spirit medium, ain't you? 'Course you're going to see things. And you need to deal with them better than you did that one in the cabinet if we're going to make any money out of you.' Pearl pouts at her. 'Well, what did you expect when you got the Power?'

Some acknowledgement, maybe, of how frightening it is. A sense of wonder, at the very least. But Myrtle's seen it all before. 'I didn't think it would be . . . like this,' Pearl says lamely.

She *wanted* to see Mother, to hear her voice for the first time. And maybe she'd hoped the ghosts would be like the friends she never had, making the house less lonely when Myrtle's out and about on her errands.

'It's different for everyone,' Myrtle reasons. 'You'll figure it out. Maybe we'll try and contact the drowned man at our next séance. See if he's all right over there. Would that make you feel better?'

It really wouldn't, but Pearl finds herself nodding. She drinks the tea, hoping it might dilute the power that's inside her body.

'Myrtle?'

'What?'

Pearl looks down at her cup. 'D'you think it was the same killer? Who murdered Mr Boyle then drowned that man? Because a sailor would've been able to swim . . .'

'Might've been.' Myrtle considers. 'Or maybe the sailor was just drunk and hit his head before he fell in the river. You can ask him, can't you?'

'But Myrtle . . .' Pearl's feet are growing numb beneath her. She adjusts her position in the chair. 'What if I'm . . . *seeing* him? The murderer? Seeing the ways he's going to kill people. First it was water, when I was so thirsty, and now I'm cold. What if he's going to freeze someone to death next?'

Myrtle rolls her eyes. 'Don't be daft. You're just poorly.'

But Pearl can't stop talking now; she's opened the dam and her thoughts are spilling from her. 'Maybe that's it. *That's* why I've got this Gift, and we can use it, use it to catch him—'

'Enough!'

Myrtle slams her plate down. It makes Pearl jump. 'Listen to me.' Myrtle's voice comes tight and low. It's how she speaks to the Society when she's angry but trying to sound polite. 'This is silly. You've got a fever and you're raving, Pearl. You'd better go to bed.'

'But I—' she starts.

Myrtle's eyes fix upon her, snuff out the rest of her sentence. 'Bed. And no more talk about stopping killers. You're a spirit medium. People getting knocked off is your bread and butter. Do you understand me?'

It's an awful thing to say. Pearl knows it deep down, and yet somehow . . . It makes sense.

All her arguments melt like sugar on the tongue before Myrtle's gaze. She touches her forehead, starts to feel that she's been the one in the wrong this whole time. 'You're right. I think I've got a fever. I'd . . . better go to bed.'

Chapter 9

Walcot Street is not far away. About ten minutes by foot – or at least, it used to be. Even if it takes her failing body twice as long, Agnes would rather make the walk than face the ordeal of riding in a fly or an omnibus.

But although the physical distance is short, there is a great social divide between her home, flanked by the abbey and the banks, and this bustling area of commerce. Everyone hurries: to the dyers, to the locksmith, to the grocers, to the chophouses that issue a malodour of hot beef fat. She cannot keep pace. And none of the men emerging from their work at the brewery possess enough gallantry to grant a lady a wide berth on the pavement.

Coal dust flecks the atmosphere. Buildings are white, yellow and black, like a set of progressively mouldering teeth, some with clapboard fronts and papered windows.

Struggling against the throng, who jostle her, Agnes checks the address she has written down one last time. She *could* travel further, to the coroner at Walcot Parade, or visit the men at the Humane Society, or even contact that boorish policeman, Redmayne, for information. But she feels that this Miss West, who found the body, will be more likely to give her assistance; the woman will probably have observed more than all of the men put together.

Only yesterday she walked to church trying to convince

herself that the man she had seen in the cocked hat was indeed Montague. Now, she would give worlds to be certain he was *not*.

The house she seeks stands just short of Ladymead Penitentiary, beneath the stern gaze of Paragon Buildings, its windows shrouded in soot. Behind the black smudges, she makes out a card advertising something, but the words are indecipherable.

Pedestrians push on behind her and tut. Taking a deep breath, she screws up her courage and knocks.

No footsteps sound behind the door, but it is opened instantly by a striking young woman, comely and golden-haired, perhaps twenty years of age. She stares at Agnes, all piquant features and bright, questing eyes.

'Yes?'

A London accent.

Agnes feels absurd, and very, very old. 'I . . . Good morning. Forgive me for disturbing you. I daresay this is going to seem a trifle odd, but . . . Are you – by chance – the Miss West who found the drowned man?'

An eyebrow arches, its shape unnervingly reflected in Miss West's widow's peak. 'Knocked on this door *by chance*, did you?'

'N-no,' Agnes stutters, face aflame. 'Of course I discovered Miss West lived here, but I did not like to assume that you . . . She might not be the only resident.'

Miss West stares at her.

'Pardon me for interrupting you,' Agnes repeats. 'It is only that . . . They do not seem to have identified the body yet. I am anxious for a friend of mine and I wondered if I might . . . ask you a few brief questions about what you found?'

'Why don't you just go to the mortuary chapel? Have a look at him?'

The mere concept sends Agnes dizzy. 'I cannot do that.'

Miss West sucks her teeth, looks Agnes up and down. 'Well, I suppose you'd better come in, then.'

The light is strangely muted inside, not unlike Mrs Boyle's house of mourning. Agnes has a dim impression of a thinning carpet and cracks in the ceiling. What strikes her most is the odour: sulphur and rot.

There is no obvious sign of its origin. The parlour Miss West leads her to is clean, if rather worn. Faded lilac paper peels at the edges of the walls. A black walnut cabinet skulks beside the fireplace. There are several chairs grouped together in dark communion, a sofa and a circular table covered in cheap red plush. Rather than flowers, the table has a glass globe as the centrepiece. Agnes has never seen anything like it.

Miss West seats herself upon the sofa and flicks her eyes towards one of the chairs.

Agnes takes it. 'Thank you.'

'Keep your voice down,' Miss West warns. 'I've a sick man and child to look after.'

'We are alike, then.' Agnes jumps upon the common ground, grinning rather foolishly. 'Since my sister passed, I have been caring for my nephew and aged mother. It can be a trial to—'

'You said you've got questions.'

She was going to begin with a preamble, apologise for dredging up unpleasant scenes, but it seems Miss West was born without a sense of delicacy. She imagines this bold young woman touching Montague's drowned body and her stomach turns over. 'Yes. I-I wondered if you happened to see, from the coat of this naval man you found, whether he was an officer? And of which rank?'

Miss West cocks her head. 'My dad was a soldier. Dunno about the navy, though I should. Had an uncle in the service.' Agnes opens her mouth to speak, but Miss West cuts her off again. 'And it's no use you explaining all the stripes and what-not now, ma'am. To be honest, the coat was that torn up, I didn't even realise what it was until later on.'

Agnes grips the arm of her chair. She must see this through, no matter how painful the details. 'Perhaps . . . the age of the man?'

A sigh. Miss West's expression softens, along with her voice. 'The thing is . . . A drowned body ain't a pretty sight, ma'am. It swells something awful. Don't look like the person no more. Even the hair . . . I mean it's darker when it's wet. Looked kind of sandy to me, but . . .'

The girl speaks with her hands. Not nervously; these are no fluttering birds but swift, decisive motions that sweep Agnes with them. She is grateful to have them to focus upon. The words are a buzz in her ears, for she knows exactly what Miss West is talking about: she too has seen a corpse pulled from the water.

Softened, puffy. The flesh spreading out of its firm lines.

'. . . do you see what I mean? Ma'am?' Then, sharper, 'Ma'am?'

Strong arms catch her out of the swoon. Agnes has a vague sensation of being moved and having her feet elevated. The next thing she feels is water against her lips. Forcing its way in, as if she is back in the river . . . She splutters.

'Easy, now,' Miss West croons. 'Take a drink. It'll bring you round.'

Reluctantly, Agnes does. Her vision returns. Miss West offers a teasing smile.

'I see, now, why you didn't go to the mortuary.'

She is not amused; she feels like a colossal fool. Why does she keep charging about on these mad errands, instead of following Simon's advice to stay home and rest? Perhaps he has been right all along. Perhaps she *does* need someone to care for her, to tell her what to do. She makes such a hash of things alone.

She tries to sit up, but Miss West pushes her back down. 'Not yet. Give it a minute.'

'Sorry,' Agnes murmurs. 'I must seem terribly weak.' Then, feeling some explanation is necessary, 'That was how she died, you see. My sister. She . . . well. Her body was recovered from the Avon.'

She is surprised to see Miss West's face, which until now she thought rather sharp, melt into understanding. 'Terrible thing for you.' After watching her a moment, Miss West adds, 'I can see it. That dusky, ash of roses colour. Like a wound slowly bleeding in water. It left its mark on your aura, didn't it?'

Agnes is too astonished to reply.

Miss West chuckles. 'Ah. You didn't read the card in the window, then? This is a special house.'

Agnes sips at the water, giving herself time to think of a response. Either she has lost her wits, or Miss West has. Given her fainting fit, the former seems likely.

'Special how?'

Miss West considers. Just when Agnes thinks she will not answer, she says, 'Tell me, ma'am. Would you like to speak with your dead sister?'

'Good heavens, no.' She drops her cup. Miss West lurches forward to save it, her brilliant eyes widening.

'Careful. I didn't mean to scare you. I know it ain't for everyone.' She hands the glass back to Agnes. 'I was just trying to explain what we do here. I read auras. Cleanse and heal them with my Mesmerism. That's not much good to you. But the Sylph . . . I thought the Sylph might be able to help.'

Agnes struggles to get her bearings. *Sylph* . . . she has heard this somewhere before. But it does not help her make sense of the strange words this girl is saying. Mesmerism? Was that not proved to be quackery? She remembers Simon speaking of it once, after he attended a demonstration. He had been impressed by one aspect, although she is at a loss to remember what . . .

'The truth is, ma'am, that I can't help you identify your friend. You'll have to go see the corpse, or else wait until someone else does. That might take months. Or' – she looks straight into Agnes's eyes, unabashed – 'the other way. We ask the man himself.'

'I do not have the pleasure of understanding you.'

Miss West points. 'Behind that door, asleep, is the White Sylph. She can speak to the dead.'

Prickles run all over Agnes's skin. *The White Sylph*. She remembers now: Mrs Boyle. Mrs Boyle spoke of contacting her murdered husband through a spirit medium of the same name.

It all crashes together in her head: the large cabinet, the crystal ball on the table. Necromancy.

'I . . .' she begins, but it transpires there is no adequate response when people talk of communing with the dead.

Can it really be possible? *Can* it?

Agnes imagines skeletons, ghosts and ghouls. The pictures fill her with an abject, quivering dread, until she thinks of Papa and her heart stutters. If it was true . . . If she could actually *talk* to him, one last time . . .

She clears her throat, raises herself to a higher position. 'I thought you said that your sister was unwell, Miss West.'

'She is,' Miss West agrees. 'The Power comes after a spell of bad illness, and it can make you sick too. That's the price you pay for the Gift. But in a few days I'm sure she could do a séance for you.'

'And – and your father? You said you had two people to care for. He was in the army . . . He is wounded from a battle, I daresay.'

Miss West's pretty lips set. 'The man in there ain't my father.'

'No?'

'No.' The harsh London accent returns. 'My dad bit it when I was seven. Cannon fodder. I pleaded with Mother not to marry again, but what could she do? There was no one to help us. Neither hide nor hair of my uncle. And you see how it's worked out for me. She's popped off and I'm stuck caring for everyone.'

Agnes pulls a wry expression. She knows exactly how that feels.

'And what afflicts the poor man?'

Miss West puffs out her breath. 'Matches.'

'I beg your pardon?'

'He got us into matches. The hours I spent, miss, in that stinking factory, dipping the lucifers. They're right, you know, to name them after Old Nick.' Her hands gain animation once again. 'That work don't do you no good. All them fumes, they eat away at you. He got sick. And of course they don't care, do they, factory owners? Just paid him off. They said they'd keep me on there if I wanted, but would you fancy it, after seeing the work take his face away like that?'

'Oh. I think I may have heard of this malady. The corrosive effects of the phosphorus . . . Phossy jaw, do they call it?'

'They can call it what they like,' she scoffs. 'It's me what has to deal with it. I brought him all the way here to Bath because a doctor said the waters would cure him, but that's a cock and bull story, ain't it? Bloody doctors. They didn't help my mother and they can't help him.'

Poor Simon. For all his authority, she doubts he would fare well, pitted against this young woman.

Miss West seems to catch herself. 'I'm sorry. You didn't need to hear all that. I don't usually lose my temper, but it's been a trying week. That body and all . . .'

'I quite understand.'

'Like I said, my uncle was a sailor too, and he left us. Thinking of them always makes me angry.'

Agnes feels ashamed of how silly she has been. Neither the waterlogged corpse nor the river are here; they cannot touch her. And Miss West is not a wicked heretic, only a frustrated and poorly educated girl.

She drains her glass and, for want of a side table, places it on the carpet. The fibres are unpleasantly stiff and coarse, like sackcloth. 'Thank you so much for your kindness, Miss West.'

Slowly, she sits up. 'I am sorry to have troubled you. Please accept my best wishes for your family's return to health.'

Miss West watches her stand, one hand outstretched to catch her in case she should fall again. 'That's all right. And what will you do, ma'am? About your friend?'

'I am not certain.'

She touches Agnes's shoulder. Her flesh feels startlingly warm through the black fabric of her gown. 'You should talk to the Sylph. Honestly, ma'am. Just to know for sure.'

Agnes gives a thin smile. 'And what is the price for a consultation with the dead, these days?'

'For you? I'd take sixpence. Just this once, mind.'

Half a shilling! Half the price of a shade, for a piece of mummery. But she must not be rude to Miss West in her own house.

'I will think upon it,' she says.

'Make sure you do. Miss . . . ?'

It surprises Agnes to realise she has come inside Miss West's home, heard her secrets, and not even given her own name. She was taught better manners than that.

For a second she considers inventing an alias, just in case the police come to hear of her visit, but her imagination fails her. 'Darken. My name is Agnes Darken.'

It is clear she has made a mistake.

Miss West removes her hand from Agnes's shoulder. A change comes over her, like a veil dropped across a bonnet.

Is the young woman literate? Could she have read the newspaper article describing Mr Boyle's murder?

'Well, you know where I am if you want me, Miss Darken,' she mutters.

Chastened, Agnes leaves the house. She thought she would enjoy being free of that close, stale air but the streets are as chaotic as ever: the rattle of wheels and the cries of the hawkers a rude awakening.

There was something soothing about that parlour which

she cannot put her finger on. A feeling of being outside of herself, wrapped in Miss West's voice.

Agnes had thought that she was lying when she told the girl she would think about the séance. But she does.

She thinks about it all the way home.

Chapter 10

Most girls of Pearl's age and station share a bed with their sisters. She'd like that. But Myrtle's always reluctant for them to bunk together, even when Pearl is poorly. She says it's important that they each have their own space.

The problem is, Pearl's bedchamber isn't exactly a space to boast about. The wainscot is chipped, mould buds on the ceiling and a thick, dusty curtain covers the small window – Pearl's not sure it's ever been washed, or even drawn back. There's a dark wardrobe, which looks alarmingly like the cabinet in the parlour and is mostly full of Myrtle's belongings.

There's just one good thing about being alone in her twilit room: she can pray. Not like Father taught her, exactly; she doesn't know much about God other than His name. But she likes the idea of someone hovering beyond her sight, watching over her. Someone she can talk to who will maybe – maybe – talk back.

She sits on the bed, crosses her legs. This time it will work.

She can't stop the murderer or explain the shivering on her own, but there's a person on the Other Side who can help her: Mother. If she can contact Mother, they'll catch the killer together as a team. The idea fills her with a sweet glow. Not only the prospect of finally meeting her parent, but of being of use to the world outside for a change.

If she managed to call up that phantom in the cabinet and

make the fishbowl explode, surely she's strong enough to find Mother now?

She closes her eyes. Waits.

Horseshoes clack distantly outside.

The colour behind Pearl's eyelids has a brownish tinge, it isn't as dark as it should be. Frustrated, she takes off her shawl and wraps it around her head. That's better. Warm, muffled. She can hear her own breath. It dampens the wool that presses to her face.

Where are you, Mother?

She tries to recreate that sensation of falling into an abyss that comes so easily in the parlour. Showers of light and stars usually spill from her, beyond her control, but now she actually wants to reach out and pluck something, there is . . . emptiness. Just her hot breath and the terrifying blankness.

What would help? She hasn't anything that belonged to Mother. Doesn't even know what Mother looked like. But surely she'll know when she comes, she'll know instinctively.

Pearl holds out her arms like she's playing blind man's buff. She gropes into the darkness, concentrating with all her might.

'Please, Mother.'

Nothing happens.

'Where are you?'

Why can't she feel the ghosts? Normally, they scare her with their whispers and their butterfly touch, but in fact this void is worse. Calling out for help in a pitch-black cave and hearing nothing come back to her but her own voice.

The shawl itches her face.

Reluctantly, she unwinds it and tosses it aside, but keeps her eyes closed.

Maybe she's been too alert, too desperate? Myrtle says you don't catch ghosts with stomping feet. Pearl tries, tries so hard, to compose herself.

But still the blankness taunts her.

Slowly, she inches her eyelids open, hoping that by some miracle Mother will be standing before her, covered in a white shroud.

She isn't. There's only the wardrobe and the scuffed walls.

For the first time it strikes her that maybe Mother doesn't appear because she doesn't *want* to be seen. Not by Pearl.

'I didn't mean for you to die,' she whispers. 'I was only a baby. I didn't know. I couldn't help it.'

But it seems she is unforgiven.

Chapter 11

Agnes first met Montague over a table like this. Of course they went to Molland's in those days, but the essential layout of the refreshment room is the same here in Marlborough Lane: circular tables with sprigged cloths, pale green and white crockery, spiced steam in the air. They even have a similar bell over the door. It tinkles sporadically, making no impact on the chatter and clinking spoons.

When she thinks back, her memory is hazy. To tell the truth, she had no indication at that first meeting of what Montague would come to mean to her. She was more interested in sponge cake and cocoa than the two young men Captain Darken had rushed across the shop to shake hands with.

Bedford and Montague had served under him as midshipmen, her father explained. They were due promotion any day now, and he would put in a good word for them, if his word still meant anything to the navy. It had meant something to Agnes. When the engagement was finally formed, after Captain Darken's death, one of her chief pleasures had been the certainty that Papa would have approved of her match.

But on that day, John Montague was simply an agreeable young man who shared stories of life below deck. The only virtue to recommend him over his companion Bedford was the honour of his attention. For Bedford relished a challenge and had set out to engage Constance in conversation.

Although the sisters were similar in appearance, it was generally agreed that Constance's visage lacked the prettiness Agnes's possessed. Constance's chin was more pointed, her nose like a freshly sharpened pencil. Beside the rest of the family's brown eyes, her blue ones struck as particularly cold. But still there was something that drew gentlemen to Constance. That face: provocative, even at repose. Daring you to animate it.

Bedford did not succeed.

Was it that day, or later on, that she discovered Montague's fondness for marchpane? A box of it sits on Agnes's lap now, ready to take home for Cedric. It emanates a scent of almond that is almost unbearably sweet. Like her memories – one can only indulge in moderation. A surfeit is sure to cause rot, somewhere down the line.

The bell tinkles. Simon steps into the room, carrying his small black dog under one arm. The animal has a ribbon tied around his neck that matches Simon's best waistcoat.

She is oddly touched. He always remembers the day.

'Miss Darken!' He walks over, takes her hand and raises it to his lips. 'Many happy returns to you. Forgive my tardiness. A gentleman should never keep a lady waiting.'

'So why did you?' she enquires archly.

'A patient.' He sits opposite her, placing the dog upon his lap. 'This snow has caused a flare in all the rheumatic complaints.' The dog yawns. She suspects he would rather be home by the fire than trussed up for her benefit.

'Well, you see how extravagant I have been in your absence: a whole box of marchpane!'

'On the anniversary of your birth, I believe you may do whatever you wish.'

This is not something she often hears, especially from Simon. 'Anything?' she teases. 'You would let me order a cup of coffee without a warning that it excites my nerves?'

Concern flickers across his brow. He quickly wards it off with a smile. 'For today, I believe I would.'

But Agnes can be kind too, and she places an order she knows he will approve of: ginger tea and a small apple tart in honour of the occasion. If one can call it an *occasion*.

They amuse themselves by feeding sugar lumps to the dog while they wait for their refreshments. She wonders why it never seems to strike Simon that this is also the day that Constance was born. *That* would be reason enough to dampen the celebrations. Yet each year they re-enact this charade: him, so desperate to treat her; she, trying to appear pleased for his sake, as if growing older were a privilege rather than the burden it feels.

She has stopped counting her age with any accuracy. Simon could probably tell her the exact figure, but his gallantry would never allow it.

'That is enough, now, Morpheus,' Simon finally says as the dog's tongue works busily at his fingers, trying to lick off every stray grain of sugar. 'We are both of us portly already.'

'But you are strong,' Agnes tells him. 'Whereas I do not think Morpheus can say the same.'

The dog answers with a burp. They laugh.

'It is true, of course,' Simon chuckles. 'I indulge him. He is a greedy, lazy little brute. But I do so enjoy seeing him content.'

Morpheus is content, she thinks, because he never met Simon's wife. His previous dogs were not so fortunate.

She gestures to the box beneath the tablecloth. 'Perhaps I am the same with Cedric. Taking home treats although he *never* remembers to wish me a happy birthday. And Mamma cannot remind him. You know how her mind wanders these days.'

He shifts uncomfortably, but is prevented from replying by the arrival of their victuals.

The aroma of her ginger tea is pleasantly warm. She has not drunk it in a while, but she remembers now it was always her sister's favourite. That kick of spice, just like the woman herself. Simon has ordered coffee, proving that physicians never follow their own advice. To be fair, he looks as if he requires a whole vat of the liquid. Despite his attempts to dress smartly and oil the remains of his hair, Agnes can see his fatigue. In the moment he pauses to lift his cup, the mask slips, and what she glimpses beneath is exhaustion.

It frightens her. She has become so reliant upon him.

Morpheus's round eyes grow large at the sight of the apple tart. Agnes pulls it to her side of the table.

'Simon,' she begins. She does not look directly at him but stirs her tea, round and round. 'I did wonder if . . . with it being my birthday . . . I might ask a favour from you?'

'As ever, I am at your service.'

Her heart flutters its wings inside her chest. It is only Simon; she should not be afraid to speak candidly before him. But the problem is, Simon knows her better than anyone; he sees the things she keeps hidden, even from herself.

'There was a man. He drowned in the Avon not long ago. You may have read of it.'

He clears his throat. 'I did, yes.'

Her spoon is moving very fast. Morpheus watches it, his eyes flicking forward and back. 'With your medical connections, I wondered if you might . . . make some enquiries for me. See if they are any closer to establishing his identity.'

The sound of cups and plates moving only exaggerates Simon's silence.

He is so quiet that she thinks he may have stopped breathing.

At last, he says, 'And may I ask why . . . ?'

She must concentrate. She cannot let either feature or voice betray her. 'He was a naval man, it seems. I very much doubt he ever served with Papa, but I should like to know if—'

'Miss Darken, it is not *him*.'

Her cheeks scald, as if he had thrown his coffee in her face. 'You mistake me,' she snaps.

'Do I?'

Morpheus whines.

Agnes lets go of her spoon. It chimes loudly against the cup. Without it to clench, she notices that her hand is unsteady. 'Yes. This is not about Montague, precisely. But I was not being wholly honest when I said it was about Papa either. The truth is, Simon . . . Something very strange is happening. Do you remember when the policeman came around? Asking about Mr Boyle?'

'Naturally, I recall it.'

'That very same day, I took a study of a naval officer by Sydney Gardens. Do you understand? The silhouette – and then – the man – he drowned! What if it was *him*, Simon? What if it was the same man?'

She pants, short of breath.

Simon scrubs a hand over his chin. 'Well,' he says slowly. 'What if it were? What would that mean?'

She flicks a glance around the crowded tables. She must try to comport herself with more dignity; already an elderly lady is peering at them through her pince-nez.

She takes a sip of ginger tea, which lights a flame in the back of her throat. 'It would mean, Simon, that my sitters are dying. That may be a given in *your* profession, but it is rare in mine. What if people find out this death also had a connection to my business? The customers . . . And that dreadful Sergeant Redmayne would come back, upsetting me.'

Simon draws his lips together, pats her hand awkwardly across the table. 'Do not fret. I would never allow that upstart to hurt you. And let us consider. You say this man was just a study you took? In the gardens? Then no one will ever know. He will have no appointment scheduled, nothing that links him to you.'

This is true, but she is not appeased.

'All the same, it makes me uneasy. I should like to know for sure whether it was the same officer. I know it sounds superstitious and dreadfully silly, but I shall be frightened to cut another shade in case the sitter is . . . hurt . . . again.'

A pause. Steam hisses.

'You could not . . . retire from cutting silhouettes?' he suggests gently.

'We would starve!'

'I would never allow that to happen. Do you need more assistance? You have only to ask. Let me extend my surgery, shoulder more of the load. Given our relationship, it would not be improper . . .'

Her eyes begin to sting. When all else in life has been taken from her, does Simon really think she will surrender the one occupation that was ever truly hers? Her studio is the last room in the house where she feels *herself*; the only one that does not require Cedric's presence to enliven it. She will not relinquish her last means of independent joy.

Simon seems on the point of saying more, but Agnes pulls back in her chair.

'Use your money to help Cedric establish himself, Simon. That is all I ask of you.'

He hangs his head. Deep down, she thinks she knows what he was going to say next.

He has been not saying it these ten years at least.

'Thank you for the tea.' She pushes the plate away. 'I do not think I can manage the tart. I seem to have lost my appetite.'

Morpheus swoops in and gobbles it up.

———

Fresh snow has fallen outside. She is tempted to accept Simon's offer of a sedan chair home simply to avoid the awkwardness of walking by his side. But when it comes down to it, the enclosure and its movement are too similar to that of a carriage. Any social discomfort is preferable to being reminded of the Accident.

'We will walk slowly,' he decides, setting Morpheus down on the pavement.

The dog's stubby black legs disappear beneath the drift, which reaches his belly. He whines. Simon ignores him and holds out an arm for Agnes to lean on.

She takes it carefully. The friction of their disagreement seems to prickle through his coat.

'You are not cold, Miss Darken? I will not have you catch pneumonia again.'

Agnes assures him she is wearing her chest preserver and thickest boots. How does he suppose she managed to make her way to the tea shop in the first place?

'We used to enjoy weather like this,' she reminds him. 'When we were young. Let's wander up a little and see the gardens. They will look so pretty in the snow.'

She had hoped to soften Simon with the memory, but the muscles in his arm tense. 'Not the gardens. They are too far and perhaps treacherous. I would not wish for you to slip. In these low temperatures, we really should get you home as quickly as possible.'

'So much for pleasing myself on the day of my birth.'

The frown deepens on his face. 'Well . . . Perhaps just to Crescent Fields.'

Morpheus huffs and begins to push his way through the snow. It cuts a track for them to follow.

Bath is a different city in the snow. White smothers every soot-stained building, every dung-heaped road and every skeletal tree. This is how it must have appeared when the limestone mansions were freshly built and full of promise: a dazzling expanse of unclaimed space.

Well, not quite unclaimed. Even in this enchanting tableau, the iron railings at the top of the Crescent show dark against the glare. It is the divide between the private lawns of the rich and the public ground below. Everyone carefully contained and in their space.

Today, Agnes is content to be on her own side. Those braving the fields do so with genuine glee. Laughter peals through the frigid air. She smiles at the children, who pelt each other with snowballs. Nurses scold and run after them, but they are powerless to stop the fun.

'Do you remember . . .' she begins, turning towards Simon, but the sentence dies in her mouth. The tears shining in his eyes tell her he recalls only too well.

She lowers her head, chastened. Simon was born to a large family. Sometimes it seems impossible to believe that there is only him left. She pictures the little Carfaxes running in the snow as they used to do. Their faces live in her memory, but she cannot reach all of the names. Nancy, the eldest, who used to hold Constance's hand when Agnes would not. Edmund. Or was it Edward? There was certainly a Matthew.

Now they are only silhouettes hanging in Simon's hall.

Morpheus wades past a trio of men in knee-high boots, then another cluster of young people building walls out of snow. In vain, Agnes searches for Cedric amongst the red-cheeked revellers. He should be out, on a day like this, playing with children his own age. She wishes she had the energy to pull him on a sled or teach him how to skate.

The air smells pleasantly clean. While Simon is lost in thought, she steers him gently in the direction of the Victoria Obelisk. It wears a lace cap. She can almost make out the lions beneath, sprinkled as if with sugar. It gives her a strange satisfaction to see everything in chiaroscuro. She might have painted it herself.

Trudging through the snow *is* tiring her and the box of marchpane now seems full of rocks, but she is determined to reach Victoria Gardens ere her birthday is done.

Before they come within full view of the Victoria Gate, a sound snaps Simon from his reverie. Morpheus cocks his head and listens alongside his master. A man is calling Simon's name.

Releasing Agnes's arm, he turns. A gentleman of perhaps

thirty years of age, ill-dressed for the weather, is stumbling towards them. 'Dr Carfax!'

Two women titter and clear themselves from his haphazard path.

The man sports a thin, dark beard which only serves to show the dreadful pallor of his face.

'Mr Oswald?' Simon cries.

He skids to a halt and nearly collapses, but Simon catches him under the elbows.

'Dr Carfax,' he pants. 'Thank heavens I have found you!'

'Calm yourself, sir. Whatever is the matter?'

'Mrs Oswald.'

Simon blanches. 'The child is not . . . Not already . . . It is so early . . .'

'I pray to God, no!' The man gasps, trying to catch his breath. 'But she slipped. She slipped on the ice and she fell.'

'Where?'

Mr Oswald throws out one arm. 'Just there, further down the Royal Avenue. I knew I saw you, in the distance. Thank God I *did* see you! Will you come to her?'

Simon hesitates. Glances at Agnes.

'Go, go,' she orders. 'I shall come to no harm waiting here.'

'But—'

'The dog will protect me.'

It is a bold claim to make on behalf of a fat pug, but Simon seems mollified.

'Please,' Mr Oswald urges, tugging at his sleeve.

Simon nods and takes off through the snow.

It is blissfully quiet after they have left. Agnes stands for a while, watching the breeze skim a fine layer from the top of the drifts. White specks wheel into shapes that abruptly collapse. If she listens hard enough, she can hear the snow melting in the tops of the evergreens, crackling against the leaves.

It seems the Royal Victoria Gardens are hers, after all.

She walks to the gate and pushes it open. Snow falls from

the black iron bars as they swing on their hinges; Morpheus whuffs and grumbles at her feet.

No one else has braved the park. The lawns stretch pure as a freshly starched petticoat. There are no blemishes, no indication of where the footpaths and carriage drives lie buried. Agnes may choose her own route.

She sets off straight, towards the lake, hugging a belt of mature trees. The earth is uneven underfoot. Somewhere down there, life slumbers, waiting to burst forth again: green shoots, daffodils. They will be a long time coming. They have not even made it through October yet.

It is early, for snow, but then it has been a tumultuous year, what with the war breaking out and cholera in London over the summer. Everything is out of sorts. At least here there is beauty and peace.

Morpheus toddles on ahead, curly tail twitching. She watches him sniff and forage, following a pattern of twig-like bird tracks underneath the trees.

If she is reasonable – and she tries to be – she can understand why Simon grew prickly at the mention of Montague. His objections against the man are probably just. Her own should be stronger. But the difference is, she forgives him. If that makes her despicable as a woman – well, she would rather be happy than prudent.

Let her assume Simon is right: the drowned man is somebody else entirely. It hardly makes circumstances much better. She is still faced with the question: why are her sitters dying?

Agnes regards the humped shapes of box, laurel and privet hedges. They look like furniture covered by dust sheets, or perhaps ghosts in their shrouds. Her mind returns to that strange, vibrant young woman in Walcot Street and her outlandish claims of seeing auras. What colour did she say Agnes's was? Ash of roses. She imagines the pink seeping out from the bottom of her skirts into the snow, a circle spreading to reach Morpheus who is digging beneath the trees. It must be interesting for Miss West to see everyone like that: tinged with their own hue. Agnes views them in lines of black and white.

You should talk to the Sylph. Just to know for sure.

It might be that Miss West's sister *could* contact the dead and tell Agnes what happened to her clients. But even if Spiritualism is real, it is wicked, a kind of devilry that should not be meddled with. She knows this. She tries to remind herself.

A pigeon breaks free of a group of conifers and takes wing.

When all is said and done, Agnes should trust Simon. Accept that both deaths were unfortunate mischances and no incidents like them will ever occur again.

Morpheus barks.

It is odd, because Morpheus is not usually a barking dog; he vocalises through grunts instead. Yet here he is, yowling over and over in distress. His paws scrabble wildly, flinging up powdery snow.

Agnes doesn't know what she is supposed to do.

'Bad dog,' she tries. 'Come here!'

He starts to obey but then dashes back yapping.

After four repeats of this charade, Agnes realises the dog wants her to follow him.

'For heaven's sake.'

She pulls up her skirts. The snow is deeper at the edge of the gardens. She will struggle to wade out there, and for what? A rabbit hole? A half-eaten squirrel? But she can hardly return to Simon without his precious dog.

'What is it, then?'

Morpheus is barking so hard that his feet seem to lift off the ground. She proffers the box of marchpane, hoping it will tempt him out to her. It doesn't.

Morpheus never refuses food.

Ducking beneath a snow-laden branch, she toils towards the dog. He looks half-frantic. His eyes roll.

There is a sharp, fungal smell. She glimpses the frozen earth

Morpheus has uncovered and the pale tree roots writhing up from the ground.

'What—?'

She cannot finish her question.

The box of marchpane falls silently from her grip into the snow.

Erupting from the white hill in front of her are three grey-blue fingers of a human hand.

Chapter 12

Sergeant Redmayne has brought company to the house this time. His fellow officers are no more courteous than the man himself; their voices bray so loudly from the parlour that they carry up the stairs and through the open door of Agnes's bedchamber.

Morpheus has flattened himself against the landing, cowering with ears back, while Cedric pets and tries to comfort him.

'Fancy seeing you here, sir. Again,' she hears Sergeant Redmayne say drily to Simon downstairs. 'And you just *happened* to be in the park when the lady discovered the body too?'

Chuckles from below. One of the other officers pipes up with: 'Quite the old beau, ain't you?'

Agnes is grateful they cannot see her angry blush. When Simon replies, his tone is dangerously polite. 'Yes, I was escorting my *sister-in-law* on a constitutional walk. And thank goodness I was. She took ill at the sight of the dead man, as any lady might.'

The police stop laughing. 'You didn't mention your relationship last time I called,' Redmayne points out. 'Said you were her physician.'

'I act in that capacity also. What does it signify?'

'Everything matters, sir. And where might your lady wife be?'

'Deceased. I am a widower.'

Snow drops down the chimney and makes the fire hiss.

Agnes lays her head carefully back on the pillow. She doesn't want to listen to the discussion taking place downstairs, but nor does she want time alone to think. Sleep is no relief. Each time she closes her eyes she sees again the frozen rictus of horror.

He must have been there since the early hours of the morning, at least. Maybe days. She cannot remember when it first started snowing. Someone must have dug in the drift to bury him, knowing that any later snowfall would further conceal their sin. Out there, on the edges of the park, he would not have been discovered until the thaw, were it not for one busy little dog.

The abbey bells toll.

Part of her is glad they found him. His poor remains did not deserve to lie alone in an icy grave for any longer. But she wishes she had not seen the face. How it had changed. The eyelashes and brows flared shockingly white. His hair had clumped into one semi-transparent shape, like wax that had melted and set. Patches of the skin showed black. Scorched by fire, she thought, until she realised: the cold can burn too.

The floorboards creak. Simon's voice rumbles downstairs. 'I can answer for Miss Darken. Neither of us has seen the unfortunate gentleman before in our lives. Did he have nothing about his person to suggest his identity?'

'We've a lad reported missing. The family are on their way to view the body.'

'Well, then. We can hardly be of further assistance.'

'But if we could talk to Miss Darken herself—'

'Absolutely not. I made it clear to you that the lady is unwell.'

'It's a murder inquiry, sir. Can't stand upon niceties.'

Simon fumes: 'So you would have another death upon your hands, would you? I am telling you that as her physician, I advise against it. She very nearly died in '52. Can you not wait a few days until she is recovered?'

'We'd prefer to—'

'I see I will have to speak to your superior. But let me make this plain now: if you continue to harass my sister-in-law, I will not be answerable for the consequences to her health.'

Agnes's hand grips the bed sheet. Simon is exaggerating, but she really does feel ill. The walking, the cold and the shock have overwhelmed her. If Sergeant Redmayne appeared in her room, she thinks her heart would stop.

There is more movement downstairs. Cedric leaps up from his position beside Morpheus on the landing floor and scurries back inside his own chamber.

She hears some last, muffled words and the slam of the front door. The stairs groan. Morpheus's tail begins to thump as Simon makes his way up, a mug in hand.

He enters the bedchamber with eyes respectfully averted. Sweat beads his brow. She detects its slight tang beneath his usual scent of carbolic soap as he approaches the bed and offers the cup.

'Drink this. It is not laudanum, I promise, just hot flip. It will help you sleep, without the dreams.'

Agnes shuffles into a sitting position and takes it from him. His manner is odd, and she senses it is not just because he is inside her bedroom. She feels as if she has misbehaved, disappointed him in some way. 'I forgot to ask after Mrs Oswald.'

'Hmm?'

'The lady who fell.'

'Oh, she will recover. Merely a sprained ankle. Her child is unharmed.'

Agnes takes a sip of her drink, wincing at how alcoholic it is. 'Small mercies.'

He remains silent. Concentrating, although she does not know on what.

While she drinks, her eyes shy away from Simon to survey the room. It is in a bad state. She needs to dust the dressing table and pull the hair out of her brush. Some pencils have found their way in here, and the silhouette of Constance . . .

She frowns.

The shade that fell from the broken frame is propped up, beside her mirror. She could have sworn she put it away in her book.

'I imagine the police will return,' Simon sighs. 'Especially if no one identifies the body.'

'Ned,' she whispers. 'His name was Ned.'

Now the moustache shading his upper lip will never grow. She remembers his self-effacing smile, even his pomade, and it is impossible to reconcile them with the *thing* they pulled from the snow. But Agnes was not mistaken. The body was certainly his.

'Why would you not let me tell them I had met him and knew his name, Simon?'

He bridles. 'You ask me *why*? What of the business you were so worried about at teatime? Do you think this news will help matters?'

He has rarely been this short with her before. A tear slips down her cheek as she takes another mouthful of drink. 'I just . . . I worry they will find out he was a client here anyway.'

Simon shakes his head. 'You said it was a drop-in appointment, unrecorded—'

'Unless he already gave the shade to his grandmother?'

'I doubt that is the case.'

She takes a shuddering breath. 'It was . . . some of my best work, Simon. I was so proud of it. And now . . .'

He places a hand on her shoulder and lets her cry.

'You must believe me *now*,' she sniffs. 'You must see.'

'See?'

'Three people, Simon. Three people have died after sitting for my art.'

Simon appears at a loss for words. He brings his watch out of his waistcoat pocket, puts it back again.

'It is . . . true that three gentlemen have died,' he reasons. 'But I believe it was a mere coincidence that you happened to cut their profiles. Consider. How would this murderer have known about you? What motive would he have to interfere with your livelihood?'

She looks at her hands, swollen and arthritic around the cup. 'I cannot explain it, Simon. I feel somehow responsible. As if my gaze has cast a shadow over them.'

People did say, when photographs first appeared, that there was danger in having your image captured. Part of your soul would remain forever imprisoned in that glass lens. Sit for too many and you might be . . . depleted. More alive in the photograph than in real life.

She never suspected the same could be true with art, until now. For isn't that what she has been trying to do: reduce someone to their essence, and capture it?

But Simon is staring at her with utter dismay. She has never seen him look so wretched, and she feels like a simpleton.

'Oh dear. I can see from your expression that it is Kingsdown Lunatic Asylum for me.'

'That is beneath you, Miss Darken.'

He *did* commit a patient to a madhouse once. A lady. He will not speak of it, he only tells her, darkly, *never again*. Whatever happened to her must have been terrible.

'Simon,' she says slowly. 'If you truly will not consider me mad . . . Can you tell me what you think of Mesmerism?'

He blinks. 'Mesmerism? Why?'

'Is there a science to it?'

He wets his lips, seems to think. 'Yes, I believe there may be. Not that it has been conclusively proven. They theorise that a vapour flows from every living thing, which a trained operator can manipulate. If he does so correctly, he may exert the power of his mind over another person's body. I have seen a mesmerist put a patient into a trance and tell them that they will feel no pain. The patient then underwent a surgical procedure without making a sound of protest. Before we had ether and chloroform, it could be useful. Not that I ever practised it myself.' A cloud passes over his face. 'It struck me as distasteful to see a patient under the power of a stranger's will. Entered and dominated, as if by a parasite . . .' His gaze sharpens. '*Have* you been mesmerised, Miss Darken? Is that why you are asking me this?' He leans down towards her so quickly that it startles her. 'Is *that* what has happened? Tell me.'

'No! It was only a question, and I do not know why you should be so nettled by it.' She pulls away from him to the other side of the bed, spilling some of the flip. 'I saw an advertisement in someone's window, that's all.'

'Well, I' – he tries to gather himself – 'I am sorry. I spoke hastily. But you must understand that there are charlatans about. People who meddle with forces they should not. In the mesmeric trance, a person is subject to a lower and more automatic level of functioning. They are permitted – nay, encouraged – to renounce their consciousness and let their usual personality fade away. The brain is a powerful organ, Miss Darken, but delicate. One should not . . . tamper.'

'And I expect you feel the same about Spiritualism?'

'Good God! Is it possible you have been bitten by that nonsense?'

It is a relief to feel annoyed with him. Anger is something she can grip onto. 'Nothing has *bitten* me, Simon. I am considering possibilities, asking questions. If you cannot help me understand what happened to these men, I must find someone who will.'

He puts a hand to his forehead. 'Forgive me, forgive me. I *shall* help you. Only do not visit a spirit medium. I beg of you.'

'Well, perhaps I shan't. It is bad enough with the police coming here. I do not want you calling the alienists in on me too.'

Simon flinches, turns from her. 'Do not try to provoke me. That was your sister's trick.'

'Simon . . .' She was only being flippant, she did not mean it, but it is clear she has wounded him. 'I apologise.'

Without answering, he leaves the room.

She hears him plod downstairs. Morpheus thumps after him.

She casts the mug of flip aside and falls against her pillow, miserable. She has ruined everything, but it is not her fault, she is not well. The shock . . . Her temples pound so fiercely she thinks that they will crack.

The bells chime again.

When their peal dies out, the hinges of her chamber door creak open. 'You mustn't worry, Aunt Aggie.'

Cedric stands at the threshold, watching her. He is the only person whose presence can bring her comfort. She opens her arms to him.

He trots over and pulls his gangly legs up on the bed. He is still wearing his shoes, but she does not scold; it's rare that she gets to cuddle him like this nowadays.

'My father's just scared,' he explains. 'People get cross when they're scared.'

'Really? And what makes a grown man like Simon afraid?'

'Spirit mediums,' Cedric replies simply. He raises his chin to look up at her. 'He never liked reading me ghost stories.'

'I daresay he didn't.' She winks at him. 'Penny dreadfuls are *our* little indulgence, are they not?'

He chuckles. 'You read them much better, anyway. But do you know . . . When we lived with Papa in Alfred Street, I found these great big hooks he kept in a box. They were really heavy. I couldn't lift even one of them.'

She is thrown by how suddenly he shifts topic. 'What – Cedric, I do not understand how hooks relate to spirit mediums . . .'

'Listen! I'll explain. Papa told me he'd used the hooks when he was studying medicine in Edinburgh. He went fishing.'

'Again, how do fish have any bearing on—'

'Not for *real* fish!' he laughs. 'That's just what they *called* it. The medical students used to go fishing for coffins.'

She starts. 'Coffins?'

'They dug the earth at the head end. Then they inserted the

hooks, you see, under the lid. Tied them to big ropes and hauled them up through the soil. They needed the bodies. You know, like Tidkins in *The Mysteries of London*.'

She never equated Simon with this diabolical practice. In a story, bodysnatching is horridly entertaining, but in real life . . . She can only hope this is an exaggeration Simon employed to quench the boy's thirst for gruesome tales.

'Papa didn't have a fresh supply of bodies for his anatomy classes, like students do today. He said everyone was forced to do it. He looked so sad when he told me. Poor Papa. He hated the time he spent away studying. That's why he didn't want me to learn to be a doctor too.'

Well, that was possibly one reason. Heaven knew the young Simon who went off to Scotland was a very different creature to the one who returned to find his entire family either dead or dying of cholera.

'He's scared,' Cedric repeats. 'Because he dug up dead people. So he doesn't want to believe they could come back and haunt him.'

How did this sweet, perceptive boy come from Constance? Agnes had been so afraid that the apple would not fall far from the tree. But Constance's vindictiveness has not been passed on. Her son has inherited nothing except her taste for the macabre.

'You are very wise, you know, Ced.'

He grins. 'I know. I'll probably be prime minister one day.'

She plants her lips on the top of his sandy head, wishing she could give him that chance.

Chapter 13

Pearl cries deep into her pillow. She's exhausted and would rather save her breath, but she can't seem to help the sobs. Myrtle's words go round in her head. *You're a spirit medium. What did you expect?*

She only knows what she *didn't* expect. She never bargained on feeling this ill. Being in pain every day is wearing her down, like the seams on the easy chair in the parlour. And what has it got her? She still hasn't met her mother, still hasn't been able to discover who is killing people around Bath.

They call what she has a gift, but Pearl doesn't want it any more. She doesn't want it at all.

Beneath her quiet snuffles, she can hear Father in his room, fighting for breath. Shame fills her to the brim. How dare she lie here thinking these selfish thoughts? Using the Power was never about *her*. It was about making money, so that Myrtle could concentrate on her Mesmerism and heal Father.

All her family want her to do is sit still in a dark room and give up control. It isn't so much to ask.

Except it is.

Some days it feels as if it's sapping her very soul.

She needs guidance. It's times like these that she really wishes Mother hadn't died. In stories, the mother characters are always kind, with words of wisdom to bestow. Myrtle's not like that much. She can be wise, but she has a limited supply of pity, and most of it is used up on the mourners.

As for Father . . . She misses the sound of his voice. They hardly communicate now, and while his presence still brings some comfort, it's also harrowing to look upon his face. Or what's left of it.

She scrubs the tears angrily from her eyes. She *should* look at his face, and remind herself why she's doing this. Her pain is bad, but it must be nothing compared to his.

Pearl stands up, opens her door and stumbles out, past Myrtle's room and towards the sick chamber. Already the stink is bubbling. She takes a deep breath and forces down her biliousness.

It's far too bright inside. Pearl yelps. 'Myrtle!'

Myrtle's sitting at his bedside, reading penny papers by the light of an open window.

'I was taking a rest,' she says defensively, clearing the papers away. 'See that water he's just drunk? I magnetised that.'

Pearl doesn't answer, just pulls at the curtains.

'Does him good to get some daylight. We don't all want to be shut up in the dark like you.'

In deference to her sister, Pearl only closes the curtains partially, leaving a sliver of burning sun. It doesn't *look* like it's done Father any good.

The hinge of the jaw is fully exposed, all gristle and string, but she takes care not to dwell upon that. She just kneels down on the opposite side of the bed from Myrtle and takes his hand in her own.

She must help him. She *must*.

'Don't look so glum,' Myrtle cajoles. 'We'll have punters knocking down our door for séances soon. They've just found another body.'

Pearl holds her tongue. She yearns to ask how, where, if it had anything to do with her uncontrollable shivering, but she remembers their previous argument.

Besides, the murderer doesn't seem important any more when

she's kneeling here, listening to Father's struggling, gummy breath.

'When will you treat him again?' she asks.

'In a minute. With a new technique. I was just reading over it. Business has been that good, I've been buying *The Zoist*.' Myrtle flourishes one of the rustling sheets in her direction. 'I'll be a proper expert soon.'

'But . . .' Pearl glances down, unwilling to meet her sister's eye. 'Will it *work*? Promise me it'll cure him.'

Myrtle tuts. 'Of course it will! Look at this. If Mesmerism weren't real, would they have opened a special hospital for it? The London Mesmeric Infirmary. Says right here. And the women, Pearl.' Her voice climbs a notch in excitement. 'They've got women mesmerists. Working right alongside the other doctors. Like equals. That'll be me, one day.'

Pearl can see it. She's never been in a hospital, but she can imagine a lot of beds lined up with people like Father in them, and Myrtle striding confidently down the aisle between them, waving her pretty hands.

The only problem is, there's no room for Pearl in this dream.

'You wouldn't just . . . leave me alone here, would you?'

Myrtle laughs. 'Don't be daft. When your dad's better, he'll look after you, won't he? Then I can go off and do what *I* want to do. That'll make a change!'

Father's hand squeezes Pearl's. She glances up and shrinks from the expression in his tortured eyes.

She wants to believe Myrtle. She *does* believe. Her sister can do anything.

But she knows that Father isn't so sure.

Father thinks he's going to die.

Chapter 14

Agnes makes the practice cuts in waves: peaks and troughs that roll smoothly like a black ocean. Papa and Montague would have seen the sea at night many a time during their travels – she wonders if it looked anything like this. They were brave men; Agnes would find such pitch-darkness utterly terrifying. It is true that she likes shadows – but even shadows need light to exist.

Today's light is sodden and pale. It seems to hesitate at the window, irresolute.

Her studio, on the top floor of the house, is not in the direct eyeline of any other residence, yet as she sits curving the sable paper with her second-best pair of scissors, she has the uncanny feeling of being watched. It is as if her work and her person are under scrutiny – and both have been found wanting.

She pauses, flexes her fingers. She is not used to feeling this way inside her studio, her refuge. Perhaps it is a magpie observing her from the window. The birds have been clattering away on the roof all morning; she dare not imagine how much of the property is infested with their nests.

She starts to cut again. None of her usual joy sparks. It must be these scissors – they are of no use. How did she manage to make Ned's hollow-cut with such a clumsy instrument? Poor, poor Ned. She sighs, shakes her aching hand. After all that has happened, maybe it is time she stuck to painted shades instead.

She is an accomplished painter: that is a fact, not a boast, but it was always the papercuts that were her real talent, even from a child. Must she relinquish them now? The stubborn part of her refuses; she expects that when her hands have given up entirely and she is physically unable to make a single snip, that portion of herself will still be there, clamouring to get out.

She puts the inferior scissors down, defeated by the burning in her fingers.

The woman she knew as Agnes is fading day by day. Determined to remember there is *something* of her left, she crosses the landing to her bedchamber, retrieves the shade of Constance from beside her dressing-table mirror and brings it back to the studio.

Yes, she captured it well: the curious way her sister's head sat upon her shoulders. You can see, even without bronzing, where the ears and eyes should be.

It would be wrong to consign such a good piece to the back of the duplicate book – although she could swear she had done so previously. Agnes opens it again, at the front this time, where her collection of earlier Constances live. Page by page they grow, become taller, the lines of their faces more defined.

Looking back, she realises how often Constance offered herself as a model. Was it a kindness, or was she just trying to keep Agnes's focus trained upon her? Constance never could endure competition for Agnes's attention; even her papercuts were viewed as rivals.

Perhaps she is judging too harshly. Constance *could* be agreeable at times, only . . . there was an uncomfortable intensity to it. She was *too* nice, a person playing at being nice.

Then came the betrayal. It was hard to believe any good of her after *that*.

Agnes is still at a loss to say exactly why Constance did it. Was it spite, jealousy – or just to prove that she could? Somehow she would feel better if love were involved in the matter, but evidently it was not. The whole affair was about power, manipulation, ownership.

There is no use going over it again. Constance is dead now, and a dead person cannot control her any longer.

She slots the paper Constance amidst her twins and lets the book fall open to its wonted page.

Montague's shade faces to the right. Symbolically, this means he is looking forward to the future – and that was apt for the man – but now she wishes she had cut it facing the other way. Because the future, when it came, held only sorrow for them.

Montague is the one full-length in her collection with added colours. When he made first lieutenant, he showed her his uniform, and she recreated it from memory: a bold, blue coat with white breeches. Only the face remains shadowy and inscrutable. Agnes runs the tip of her finger over it.

'Where are you? Do you think of me?' she asks.

Forcing herself to turn the pages, Agnes leafs to the forlorn little physiognotrace Ned was so impressed by. Her throat tightens. Mr Boyle's death saddened her, but Ned's seems even worse: a boy full of promise, cut off in the bloom of his youth. She remembers thinking that Cedric might resemble him in another five years. Who could want to hurt such a nice young man?

Outside, the abbey bells toll.

'Agnes!'

Mamma's usual screech. She closes the book gently and puts it away.

In the parlour, the grandfather clock falters on. It needs winding. She forgot to lay the fire too, but somehow Mamma has found a way. Agnes frowns at the blaze as she steps inside. It is sweltering, extravagant. All that precious, expensive coal . . .

'There you are!' Mamma's cheeks are alarmingly red above her newspaper. 'When were you going to tell me about the scrapes you've been getting yourself into?'

'I do not—'

'Right here!' Her eyes seem to bulge behind her spectacles. 'A body, Agnes? You found a *corpse*?'

'What is that? What are you reading?'

She wrests half the paper from her mother's grip.

There it is in black and white: every self-respecting lady's nightmare. Simon said he would keep her name out of print and make them use his instead, but evidently there is one reporter who has given both.

'Really, Mamma, it was nothing.' She quells the tremor in her voice. 'They do exaggerate in the newspapers. Simon's dog found something and we alerted the authorities. I am quite safe.'

Mamma's hot hand clamps on hers. 'My poor Agnes! Splashed all over the papers . . . It is one thing to have an advertisement, but this! Whatever would your father say?'

'Hush, now. Papa would be pleased I have performed my duty in reporting the discovery. And you see, I appear next to Simon's name, which will always be respectable.'

How easy it is to lie to Mamma. The truth is, this article is a disaster, the death kiss for her business. She has not had a customer since Ned, and maybe she never will again.

Her eyes catch the price of the paper. Simon must have paid off her debt at the news vendors without telling her. She should be thankful for his benevolence, but it only feels like another shackle preventing her from making her own way in the world.

Yes, that is the sensation: one of being chained or trapped. She has been feeling it ever since the killer started targeting her business. How can she countenance a future in which she has no money of her own, and no opportunity to practise the art that has been the pleasure of her life? She shudders to think of being a burden to Cedric in her old age, of him waiting upon her in the same way she is tending to Mamma.

'No more policemen will be coming here, will they?' Mamma continues to fret. 'Agnes, I don't think I could bear to see a policeman after—'

'No, no.'

She blesses her lucky stars that Mamma was in bed asleep when she and Simon arrived back from the gardens and the discovery of Ned's body. Quite how she managed to doze through the ruckus of Simon's argument with Redmayne is a mystery, but Agnes is not about to look a gift horse in the mouth.

Mamma's breath saws.

'Try to be calm, Mamma. *This* is why I did not tell you. It was a trifle, and I knew you would get upset. Sit there. I will fetch you some tea.'

She walks out of the heat into the coolness of the kitchen. A plague on those reporters, and the policemen too. As if she did not have enough trouble without them.

Locating the key, she unlocks the caddy. There is no tea.

Agnes slides down against the cupboard and sits on the floor.

It will not do. She cannot endure this any longer. Simon's promised help is not forthcoming: she must take matters into her own hands and rescue her silhouette parlour.

But she can think of only one course of action.

———

Naturally, the event must take place in the evening; wicked deeds require the cover of darkness. The abbey bells toll seven as Agnes slinks out of the front door and locks it behind her.

She shivers from cold and fear. It is not exactly late, but at this time of year, seven o'clock might as well be the middle of the night.

Her senses sharpen. People she would scarcely notice crossing the churchyard by day now carry an air of menace. Do they regard her with disapproval? A lone woman out at this hour is unlikely to be virtuous, and Agnes feels that she is not: she is about to do something repugnant to her feelings and decency alike.

Twice, she nearly turns back. What is it that makes Bath so

eerie when the sun goes down? It could be the mounds of snow, pale as flesh against the black sky, or it might be the buildings that tower over her, conspiratorial and worn. More likely it is the frightened whispers of her own conscience.

But what else can she do?

She listens to her heartbeat and her footsteps. Both strike too rapidly. The pointed spire of St Michael's looms up, making her feel helplessly small.

She tries to remind herself that this anxiety is simply a sign of her own weakness, not an indication that she is making an error. Attending a séance is the only way to obtain answers: the definitive identity of the drowned sailor, and the name and motive of the person who is killing her clients. The knowledge of the dead is useful beyond measure: that is why it is forbidden.

The house on Walcot Street is clothed in darkness, its parlour curtains drawn tight against the light of the street lamps. A mere passer-by would think all of the inhabitants were long asleep.

Agnes raises her fist to knock on the door, but she cannot quite bring herself to let it fall.

What if she peers beyond the veil and sees a sight she is not able to bear? It is not too late to turn back. She really *should*. But there is a nightmarish inevitability to her actions. Somehow she knew she was going to come here, from the moment she first heard Mrs Boyle mention the White Sylph.

Releasing her breath, she finally knocks.

As before, Miss West steals noiselessly to answer the door. That is the one aspect familiar to their last meeting. Tonight the young woman is dressed from head to toe in jet, her flaxen hair extinguished by something like a widow's cap. The only feature alive in her face are those simmering, witchy eyes. Their expression is far from friendly.

'Miss Darken. Good evening. Do step inside.'

This is not the woman Agnes spoke to about the corpse. She

is a polished version with better diction. Speechless, Agnes follows her into the house, which is even darker than on her previous visit. A powdery, sickly aroma overlays the rot she detected.

As she turns into the parlour, she sees bunches of open lilies glowing like pale, white hands by candlelight. Lilies and wax – that explains the cloying scent.

'May I introduce the White Sylph?' Miss West gestures to the far side of the circular table, near the drawn curtains.

For a split second, Agnes thinks she has already glimpsed a ghost.

The child sits behind a flickering barrier of black candles. She is an albino, entirely without pigment. A white gown bleeds seamlessly into the alabaster of her skin and ivory hair falls loose over her shoulders. Her lips and brows must be powdered, for Agnes cannot make them out. Even the girl's eyes show clear as glass marbles.

'Come. Be seated.' Miss West has the air of a housekeeper revealing hidden rooms. She sweeps Agnes effortlessly towards a chair she does not want to take; there is no resisting her.

The White Sylph watches with uncanny serenity. She must be even younger than Cedric but there is an agelessness to her: it does not feel like sitting opposite a child.

Miss West takes the third chair, closing in the circle.

The Sylph reaches out and offers Agnes her bloodless palm. It is cold to the touch. By contrast, Miss West's feels warm and dry.

There is no escape. Agnes is in their power now.

'We'll start with a hymn,' says Miss West. She opens her mouth and sings.

> Jesus, full of truth and love,
> We thy kindest word obey;
> Faithful let thy mercies prove;
> Take our load of guilt away.

She has a beautiful singing voice. Agnes knows the words and tries to join in, but her vocal chords are taut.

> Weary of this war within,
> Weary of this endless strife,
> Weary of ourselves and sin,
> Weary of a wretched life.

The White Sylph does not sing. She stares into the candle flames, her pupils shrinking to pinpricks as she retracts, further and further inside herself.

> Lo, we come to thee for ease,
> True and gracious as thou art:
> Now our weary souls release,
> Write forgiveness on our heart.

The last notes of their hymn hang suspended for a moment, then everything falls still.

One of the candle flames silently dies.

Slowly, the Sylph lifts her chin. Material whispers as her head lolls backwards, strangely contorted. Her glassy eyes roll to the whites.

Agnes's hand twitches involuntarily.

'Yes, come,' Miss West murmurs.

And they do.

An invisible bell rings. Agnes's heart leaps into her throat. The Sylph's neck grows turgid, her white cheeks flush and she is glowing, actually glowing with light from the afterlife.

Her lips begin to move. Agnes leans forward, desperate for the words, but this is not language it is . . . bubbles. Kisses popping from a fish's mouth.

'Spirit.' Miss West's hushed tones are calm. 'Welcome. Have you heard Miss Darken's call?'

The Sylph's head jerks in a nod. Agnes did not realise it

would be like this. She thought the spirit would speak to the child, not take possession of her.

'You are the man I found in the river?' Miss West confirms.

Agnes watches, transfixed, as the lips try to form a reply. All that comes is a heaving gasp.

He is drowning. He is still drowning after death.

The Sylph tosses her chin, trying to break above the surface. It is difficult to keep hold of her hand. Agnes feels something wet pool in her palm and hopes it is sweat. But why can she smell something brackish, like river water?

'It's him,' Miss West hisses. 'Ask your questions. We will not keep hold of him for long.'

Her tongue has never felt so dry. All she wants to do is reach out and help, to pull whatever suffers there from the water.

'His . . . his name?' she croaks.

Fluid gurgles in the Sylph's throat as she struggles for air. 'H-h-h-harg . . . reeeaves.'

'Hargreaves?' Miss West repeats.

The Sylph exhales like a load has been lifted from her. Then she keels forward, her head landing on the table with a smack.

Another candle puffs out.

Agnes breaks their circle of hands, reaching out to see if the child is hurt, but it is not over yet.

No sooner does one spirit discard the marionette than another picks it up. The Sylph's thin shoulders quake beneath her white gown and the table moves with her.

For the first time, Miss West looks afraid.

'Sp-spirit?' she ventures. 'Look at me.'

Trembling, the Sylph raises her head from the table. Her jawline is in constant motion and Agnes realises the girl's teeth are chattering.

The temperature plummets. Breath steams not just from the Sylph, but from all of them.

Miss West swallows audibly. 'Spirit, name yourself.'

Agnes does not need the answer.

'Dear God,' she breathes. 'It's Ned.'

The Sylph turns to face her. It is not the girl's physiognomy, nor even Ned's, but a death mask with staring eyes.

This is what Agnes wanted: to converse with the dead, yet she is speechless before their eternity. She tries desperately to remember the easy-going young man in her studio, what she would say to him if she still had the chance.

'Oh Ned, what happened to you? I am sorry, I am so, so sorry. You were so young, and—' The fixed, glassy eyes seem to look right through her. 'Was it my fault? Did someone murder you just to hurt me?' she whispers.

At first there is no reaction. The Sylph – or whatever moves the Sylph – seems to consider. Then it says in a low, creaking voice, 'Y-y-yes.'

She nearly sobs.

'Poor Ned! Stay a while. Are you so cold? If only I could warm you! Won't you tell us, dear? Tell us what monster did this?'

Abruptly, the eyes slide to the right. Agnes starts back. The Sylph is still shuddering, but she seems to be taking furtive glances about the room.

'A-f-f-fraid.'

Miss West flexes her fingers nervously, regarding her sister as if she has never seen her before. 'What of?' she demands in her natural voice. 'Whoever killed you can't hurt you no more, can they?'

The Sylph's lips are turning a sickly shade of blue. She is losing the power to move them. 'S-s-s-sent Ag-agnes m-m-message.'

Agnes gasps. 'The killer sent a message to me? What message?'

But the mouth is freezing up, too numb to speak. The Sylph distorts her face to no avail.

'Tell me the message!'

Agnes is trembling so fiercely that it takes her a moment to realise that the room is shaking too; the picture frames are rattling on the walls.

Miss West releases a strangled shriek.

The lips. She must focus on those dead lips and read the words, or all of this will have been for nothing. Straining with all her might, Agnes manages to catch the last word.

'. . . m-mine.'

All of the candles blow out.

As quickly as it dropped, the temperature returns to normal. A chair scuffs against the carpet and Miss West lights the gas. Her face is almost as pallid as her sister's.

'She's . . . never done that before.'

Both of them glance at the child, flung back in the chair with her arms hanging loosely by her sides. Cataleptic. Helpless. Is it Agnes's imagination, or has the Sylph physically shrunk? Her white gown seems loose upon her.

Tentatively, she leans forward and touches the ivory hand. It is cold as marble. An acrid smell breathes from the skin, a sort of tang that reminds her of the charnel house. She wrinkles her nose.

'Spirit smells.' Miss West brushes down her gown repeatedly, although nothing marks it. 'That . . . that happens.'

Agnes watches, tensed, expecting the girl to snap up again any minute, possessed by another spirit. But she seems to be in a deep swoon. Miss West places cushions behind her, covers her with a blanket and wipes the disarrayed hair from her forehead. The young woman's mouth is set in a hard pout Agnes cannot interpret.

She completes a nervous survey of the room, wondering if ghosts are lurking in the dark corners. The few cheap prints hanging on the wall are all aslant and the table itself seems to have moved a full six inches to the left.

It is horrendous and evil, even worse than Cedric's books, and yet it is undeniably true: the dead walk. They have burst from the tomb.

She wants to laugh and to cry.

Here is all she sought: the drowned man's name – not Montague! – and a chance to speak with poor Ned. She has confirmation from his icy lips of what she knew from the start: that the murderer is hounding her, trying to send her a message through her clients.

But that knowledge is no relief.

'The séance is over,' Miss West says. 'She needs her rest now.'

Agnes's legs have turned to water. With great difficulty she rises from the chair and fishes in her reticule for the coins, all she has left from Ned's commission. Miss West snatches them.

This séance, she senses, was not like the others. The young woman is twitchy, on edge, as she leads her into the hallway and towards the front door.

Agnes hesitates. 'If . . . I wanted to come back . . .'

'Back?' Miss West repeats, her eyes wide and tinctured with loathing.

'To . . . hear the rest of the message.'

Miss West shakes her head. 'It won't be cheap. Cost you one and six.'

Even after the horror of the evening, a laugh escapes her. 'A shilling and sixpence? Do you know how long it would take me to earn—'

'I don't care! Didn't you see the state of her? She'll be like that for days now and we won't make a penny. You're no good for us. I should never have asked you here.'

Miss West has dropped her act so completely that she is practically trying to push Agnes out through the door.

Perhaps it is a business tactic. Agnes doubts it, though. Reluctantly, she steps out onto the cold street. If she leaves now, she will be in a sorrier condition than the one she arrived in: knowing that she really is a target, but not what the killer wants from her.

'I do not have the money, but we could come to some arrangement,' she pleads, turning back. 'I am a silhouette artist.

I could cut you a shade for payment. They usually cost a shilling apiece. I would do one of each of you. Two shades – that's worth even more than you asked for.'

Miss West shakes her head darkly. 'We've got enough shadows in this house.'

She shuts the door with a bang.

Chapter 15

It's coming again. Burning, corrosive. Myrtle holds back Pearl's hair as liquid fire spills from her lips into the chamber pot. There's no other pain like it. She's doubled up, squeezed together.

Wasn't she cold, a while back? She'd give anything to shiver now. The heat is unbearable, inside and out. Sweat pours from her skin as freely as the vomit issuing from her mouth. Why won't it stop?

Tears half-blind her. She's already felt the chill of the grave; maybe she's gone further still: deep in the ground – like those do-gooders warned Myrtle – into the fires of Hell.

Bile dribbles from her chin and Myrtle wipes it with a rag before crossing the room to push open the sash window.

Pearl's got a horrible compulsion to see what's come out of her. Struggling for breath, she opens her eyes and instantly wishes that she hadn't.

The chamber pot steams with white smoke, the same as the stuff that rises up from her during the séances. The ghosts have got right inside her. It's like she's eaten them for supper.

Myrtle hands her a glass of water. Pearl's mouth is parchment dry but she swallows slowly, carefully, afraid to set her stomach muscles heaving again. Drinking doesn't dull the scorch within. The flames are still there, simmering.

'Myrtle,' she wheezes.

Her sister clenches her free hand. 'Another mess I'll have to clean up,' she jokes.

Pearl tries to smile and holds on tight. Myrtle is one of the living. She needs to anchor herself to that.

'You gave me a scare,' Myrtle admits. 'Getting too powerful for your own good.'

'I don't feel powerful.'

Even speaking tires her. She's never been weaker in her life. That's how it seems to work: the stronger the spirits get, the more listless she becomes. There's only room for one or the other.

She struggles to hold the glass upright in her feeble hand. This isn't a fair fight. The dead – they are legion. Pearl's all alone.

'I want us to try,' she bursts out.

'What?'

'If you think my powers are strong now. I want us to try and reach . . .' She bites her lip, waiting for courage that never comes. It's almost as painful as pushing the vomit from her mouth. 'Mother,' she finishes in a whimper.

Myrtle lets go of her hand.

Why can't her sister understand? If Pearl could contact Mother, she'd have an ally, someone to protect her from the bad spirits and stop her getting sick like this. She longs to feel Mother's cool hand on her burning brow.

'I ain't stopping you from talking to her,' Myrtle says eventually. Her voice has gone gravelly and she's got that puffy look, as if she's about to cry.

'But you are. I need a circle. I can't do it alone. I never see ghosts when I'm on my own.'

'No. I won't do it, Pearl. Let her rest in peace.'

Pearl slumps. She's so exhausted and so hot, she hasn't the strength to fight, but she must. This is the only thing that really matters to her.

Mother's the only one who can help now.

'Please, Myrtle. Don't you think she'd want to meet me? She can be my spirit guide.'

'You don't need one.'

'But I never knew her!' Pearl bleats.

'No, you didn't,' Myrtle fires back. 'So you never had to lose her. You can't even imagine what it's like. Every day . . .' She glances away, trying to hide angry tears. 'Nobody suffered like I did.'

'Father lost her too.'

Myrtle scoffs. 'Right. Someone he was married to for a couple of years. That ain't the same as having your Ma ripped from you. But what would you know?'

Pearl can't bear to have her father talked about like he doesn't count. 'He loved her,' she whispers.

'He *killed* her!' Myrtle erupts. Her eyes aren't beautiful now; they're frightening. 'If it wasn't for him putting a baby in her belly, she'd still be alive. And look what he's gone and done to himself. I *told* him we shouldn't work in a match factory. Now here we are. I'm the mug, busting my guts to cure the man who murdered my own mother.'

Pearl's still hot, but she's shaking, furious and heartbroken all at the same time. Maybe it's true: maybe she's the offspring of a feckless man and a mother who resents her every bit as much as Myrtle does. But Father didn't *mean* for it to happen. He'd never hurt anyone on purpose, and if he's done wrong, isn't he paying for it now?

She finds a thread of voice. 'It's not Father's fault. You have to help him, Myrtle. Don't take your anger out on him. Blame me instead.'

Myrtle's nostrils flare. She peers down at Pearl, still crumpled on the floor by the chamber pot. 'D'you know what? Sometimes I do.'

With that parting blow, she strides off and shuts herself in her bedroom.

Pearl's free hand grips at the carpet. It feels as though the floor is moving. She wants to cry, to really howl and weep, but her head's just too painful.

Everything hurts so much.

For a moment she sits swaying, utterly hollowed out by her sister's words.

Then she's sick again.

Chapter 16

'You should not be here!' Agnes cries once more, but the lady is impossible.

Her dome-shaped skirt takes up most of the studio. Wide, fringed sleeves send paintbrushes clattering to the floor as her busy hands explore every surface.

Her daughter, about sixteen years old, lurks on the landing with her arms crossed. Her expression carries all the disdain Agnes feels, but must not show.

'Is this where it happened? Where Mr Boyle sat?' The lady tries the chair for herself. 'And that young gentleman you found? Did you take his shade too?'

'No,' Agnes lies. 'That was an entirely separate matter. Please, Mrs . . .'

'Campbell. I already told you my name. I hope you observe better than you listen.'

'And I have told *you* that you must leave this place, Mrs Campbell. It is not safe for you to be here.'

The lady's eyes twinkle. 'Now, now, I know what you are about. I won't pay more. Two shillings apiece is a fair price for a silhouette from the *parlour of death*.'

'Please, stop calling it that!'

A magpie cackles.

Agnes had anticipated whispers and avoidance after the newspaper article, but not this. She had not reckoned on the ghoulish crawling out from their holes to revel in all the morbid detail.

'Look, Lavinia!' Mrs Campbell takes off, knocking over the chair she has just sat upon. 'Look at the Etruscan pieces. So classical. I am minded to have one of them.'

These are the silhouettes where either the profile or the background has been worked in terracotta to resemble ancient pottery. Agnes always thought it was a cheerful colour; now she looks at the specimens hanging on her walls, and it seems as if they have been smeared with blood.

'I will not do it!' she repeats. 'I cannot. I have reason to believe my customers are being persecuted and until I—'

'But then the bronzing is charmingly quaint,' Mrs Campbell rabbits on, moving to another frame. 'A nice ethereal, ghostly quality, don't you think?'

Like Mr Boyle's shade, these pieces are black profiles with little details, like the hair and the collar, sketched on in gold. Agnes remembers how these features glittered by candlelight in the house of mourning at Queen Square, and her sense of foreboding deepens.

'Really, I must insist—'

Lavinia catches her eye from the doorway and shrugs her shoulders. 'You had better do as my mother says,' she tells her wearily.

'Do you not understand the danger?'

Mrs Campbell laughs. 'And do *you* not understand four shillings, my good woman? Come, you could use them. I see that you could. Get inside the room, Lavinia, for heaven's sake. Pick up that chair. Let the woman take your likeness with this nice machine here.'

Four shillings. It is blood money, and yet . . . they would certainly prove useful. Agnes needs to buy tea, and to make up for that sixpence she spent at the séance.

Can she in good conscience turn down four shillings, when poor Cedric has spent all morning complaining of hunger?

Mrs Campbell is not a pleasant woman, anyhow . . .

But the daughter. She sits where Ned sat, albeit far less eager. A pretty, sullen thing. Long, lace-trimmed bloomers show at her ankles and an innocent white ribbon threads through her hair.

Young Lavinia does not deserve to come to harm.

'I beg you to reconsider—'

'Do it!' Lavinia groans. 'I'll never hear the end of it if you do not.'

Agnes hesitates. She sees it now: she is a coward. Has always been. She might put up a fight, but eventually she will let others' actions control her own, just as she used to let Constance dictate their games.

'Four shillings?' she confirms.

Mrs Campbell beams. 'Let us say four and six if you sign them both nice and clear.'

Everyone has a price. Agnes honestly thought hers would be higher.

Hating herself, she loads the physiognotrace with paper.

It is a very different experience to tracing Ned. There are no smiles or suppressed giggles. Agnes holds herself stiff, not savouring every dip and hollow this time but moving the pole mechanically, as grave as a torturer turning the handle of a rack.

The abbey bells sound.

Could the murderer be watching her do this?

Working used to be a pleasure. Now some unknown person has found a way to turn it against her. It is as though they want her to have nothing of her own. Why? What threat could she, an impecunious spinster, pose to anyone?

'Done,' she announces shortly.

Lavinia heaves a sigh and vacates the chair. She shows no interest in the results, but Mrs Campbell already has her fingers on the box, trying to unfasten the hatch.

'Careful,' Agnes warns. 'Mind the pole. Let me—'

'I wish to see it!'

Agnes shoulders her out of the way. This lady might be paying twice what her art is worth, but by God she is making her earn it.

'There will be little to see at present,' she explains as she opens the instrument and reaches inside. The paper unclips easily. 'I will need to enlarge it with a pantograph before—'

She has barely withdrawn the sheet from the machine before Mrs Campbell snatches it.

As she inspects the tiny sketch, her smile rapidly subsides to a frown.

'Is there a . . . problem?' Agnes ventures.

Wings beat as the birds squabble on the roof.

'It looks nothing like her.'

'It will not, until I have—'

'Really, it might be a different person altogether. Do it again.'

She drops the page. Agnes lunges for it.

'I'm sure it's not so bad, Mamma,' Lavinia says languidly.

'It truly is. Look for yourself.'

Agnes turns the paper over for the girl to see. Freezes.

There is no mistake, small and faint as the profile is. Mrs Campbell was right: it is not Lavinia.

The physiognotrace has drawn Constance.

'That's adequate for me,' Lavinia yawns. Her perfectly manicured fingers tug at the paper but it is a moment before Agnes can force herself to let go.

What is happening? How is this possible?

'I will enlarge it, cut it out—' she starts but Lavinia waves her off.

'Really. Do not trouble yourself.'

Mrs Campbell sniffs. Her mouth has pinched, highlighting the wrinkles around it. 'I *did* have something better in mind. I take it you will not be using that incompetent contraption for my own shade.'

'No, no.' Agnes hurriedly pushes the physiognotrace aside, disengaging the pole and propping it up in the corner. 'I did not wish to use it in the first place. Please, have a seat. I will . . . Let us use paint! I will paint your silhouette onto plaster, how about that?'

She hopes her hand will be steady enough. The prospect of four and six seems to be drifting further and further away.

Why Constance?

She cannot begin to comprehend how a machine, an actual machine, could make this error. Her own hand might cut something from memory, yes, if she lost concentration. But the physiognotrace? She is tempted to take the paper from Lavinia and pore over it, see whether her eyes were mistaken.

It must be the séance – all that talk of ghosts is making her see them everywhere.

Mrs Campbell spreads her skirts and descends upon the chair.

Agnes gathers her apparatus: not really paint but India ink, water and soot blended together to make the perfect consistency of black, and a white oval of plaster for the background.

Her trembling fingers select a round, soft brush. Then she begins to work.

It is soothing. With scissors, she is forced to cut away from her body, but now she can pull the brush towards herself. The lines are soft, oily smears. There are two edges to her brushstroke and she focuses on the left, the clearer one, ignoring the other that encroaches into the white space she will later fill.

Forehead, nose, mouth, chin.

These are not Constance's features. She makes sure of that. But the machine's drawing still flashes before her. Impossible, as were the things she saw in Miss West's parlour on Walcot Street.

Perhaps this is what happens when you meddle with the natural order. She did not stop to fully consider the consequences before she called up spirits, but of course it makes sense: if *one* ghost can wander, surely they all may.

Constance always wanted to be her only sitter.

Agnes adds more water, makes the ink thinner and thinner as it reaches the back of Mrs Campbell's head. The woman appears to be falling through an empty, white space. She picks up a needle, ready to scrape in some finer detail.

'Are you nearly finished?' Mrs Campbell complains.

Maybe Constance has *actually* appeared to help defend her against this fussy customer. It amuses her to think of how icily her sister would have treated a woman like Mrs Campbell. Mamma once said: 'If Constance loves anyone, it is you, Agnes.' But she is not sure if that was true. She only remembers feeling tied to her little sister. As if she were a doll Constance wanted to carry about with her everywhere: something to own and control.

On the day Montague left, Constance took her hand and said, 'Now he will never part us.' As if that were some kind of comfort.

Well, death has parted them. And although her ghost might be trying, Constance cannot *really* get back to her now.

Agnes is no spirit medium. She cannot be possessed.

'Is it ready?' Mrs Campbell persists.

'Almost.' Agnes lays the needle down and signs her work. It is charming, despite its subject. The painted woman is silent and without Mrs Campbell's haughty expression; she has even managed to capture the wispy lace in her hair. 'Here. Please be gentle with it. Some parts may still be wet.'

Mrs Campbell comes over to the table and beams down at her shadow self. 'Well! *That* is more like it. What do you think, Lavinia? Is not Mamma very handsome?'

Lavinia just blinks.

'A treasure,' Mrs Campbell continues, scooping it up. 'Wait until my friends see! An actual silhouette from the infamous Darken's Parlour. I will be the envy of Laura Place.'

Agnes grimaces. 'Allow me to show you out.'

When they gain the hallway, Mrs Campbell produces her purse. 'Make yourself useful, Lavinia, hold the shade.'

Her smooth, pale hands tell out the coins, four and six as promised, without the slightest demur about Lavinia's failed portrait. How rich she must be, to fritter money away like that.

Agnes closes her fist tight over the treasure.

'You should take a cab home,' she advises. 'The streets are filthy.'

Opening the front door illustrates her point. Greyish-brown mush heaps the pavements. What was beautiful and snowy has melted into formlessness once more. It smells too, possibly the effect of thaw water running down the drains.

'Nothing like a walk for the constitution,' Mrs Campbell announces, striding out without a backwards glance.

Lavinia raises her eyes to heaven and mopes after her, still carrying the shade.

Agnes watches them nervously from the threshold. She ought to shut the cold out, but how can she? She must see her customers safe, at least until they have turned the corner. She has a dreadful feeling that she has just signed their death warrant.

Few people have ventured out into the dirt. The young girls stay firmly inside Mrs Box's seminary, yet there are still servants carrying packages from the butchers, and clerks scurrying around the banks. Agnes hunches behind the door. Any one of them could be the killer, spying on her house.

Mrs Campbell has nearly disappeared from sight but Lavinia dawdles, no doubt enjoying a respite from her mother's company. She is drawing level with the abbey when Agnes glimpses something hurtling towards her from the opposite direction, throwing out spray as it goes.

Agnes rubs her eyes. The object is too small to be a cart, but part of it does resemble a wheel . . .

It *is* a wheel – or to be exact, a hoop, Cedric's hoop, jouncing along while he dashes after it with his stick. In this slush! She represses a groan, foreseeing hours spent over the sink scrubbing his trousers.

He pays no heed to where he runs. People seem to miraculously sidestep out of his path and he does not falter, not even when he is nearly upon Lavinia.

The girl has not noticed him. Agnes raises a hand, lets it hover uselessly beside her mouth. She ought to call out but the last thing she wants to do is attract attention to her customer, to Cedric . . .

Now it is too late.

Cedric weaves, skims past Lavinia with barely an inch to spare. The girl gives a violent start and drops the shade.

Even from this distance, Agnes can hear the *crack* of plaster splitting into a jigsaw.

'Whoops,' Lavinia says dispassionately.

Agnes casts about wildly to see who observed the accident – did that lady, wrapped in fur? No, she only gave the merest twitch of her head, but what if the killer is out there somewhere, and this has drawn their eye . . . ?

Cedric barrels in through the door. His clothes are wet against her skirts and she leaps back with a shriek.

'Cedric! Careful, dear! What are you running away from?'

'Have we got any food yet?' He makes to push past her into the kitchen.

'Wait just a moment, young man.' She grabs hold of his shoulder and snaps the door shut. 'You should have stopped to apologise to that lady in the street, and helped her pick up her parcel. You made her drop it and now it will be broken. It is not like you to forget your manners.'

He blinks up at her from under his sandy fringe. 'Sorry, Auntie Aggie.'

'You really *do* need to be more careful, Cedric. Watch where you are going, at the very least. There are dangerous people about. I often worry that you will—' She loses her train of thought, caught suddenly by the state of him. 'Goodness me. What on earth have you done to your coat?'

He looks down at his feet. They too are caked in grime. 'I fell over. Tore it.'

It must have been a prodigious fall. The material is blotched all over with dirt as if it has been trampled underfoot. One tear is a crescent shape and the other gapes wide at the shoulder; the sleeve is almost hanging off.

Her anger flicks quickly to worry.

'Darling! Are you hurt?'

He glances up as if it is a foolish question.

'Come here. Give me that. That's it, dear, take it off.' She coaxes him out of the coat, both relieved and amazed that she cannot see any bruises on him. He is unharmed – that is the important part – but she cannot help grieving over the garment. She does not want to ask Simon to pay for another; she must sew it up as best she can.

She drapes the ruined coat over her arm and places a hand upon his head. 'This is precisely what I mean, my love. I do not scold to be cruel, but for your own good. Please be more careful. I do not know what I would do if something were to happen to you . . .' A chilling possibility occurs to her. 'It *was* a fall, Cedric? No one pushed you, did they?'

He looks a little tearful. Her heart clenches. It is one thing for a killer to victimise her practice, but if they were to touch Cedric . . .

'I'm sure it was my fault,' he whispers.

Please God, let him be right. For if this assailant really is trying to take the things that she loves, it makes sense that they would move on to her family after her art. The idea makes her feel like she is in the river again, fighting desperately for breath, but poor tattered Cedric gazes remorsefully at her and she does not want to give him further cause for fright. She dredges up a wobbly smile. 'Never mind,' she says. 'Look what I have for you here.'

'Food?'

'Almost as good, my dear: money.' She pretends to produce a coin from behind his ear. 'Why don't you run to the Cross Keys and see if they have any pork pies left? And could you pick up an ounce of tea from Mr Asprey for your grandmamma?'

His troubled face lights into a grin. When she sees that smile, nothing else in the world seems to matter.

'Thank you, Auntie Aggie.'

He seizes the coin but makes sure to leave the house more slowly than usual, showing her that he has heeded her warnings.

Agnes lets her false smile drop. Her lips purse in worry instead. At least she knows where Cedric is going, and he is familiar to the tradespeople he will be buying from: they will keep an eye on him. But if her fears are correct, she will not be able to let him gad about with his hoop and stick any longer. She must keep him indoors.

It feels wrong. He is too bright, too noisy and busy for this gloomy little house. He has already read all of his chapbooks; she will have to visit Milsom Street and see if she can get any more.

But first: the coat.

Her workbox is in the parlour. She opens the door and tiptoes inside. Mamma is slumped in the wing chair, snoring alongside the grandfather clock. Her poor swollen skin looks red, but perhaps that is a flush from the fire and not a result of the dropsy. If only Simon would examine her again. He is always so reluctant.

Agnes sits on the sofa, opens up her workbox and selects a spool: a dull brown. It does not match the colour of Cedric's coat exactly, but it will have to suffice. She spreads the garment out on her lap. All these torn, tangled threads look like the roots of a felled tree. She snips them into shape, threads her needle and begins to sew.

It is difficult to concentrate. There are too many concerns swirling around her head. Not just Cedric and Mamma, but the Campbells. Are they still safe, out there? Perhaps she did the wrong thing by giving in to that overbearing woman's requests. Maybe she should have tried to remove them from her premises by force. She pricks her finger, curses under her breath. She cannot think of it. She simply must not allow herself to dwell upon anything but the stitches.

The crescent-shaped rip is finally repaired. As she picks up the coat and turns it over to reach the torn sleeve, something drops onto the floor. A piece of paper. It must have been tucked in Cedric's pocket.

She bends to scoop it up. The edges are rough; it was probably torn from a book and folded twice into this vague square. She hesitates. It belongs to Cedric. Young as he is, he deserves some privacy. She should put it back into his pocket and forget about it.

But she doesn't.

She sets down the needle and begins to tease apart the damp folds of paper.

Pencil, just like the note pushed under her door. The same handwriting, Agnes realises, as she opens the scrap in full, revealing a single word.

The same word she heard at the séance.

Mine.

Chapter 17

Agnes has locked Mamma and Cedric in the house. It is hardly a foolproof plan, but she can think of no alternative while she runs for help.

Her footsteps clack against the pavement. She is walking too fast, striding right through icy puddles. She wheezes, but carries on. Wet feet and shortness of breath do not signify; after receiving that note, the prospect of catching pneumonia again seems like the very least of her troubles.

She turns through alleys plastered with handbills for coach builders, boarding houses and a lamp depot. Pasted fresh over the last is Ned – or *Edward Lewis*, as the police appeal for information calls him. There is a lifelike drawing of his face, clearly copied from a photograph. It seems the picture he had taken for his grandmother came in useful in the end.

Agnes averts her eyes from the poster with a fresh spurt of horror. If it were Cedric, in his place . . .

She has no good likeness of her nephew, nothing beyond a silhouette. She has always resisted daguerreotypes, but now she sees why a relative might pay good money for such a clear record. It is insurance against a failing memory. For if Cedric's face were not before her every day, she would lose not only his precious features, but those of someone else dear to her heart.

She would lose sight of the resemblance to his father, Montague.

It is mainly uphill to Alfred Street. Her lungs heave for

breath. Simon has established himself in a good location, close to the Circus and the Assembly Rooms, where his rich patients recline on chaises longues and sip languidly at the Bath waters. She stumbles up to the black iron railings that surround his house, pausing to blot her brow with a handkerchief and pinch her cheeks so she looks less like a person on the verge of collapse.

The more reasonable and collected she appears, the greater chance she has of persuading Simon.

She knocks. The charwoman answers the door – or, rather, sees Agnes and shuffles away again, uninterested by such a regular visitor. Perhaps she was hoping for a gory injury to brighten her day.

Agnes wipes her feet, takes off her bonnet and gloves and lays them on the console table beside the door. This house always smells of herbs and carbolic soap. Impersonal, sanitised. The silhouettes of the dead Carfax children that line the staircase are the only decorative touch. It is the home of a man without substance, lacking flesh and blood.

Simon could surely afford to hire one or two live-in servants, but he seems to prefer his isolation. The charwoman, Mrs Muckle, comes in for a few hours each day to tackle the worst of the drudgery – everything else, he does himself.

She recalls what Cedric said about Simon's time in Edinburgh. Maybe it *was* digging up bodies and anatomising them that changed poor Simon from the eager, ambitious young man that he once was. She always assumed it was his marriage. That was certainly when he started to lose his hair.

His consulting room is on the lower floor, in concession to his less perambulatory patients. Agnes makes her own way there, collecting Morpheus as she goes. Simon's previous dogs would not walk confidently beside her skirts inside the house, but cringe in anticipation of a kick. The pitiful things did not have wit enough to distinguish one Darken sister from the other; all they heard in the rustle of a gown was danger.

She taps on the door in case a patient is within, but Morpheus butts it open before Simon can respond.

The consulting room is papered in a damask the colour of potatoes and beef. Walnut furniture houses inkwells, empty glass domes, a magnifying glass and piles of paper tied neatly with string. Beside a row of leather-bound books, a chipped phrenology bust gazes impassively down at them.

Simon's desk is lit by a brass lamp with a tall, glass chimney. He sits behind it, reading a newspaper, but her entrance raises him to his feet.

'Miss Darken! I did not expect you. Have you been walking in all this damp?'

He pulls out a chair for her and rings the bell for tea. Her prepared speech thickens on her tongue; it is not possible to be eloquent while he fusses about her. 'Simon – I must . . . I had to . . .'

'I suppose you have already seen,' he cuts in, as Morpheus settles down by her feet. He gestures at the newspaper. 'It has been a busy morning and I only just read it myself.'

She stiffens. 'Not another death?'

'No. Did you not hear? They have identified the man.'

'The killer?'

He shakes his head. 'Oh, no. The man who . . . drowned. The one you asked me about.'

She had almost forgotten. Looking back, her former worries seem insignificant.

Noting her silence, Simon speaks gently. 'It was not . . . Lieutenant Montague.'

'No.' She shudders, remembering the Sylph's frantic gasps. 'His name was Hargreaves.'

'So you *have* read it?'

The charwoman interrupts them, thumping inside with two cups of a questionable-looking beverage. Chagrined, Simon stops leaning over Agnes's chair and returns to his own seat.

'I put sugar in it, Doctor,' the woman informs her employer as she sets the cup down on his desk. 'Thought you might need it after this morning.'

'What happened this morning?' Agnes asks.

Simon waves the question away with a pained expression, but his charwoman is only too keen to elaborate. 'Suicide, weren't it, Doctor? Is that what you found?'

'Indeed, the contents of the stomach lining would seem to suggest it was not accidental. Now, please, Miss Darken is—'

'So he ate them? A whole box of matches?'

'It would appear so. That will be all, thank you, Mrs Muckle.'

Still she hovers. 'I'll be off home for the day, then?'

'Yes. Thank you.'

The charwoman raises her eyebrows at Agnes, as if she has revealed a great wonder to her, and makes her exit.

'My apologies.' Simon grimaces, sips at his tea and grimaces again. 'That was not intended for your ears.'

It is endearing how he still thinks to protect her. She saw things at the séance in Walcot Street that would make his hair stand up on end.

Death is not the conclusion, but the alternative she saw is hardly comforting. If Hargreaves is still drowning, and Ned is still cold, she dare not think how this other man, who died feasting on phosphorous, will linger through eternity.

'I am not so *very* fragile, Simon. I do encounter sad stories in my work too. In fact, I lately met a woman who worked in a match factory.' She pauses, conscious she must not reveal the full circumstances of the meeting. 'She worked there with her stepfather, and he suffered terribly from the chemicals, even without ingesting them.'

'Ah. The jaw, was it?'

'Yes. What is the cure for that? Is there anything a physician can do for him?'

'Not a physician, but a surgeon.' He mimics with his index finger and thumb. 'Removing the mandible – the lower jawbone – is the only way to give the poor fellow a fighting chance. One must cut out the rot before it can contaminate the entire body.'

'Have you ever performed that operation, Simon?'

'I have,' he replies on a downward note, closing the topic. As with Edinburgh, as with the lady sent to the asylum, Simon does not speak of his surgical days. Sometimes Agnes wonders if that is why he has become so plump in recent years: he is swelling with all the words unsaid.

Feeling uncomfortable, she picks up her cup. The tea looks pale and insipid. Come to think of it, that is what has always troubled her about the atmosphere of this room and its dull decoration: it is like a cup of weak tea.

She pours some into a saucer and offers it to Morpheus, who laps it up without hesitation. His forebears would have been warier. Of course, there was no *proof* that Constance poisoned them . . .

It will be better if she does not mention Constance at all today.

'Simon,' she says, crafting his name carefully. 'I know you try your best to shield me from all delicate matters. But you see, I can talk to you quite composedly about a suicide and a jawbone extraction, so I hope you will realise there is no danger in being candid with me today. We must face a topic we have long been avoiding.' She draws in a breath. 'We must speak about Cedric.'

He blanches, reaches for a paper on his desk. 'This is not the best time to—'

'Listen, Simon. Please put that down and listen to me. I understand why you do not wish for him to inherit your practice – that would be, well, I understand your objections. You did him a great kindness in giving him your name. But you must give him something more!' He tries to screen his face with his hand but she sets her tea down by Morpheus and goes over to him. 'Please, Simon. Apprentice him to someone else, send him from Bath. I know you do not have a vast fortune . . .'

'His mother saw to that,' he laughs bitterly. 'Even before the separation.'

'I know, I know. But none of it is *his* fault. He is fond of you, he believes you are his parent, and you avoid the boy.'

Simon's watery blue eyes do not focus on her, kneeling beside his chair, but on the bookshelf, as if it were telling the story of his pain. 'It was difficult,' he croaks. 'His father . . . I did try. But his father was stamped on his face the moment I delivered him.'

'You saved the whole family by marrying Constance. None of us are in danger of forgetting your goodness. The scandal she would have faced, the shame upon my mother . . .' She takes his hand.

'I did it only for you.'

'Then do *this* for me too. Perhaps Cedric can train for the army? He needs to get away from here, some place safe. It is *better* if he goes. I can be brave, for him . . .'

Finally, Simon regards her. 'Can you, Miss Darken? I am not convinced you can make up your mind to live without your nephew.'

She bites her lip.

'Come, now. Whatever has brought this talk on?'

'I am afraid, Simon! The killer is drawing closer to me. They will not stop at my clients, they will take the people I love next. They want me to be all alone.' Simon's hand turns rigid beneath hers. 'I have received a note – two notes, in fact. One was pushed under my door and then I found one in Cedric's coat pocket! They want me to know how near they are, how easily they can destroy everything . . . Should I go to the police?'

'No!' he exclaims. 'There is no call for that yet, I am sure, but . . .' He pulls at the tiny flecks of stubble on his chin, thinking. 'But what did these notes say? Was there any indication of who they were from?'

She rubs at her forehead, as if she could erase the image of that slanted writing. 'No, it was just pencil words ... One asking if I had missed someone, and the paper in Cedric's coat said *Mine.* As if they would claim our dear boy! I thought ...' She looks sheepishly at him. 'There was a moment when I thought it might be Lieutenant Montague. That somehow he had found out ... But he has no right, has he, no legal right? Nobody can prove ...'

'No, no,' he says distractedly. 'In the eyes of the law, Constance gave birth to my son. And much as I despise the man, I must do Lieutenant Montague the justice to say I do not consider him capable of *murder*.'

No. The pain he caused Agnes may have felt like death, but even his betrayal cannot convince her that he was a thoroughly bad man. He was young, easily swayed, far more equipped to navigate the ocean and the demands of a ship than the tempests of human relationships.

'Yet *someone* is capable of it, Simon, and now they have turned their eye upon my family! Please, find the boy some work safely away from Bath. I do not care about anything else, so long as Cedric is not harmed.'

Simon seems to realise he is squeezing her fingers. He lets go of her hand, pats it. 'Leave it with me. I will make enquiries.'

'Is that all? And what am I supposed to do in the meantime? You are sure I should not take these notes to the police?'

'On no account. That would only fuel gossip. Besides, a single word written in pencil cannot aid the investigation in any meaningful way.' Always the slow crawl of a snail with him. It drives Agnes distracted. 'Have some patience, Miss Darken,' he counsels. 'Wait for me to call upon you with more information.'

'*Wait*?' she echoes, indignant. 'When my clients are being

killed and my nephew is in danger – you expect me to just wait?'

Simon burdens her with a sad, sad smile. 'You have waited all these years for Lieutenant Montague. You might at least give me a few days.'

Chapter 18

Pearl curls her fingers into her palms, fighting the urge to open her eyes. Just when she thought all her hope had tired, there's this: a patting, a tapping.

This is the moment everything will change. Mother's answering her at last. She just has to concentrate a little bit harder . . . But she's already focusing so intently that it feels like her head will burst.

The tap comes again, in the same rhythm but louder, like the telegraph machine Myrtle told her about, beating out messages from important men in London to important men in India. Only this message is travelling further – not just across water but through the veil itself.

She hones in on the sound, leaning forward.

All at once there come three loud thuds.

A female voice calls. 'Hello?'

Pearl can't breathe.

'I say, hello?'

It isn't Mother. It's just someone at the front door.

Miserably, Pearl gets up from her cross-legged position on the bed and walks out into the hall. Myrtle's gone on an errand and she's not meant to make a peep while she's out. But the woman sounds so forlorn . . .

'Please, I am desperate for your help. It is wet out here and people are beginning to stare at me,' she wheedles.

Pearl dare not speak above a whisper. 'Who are you?'

'Miss Darken, dear,' the voice says. 'We met at the séance.'

A swell of giddiness overcomes her. Miss Darken must mean the séance that took place before she became so ill. Her body still hasn't fully recovered from that evening and what's worse, she remembers so little about what happened.

'My sister's out,' she stammers.

'I know that. I saw her leave.'

'You must go away,' Pearl calls. 'I'm not supposed to open the door.'

'But I need to speak with you.'

Nobody ever wants to talk to *her*; it's always Myrtle they're after. And if Myrtle finds out that she's spoken to someone at the door, she'll be in a whole heap of trouble.

'I'm not allowed.'

'Please.' The lady is taken by a cough.

Pearl's within an ace of turning back and running to Father's room for safety, but something stops her. Her hand grows cool and tingly, like it does when a spirit's about to come, and suddenly it's moving, sliding the bolts and turning the handle to open the door a crack.

'Ah! Thank you, my dear.'

Pearl squints. The lady standing outside does look vaguely familiar. She's petite and fine-boned. Her eyes are not big like Myrtle's, but they grab Pearl's attention because they're so lined and troubled. She must be nearly fifty years old.

'What d'you want?' she asks.

'Please let me inside. I am tired and rather cold.'

Pearl hesitates. She can smell the rain, and she doesn't want to be stuck here talking at the door where the light's too bright. Reluctantly, she steps back to let the slender lady and her carpet bag into the hallway.

'Thank you,' the visitor wheezes, shutting the door behind her. She removes her gloves and a drooping bonnet, revealing dull brown hair with a streak of brilliant white through it.

Pearl's fingers stray to her own loose tresses.

'May I sit down for a moment?'

'I suppose you'd better come to the parlour, ma'am.'

The lady clears her throat. 'I hope that we shall become friends, so I am happy for you to call me Agnes, dear. And you – well, I only know you as the White Sylph. I am certain that is not your real name.'

'It's Pearl,' she tells her shyly.

The lady smiles. Her teeth are clean but slightly crooked. 'How pretty.'

Pearl's not meant to be doing this. Walking to the parlour feels like running a race, because her heart beats so fast and her breath's all ragged. She subsides into her usual chair, while the lady who calls herself Agnes puts down her carpet bag and perches on the edge of the sofa.

'Pearl,' she begins. She folds her hands together on her lap and stares at them for a moment. 'Pearl, I need to talk to you about your Gift.'

'I don't remember,' she blurts out. Seeing Agnes's confused glance, she hurries on. 'I mean, I remember you a bit. But not the séance we had. When I contact the spirits, it's like . . . They possess me. Take over my body, make it do and say things, but I'm not there. I don't know where I go . . . It feels like a dream. A mad dream you have and then you wake up in the morning and parts of it are gone forever.'

'Yes, I understand,' Agnes replies seriously. 'I have those kind of dreams sometimes. Especially since I was ill. I forget an awful lot.'

Pearl notices the lady's sleeves. They're worn thin at the elbow, going from black to mackerel skin. For all her airs and manners, she can't be that wealthy.

'Maybe you have the Gift too.'

Agnes presses her lips into a closed-mouth smile. 'You jest. But no one else has a talent quite like yours, Pearl. When last we met, you performed an . . . extraordinary séance. It was remarkable. And what is more, I now have confirmation that your revelations were accurate. You correctly identified a man who had drowned – why, you must know this already. Your sister, Miss West, found his body.'

Pearl's ears prick. Myrtle *hasn't* told her that. She doesn't tell her anything important.

'Good. I'm always glad to help,' she murmurs.

'I hope that is true. For I need your assistance once again.'

'You'll have to make an appointment with Myrtle, I don't—'

Agnes holds up a hand. It is knobbly; all joints. 'I would. But since you became so unwell . . .' She fidgets. 'Well, the truth is I cannot afford the price your sister is asking for a second sitting.'

Pearl's gripped by a sudden panic. 'I can't change her mind for you. Don't ask me to talk to her, because she won't do it. She never listens to me. And she'll kill me if she finds out I spoke to you or let you in the house—'

'Hush, now. Hush, dear child. I do not wish to cause you trouble. But you see, there was a message for me, from the beyond. You began to tell me at the séance, but unfortunately you were taken ill and I did not have the opportunity to hear it in full.'

'Sorry. I don't remember what that message was. It wasn't me speaking. I can't just turn it on and off like the gas. I wish I could . . .' Her throat's closing up. What a failure she is. Don't let her cry. Not in front of this nice lady.

'Oh, come now. None of this!'

To Pearl's astonishment, Agnes gets up from the sofa and holds out a hand to her. She freezes, wanting but unable to accept it.

Her hesitation doesn't matter in the end, because the lady crouches down beside her chair anyway and wraps one arm around her shoulders.

'I imagine all these spirits must be rather frightening for

you. I was scared of them myself, and I am . . . well, a woman grown! You can only be about the age of my nephew. He is twelve years old.'

'I'm eleven,' Pearl snuffles.

'Eleven! My, oh my. And so accomplished already! Your father must be very proud of you.'

She worms a little closer to the lady who smells of faded paper and dry ink, like a well-thumbed book. 'Does he look like you? Your nephew?'

'Oh, no. Cedric is handsome, like his father. He was a naval officer and every bit as dashing as you can imagine.'

Pearl grins. She'd like to see this nephew. Young men rarely attend the séances, and none of them are comely. Mr Stadler thinks he is, but he's not. 'Just like my uncle. I never met him, but Myrtle says he was in the navy.'

'As was my papa. Many naval men settle in Bath.'

'Maybe all three of them were on the same ship, once upon a time. Where's Cedric's father stationed now?'

The muscles tighten in Agnes's face. It looks like she's about to say something, but then she just shakes her head. 'Cedric is an orphan. I look after him and his grandmamma. So you understand why I do not have a great deal of money . . .'

'Neither do we,' Pearl points out.

'However, I *can* offer you something. A useful service in exchange for your own. Altogether, it is probably worth far more than you can earn in a dozen séances.'

'You'd have to ask Myrtle . . .'

Agnes shakes her head. 'Oh, no, my dear. This would be just between us. Our own séance, in secret.'

Her chest constricts. She feels as scared as if Myrtle were sat opposite her, listening to this conversation. 'I can't—'

'I doubt Miss West would approve of my tender. She dislikes doctors. No doubt she means to treat your father in quite another way . . . Although I am sorry to say, her experiments will be doomed to failure.'

'My father?' Pearl echoes, confused.

'Yes. Miss West told me that the unfortunate man suffers from phossy jaw as a result of his work in a factory. A terrible, terrible condition.' She tuts sympathetically. 'But all is not lost. My brother-in-law is a renowned surgeon. At a word from me he could perform an operation, free of charge, to cure your father.'

It's like a ray of sun has come out from behind a cloud: beautiful – but terribly painful. Pearl flinches as she would from the real thing.

'You could . . . do that?'

'Together we could. It is the only way to help him, you know. He cannot be saved without an operation.'

A cure for Father.

A *cure*.

Myrtle's voice snaps in her ear: 'Butchers, the lot of 'em.' Yet Pearl's never believed that. Father was happy to see the doctor who sent them to Bath in the first place, and he told her, before he lost the ability to talk, that he wanted to consult a surgeon.

She's dizzy. An hour ago, she would have said she'd never dare to cross Myrtle for anything.

'How would we even . . .' she starts.

'The operation could not be performed here, of course,' Agnes acknowledges. 'We would wait for your sister to leave, like I did today, and then the doctor and I would come to take your father somewhere more . . .' She casts an eye around the parlour, searching for a word. 'Salubrious.'

Pearl doesn't know what that means, but she understands Father would be somewhere safe – maybe like a hospital – and Myrtle wouldn't be able to do a thing about it.

What a traitor she is. But Father . . .

It feels like she's being split in two.

'Won't Mesmerism cure him?' she asks hopefully. 'Myrtle says it can.'

Agnes turns down her mouth and shakes her head. 'Oh, my

dear. Mesmerism is all very well in its way. But diseases of this nature are rather more complicated than that.'

Are they? How would Pearl know? She's never felt so stupid in her life. She can't read, and Myrtle doesn't tell her everything. Even the ghosts say their piece while she's in a trance.

'Your sister is remarkably talented within her remit,' Agnes says kindly. 'Yet even you must admit that she has never studied medicine, or attended a university.'

'She taught herself.'

Agnes observes her with pity. What must she think? That Pearl's some poor simple girl with no brain between her ears?

How her head aches. It's hard to think straight. She can't believe she's even considering putting her faith in this stranger, rather than her own sister, but she finds herself asking, 'Your brother-in-law would really do the operation for no money? Just for one séance?'

Agnes removes her arm from Pearl's shoulders and sits back on her haunches. It looks like it hurts her to kneel down. 'Perhaps more than one; it all depends on our success. The truth is, I am trying to contact several of my clients. They are . . . well, I suppose I do not need to mince words with a brave girl like you. They have been killed, Pearl. First Mr Boyle and then the sailor Hargreaves, drowned in the Avon. Last was poor Ned, whose body they found frozen in the snow.'

Mr Boyle. Wasn't that the very first spirit Pearl reached out to? And what did Agnes say, about the last man? *Frozen* after her shivers.

'I need to contact their sad murdered spirits,' Agnes continues to explain. 'Oh Pearl, I must. How else can I find the vile wretch who hurt them and put a stop to his crimes?' She presses one of Pearl's hands. Her touch is dry. 'And consider, my dear. Why would Providence bestow such a gift upon you unless it was to help your fellow men? Catching a killer, saving lives – why, I am sure that is the noblest action anyone can perform!'

They're her own words. Better words, obviously, but they mean the same thing. This is the argument Pearl had with Myrtle. She could use her power to stop the killer.

Everything's spinning. There's too much to think about, too much to hold in her head, so she grips on tight to Agnes's hand.

She wanted to hunt the murderer with Mother, but since she hasn't appeared . . . Mightn't this nice lady do just as well for the time being?

'I saw water,' she gabbles. 'Before the drowned man. Then I was cold. Perishing with cold. Did they really find someone all frozen?'

Agnes nods, mouth slightly ajar.

So she was right. *She* was right, and Myrtle was wrong. Thank God she's holding on to Agnes. If she weren't, the force of that would sweep her away.

'Do you . . . feel anything now?' Agnes probes.

Nothing she can put into language: just pain.

Pain, Pearl believes, should have its own vocabulary, because no one else seems to feel it like she does. Up until now her experience of pain has been mainly bodily hurt: her continual exhaustion and the sense that all her bones are on fire. But now she feels . . . shattered. Like her mind is cracking apart into jagged fragments.

If Myrtle was *wrong* . . .

Myrtle.

Oh, hell.

Pearl jerks her hand away and climbs speedily to her feet. The parlour wobbles. 'You need to leave,' she frets. 'She'll be back soon. She'll come home and find us.'

Agnes does not budge. 'The séance . . .'

'There's no time *now*! What will I do if Myrtle catches you here?'

'We could make up an excuse.'

Pearl doesn't think she could lie to save her life. The few

times she tried, growing up, she bungled it terribly. Myrtle always caught her out.

She opens her mouth to explain, but then she hears a horribly familiar step.

'It's her!' Panic strangles her voice. *'Hide!'*

'I beg your pardon?'

'Shh!' She hears a jangle; Myrtle must be getting out her keys. Pearl thinks she's going to faint. 'Oh God, please hide, ma'am. I'll never, ever help you if you don't hide right now.'

Agnes purses her lips, but suddenly she moves. If she hadn't seen it, Pearl would never believe this lady could move fast, but she does, nipping quick as a bullet from the parlour to Pearl's bedchamber and shutting the door behind her.

A mere second later, Myrtle comes in. Her cheeks are flushed from walking. She looks impossibly tall and bright as she stands there in the hallway and removes her bonnet. 'All right?'

Pearl makes a squeak.

'What you looking all het up about?'

'Nothing.'

Myrtle narrows her eyes.

It's one thing to act a part when your face is painted in ashes and everyone thinks you're the spirit of Florence King. But here, in the light of day, dressed only as herself, Pearl can't do it. The secret's heavy in her chest, and she can practically taste her heartbeat.

'I did a bad thing.' The words spill out.

Slowly, Myrtle enters the parlour. Her presence is totally different to Agnes's – youthful and almost overpowering. 'What did you do?'

'I – I . . .' Pearl's gaze drifts to the carpet bag, still beside the sofa. Myrtle's follows. 'I went upstairs,' she invents. 'While you were out. I was nosing about upstairs and I found that bag.'

Myrtle sniffs. 'Well, what's in it?'

'I dunno. Haven't opened it yet.'

Myrtle herself once told Pearl that all the best tricks are based on truth.

Her sister glances at her, at the bag again, and laughs. 'You're a rum one, ain't you?'

'Sorry.'

'Well, you'd better put it back. *I* don't care if you want to poke around upstairs, but if the bloody landlord finds anything missing he'll chuck us out in a flea's breath.'

'Yes, Myrtle.'

Myrtle rakes her with one more searching look. Pearl's guilt shifts and stings.

'Guess I'll make us a bit of supper, then.'

Pearl tries her best to smile. 'Thanks.'

Her sister walks leisurely to the kitchen. Pearl closes her eyes, releases her breath. The danger isn't over, she can't relax.

She inspects the closed door of her bedroom. Agnes is hiding there, just like Pearl used to hide in the cabinet, unable to cough or sneeze.

But Pearl's no showman with hidden trapdoors.

How on earth is she going to get Agnes out?

Chapter 19

Time is a strange concept. Ticking clocks and the slow creep of their hands mean nothing in the dark, where you cannot see them.

At first, Agnes did not dare to bend her knees in case she made a noise, and now she is uncertain whether she still can. She thinks this must be how corpses feel in their coffins.

The wardrobe seemed the perfect hiding place. Hardly any clothes occupy the cavity and there are no shelves inside, but the wood smells musty and small chinks of light in the door show where worms have eaten through it. She dare not muse upon what manner of bugs make their home here, or upon the few garments that hang on pegs beside her. Her skin itches, yet she cannot scratch it.

She has no idea how long she has been standing here. It was past midday when she called upon Simon, and then she returned home to check on Cedric and fetch her carpet bag. It must be reasonably late. There is no timepiece in Pearl's bed-chamber and in this part of the city she cannot even hear the toll of the abbey bells.

Of all the days to get stuck away from her family! She should be watching Cedric like a hawk, guarding him at every turn after finding that note, and instead she has left him in the care of his feeble grandmother. The doors to the house in Orange Grove are locked, but what does that matter? Someone determined could find a way in . . .

She peeps through the holes in the wardrobe door. The tiny bedroom window is swathed in heavy curtains. Everything remains static and unchanged. Time is not passing. It is holding its breath, encapsulating her.

When the wardrobe door finally creaks open, she cannot trust that the sound is real. A flame wavers, releasing the scent of tallow. Finally an ashen face comes into focus behind it.

'She's asleep,' Pearl whispers. 'You can go now. I've fetched your bag for you. You left it in the parlour! Nearly got me in all kinds of trouble.'

Night has fallen. Agnes has been inside this wardrobe all afternoon! Her feet have forgotten how to move; she half-climbs, half-falls out.

'Shhh!' Pearl urges.

By daylight, it was easy to treat this girl as a regular child. Other than her pallor, there was no material difference between her and Cedric, or even someone like Lavinia Campbell. But there is something ethereal about Pearl's albinism at night. Her shape seems to be pinned against the darkness, the reverse of a shadow. Agnes could swear that she trails a fine mist as she moves.

'Can we do it now?' she asks. 'The séance?'

Pearl hesitates. 'I'm tired,' she replies softly. She does look it. 'And Myrtle might hear us.'

'Then you will have to come to me.'

'What?'

Agnes feels like a pressed flower, sapped of her essence, but she needs to recover her wits quickly. She'll be damned if she's spent hours in that worm-eaten wardrobe for nothing.

'Where did you say my carpet bag was, dear?'

Pearl moves the light and shows her where the bag sits, beside her narrow little excuse for a bed.

'Come and look.' Agnes gropes her way forwards, struggling to keep her movements quiet and her voice hushed. Now that she is out of captivity, she is aware of the rotting smell again: an odour somewhere between potato peelings and a spoiled egg.

Her carpet bag contains a set of Cedric's clothes and a large cap that belonged to Agnes's grandfather. One of Papa's great-coats sits under the collection, still faintly speckled with to-bacco.

'If you could not do a séance today, I was going to ask you to creep out and come to my house at a later date,' Agnes ex-plains. 'I have drawn you a detailed map of the buildings, you see. You can understand where to go even if you cannot read the words. I thought that if you dressed as a boy, there would be less danger in walking alone . . .' Only now does she realise how absurd this plan sounds. Hurriedly, she puts the map away. 'But tonight I can bring you there myself. If I wear the greatcoat, we will pass for a man and his son, no one will re-mark upon it. And our séance will not be disturbed at my house. My family sleep deeply, believe me.'

'I'm not going anywhere with you,' Pearl asserts.

Of course she isn't. The girl may be young, but she has a steady head on her shoulders, which is more than Agnes can say for herself. What was she *thinking*? Has she really grown desperate enough to come up with this half-baked scheme?

She nods, defeated. 'I understand.'

Pearl watches her repack. The small, white face shows reluc-tance, but there is something harder under there, pushing against it.

'We could . . . go upstairs,' she suggests. 'Further away from Myrtle. Maybe we won't wake her.' The light is burning dan-gerously near to Pearl's fingers and she blows it out. 'But there's a condition.' Her whisper continues from the pitch-blackness. 'I won't do any séances unless you agree to it.'

'Anything, my dear.'

'These circles won't just be for you. We'll talk to your dead men, but then I want to contact my mother.'

Agnes feels a flicker of annoyance; she does not see why the girl cannot do *that* in her own time, but in the grand scheme of things, what is one more ghost amongst so many? She does not hold the power here; she must remember that. 'Very well. I agree.'

Small, hot fingers thread themselves through her own. The little hand tugs at her, forces her to walk onwards into the dark.

The bedroom door opens softly. Pearl seems perfectly comfortable in this twilit world, pulling her down the hall and up the first few stairs with ease.

Agnes reaches out a hand for the bannister. She cannot see her feet.

'Shhh!' Pearl hushes her.

Shabby as the house is, the stairs are actually in better condition than the ones where Agnes lives; they have endured less use and the treads hold their tongues.

On the landing, Pearl loses some of her confidence. She does not seem to know which way to turn. Choosing a door on the left-hand side, she drags Agnes into a room that is bare of furniture and even carpet. Ash stains the maw of the fireplace. There is one bottle-glass casement, blinded by dirt, but it lets in a faint tint of lamplight from the streets.

Pearl scowls. 'I'd prefer it to be completely dark.'

'Oh, but we had candles at the séance. Surely this light is comparable? I am positive a talented girl like you can manage.'

Pearl shrugs and seats herself cross-legged on the floor. Apparently it does not occur to her that Agnes cannot do the same with ease.

She holds out two lily-white palms. 'Come on, then. Form the circle.'

Painfully, Agnes lowers herself onto her knees. Her dark skirts pool around her. She hopes there are no mouse droppings on the floorboards.

She reaches out, clasps the child's hands in hers.

There is a connection.

She remembers standing like this with Montague, ready to lead a dance.

'Do we . . . sing?'

Pearl shakes her head. Locks of hair pale as lint rustle. 'We're doing it my way tonight.'

Agnes attempts to concentrate, shut out the squalor and focus upon the little girl who, in another life, might have been her own. She notices there is a yellowish tinge to her, like the first rays of a rising sun.

'No talking through me,' Pearl orders whatever she sees in the darkness. 'I don't want to be possessed this time. You can speak *to* me with knocking. Three raps for yes, one for no. Two if you're not sure.'

Agnes feels a tremor in the small hands – or is it in her own?

Pearl closes her eyes and waits. Agnes does not feel comfortable doing the same. Whatever takes place here tonight, she needs to see it.

'Is anyone there?' Pearl calls softly.

Silence replies.

Time seems to stretch. The house groans, settling. Five, perhaps ten minutes pass.

Eventually, Agnes tires of staring at Pearl and begins to study the leprous walls of the room. They are misty, blurring together. She can just make out a faint outline where a cupboard must have stood, and dirty prints smeared across the floorboards.

Nothing in this abandoned chamber reminds her of the downstairs parlour with its theatrical paraphernalia, but there is a similar sensation: a current seething beneath the surface, just waiting for someone to tap into it.

Pearl's breath comes in gentle bursts.

The hours of standing in a wardrobe are beginning to take their toll. Agnes feels her own eyelids begin to close in spite of herself. She could, she *could* let them fall, ever so briefly . . .

But then the atmosphere shifts.

There is no sound, no movement, yet all at once it feels as though someone has stepped inside the room.

'Are you there?' Pearl asks again. This time, her voice shakes.

Knock. Knock. Knock.

They flinch so violently that they nearly break the circle. The sound comes from the wall behind Pearl and ripples out to where they sit; Agnes feels the vibrations in her knees.

'Mother?' Pearl gasps.

Knock.

Desperately, Agnes tries to gather her scattered thoughts. One rap meant *no*. It is not Pearl's mother. That can mean only one thing. She pushes words through the fear that congests her throat. 'You are here for me.'

Knock. Knock. Knock.

Each tap hits her like a physical blow. Her hands are drenched in sweat and slip within Pearl's.

'Ned—'

Knock.

'Mr Boyle?'

Knock.

'Please! I need your help. I need you to tell me who killed you and—'

Knock. Knock.

Pearl's glassy eyes shine out of the darkness, wide with amazement. 'Two knocks. That means they don't know.'

'You must know something! Anything. Why else would you be here?' Agnes is speaking too loudly but she cannot control herself; the words will either come with force or not at all. 'Please help me. Give me some clue! My nephew, my little nephew may be in terrible danger—'

The ash in the fireplace ignites.

Agnes's voice drains away. She can feel the heat from across the room as the flames leap and claw upwards.

'What's that?' Pearl twists around to see, pulling Agnes with her.

Shadows flee across the plaster like a fantascope.

Pearl squints and lowers her chin to protect her eyes. 'There's no kindling,' she squeaks. 'There's nothing in that fireplace.'

But they can hear it crackle and pop.

The dark patterns begin to take form: they flatten out, grow edges, spread into faces – no, profiles. They are shades; the shades Agnes has cut with her own hands. Astonished, she watches them flick past as quickly as the pages of her duplicate book.

The Carfax children, Montague, Mr Boyle, Ned – and other faces with names she has long forgotten. Was that Mrs Campbell, there? She cannot be sure, the images are cycling by so fast . . .

But the last shape she knows.

It flickers, suspended, as if held underwater.

'Constance?' she cries.

Soot rattles down the flue, raining black over the flames. Constance's profile breaks and scatters.

As quickly as the fire burned, it winks out.

The room falls into darkness and whoever it was – whatever it was, it has gone.

Pearl releases her hands. Without their support, Agnes topples.

'Careful!'

She catches herself just before she meets the floorboards. Her arms shake under the strain; her knees feel like they have had knitting needles driven through them.

'Here, let me help you stand up.'

Looking at the room, Agnes can barely credit that any of it really happened. The house around them seems tranquil. Their noise has not awoken Miss West or the neighbours.

Pearl steals up to the fireplace and pokes one of her fingers into the ash heap.

'It's cold,' she marvels. 'How can it be cold after that fire?'

The entire place feels cold to Agnes, even though she is slick with sweat. She keeps seeing the way those flames rippled, more like water than fire, and Constance's face beneath the river.

'Are you sick, ma'am? It's usually me what gets ill after a séance. Take a big breath. I'd give you a glass of water if I had any.'

At the mention of water, Agnes shakes her head.

'Who . . .' Pearl starts cautiously. 'Who's Constance? You called out her name. Was that your sister?'

'Yes.'

'How did your sister die?' Pearl whispers.

Agnes closes her eyes. 'She . . .' She is about to say *drowned*, but she bites the word back. That is only the socially acceptable version of the story. This girl who has hidden her all day and risked so much for her sake deserves honesty.

'No one was able to tell us exactly what killed her. Whether it was her injuries or . . . You see, there was . . . an accident. We were in a carriage when the horses bolted. It ended up in the river. They say my friend Simon rescued me but I cannot recall that. I lost consciousness underwater. When I came to myself, I was safe and Constance was . . . gone.'

Pearl clutches her hand. 'I'm sorry.'

But here is the nub of it: *they* were not sorry. Simon was released from a loveless marriage that had led to embarrassment and financial loss. Cedric had always been closer to his aunt, anyhow. The family had been . . . relieved that Constance had died.

It eats her with shame to think of it now.

And yet death has not altered her sister. She is still enigmatic and infuriating, pushing in front of the other spirits to claim Agnes's attention. Why? It is next to no use for her to be popping up here, there and everywhere; if she truly wants to contact Agnes, why does she not use words?

She shakes herself. 'It does not do to dwell upon these tragedies. I must return home now, I have been away too long.'

'It's very late. Will it be dangerous out there?'

'I will wear the greatcoat in the carpet bag. I will pass for a man in the dark.'

Still, Pearl clings on to her hand. 'You'll come back?' she pleads.

Agnes wonders if it is worth the effort. She has learnt no more tonight than she did in the last séance, and that was precious little. Ghosts, it seems, are contrary creatures. Not the oracles she had hoped for but imps, out to tantalise and tease.

No wonder Constance fits in amongst them so well.

'I did not receive any answers,' she says, non-committal.

Pearl's teeth show as she smiles. They are discoloured, darker than her skin. 'Then you've got to come back, haven't you? We'll find your killer, and we'll talk to my mother. I can't . . .' She sweeps an alabaster arm towards the fireplace. 'I can't do *that* alone.'

But Agnes is no longer looking down into the girl's eager face. A slice of lamplight near the window shows the dust on the floorboards has been disturbed.

'Are those mouse droppings, Pearl?'

'Where?'

'Or did you do that when you . . .' She trails off, frowning. Pearl would not have passed across the area when she went to the fireplace, although she was near it.

Slowly, Pearl follows her gaze. Gasps.

'What is it, Pearl?'

'I . . .' She finally lets go of Agnes and steps closer. 'I can't read, but they look like some kind of letters?'

Dread is a leaden ball behind Agnes's ribs. She wanted words, and now she has them. She ought to be more careful with her wishes.

She slinks up to the child, peers over her shoulder. It's the same writing. The very same as on the notes pushed under her door and hidden in Cedric's pocket, only this time a finger has traced the words in the dust.

'What does it say?' Pearl urges.

Agnes blinks. She would give worlds to believe that her cataracts have deceived her, and she read the wrong message.

But it is still there, defiant in the dust.

'Ma'am? What does it say?'

'Too late,' she croaks. 'The writing says: *Too late.*'

Chapter 20

Agnes does take the greatcoat in the end, for warmth more than anything else; being seen out alone or accosted by a rough man no longer register as legitimate fears in her mind. The writing has warned her that something far worse waits ahead.

Too late.

Walcot Street lies deserted. Shutters cover the shops and night has dulled the cheerful gilt letters on their signs. A breeze slips down the road, flattening the lights in the street lamps. She hears her weary footsteps – just the one pair, stumbling along – and yet she has the peculiar feeling that she did not leave that house alone.

Shadows flee across the cobbles and climb up walls. Agnes has spent her life studying them, but she has not appreciated their sheer number until tonight. She sees shadows thrown by a dancing flame, the shadow of a tree branch, of an alley cat, shadows from nothing at all.

Twice she winces at the sight of a figure rising up a wall. Each time, it turns out to be her own. The shape of the greatcoat changes her silhouette, confuses the eyes. She curses herself for a coward. *Afraid of your own shadow* – that is how the saying goes. Cedric scoffs at this. He says the real monsters, like vampires, do not even cast a shade. You never see them coming.

Well, Agnes can certainly feel *something* approaching fast

behind her: a terrible premonition that bites at her heels as she walks. She will not turn and examine it, will not let it develop into a clear thought until she is home.

Too late, too late.

Her mind has never felt so disjointed and febrile. A crescent moon curves behind tattered clouds and she finds herself absurdly grateful that it is not shining full – why should that be? A large moon would help her to see. She does not believe in Cedric's ghouls and lycanthropes.

But then, a few weeks ago, she did not believe in ghosts.

In another turn, she is greeted by the welcome sight of the abbey, a bulwark of protection. If she had the strength, she would run to it. No murderer or monster would dare attack her *there*.

Panting, she crosses the churchyard and looks up at the place of worship. Angels are carved on either side of the great arched doorway, where they climb Jacob's Ladder. They seem to be leaning in, offering Agnes a hand. Their stone faces are mottled the colour of decay; she notices for the first time how stern their features are. Perhaps they are not going up to Heaven at all. They might be spirits climbing *down*.

The house she has lived in nearly all of her life appears from the darkness, just the same as it always was: with its portico and sleeping magpies, its sightless windows locked secure, and the little whiskers of foliage that grow between the lintels. Nothing has been disturbed.

She breathes a sigh of relief.

Tiredness makes her all fingers and thumbs, but she finally manages to fit her key in the lock and turn it. She opens the door and steals inside.

What strikes her most about the house is not its lack of light but its silence, weighted and profound. She finds herself closing the door behind her with infinite care, so as not to disturb it.

Why does everything seem so airless and strange?

A smoky, charred smell breathes across her face as she passes the parlour door; Mamma must have doused the fire before going to bed. Agnes cocks her head, considers the stillness of the room. *That* is the anomaly: Papa's grandfather clock. It has stopped ticking.

She stifles a childish plunge of panic. She liked to hear the clock's steady rhythm, always in the background, as if dear Papa were there watching over her. Without that wheezing tick, it feels like the heart of her home has ceased to beat.

But there is no real cause for alarm; the clock may not be broken, she may simply have forgotten to wind it. She will investigate further in the morning.

Perhaps it *is* nearly morning already; she has lost all sense of time. Even her full bladder, hitherto so imperious, no longer complains.

Groping for the bannister, she pulls herself up the staircase. Each tread offers a feeble creak. Beneath this noise, another sound: Mamma's rumbling snore.

Proof at least that Mamma is safe and fast asleep. The nerves that have fluttered through Agnes like so many moths still their wings. Nothing is wrong, no one is hurt and she is certainly not *too late*.

Perhaps she has let her imagination run away with her. Seeing Constance's shadow again at Walcot Street flustered her. Maybe the words said something else entirely? They had *looked* the same as the handwriting on the notes, but it was dark, and Agnes's eyes struggle in poor light: there is a chance they were just incidental marks in the dust.

The door to her own chamber stands wide open. Tempting as it is to enter and fall straight upon the bed, she knows her mind will never settle to sleep unless she checks on Cedric first.

Carefully, she creeps past Mamma's room and edges the door of Cedric's bedchamber open. Dark shapes litter the floor: the toys and books she has bought him over the years.

She is pierced by the contrast with the hovel that Pearl calls her *room*. Agnes suspects it was converted from a maid's cabinet. There were certainly no ornaments or trinkets there, no little touches of decoration to make a child feel loved.

At least Agnes has given Cedric *that*.

She steps inside and navigates her way towards the small brass bed. The boy does not snore; he always sleeps quiet as a lamb. Even as an infant, she does not recall him wailing in the night; perhaps he did not dare to, with Constance as his mother.

She never wants him to feel fear like that again, or to feel unwanted because of Simon's behaviour. Cedric may not have been conceived in wedlock, and his parents may have had no attachment to each other, but he is precious: the only gem snatched from all the misery.

Agnes reaches out a tender hand to place it upon the lump beneath the covers and watches it sink, slowly, to the mattress.

Nothing. There is nothing there.

The floor seems to pitch under her. Her hands tear at the covers, the pillow, even push the mattress from the frame as if her nephew might somehow be concealed beneath.

He is not.

'Cedric!'

She starts to rip the sheets, hoping to find him hidden inside.

'Cedric!' she screams. 'Ced!'

He could not have left the house: it is not possible, everything was locked up tight.

She drops to her knees with a cry. She can hardly see, can hardly breathe for tears, yet her hearing is not at fault for her ear catches a distinct rustle of paper as she pounds the shredded bedclothes.

Searching, she feels a torn page at the bottom of the mattress. A note.

She snatches it up and staggers over to the window. The

note is rumpled and a little smudged, she cannot make out the words . . . Moaning with frustration, she pulls the window shutter back and leans greedily into the light from the street.

She feared she would read *too late* again, but this is worse. That slanting hand, now as familiar as her own, has written: *You both belong to me.*

Chapter 21

Pearl thought she'd got off pretty lightly, all things considered. No spewing or fainting. She'd been tired when Agnes left, but not too tired to sleep, and after a few minutes tossing and turning feeling guilty about disobeying Myrtle, she'd drifted off.

This morning is different, though.

She feels queer, like the food she ate for breakfast was an ember that's tracked a fizzing path down her gullet, into her belly, where it's setting light to everything.

Myrtle eyes her across the table. 'You peaky?'

'A bit.' She still can't look Myrtle in the face. She's going to have to become an awful lot better at this lying business if she's really going to get Father out of here, to a real doctor . . .

Her innards lurch. It's not just the fear of getting caught that causes her stomach to ache; it feels as if there's something *alive* in there.

'Well, see you recover before tonight,' Myrtle orders. 'I'm not cancelling this séance. These ones have money, and connections. We'll clean up if we can impress them.'

Pearl stares at her jam-smeared plate. The crumbs on it seem to dance. 'I didn't sleep all that well,' she excuses herself.

'You still need to work. Christ! I don't ask a lot of you, Pearl. You're lucky you've got me for a sister. Others would be selling tickets to let people gawp at an albino like you. Maybe

I should just bundle you off to the circus – you and your dad, both.'

Her stomach pitches and this time, there's no controlling it. Pearl crashes down from her chair and hurries into her room, where she manages to sit on the chamber pot with just a second to spare.

It's agony: ripping her body just like she rips away the veil to enter the land of the dead. Pearl folds in half, her head between her knees and her lips parted in a soundless scream.

The pain doesn't go away when she's done, but it does dull to a simmer. She's left with a brand of disgust and shame. Who would've thought her body was capable of making those sickening noises, those *smells*. The room stinks nearly as bad as Father's wound.

Nearly.

She uses the old copies of *Missives from Summerland* to scrub herself clean: it seems fitting. All those writers harp on about the beauty and the wonder of the spirit world. What's that word they use? *Ethereal*. Myrtle says it means pretty and airy, but there's nothing pretty about the ache pulsating deep in the pit of Pearl's belly, or the contents of this chamber pot. Contacting the Other Side isn't a pleasure cruise. If you want to talk to the dead, you have to go digging amongst the worms and maggots.

Grimacing, she manages to stand and holds the pot at arm's length by its handle. God forbid someone should walk down the street while she empties this out of the window. She couldn't bear the humiliation if anyone else were to see . . .

She blinks, her eyes watering. Is *she* really seeing this?

Fumes drift up from the pewter rim: spirit matter trying to make its way back to Summerland.

Every inch of her skin crawls. It was bad enough with the smoking vomit; now they're in her evacuations too. Spirits and ghosts are tucked into her every nook and crevice, seeping through every pore. She's never felt so dirty.

She looks down at her slender trunk and wonders just how much of herself is left under the skin.

She twitches the curtain aside and raises the window sash, not even cringing from the daylight. She's so full of pain, her body simply won't absorb any more of it. Her waste sloshes out of the chamber pot onto the pavement outside and she shuts the window quickly, before the fumes can get back in.

Drained, Pearl staggers back to her bed and lies down. Even with her eyes shut the world is spinning. Dimly, she hears Myrtle cleaning up crockery and padding softly to Father's room for another session of Mesmerism. Another waste of time, she adds mentally, before a bolt of pain erases the thought.

The fact of the matter is, she doesn't know who to believe. Myrtle says doctors are useless butchers; Agnes says Mesmerism won't help the sick – they can't both be right. The only sure way to save Father is to play both sides.

Everything depends on Pearl now. She must keep doing her regular séances so Myrtle doesn't suspect anything's afoot, and she must put in extra work for Agnes in secret so that the doctor will come and help Father.

But all that means she'll be giving herself over to the misty hands of the dead more and more each day, and her body's telling her, louder than the spirits ever speak, that it's too much.

If she keeps pushing herself, she can save Father's life. Maybe she'll save *lots* of lives, by catching the killer. But she has to be brave and accept the truth: that all this hard work might just claim her own.

Chapter 22

The police station waxes various shades of brown. Drab beige plaster coats the top of the walls; below the dado rail it darkens to umber. Someone has tacked up handbills announcing rewards, items lost and found, but these too have become parched, curled up like decaying leaves.

Behind a walnut structure that resembles the bar of a public house, a policeman stands, avoiding everyone's eyes, looking only to his vast, leather-bound book. A brass lamp shines on him; he has a brass bell at his side too, as if he might call for assistance, or tea.

Agnes thinks she may scream.

Some people do. They are all here: the dregs of Bath. Men with black eyes and cuts; guilty-looking, flea-ridden youths; women wrapped tight in their shawls, rocking back and forth. The din would be unbearable, if it were not in tune with Agnes's inner wail.

The police are too slow. Their station looks like it has been dipped in treacle and that is how they move: painstakingly, with no comprehension of how urgent her errand is, even though she has impressed it upon them several times. No doubt everyone is here on important business. But Cedric—! A missing child! Why are the policemen not galvanised with horror?

Perhaps she has gone mad. It feels possible: she is living at a rate twenty times faster than their insipid pens can scratch.

Where, oh where is Sergeant Redmayne? Anyone of importance is shut away from her, behind doors with panels of frosted glass.

This place sparks memories of the Accident. How different *that* was. Back then, the policemen seemed to be ricocheting around the room at speed, firing questions with the rapidity of a locomotive train. Even the kindly inspector with a moustache, who had tried to prepare Agnes for the sight of her sister's body, had spoken quickly. She only absorbed a handful of his words: *caught up . . . dragged behind . . . spokes . . . axle . . . velocity*. None of them were adequate to describe the smashed, skinned wreck she had finally identified.

Papa had once complained that Constance must be pure black inside. She was not. She was very, very red.

'Miss Darken?' Her head shoots up. Sergeant Redmayne has materialised from nowhere. His face is as large and stony as she remembers; it does, however, register a hint of surprise to see her. 'This way, please.'

She stands up so fast that she nearly trips over her skirts.

'My nephew,' she begins, before they have even reached the little room he is escorting her to. 'Sandy hair. About . . . four feet, three inches tall?'

Now that she has someone to listen to her, the words come confused and garbled. She has not slept. It *must* have only been yesterday that she stood in the wardrobe, but it might as well have been years ago; she feels that she has died, come to life and died all over again.

Sergeant Redmayne ignores her rambling and opens a door. Nothing much lies inside: a deal table and two uncomfortable-looking chairs, plus a pair of iron cuffs on reserve in case conversations should grow too heated.

'You've remembered something about Boyle?' he enquires, showing manners at last by letting her enter the room first. 'Or Lewis? Your brother-in-law said he'd bring you down here for questions when you were feeling better.' He produces a pocket notebook and throws it on the table before closing the door behind them. 'There's a few things in there I want you to help me clear up.'

'Anything. I will tell you anything you like, only please send someone to search for him this minute! He could be in danger, he is all I—' Tears throttle her. She is so exhausted that she has no defence against them.

The sergeant catches her out of a swoon and guides her to a chair that creaks as it takes her dead weight.

'Dr Carfax told me you'd been seriously ill,' he says with a gruffness that is very nearly concern. 'I suppose he's right. Should you be back home, miss?'

She shakes her head. 'Cedric,' she gasps.

'Who?'

'It's my nephew. Sergeant, he has been taken. Abducted.' She raises her chin, gulps in breath. 'The killer was targeting me all along, I can prove that now.'

Were she not so wretched, she would triumph in the fact that she has finally managed to make the impassive sergeant blink.

'I'd better fetch the Inspector.' He stands, strides for the door and swings it open.

Simon is waiting there. Redmayne sighs. 'I was wondering when *you* were going to show up.'

'Where is she? Where is Miss Darken?' Simon pushes inside, red and sweaty. When he sees her, he picks up her hands and clasps them in his own. 'I have just this moment received your note.'

'Oh Simon! They took him. *Took* him. Why would you not listen to me?' For all her scolding, she is relieved to see him. Simon will take charge, he will make everything right, somehow. 'Dr Carfax is the child's father,' she tells Sergeant Redmayne. 'It was too late for letter carriers, so I sent him word by the first boy I could grab. I was not certain my message would get there.'

'All right. Good. The Inspector will want to talk to both of you.' He turns to leave, but Simon's imperious voice arrests him on the threshold.

'Wait!' More softly, he adds, 'A moment, Sergeant.' He pats Agnes's hands, returns them gently to her lap. 'Alone, if you please.'

The policeman's chest heaves beneath his uniform in another weary exhalation, but he gestures to the corridor, as if to say they may speak outside.

'But Simon—'

'I know, I know. Have no fear, Miss Darken, we shall return presently.' He has regained his poise. Smoothing back his scanty hair, he follows Sergeant Redmayne and shuts the door behind him.

Once more, Agnes finds herself on the wrong side of the frosted glass.

It would be enough to vex any woman. What can they be speaking of, if she must not hear it? Vague mumbles reach her: a droning she recognises as the base note of Simon's professional voice. Had she more strength, she would stand up and press her ear to the door.

She is Cedric's real blood relation. She has spent more time attending to his welfare than either of his parents ever did; she has earned the right to be involved in this conversation.

A conversation that is apparently going to take a long time.

She hears the words 'terrible accident,' and 'loss of mother,' then 'dredged up old associations.' Simon is clearly explaining how Cedric came to be in her care, rather than his own.

She rests her elbows on the chipped table. Misery and guilt seem to be ingrained within the wood. She wonders how many people have sat here in utter despair. One of her predecessors has carved shapes with their fingernails; another has left a stain that looks like blood. She shudders, imagining the miscreants and blackguards who must have occupied this very same chair.

Her stomach growls. She cannot remember when she last ate. It is hard to focus on anything except Cedric. What is she going to tell Mamma? Anything but the truth. She shakes her head, unable to believe she has been such a colossal fool.

Each time she has an item or person of value, she loses it.

The door creaks, making her jump. Simon enters, alone.

'What is it, what did he say?'

Simon spreads his hands in that conciliating gesture of his. 'The police will do everything within their power. They have instructed me to take you home, in case the boy returns.'

Go *home*? That would feel as bad as giving up, resigning Cedric to his fate. 'But I have not told them—'

'I knew how upsetting it would be to explain the . . . circumstances surrounding Cedric. Consider the matter in hand. The police shall deal directly with me from now on.'

Her mouth falls open. She has never felt more impotent, more inconsequential. Does Simon really expect her to sit at home and do *nothing*? It was his reluctance to act that caused this mess in the first place! And he *cannot* have given Sergeant Redmayne the full story, because he does not know it himself. There is so much she has not told him.

Her shaking fingers fly to her reticule. 'But the proof! The notes. Surely they need this? It is evidence!'

Simon examines the heap of paper she has tipped out upon the table. His face turns white. 'Where – where did you find these?'

'I told you before: in Cedric's bed, in his pocket, under the door. I *told* you the murderer was writing me notes.'

He is holding himself remarkably stiff and still. His eyes do not leave the pieces of paper; it is as though they have turned him to stone. Agnes has a wild urge to slap him, spit at him, do *something* to shake him out of this lethargy. Any other man would be frantic with worry for his missing son, even if he is only a son by law.

'Do you recognise the writing, Simon? It is familiar to me, although I cannot place it . . . We both agreed it could not be Montague. He would not do such a thing.'

Simon draws out the other chair from under the table and sits down opposite her: she the culprit, he the interrogator. He even looks a little like Sergeant Redmayne now, with his frozen features.

'No, it cannot be Montague,' he says at last. 'I can assure you that he will never make a claim upon the boy now.'

'How can you possibly know that?'

He hesitates. 'I took the opportunity to consult the naval lists after our last conversation. I wanted to put your mind at ease on one score, at least.' A forlorn smile plays about his lips. 'You used to check them yourself, constantly. You were always looking for Lieutenant Montague . . . Tell me, when did you stop?'

She lowers her gaze to the table. 'I cannot recall. I suppose I listened to you, Simon. You said that it was not a healthy occupation for me.'

'Nor was it.' He drums his fingers upon the wooden table. They both stare at them, seeking answers in the rhythm. 'I have been considering how best to tell you this, Miss Darken. At times, I doubted whether I should tell you at all. But I think you have a right to know.'

Her breath catches. 'You found him?'

'I found a *Captain* Montague, of the HMS *Raptor*.'

He made captain! Why does that still cause Agnes's heart to swell with pride? 'Good God,' she gasps. 'You have really found him, after all these years. Where?'

She must write to him. Tell him that her nephew is missing – she need not explain the full truth. She could simply beg that he use his influence and put pressure upon the police. With a naval captain and an eminent physician demanding answers, surely they will make it a priority to find Cedric?

The man she knew would not hesitate to be of assistance. He had possessed a great regard for her father. He only went away because he thought it was best for the family, but now it is clear that Constance has gone and Agnes needs him . . . Is she being too optimistic to believe that he might sail back?

But Simon is biting the peeling skin on his lower lip. He has not answered her question.

'Please tell me where he is stationed!' she urges.

'My dear Miss Darken . . . I cannot.' Simon bows his head. 'He has recently . . . passed from this world.'

All air leaves the room.

'H-he what?'

'I am afraid he succumbed to yellow fever.'

She can feel nothing, which makes no sense, for this is the most pain she has ever been in.

Montague is gone. Gone forever.

She cannot make herself believe it.

'Miss Darken? Do you need me to fetch your salts?'

Salts! She nearly bursts into laughter. What use are salts? Simon may be a doctor, but he cannot stitch up what is beyond repair. To lose Montague and Cedric both, in one day!

Wearily she leans down, places her forehead on the rough wood of the table.

'Let me take you home.' Simon's worried voice sounds far away. 'The shock has been too great. I should not have told you. You must rest . . .'

As if she possibly can.

Everything is slipping through her fingers: each person or occupation that ever brought her cheer. She does not feel as if she is only fighting against a killer; it seems like a battle for her soul.

Who can she be without her art, without her dear nephew, or even the hope of being reunited with the man she once loved? She tries desperately to picture Montague as she knew him, to conjure the sound of Cedric's voice, but already they are fading away.

Soon, there will be only Simon left.

Thank heavens for his kindness, for his warm touch upon her arm. Her other joys are mere shadows, retreating into the darkness when the lamp is blown out.

Chapter 23

Days have passed and Agnes still hasn't come back.

But she left her carpet bag behind, and Pearl has hidden it inside her wardrobe as a kind of talisman: the only proof that Agnes *was* here and promised to help her. Most days it's easier to believe in the spirits than it is to believe that Agnes will return.

Pearl spends her hours fever hot, bone dry, thrown from one encounter to the next. It's getting difficult to tell all the séances apart. So many clients, so much money changing hands. Her ears ring with wails and sobs and some of them are her own.

She trawls through the carpet bag and pulls out the map; she's already memorised its twists and turns. Agnes was right, she doesn't need to read in order to follow its directions, but she needs another talent that she doesn't have: courage.

The paper shakes in her fingers. Her whole hand looks as if it might shake to pieces. It's been like that all the time since the ghosts started sucking her dry. The only steady objects in her life are Myrtle's eyes, watching, watching.

She tucks the paper away, fastens the bag and closes it in the wardrobe. She'll give herself a few more days. If Agnes doesn't return by then, she'll put on the clothes and follow the map.

Maybe.

Her pulse beats so hard she can see it in her wrists.

Donning the green-glass spectacles Myrtle has brought her

to help shut out the light, she ventures from her darkened room. Everything looks emerald-coloured, which doesn't help her sense of unreality. The house is prettier through the lenses, but it still smells the same and is smelling worse day by day. The stink plagues her wherever she goes, like someone's shoved a piece of bad meat up her nostrils.

Maybe *she's* rotting, being pulled down among the dead.

Father definitely is. When she pushes open the door to his room, she can see a halo of spirit matter circling his sleeping head. She wonders if that's how the reaper plans to take him: if he will drag poor Father to the afterlife headfirst.

She has to stop it.

Myrtle sits in a chair beside the bed, not reading for once, or even doing her Mesmerism, just looking. Her face is sad when it's relaxed; you can see creases in it, lines she shouldn't even have at twenty. Her wide eyes are glazed over.

It scares Pearl, to see her like this.

'What you doing?' she asks loudly, hoping to snap her out of it.

Myrtle blinks and turns her head, but she doesn't look that much brighter. Her attempt at a smile is more like a grimace. 'I'm thinking of my dad.'

Pearl hovers near the door, irresolute. Myrtle doesn't often talk about her father, still less their mother, and if she shows too much interest, her sister might clam up again.

'D'you remember him much?' she asks softly.

''Course I do,' Myrtle huffs. 'I remember him better than anyone. Even . . .'

She trails off, but it's another one of those times when Pearl can hear the unspoken words inside people's heads. Myrtle was going to say that she remembers Private West better than she remembers Mother.

Pearl creeps forward, interested. 'What was he like?'

The grimace finally turns into a smile, but it's a sorry one, tinged with pain. 'He was brave. Wouldn't let anything stop him. Used to say he'd make major if ever a common man did.' She grits her teeth. 'And he would have. He *would*. Life just didn't give him enough time.'

You could say the same of pretty much anyone who died young, but if this soldier was like Myrtle, Pearl has to admit he'd stand a good chance of getting promoted somewhere along the line.

'Lord,' sighs Myrtle, 'I miss that way of life. Following the army. It was tough at times, but . . .' She flicks her eyes over the room. It was built to be a second parlour; it's the largest bed-chamber in the house, but she seems to view it like a cage.

'There were men who should've treated us better. My dad saved their lives. They should have helped us out when he bit it, or married Mother if it came to that. They'll all be in the Crimea now and it serves them bloody right.' She knots her fingers together. 'But it's my uncle who gets me most. I'd never *be* in this mess if my uncle had been around to look after us.'

Pearl glances at Father: his eyes flicking beneath their closed lids. She thinks he's just as brave as any soldier – more so, in fact. Surely it would be easier to be shot down by a cannon than to waste away like this.

'We're not in a mess,' she says quietly. 'Are we? I thought the séances were going really well.'

Myrtle makes a harsh guffaw. 'You don't know the half of it, do you? You just sit there and close your eyes and it all happens for you.'

'I'm trying, Myrtle—'

'D'you know, I've envied you every day of your life?'

Pearl stares. Myrtle, the astonishing Myrtle, is jealous of *her*? What for?

'You don't have to *do* anything, Pearl. Plan for what we're going to eat, or beat out carpets, or fetch coal and haggle over it, or keep a book of everything that goes out to the laundry, or cook, or charm the landlord into giving you a few more days, or bloody anything except the séances, and I arrange those too!' Myrtle's angry voice pinches out, strained by the effort of trying to keep it at a low volume.

Pearl stands there, stunned. She didn't even notice that Myrtle did all those things. Wouldn't know that they *needed* to be done.

Father tosses his head on the pillow but he doesn't wake up.

Myrtle glares daggers at him. 'Maybe it's not your fault. Maybe you just inherited it from *him*. He's not helping me either.'

'He's so ill—'

'He's resisting me. The Mesmerism. I shouldn't be surprised. I've had it up to here, Pearl, I can't feel sorry for him any more. He doesn't *want* to get better. It's too much effort for him.'

Even in her weakened state, Pearl manages to snap at her sister, 'You take that back.'

'I can't. He lost his wife, but I lost my ma. And he went all to pieces. Didn't take charge of the house, the funeral, even the wet nurse for you. He expected a nine-year-old girl to do it all. And I did. I've been doing *everything*, ever since.'

Myrtle's always been capable. Pearl assumed that was her character. But now she imagines Myrtle at nine, two years younger than she is now: grieving, looking after a sickly baby, running a house and working in a match factory.

Myrtle has done her duty ten times over. It's *Pearl's* responsibility to fix Father. She's his flesh and blood. She can't just leave it to Myrtle, like she has done everything else in her life.

She sits down on the edge of the bed, fighting for some strength. Just an inch of it will do. She feels utterly, utterly useless.

Myrtle watches, and her features fall slack. 'I wish,' she says raggedly, 'I wish I could just've been your sister, Pearl. I think I would've been much better at that.'

Chapter 24

It is the silence that wounds her.

No pattering feet, no half-whistled tunes. Cedric's hoop and stick stand propped up against the old grandfather clock, which still refuses to tick. Even the magpies have ceased their chatter on the roof. The whole house holds its breath.

Mamma raises the trumpet to her ear. For once, it is not her hearing that is at fault.

'*Why* should Cedric be with Simon?' she asks for the third time this morning. 'He was perfectly well here with us.'

'You know why, Mamma. He is a Carfax.'

'He is *not*.'

The perquisite of grief is that it dulls all other emotions, even the temper. Agnes finds she can lie to her mother again and again, without the slightest compunction. She will keep saying Cedric is staying at Simon's house until the police return him. And they *will* return him. If she repeats it often enough, she may even believe it herself.

'According to the baptismal records and the law of this land, Cedric is Simon's son.'

Mamma snorts. 'That may be so. But the child was to live with us, after the separation. We agreed to it.'

'And he has. Now he is almost a man. He needs an occupation and an education. Simon will provide him with both.'

Mamma lowers the ear trumpet, unsatisfied with its message. 'What I don't understand,' she mutters, 'is why my grandson would go away without saying goodbye to me. And he didn't even take his books with him!'

'Because he is not far away,' Agnes says to herself. 'He will be back soon.'

How dull the parlour feels without him; cluttered and poorly kept, occupied only by a spinster and a widow. Rather than providing a place to rest, it offers a crushing weight of banality.

Agnes remembers leaving the police station, and how Sergeant Redmayne watched her departure with an altered manner. No doubt Simon told him the whole sorry story to gain his assistance: how she lost her father and supported the family; how the man she loved jilted her; how her sister died in the Accident; how she nearly succumbed to pneumonia two years ago.

A failing business, two scrapes with death and a legacy of fragile health. Even the police would pity a person with this history.

Agnes finds it difficult not to pity herself.

'I am going upstairs to work,' she announces.

Mamma mumbles something incoherent and stares into the fire.

Agnes touches a hand to the grandfather clock as she leaves. Papa would have helped her through this mess. In fact, Papa would have stopped all of it from happening in the first place. He was the only one who could keep Constance in check. She would never have dared to seduce Montague while their father breathed.

The stairs wail like the miserable damned as she climbs them and goes not to her studio, as she said she would, but to her bedchamber. The curtains have not been drawn back in days and discarded linen lies in heaps upon the floor. It is starting to resemble the benighted little house on Walcot Street more every day.

Agnes closes the door, sits carefully upon the bed and smooths her skirts out around her. Only then does she allow herself the luxury of tears.

Her sorrow will not fit inside the small space she has allotted to it. It is not like a fish that grows to the size of its pond; the more she tries to squash it down, the more it threatens to burst out and consume everything.

How she wishes she had a confidant to talk to. Miss Grayson from church and even gossipy old Miss Betts circle through her desperate mind, but they cannot be trusted with secrets. Agnes enjoyed the company of her peers in her younger days – where have they all gone? It was not easy to keep friends, with Constance as a sister. Her jealousy became a problem. Agnes's playmates would suffer 'mishaps,' mysterious nips and burns until they eventually stopped calling at the house altogether.

The only female Agnes has spoken to with something approaching honesty since the Accident is young Pearl. Constance would have been jealous of her too.

Of course there is still Simon, infallible Simon, but she can hardly weep for Montague's fate in front of him.

The tears show no sign of abating. Her head throbs with the pressure of them. She places a handkerchief over her mouth to stifle the sound of her gulps. Did Montague ever think of her with regret? He died a lingering death overseas. There would have been enough time for him to write her a line and say goodbye – but of course, he had no guarantee that she was still living in Orange Grove. He did not know about Cedric, or about the Accident. He had been so ashamed of himself that he had cut off all connections. He seemed to believe that the only way for the family to carry on was if he disappeared entirely.

Agnes never had the chance to say that she forgave him. She was hurt, of course, and incandescent with rage for a time. But he was not the first person unable to fight against Constance's will. She had a way of making you do things.

For all his flaws, Montague was a good man at heart. Cedric

is the last whisper of his name. But *where* is he? Who would take him?

Teardrops spot the dark material of her bodice, each a tiny, bloodless bullet hole. Agnes scrubs at her eyes with the handkerchief. She has gone through so many of them lately that she's been forced to use Constance's old ones; she has picked the initials out but the ghost of the letter C still marks the corner.

Throwing her used handkerchief onto the heap of dirtied linen, she stands and goes to the press to fetch a new gown.

Her press is far better appointed than Pearl's wardrobe: floral-scented with a variety of shelves and hooks. Neatly folded stacks of jet clothing line up before her. Though there is scarcely any change in the hue, the material alters: poplin, coarse wool, smooth bombazine. Her fingers trail over each, selecting none. Instead she bends to the bottom shelf.

Constance's dresses have not been disturbed in years. On top lies a royal blue gown made from Henrietta cloth. Dust has turned it the colour of the sky on a cloudy summer's day. Underneath, better preserved, is crimson silk trimmed with black braid. Agnes pulls it out, holds it up before her.

She can move the gown, make it sway as if inhabited, but she cannot imagine herself wearing it. Nothing about the dress says *Agnes*.

Yet if it comes to that . . . What in her life truly does feel like her own, these days? There is no point left in being Agnes; there is so little to her.

Mechanically, she removes her tear-stained mourning gown and fastens herself into the crimson. It fits. She is surprised: Constance's clothes always used to be too long and tight for her.

Before donning gloves, she considers her hands. Veins rise beneath the fragile skin. Her nails are overgrown. The only vestige of beauty left is the gold band on her third finger and the glint of its small gem.

After all this time, the ring is difficult to remove; it jams around her swollen knuckle, but Agnes tugs, ignoring the pain, until it slides free.

What a tiny item of jewellery it is, to hold all the promises and hopes she bound up in it. She takes her reticule off the dressing table and drops the ring gently inside. Technically, the ring belongs to her, but *he* chose it and purchased it. It shall have to suffice. She has nothing else.

Misery still hovers over her head, but at least she feels like a different, more collected woman as she heads downstairs and walks out of the front door without bidding farewell to her mother.

The churchyard heaves with sedan chairs and it does not take long to lose herself in the crowds. There is an array of hats: proud toppers, low caps that cover the eyebrows and an aviary of decorated bonnets. Beneath them, most of the faces look cold and frustrated by their lack of progress. Each individual has become absorbed into the swarm: moving slowly forward with one accord, like a colony of ants, none acting of their own volition.

As Agnes shuffles towards Cheap Street, the feet walking in front of her own slow and then come to a complete stop. Standing on tiptoes, she perceives some movement up ahead: dark plumes wafting to and fro. When the men remove their hats and hold them to their chests, the reason for all this congestion becomes apparent: a funeral cortege is slithering through the streets.

To meet a hearse is bad luck. Instinctively, Agnes's hand seeks a button to hold for protection, but this is not her own gown and she cannot find one.

Respectful silence falls across the crowd. Only the clop of hooves echoes, like the beat of a failing heart. The deceased must have been a person of some standing.

A tall, thin mute heads the procession carrying a staff swathed in crêpe. There are so many black handkerchiefs fluttering behind him that they resemble wings, wafting the creature along. But of course that is not the real means of impetus: each carriage is pulled by a quartet of ebony horses crowned with ostrich feathers. On their backs, black-clad postilions ride without expression on the solemn road towards the grave.

The glass hearse displays a coffin suffocating in lilies. It travels feet first so that its occupant cannot look back and beckon others to follow.

Yet they *do* follow: mourners trail wearily behind on foot and the family creep along in their own elaborate carriage. They have not pulled the curtains for privacy. Each stricken and contorted countenance is on view.

Agnes knows she should lower her eyes in consideration of the family's pain, but she does not; no one does. Everybody peers into the carriage, eager to see the mark death has left on those it passed so closely by.

One of the passengers is an upright gentleman with salt-and-pepper hair. A moustache obscures his mouth, but she can tell he is clenching it tight in an effort to appear composed. It only serves to make him look like he is being throttled. His lost, dazed children stare at the streets, and an older girl . . .

Agnes's mouth falls open.

That girl.

The carriage crawls so slowly that she can take a second glance, and even a third, but none of them prove her wrong.

She knows those loose blonde curls and that habitual pout. The slope of the slender shoulders is not caused by dejection; it is there whether the girl sits in a chair or dawdles through the churchyard carrying a package, which she then drops.

The girl travelling in the funeral carriage is none other than Lavinia Campbell.

Chapter 25

Dusk falls earlier every day. They're pushing towards full winter now and Pearl yearns for it: the gentle gloaming against her eyes and hopefully more snow to soothe her heated limbs. Her skin prickles, seems to crackle with its fever.

Outside, wind slips between the limestone houses. She imagines stepping into it: feeling the cold currents strike her face and lift the hair from the back of her neck. This doesn't have to be a dream; it's possible. All she needs to do is don the outfit that rests upon her lap.

Pearl's started to do this every night: take out the carpet bag and sit waiting for bravery to possess her like the ghosts do, so she can put on the boy's clothes and follow the map. But it turns out bravery is the hardest spirit of them all to catch. She calls and calls, yet it doesn't come.

Her body's so tired. Though it's ready to give up, her mind isn't. She hasn't forgotten Myrtle's words about how useless she is, and she's determined to prove her sister wrong eventually. She'll do *something* to help.

The clothes don't smell like they belong to a boy. The men who touched Florence King were scented with tobacco, wine and bear's grease, but Agnes's nephew has his own musty perfume.

Gingerly, she unfolds the shirt and unfastens a button.

Just that daring makes her head spin.

Not yet. Not quite yet . . .

Something rattles against the window. Pearl gasps and draws the clothes towards her chest.

She knows who it is: the murderer. He's come for her at last.

Tap, tap.

It starts as a note played by one finger but then it is a hand, maybe two, patting the glass, seeking admittance.

The killer can't reach her, can he? He'd need to break through the glass. And if he did she could run into the next room, screaming for Myrtle.

She puts down the clothes and takes a deep, steadying breath. This is what Myrtle was talking about: she needs to face up to things, not run away.

She crawls on all fours, very slowly, towards the window. When she gets there, she sits on her haunches and reaches a shaking hand towards the curtain. He can't, he *can't* get to her through the window.

The frantic tapping carries on.

Here comes the faintest whisper of what she's been waiting for: courage. It allows her to clench her teeth and flick back the corner of the curtain.

A white face is pressed against the glass.

It takes her a moment to recognise the bird-like features of Agnes.

Agnes, come back to help her!

All at once Pearl is on her feet, pushing up the sash. The cool wind that she craved reaches in and strokes her forehead.

Agnes's small hand clamps on her wrist; even through her glove, it feels cold. 'Please let me in. Your neighbours will think me a housebreaker if they see me out here.' She really *does* look like a desperate woman, with strands of hair escaping from under her wind-blown hat and her papery, fluttering eyelids.

Pearl glances down the street to check no one is abroad and then helps Agnes scramble gracelessly over the sill.

'I thought you weren't coming back!'

'Forgive me, I . . .' Agnes's voice cracks.

'Why are you so cold?' she whispers.

Agnes slides the sash closed. 'I have been walking the streets for hours. Searching . . .' She swallows audibly. 'I have lost something very precious to me.'

Pearl doesn't know what to say. Her head's full of her own troubles. She so needs Agnes to be solid and comforting. 'I'm sorry. But my father's worse. Much worse. I nearly put these clothes on to come and find you.'

The carpet bag and Cedric's shirt lie on the floor. Agnes covers her mouth and stifles a sob at the sight of them.

'What is it?'

Agnes picks the shirt up tenderly. Pressing it to her face, she inhales, as Pearl has often done.

'Has . . . has something happened to your nephew?'

'I cannot find him. He is . . . Oh, sweet child! So many terrible events have occurred since last we spoke. It does me good to see your face.'

Pearl's taken aback. She doesn't know Agnes well enough for her to say these things, but she understands the lady's scared and grieving too. Mourners come out with some odd sentiments. It's not their fault, really.

'I need your help,' Pearl emphasises. 'I know we haven't found the killer yet, and I haven't got a chance to speak to my mother, but Father's that sick, I think we just need to—'

Agnes places a finger on her lips. 'One more. One more séance and you will have your reward.' Her mouth twists. 'How naïve we were. Believing we could track down a murderer with the help of ghosts. And what did we get? A few garbled messages and some shadows. Did we really think we were going to challenge the police with *that*?'

'We only tried the once,' Pearl says defensively. 'And I'm still new to this.'

'Hush, dear. I am not blaming you. Only myself. I was never strong enough to be trusted with so much, alone.' She shakes her head. 'Papa should have known that.'

Pearl shifts uncomfortably. She thought seeing Agnes again would be a cause for joy, but there's something funny about her, like her attention's fixed on a tune no one else can hear. Why's she talking about her papa, now? It's *Pearl's* father who needs help.

'Is that who you want to talk to? Your papa?'

Agnes reaches into her reticule and produces something shiny. It's gold: a ring.

'No,' she says. 'There's someone else I need to speak with, one last time.'

Chapter 26

They have barely seated themselves on the dirty floorboards upstairs before Agnes starts to see hints of the celestial about Pearl. Undoubtedly, the girl's power is growing stronger.

Agnes has not yet mentioned how Montague died, but already the child has taken on a yellowish tinge that reaches to the whites of her eyes.

His spirit is surfacing beneath.

Will he be as the others were, caught in the moment of his death? He had his faults, but it is too cruel to imagine him suffering the sweats of yellow fever throughout eternity.

'Tell me about him,' Pearl says.

Agnes places her engagement ring on the floor between them. 'His name was Montague. John Augustus Montague. Captain of a ship called the *Raptor*. This ring was . . . was a gift he gave, once.'

Pearl picks up the ring and inspects it. She is frowning, as if she has heard these names somewhere before.

Even as Agnes gazes at her hungrily, waiting for something to emerge, she's conscious of nerves. She has dreamed of Montague, fixated upon him for so many years now. She ought to have prepared what she was going to say to him.

One thing she *does* know: 'Knocks on wood will not suffice for this séance. Montague must be able to answer me.'

Pearl turns the ring over. Her pupils fatten in the darkness. 'But I don't want him to possess me. I hate the spirits using my mouth.'

Once again Agnes sees the wisps of them, teasing at the girl's edges. She plays the only card she has. 'For your father, Pearl. Think of *his* mouth.'

Pearl screws up her face. When she breathes, it comes out like mist. 'A ghost called Florence King used to speak to Myrtle inside her head. Then she'd tell me what Florence had said. Would something like that do for you?'

A flush creeps into Agnes's cheeks. There is bound to be some mortifying content to this conversation; she would prefer if Pearl *was* possessed, absent, and heard nothing of it. She takes the ring back. 'I could go to other spirit mediums,' she bluffs.

Pearl's too sharp to fall for it. 'Not for free, you can't.'

Agnes sighs. What a pass she has come to when she is the lesser power, the weaker link, even when pitted against a child.

'Very well. We shall just have to see what Captain Montague chooses to do.'

There is a snag of tension as they join hands, neither of them fully satisfied with the other. Montague's ring is pressed between their palms.

Pearl closes her eyes. 'John Augustus Montague,' she repeats.

There is a pause.

Agnes cannot bear the suspense. 'Are you there?' she whispers, but silence reigns.

What if he does not come? What if he jilts her, again?

Her face begins to tingle. She has the strangest sensation, as if threads are being drawn out from the pores of her skin. Every jagged sound of the day, from the hoof beats of the funeral procession to her fruitless cries of Cedric's name, seems to build to a crescendo inside her head.

'Please, Montague. Please.'

Suddenly, the fireplace springs to life.

The flames burn higher than last time. She can taste their smoke, but there are no shapes dancing on the wall like before. Only a single patch of black appears upon the floorboards.

Pearl makes no movement; she looks cataleptic. Whatever is taking place, she is not a conscious agent in its production.

The dark blot stretches across the room and touches the skirts of their gowns. For a moment it wavers there, then the umbra spreads and begins to take form.

Agnes knows what it will be; she has stared at it often enough. The shadow is assuming the outline of Montague's silhouette.

'Pearl! Pearl, can you hear him?' she hisses.

Pearl gives no response.

She can't breathe. The shade is life-size. Bigger, perhaps. Growing. She closes her eyes.

'H-h-hello?' The voice is faint and close to her ear. It fizzes through her veins. But these are not the words of endearment he once muttered; he sounds confused and afraid. 'Hello?'

'Montague,' she breathes.

'Where . . . Who . . .'

She promised herself she would not cry, yet the tears are already flowing. 'Oh, Montague. Don't you recognise me?'

A pause. The fire cracks.

'Agnes?'

'Yes!'

There is no immediate response. All she can hear is the rustle and snap of flames. Carefully, she opens her eyes. The shadow remains on the floor. She wants to reach out and touch it, but that would break the circle and he might disappear.

'Will you not speak to me?' she pleads.

The words come muffled and incoherent. She can only catch at odd ones: '. . . must . . . not safe . . . She . . . watches you.'

This is how Mamma must feel, listening through her ear trumpet. Agnes groans in frustration.

'Montague, I have so much to tell you! You do not even know . . .' She looks helplessly at Pearl, but the girl is clearly going to be of no use in communicating. She takes a breath, tries to focus on the most important thing. 'You had a son, John. A lovely boy. The spit of you.' Tears force her to break off. 'He is missing. I thought you could help me find him. I thought . . .'

Something bumps downstairs. For an instant, she worries it might be Miss West, but then Montague fades in again.

'. . . here . . . together . . . We . . . held . . . but she . . .' Nothing animates the silhouette; its lips do not move when Montague speaks. It is disconcerting, for the voice that comes through the interference is ardent; even panicked.

'I cannot understand you! What are you trying to say to me?'

Knock, knock.

Agnes flinches. It is the sound that came at the last séance, but what did it mean? Memory fails her; all that strikes her is how ominous it sounds.

Montague's voice pitches higher. 'Marry . . . Carfax . . . keep . . . safe.'

'What?' She frowns. 'It was *Constance* who married Simon. She made the poor man miserable, but it was the only way to save our name. You cannot think that I would—'

'. . . takes over . . . unaware . . . But if Carfax . . . husband . . . protect you.'

She feels like a piece of sable paper, being snipped to pieces. It sounds as if he is telling her to *marry* Simon. A wave of hurt and rejection hits her. After so much time, can *that* be all he has to say?

Knock, knock.

The shadow flutters.

'Montague, are you still there?'

Knock.

'You cannot think I would marry another . . . I never loved anyone but you!' The confession bursts out of her. 'Despite everything. If you had not run away like that, perhaps we . . .'

His shape is quivering wildly now, threatening to break apart. Thin black lines creep like fingers across the image.

She shoots an anxious glance at the fireplace. The flames are dipping and swooping, roaring louder than ever; their spitting seems to fill her ears, censoring anything he might say.

Then a single, terrified sentence breaks through.

'*She's coming.*'

'Montague!' Agnes flings out her left hand to clutch at him; the ring flies with it, clatters somewhere.

Montague's shadow starts to trickle away.

She sees Pearl's empty fingers droop to her side and realises, too late, that she has broken the circle. She is losing him.

'No. No, come back!'

She snatches up Pearl's hand again, but it is no good: the damage is done. The flames dwindle faster every second.

'Montague!'

The fire sputters and dies.

The sudden darkness is like the shutting of an eye.

He is gone. Gone, again.

A painful moment passes, then Pearl comes back to life with a gasp. 'What? What happened, where am I?'

Agnes cannot even speak.

Behind her comes the creak of wood. Something approaches.

Pearl's face turns a paler shade of white. 'Oh, no.'

Still winded, Agnes peers warily over her shoulder. Recoils.

Two malignant eyes burn above the thin glow of a rush-light.

It is Miss West. Her fury radiates through the room.

'What the hell d'you think you're doing?'

Chapter 27

Now she's for it.

Pearl wishes she could sink into a trance, but Myrtle's already striding across the room, puffing up dust as she goes. She grabs her by the earlobe and jerks her to her feet.

It hurts. It really hurts.

'Miss West, let me explain . . .' Agnes starts.

Myrtle thrusts the rushlight holder forward. She must recognise Agnes from the first séance, because she growls, '*You*.'

'Yes, it is me, Miss Darken. Forgive my audacity, I—' She breaks off, emotional. Her cheeks are already shining with tears. 'We can discuss this between us. The child is not to blame.'

Myrtle gives Pearl's ear a twist and makes her squawk.

'Please, do not hurt her,' Agnes cries. 'It was *I* who persuaded her to hold a séance—'

'Then you owe me a bob,' Myrtle cuts in.

'I beg your pardon?'

'A shilling,' Myrtle spits. 'You use a service, you've got to pay for it. Otherwise it's stealing.'

Agnes is aghast. 'I . . . I do not have it.'

'Guess I'd better call the constable, then.'

Myrtle hates the police almost as much as she hates doctors, Pearl knows she'll never do it, but Agnes starts to panic, pulls out a purse and offers odd pennies and farthings on an outstretched palm.

It makes Pearl feel better to see the older woman is helpless before her sister too. She isn't the only weakling.

Myrtle glowers at the coins for a long time. Finally, she drops Pearl and grabs them. 'It'll have to do. Now get your arse off my property.'

Pearl gasps in relief. She raises a hand to cup her smarting ear.

'Yes, of course,' Agnes blusters. 'But please do remember, it was my fault entirely—'

'I won't tell you again.'

Shooting an apologetic glance at Pearl, Agnes hurries out of the door.

They hear her stumbling down the stairs in the dark.

Pearl looks at her feet; it seems the safest place. Panic's crashing inside her head, but maybe the money will calm Myrtle down, maybe she won't be furious enough to . . . what? She doesn't even know what Myrtle will do. She's never crossed her this badly before.

'You ungrateful little bitch,' she snarls.

Pearl can't utter a word.

'All I've done for you, and here you are, stealing bread out of my very mouth.' When Myrtle's in a good mood, her voice can cradle you. Right now it sounds like smashing crockery. 'Get down those stairs. Now.'

Pearl's legs are weaker than water. She lurches, rather than walks, but Myrtle comes up behind her and the motion of her sister's knees against her back seems to push her on.

She should've known it would turn out this way. She's never been good at lying or sneaking about. As she totters into the darkened hallway, she has an urge to follow in Agnes's steps and flee out of the front door. But she's not strong enough to run, and she can't leave Father.

Father . . .

'Go on, then,' Myrtle demands. 'Explain yourself.'

If ever there was a time Pearl wished a ghost would take

over and speak for her, it's now. But of course they don't; they're never there when she needs them.

'It was just . . . She wanted to find the murderer. And I thought—'

Myrtle groans. 'We've talked about this before. Don't you want to earn your living?'

'We'd be popular if we caught a murderer,' she mumbles. 'It's not just ghosts that interest people.'

'No, that's right. People pay to see albinos too. Maybe I'll just put you in a cage, and we can have a menagerie instead of a séance? Is that what you want? Is it?'

Pearl shakes her head.

'How the hell did that woman even get in here?'

'I . . . It was when you were out . . .'

Myrtle's lustrous eyes spark in the shadows. 'You *opened* the door?'

It's useless. She hasn't got the words to defend herself; she doesn't even deserve them. She knew all along that she was being wicked and she did it anyway.

'I'm sorry,' she pleads.

Myrtle puffs out the rushlight. Neither of them need it. 'I should've known,' she seethes. 'You're just like your dad: out to spite me. Going under my nose, in my own house. I don't know why I bother with you. Maybe I should've left you with the cord tied around your neck.'

Pearl shrinks within herself. 'I'm sorry.'

'But *why*, Pearl? Why would you do this? Just to pull the wool over my eyes and punish me for saying I weren't going to mesmerise him no more?'

It's on the tip of her tongue to tell Myrtle about the doctor and the jawbone but something holds her back. She's in enough trouble already without mentioning medicine.

Seeing Pearl isn't going to answer, Myrtle starts to mutter to herself. 'I didn't think you could do this. Didn't think you even *capable* of . . . I messed up. What did I do wrong?'

This stings worst of all. Myrtle's not just mad, she's ashamed of her; thinks she's raised a thankless wretch, but Pearl was never *trying* to hurt her sister – was she?

Leaning against the wall, she starts to cry.

'Save me the waterworks,' Myrtle tuts.

She can't. She's too weak and ill, and still so *hot*.

It's all right for Agnes, who can just peg it and get away. All Pearl's ever known is contained inside this house. Father and Myrtle. That's it. All she's got. One's dying, and the other one hates her.

'You wouldn't . . .' she sobs. The words don't want to come out. 'I never would have . . . But you wouldn't . . . help . . . me.'

'What are you on about now?'

'Mother!' she bursts out.

The fetid, stale air rings with her cry.

Myrtle grabs her wrist and pulls her away from the wall. 'Don't you dare.'

'I only . . . did it because she . . . she promised me . . . She said we could try and . . . talk to . . . Mother.'

Myrtle's face twists into something cruel. 'And did you, Pearl? Did you and your little friend manage to call her back?'

Pearl catches her breath. She shakes her head miserably. 'We had to do her ghosts first. Both times. She never let me.'

'But you found the murderer, right?'

'No . . . I don't think so. She wanted to talk to some sailor.'

Myrtle scoffs. 'Oh, I bet she did. Don't you see? That woman is trouble. She used you, you dolt.'

It bursts upon her like Mr Collins's powder: the same agonising flash.

Agnes only talked about her sister, her papa, and the man who gave her the ring. She brushed off Pearl's concerns about Father tonight and got all snotty when she mentioned the killer.

Agnes was never going to help anyone. It was all lies.

At last, her weak legs give out. Myrtle catches her, lets her sob against her nightgown.

Berries. She still smells of berries and violets.

'I told you,' Myrtle speaks hoarsely into her ear. 'You can't trust no one. Got it?'

Her head hurts too much to nod.

She's such an idiot. How could she *ever* think she knew better than Myrtle, strong Myrtle who lifts her up and carries her all the way to her room?

The curtains are still open from where Agnes climbed in. The carpet bag and shirt lie on the floor. Myrtle kicks them out of the way.

'Get some sleep.' She plonks Pearl ungracefully on the bed. 'You've got more work to do tomorrow. Proper work.'

The pillow is blissfully cool against her hot face. She feels like she could sleep for years. Never venture out of this bed or her place again.

Myrtle turns her back on her and crosses the small room. For a minute Pearl thinks she's going to close the curtains and save her from the glare of the street lamp, but she doesn't; she picks up the pair of green glasses, which Pearl had taken off when it got dark.

'You'll get these back when you deserve them,' she says.

Then she leaves Pearl all alone.

Chapter 28

'Slow down, Miss Darken. Tell me again who is at risk?'

Simon spreads his hands on his desk and leans towards her. Agnes finds herself regarding him anew, after Montague's words. He was never *handsome*, even in his youth, but he does have a trustworthy, open face and real solicitude in his gaze.

She cannot see his blue eyes without calling to mind those of Constance. Hers were fringed with long lashes, intelligent in expression but cruel, savouring another's misery. Simon's could not be more different. They are lighter and small, yet there is a depth to them that few people possess.

'I have made such a muddle of everything,' she confesses. 'Worse than that. I have caused harm to others. But you see, I was not thinking straight. How could I, over these last few months?'

'Never mind that. I know better than anyone how severely you have been tried. Just tell me what happened. You know you can always talk to me.'

There is not much left of his brown hair. A belly protrudes beneath his waistcoat, but she must admit that both these signs of age rather suit him. *She* has altered physically, and he has never treated her the slightest bit differently.

'I am afraid you will be displeased with me.'

'I could never truly be displeased with *you*, Miss Darken.'

Dear Simon. Montague seemed to imply that he was the

proper match for her. Can it be true? Simon is not the type of man she envisaged for herself, but perhaps real love is not all romance; perhaps it is friendship and a dogged devotion that stands the test of time.

'You are kind to say so, but I am conscious of doing wrong. You advised me as a physician and a friend, and I deliberately went against you.'

Despite his assurances of forgiveness, annoyance flits across his face. Perhaps annoyance is too strong a word; it is more like a shifting: Simon making room for some new disappointment he must deal with.

What an irritant she has been to him. She irritates *herself*, with her caprices and violent mood swings. Truly, this man has been a saint to endure her for so long.

'I am sorry, Simon. The uncertainty ate away at me. I needed to be *doing* something, and I . . . I called upon a spirit medium.'

Rather than brave his gaze, she concentrates on the dark brown and beige damask on the walls. Under consideration, it is not so *very* dull a pattern; there is a stolid respectability to it, much like the occupant himself.

Simon's breath pours out. Morpheus, who is keeping aloof today, grunts from the corner.

'I see. I . . .' Simon picks up a dry pen and fiddles nervously with it. She wonders if he is remembering those plundered Edinburgh graves. 'I advised you against that practice for some very specific reasons,' he says in his professional voice. 'Foremost, I consider it a trick, but that is not my only objection. It is the . . . exposing of the mind, if you will. Those women give themselves over to a suspension of common sense. They encourage nervous agitation. No doubt there is a feeling of freedom to it all, but surrender of conscious control is not . . . something I would wish for you. Your health has never recovered from the pneumonia. It should not be tested in any fashion.'

She considers telling him what she has seen at the séances

and decides it is better not to. It is one of those phenomena a person must experience for themselves.

'You had my best interests at heart, as you always do, Simon. The elder of the women involved is indeed a grasping, mercenary thing, full of affectation. But the medium herself . . . She's a child, an innocent child, and I have caused her such trouble.'

'How so?'

Her cheeks warm to recount the circumstances. She will exclude the part where she climbed in through the window, if she possibly can. 'Oh, Simon. You will hardly credit how foolish I have been. I could not afford the fee for a séance, but I thought I might get some clue, something to help me find Cedric . . . So I persuaded the little medium to see me in private without her sister's knowledge. We were caught and I am so afraid that the girl will be treated unkindly for my error.'

'I see.' Simon turns the pen in his fingers. 'That is most . . . regrettable. Yet I suppose the child *did* disobey her guardian, and must be punished as she sees fit. Distasteful to the feelings as it is, we have no right to interfere . . .'

'The sister is *not* her legal guardian, though. The child has a father living. Do you recall me mentioning a man with phossy jaw?'

His forehead wrinkles. 'We . . . spoke around the topic, I believe.'

'And that is another blunder I have made.' She makes a steeple of her hands and leans her nose against it. This whole conversation is an exercise in mortification. 'Forgive me, Simon. It is not only strangers I have caught up in this mess. I may have implied that . . . you . . . might operate upon him . . . in return for the child's services.'

Simon presses his lips firmly together.

'It was rash of me, I know. I cannot defend it, Simon, I can only apologise. There are times when I am not . . . collected. How can I be? The police do nothing, they have not even caught Mr Boyle's killer yet, and I am expected to trust them with finding poor Cedric! I hear of such clever detectives in London, but here they do not see what is right before their eyes. I *am* being watched, Simon. Just the other day I stumbled upon the funeral for another one of my clients.'

'No.' Simon shakes his head, lays the pen back on the desk. 'That is not being investigated as murder. The police believe Mrs Campbell tripped and fell onto the railway tracks in front of a train. There is no evidence of anyone pushing her.' Seeing her astonishment, he goes on: '*I* have been watching you, Miss Darken. Whatever you might think, I did take your claims seriously. I heard through a patient of mine that Mrs Campbell intended to have her silhouette painted by you, and I have made sure to keep an eye on the Campbell family ever since.' He folds one leg over the other, making his leather chair squeak. 'The police are not quite as dull as you esteem them. I have spent a good deal of time answering their questions on your behalf. The crime scenes were evidently left by a person of some intelligence. Sergeant Redmayne believes the culprit may have had practise with this sort of thing – concealing the time and method of death, and so on.'

'But the police do not know the full extent of my involvement: we never told them of my connection to Ned or Commander Hargreaves. They have no idea I took both men's silhouettes.'

'True. And it is advisable to keep them in ignorance. That information cannot reflect well upon you.'

She throws up her hands in frustration. 'But they might be able to discover *why* this killer targets people close to me, and why on earth they would take Cedric! I have thought it over and over and it makes no sense. The only *possible* person with a claim on him is . . . well, you told me yourself, he is deceased. So unless we are proposing that a *ghost* is behind this . . . Are you sure I should not give the sergeant the notes I came across?'

Simon bites a fingernail. 'No. No, I believe those notes may

have been old, immaterial scraps that turned up by coincidence. You said that you found one in Cedric's coat?'

'You know I did, I showed it to you.'

'Yes. Well. The writing that *I* saw . . . on the note you
showed me . . . That belonged to someone else. Someone we
both knew, Miss Darken.'

'Who?'

'It was the hand of . . . my wife.'

Constance.

He is right. Memory dawns on her, sickening but irrefut-
able. *That* is why she recognised the writing. Constance has
been gone so long, she did not think to associate the notes with
her. 'But how—'

'There was not much love lost between the pair, I grant you,
but Constance *was* Cedric's mother. Do you not consider it
feasible that he might have chosen to keep a small memento of
her about his person?'

It seems unlikely. Cedric was mainly frightened of his
mother. But then Agnes *had* suspected him of playing with her
papers on the day she found the first scrap. Perhaps there is
some vestige of feeling left inside the boy that she cannot understand. It makes more sense than any other explanation.

Simon is so overwhelmingly *reasonable.*

Yet Simon does not know about the writing in the dust at
Walcot Street. *Too late.* Was that from Constance too?

She shivers the thought away. Does not want to face the
possibility that in trying to contact other spirits, she might
have accidently let her sister back into her life.

Simon's theory is far more comforting.

'Yes,' she says forcefully. 'Cedric *might* have kept a token.
Yes. I am sure everything is . . . just as you say it is, Simon.'

'Then that is settled.' He musters a hairbreadth smile. 'Nothing more to trouble the police with for the present. Now, will
you stay for dinner, or shall I walk you home?'

'You have done so much for me already. For all of us. It

pains me to beg another favour, but do you think that you could take a look at this man? The one with phossy jaw?'

He hesitates.

'Please. I have failed to protect my nephew. It would be so nice to help just *one* young person, to put *something* right. I do not want the medium girl to be orphaned. When I think of what it cost me to lose my own father, I—'

Morpheus sits up and yawns. He is ready to leave the room; he seems to know what his master will decide to do.

'This man is not under the treatment of another physician?' Simon asks.

'No! The elder sister will not allow it. The poor soul is being kept from all aid.'

Simon gives a single nod.

She *does* love him then: his goodness and his justice, even his silly dog, who is regarding her judgementally.

'Just promise me,' he says as he stands, 'that this will be an end of your spiritual adventures. Have a care for your health. Stay away from newfangled concepts that you do not understand.'

Remembering Constance's writing in the dust, it is not hard to make the pledge.

'I will, Simon. I will do whatever you tell me to.'

He offers her his arm and they walk out of the consulting room together with Morpheus trailing behind them.

Rain lashes the pavements. A couple of young ladies without an umbrella shriek and run for the cover of the nearest awning. Morpheus stops on the doorstep, takes one look at the drops bouncing off the puddles and turns tail back inside.

'A wise choice, I think,' says Simon, closing the door on his dog. He erects their umbrella – one of the old sort, with cane ribs.

Agnes lifts her skirts from the damp. Cedric must be out

here, somewhere. Is he sheltered and dry? She worries that her stitches in his coat might not hold, and if he gets wet, he will not be able to change his shoes and hose before a fire. He could catch pneumonia like she did.

She searches for his face under every dripping hat and in every saturated alley.

They walk slowly beneath their shared dome, the patter of rain upon oiled silk making up all their conversation. Simon takes the side of the pavement nearest the road and moves heavily, a man burdened with other people's secrets, while dray carts swish down Broad Street and splatter his leg with mud. Still, it is better to take this longer, more crowded route than brave the slippery hill.

The damp resurrects Agnes's old aches and pains. She will not, she *must* not think of the Accident. She squeezes Simon's arm – the same arm that lifted her from the river, all those years ago.

As they round St Michael's church and turn into Walcot Street, the fresh, moist smell of the rain takes its last breath. Here, the odour of hops rules the air.

Commerce does not stop for the weather. A determined organ grinder turns his crank, playing the shanty 'Little Billie.' Agnes pulls Simon towards a chemist's shop. The windows have steamed and the prices chalked on the slate board outside are washing away.

'It may be prudent to wait for the sister to leave the house,' she advises him, although she does not relish the prospect of waiting in the rain.

'How do you know she has not gone already?'

Agnes gestures to the waistcoat pocket in which Simon keeps his fob watch. He produces it, shows her the time. She shakes her head. She has observed this house, knows its routines.

'It needs some ten minutes more,' she decides.

Simon peers through the misty windows at the array of glass bottles the chemist has on offer. 'Perhaps I will call inside.

If this man is as bad as you say, he will need something to alleviate his pain.'

Resisting his entreaties to join him, Agnes takes charge of the umbrella and keeps surveillance on the house.

From this distance it looks pedestrian, blending in seamlessly amongst its limestone companions. No passer-by would suspect that ghouls swarm inside. It is a kind of ossuary, she thinks, holding captive the bones of an albino child and a man with phossy jaw. This is what her beautiful city has come to: the beau monde and the dandies have fled, leaving only the spinsters, the soot and the ghosts behind.

She tucks a damp strand of hair behind her ear, and notices with a jolt that her left hand is bare of all jewellery. Of course, Montague's ring must still be on the floor where it fell in the upstairs room; she did not have time to collect it before Miss West threw her out. She has worn the ring on her finger for all these years; it seems strange that she did not miss it until now. Perhaps hearing Montague's voice at the séance is finally helping her to move on. But she would feel better if she knew what had made his spirit so afraid. Or who. What were his last words? *She's coming.* Was he referring to Miss West, on the stairs? Or was he trying to tell her that the killer is in fact a female?

Agnes cannot ask him now. She has promised Simon.

Finally, the front door opens. Agnes turns to the side, letting her bonnet shield her face, and dips the umbrella a little lower. She is right to do so. Miss West leans out, casting her suspicious eyes up and down the street.

Satisfied, she calls over her shoulder – probably a warning to Pearl – and leaves the house. But then she performs an action Agnes has not noticed her take before: she turns and locks the door behind her.

'Chestnuts all hot, penny a score!'

Miss West walks straight past the man hollering his wares and weaves effortlessly around a costermonger's barrow. She has only a bonnet to cover her, but she does not bow her head under the rain. This is a woman who knows where she is going and will not let anything stop her from getting there.

Agnes watches her stride off towards Cornwell Buildings, where she is swallowed in a forest of umbrellas.

The shop bell jangles behind her. Simon emerges from the chemist's with a bottle and a brown-paper parcel.

'The sister has departed,' she tells him. 'We must move quickly.'

A boy does his best to sweep a path for them across the road and Simon tosses him a penny.

The rain has failed to wash the sooty fingerprints from the window of Pearl's house, but Simon is able to read the advertising cards aloud.

> New and scientific treatment
> The Magnetic Touch for chronic disease
> No medicine given
> No pain caused

> *The White Sylph*
> Conductress of Spirits
> Blessed with the gift of trance-mediumship
> Enquire within

He raises an eyebrow at Agnes.

'It is hardly Pearl's doing,' she points out and knocks at the door.

There is no answer.

The rain intensifies, running out of the eaves in great torrents. Agnes knocks again and again.

'Pearl,' she calls. 'Pearl, it's me. Agnes. Do not be afraid, dear. I have brought the doctor.'

'Perhaps she does not wish to see us,' Simon surmises.

'She is afraid of her sister,' Agnes corrects him, knocking until her knuckles hurt. 'Either that or . . . Oh, Simon, you do not suppose Miss West has beaten the child? Perhaps she *cannot* answer the door.'

Simon bites his lip. The crowd on the pavement has thinned; even the street sellers are seeking cover now. He glances around, then hands Agnes his medicines. She takes them awkwardly, juggling the umbrella.

'Stand back.'

Raising a foot, he kicks open the door.

It is a cheap thing with a paltry lock but all the same, Agnes is surprised by how quickly it yields. She hears a gasp from inside as the door bangs back against the inner wall.

No one on the street remarks or cares.

'After you, Miss Darken.'

She passes him the umbrella to disassemble and enters the house, where acrid fumes replace the damp street smells. If she had her hands free, she would pull out her handkerchief and cover her nose.

Her vision takes a moment to adjust to the unnatural gloom; it is only when Simon closes the front door and squelches in after her that she discerns Pearl, hovering at the end of the hallway with all the fragility of a moth.

Her pinched face is wary, unsure.

Agnes cannot make out any bruises, but the child does look ill-conditioned. Her once alabaster skin appears jaundiced and her wrists look thin enough to snap.

An arrow of guilt quivers in Agnes's heart.

'Look, dear,' she croons, holding up Simon's purchases. 'We have brought medicine.'

The girl regards them the same way Agnes inspected the cabinet and the crystal ball on her first visit.

'You're . . . not meant to be here,' Pearl croaks at last.

Simon comes forward, past Agnes, but still leaving a comfortable distance between himself and the girl. Puffing, he bends down to her height. If he is surprised to see an albino child, he does not show it.

'Forgive the intrusion, Miss . . .'

'Meers.'

'Miss Meers. My name is Dr Carfax. I understand that your father is very unwell and I should like to help him, if I can.'

Pearl looks at her feet, scuffs one against the floor. The struggle is plain on her face. The poor child wants to trust Simon, but all her education – or rather her indoctrination – tells her not to.

'Myrtle says your medicine's poison.'

'Phosphorus can be a poison,' Simon counters. He is trying to be amiable to gain Pearl's confidence, but Agnes knows him well and can hear the concern in his voice. He is grieved by the sight of this waif she has produced. 'That is the substance your father used, to make matches for his employer. The phosphorus has hurt his mouth.'

'We give him magnetised water to drink. Myrtle's going to exchange his bad energy with hers. She's strong, she's got the vit – vite – *vitality*.'

'Good. That's good.' He balls a hand by his side, the only indication of his outrage. 'Miss Meers, I would like to take a look at your father and see how he gets along. I will not hurt him, I promise. I will not administer any medicine or even touch him, if you do not wish it.'

The little body retracts like a concertina. 'He did say . . . he always wanted to see another doctor. But Myrtle wouldn't let him, after the first one sent us here to Bath . . .'

Simon nods, rises awkwardly to his feet and offers her his hand. Pearl accepts it like something that might burn her.

Agnes trails them into a chamber at the end of the corridor, which is about the size of a small parlour – an innocent-looking room to be the source of the rot she has smelt since the first day she entered the house. The stink here is not just humming but festering, choking the breath from her.

'Miss Darken, this is not a sight that—' Simon begins.

She wonders what end he intended to put to that sentence,

for there is not a word adequate to describe what lies before her. That is cruel; she should say *who* lies before her, but in all honesty she is struggling to identify the person on the narrow bed.

He is too horrible to concentrate on for any length of time. The wasted, skeletal body she can just about stomach, but the lower half of his face is dribble, corroded flesh and gaps where no gaps ought to be. Perhaps the worst circumstance is that his eyes, nose and forehead all look perfectly regular. It is only below them that he becomes a puppet with a wide, oozing grin, the teeth poking out at angles.

Has such a spectacle been a normal, everyday sight for a young girl like Pearl?

'I will help,' she murmurs, hardly knowing how.

Of course Simon is more practised. 'Mr Meers?' he asks, approaching the bed. 'My name is Dr Carfax. With your consent, I should like to examine your jaw.'

The man blinks, struggles to focus. When at last his brain registers who Simon is, he gives an approximation of a nod. One atrophied hand motions to his face. The gesture is crude, but understood. *Cut it out.*

Simon takes a breath. 'Miss Meers, it would help my inspection to clean the area a little. I will use only soda, perhaps a touch of alkaline if necessary. Is this acceptable to you?'

Pearl wavers but her Father's pleading eyes get the better of her.

'If he wants it.'

'Miss Darken?'

Agnes realises Simon is asking her for the packages, and she begins to unwrap them for him. Her hands shake. She has never seen anything quite equal to this.

'The necrosis is advanced,' Simon whispers to her as she hands him his apparatus. 'The abscesses on the gums have not even been lanced.' He turns to Pearl, in the corner. 'Miss Meers, it is conceivable this will cause your father some discomfort. Perhaps you might hold his hand?'

Pearl plaits the gaunt fingers between her own small, pale ones. 'You're brave, Father,' she says. 'You won't even feel it.'

Agnes does not want to watch. She just holds the bowl of water and soda, and passes fresh lint when Simon asks for it. She notices light, pea-sized balls fall from the jaw as Simon wipes, and realises they are bits of dead bone the body has cast out.

God above.

The man clenches Pearl's hand. 'That's it,' she whispers. 'It'll be better in no time.'

Although Pearl whispers words of encouragement to her father, she frequently breaks off to narrow her eyes at Simon. She appears to think he is a sort of dark magician who requires her constant supervision. Whatever her suspicions, she can be in no doubt that he is proving useful; when the abscesses are burst and everything is cleansed, Mr Meers looks much less swollen and discoloured.

He has proved astonishingly stoical, with fewer groans than Agnes expected. She is pleased with herself too, for not swooning. Constance always used to mock her squeamishness, but now she is stronger, capable of seeing gore like her sister was.

Simon gathers all the dirtied lint and places it into her bowl, making the water filthy. 'Could you dispose of that for me, Miss Darken?'

She cannot imagine where he intends for her to take the bowl; it is doubtful this house has its own privy and she does not know where to find the close stool. Carrying her stinking cargo out into the corridor, she dithers for a while before finally deciding on the scullery. She places the bowl beside a box of matches and walks away from it, shuddering.

How can this family bear to light a match, after all that they have done?

She re-enters the sickroom to see Simon administering drops of opium. Pearl has crept over to stand beside him.

'Agnes said you'd take Father to a hospital,' she ventures.

Simon concentrates on his task. 'It would not be advisable to move your father at present, Miss Meers.'

'Then you'll do it here? Cut the rotten bone out and cure him?'

He does not answer straight away but frowns, hands Pearl the drops and takes his patient's wrist to feel the pulse.

Mr Meers's eyes close and he seems to drift out of consciousness.

'Is it like a trance?' asks Pearl. 'Do you do it while he's sleeping?'

'Leave him to rest a while,' Simon sighs. 'We will discuss the matter outside.' He gestures to the bottle in her hands. 'Retain those for his pain, Miss Meers. I have given him five drops. I should keep it to . . . Forgive me, but can you count?'

Pearl nods proudly.

'Let us say a limit of twenty drops a day.'

After a moment of consideration, Pearl hides the bottle beneath the mattress. Her father moves in his sleep.

Simon nods and wearily trudges outside.

Agnes follows him. In the hallway, she touches his arm.

'What can be done?'

He only shakes his head.

Together, they pass into the parlour. A single black candle burns on the circular table, making a moon out of the crystal ball. Dark shapes flicker again; black claws running along the red plush tablecloth and swarming up the curtains.

Agnes wets her fingertips and pinches the wick out. She is sick of shadows.

'It has gone too long untreated,' Simon admits dejectedly, leaning against the sofa. 'I fear that the poison has entered his bloodstream.'

'Do not say so,' she begs.

'I am afraid it is true. He is beyond help, Miss Darken.'

She sits down heavily at the séance table. It feels like she has suffered a physical blow.

Pearl's father was meant to be her atonement. If *one* person could emerge from this turmoil happier than they began, Agnes would be – well, not content, but easier within herself.

Now Pearl will become fatherless.

The pain of Agnes's own bereavement comes roaring back. Not just the grief for Montague, but for dear Papa. She misses him so much. She was not there at his final breath and she will never conquer her remorse for that.

She pictures him on his deathbed, and a morbid instinct forces her to try and imagine her own. Who will be there to hold her hand at the end? Cedric? What if he is never found? She once worried about being a burden to her nephew in her old age, but she would rather that than face death alone.

From what she has seen of the Other Side, it does not seem to be a better place. How, then, can she offer comfort to little Pearl in this dire situation?

'I fear it is doubtful he would survive the ordeal, Miss Meers.'

She jerks out of her abstraction to see Pearl has entered the room and is talking to Simon. The girl looks very slight, very vulnerable.

'I don't understand, sir,' she stammers.

'What I am trying to say, Miss Meers, is that your father does not possess the strength to undergo an operation. Even with ether, the shock to his body would be more than he could stand.' He withdraws a handkerchief from his pocket and mops his brow. 'Putting that fact aside . . . I believe the performance would be futile, anyhow. The disease has progressed too far for me – for anyone – to help.'

'But you'll cure him,' Pearl asserts. 'Agnes promised you'd cure him.'

Simon's throat bobs as he swallows. 'In this instance, Miss Meers, I regret to inform you that it is quite beyond my power.'

The hush that falls is agonising.

'Miss Meers, you are unwell—' Simon starts forward, but Pearl dodges away from him.

She is shaking so much that her features seem to blur in the shadows. 'Get out.'

Is she possessed of a spirit? Agnes would like to believe so, but the voice is entirely Pearl's own. The child's weakened form cannot contain the emotions that are blasting through it; she is forced to lean upon the wall.

'Get out of my house!' she shrieks.

Agnes rises to her feet. She can feel a faint rumbling through the floor.

'Indeed, I cannot, while you are so ill,' Simon protests. 'I have been observing you and your health appears much depleted. I would like—'

'Don't touch me! We don't need quacks! I don't need you at all.'

'Pearl—' Agnes tries, but the girl is beside herself.

'Myrtle will cure him,' she insists, ferociously. 'Myrtle's curing him with Mesmerism. She was right about you lot. You don't know nothing.'

On the table, two candles ignite.

'I can assure you—'

'Bunch of bleedin' tricksters!' Pearl cries, batting Simon away. 'Get out! Get . . . out!'

A line forks through the crystal ball like a crack in ice.

'Simon,' Agnes whispers, 'I think that we had better go.'

He gives a defeated nod, but his eyes do not leave the child as they walk out of the parlour and towards the front door.

The girl slides all the way down the wall to the carpet where she sits, arms around her knees.

The last sight Agnes has before the door closes is Pearl's white face, drenched in tears.

Outside, it is still mizzling. Walcot Street goes on the same, as if it could possibly tempt them to eat sheep's trotters or buy a ballad, after what they have seen in that house.

Agnes looks into her friend's troubled eyes.

'That child is very ill, Miss Darken. Did she work at the match factory also?'

'I do not know. I am so ignorant!' She groans, hating herself. 'I did not even trouble to acquaint myself with her properly, I have simply blundered into her life and caused all this distress!'

He wets his lips, nods. 'It was only natural that you should sympathise with Miss Meers. You know what it is to have a sister who controls . . . I mean to say, you have been treated in a manner that . . . You can easily put yourself in the child's position,' he finishes awkwardly.

She pictures Miss West and Constance, side by side. He is right. There are similarities there.

'Oh, Simon. Whatever have I done?'

Chapter 29

Nine chimes of the clock and the sickroom is already rank. It stinks like cabbage soup. Pearl's opened the window, even the curtains a little bit, but the cool morning air won't come in.

They're burning up, her and Father. If anything, the December wind only fans the flames.

What is she meant to do now? Looking at Father makes her as giddy as if she were staring into an abyss. Did that fat doctor hurt him yesterday? Make it worse? She'd almost be glad to believe that, for it would mean that Myrtle was right, and all the doctor's sad *hmphs* and shakes of the head would be proved as humbug.

But she's got eyes – even if it is harder to use them without her green spectacles. And those eyes can see that Father slept much easier with the magic drops.

Their spell must be wearing off now. He's fidgety again, making that dreadful bubbling moan. The wisps of the spirit world are closing in around him; daylight scares them off, but Pearl knows they're still there, reaching out in expectation of plucking a treat.

She crosses the room and bends down to the cheap tick mattress. The bottle's still hidden under there. She pulls it out and weighs it, heavy as sin in her hands. It's got a cork in the top and a label covered in writing on the side; she squints at the weird symbols, but they don't mean anything to her.

It doesn't *look* like poison, it looks like really strong tea. But then, how would she know? Didn't the doctor say that even matches could be poison?

She can't decide what she's meant to do; who to trust, who to believe.

Father starts to twitch.

She walks to the head of his bed, the bottle still in her hand. 'You want this?'

Maybe he does, but that's not the gesture he's making; it's the one he used when the doctor came.

Cut it out.

Her eyes fill with tears.

'He's coming back,' she lies. 'The doctor's coming back and he'll do it; he's just . . . busy.'

Father gurgles a relieved sigh. Very briefly, the creases leave his forehead. He points to the bottle.

'All right.'

She wipes the sweat away from her eyes and awkwardly pulls the cork stopper out. She hasn't got much strength, and nerves are making her dizzy. The doctor said she could give him up to twenty drops, but that's the biggest number she knows and she's going to have to concentrate hard on her counting.

She aims at Father's tongue.

The drops fall slowly, landing with a tiny pat.

She gets lost counting around sixteen, so adds two more for luck – that will have to do.

Father's breathing slows. He gives her what she has always taken for a smile, though it's only in the eyes.

Cut it out, he gestures again. Then he drifts off to sleep.

Pearl leaves the room, hollow.

The Bath Society of Spiritual Adventurers are due over again tonight. It feels like a direct punishment for the broken door, but of course Myrtle couldn't have known about that when she arranged the séance. In fact, Pearl's still waiting for the real cost to become clear. Myrtle obviously didn't believe her stupid story about an attempted robbery, but she didn't do anything either; just went to the kitchen and brought back a piece of bread loaded with jam, which she made Pearl eat. Her face looked nearly black with choked-up rage.

Today, Myrtle's making the parlour ready for their guests: dusting with an old rag, while the carpet is strewn with used tea leaves. A vinegar scent lingers from where she's been scrubbing at the crystal ball. There's a line on it that won't come off – she says that's Pearl's fault too.

Myrtle has her back turned, but she seems to sense Pearl emerge from Father's room.

'Hope you're in top form,' she calls. 'Mr Stadler's going to write this one up as a piece. Who knows? We might be seeing our names in *Missives from Summerland* one of these days.'

Pearl can picture the leering, eager faces of the spirit-seekers. She wishes Myrtle would care less for the dead, and more about the man on his last legs in the very next room.

'Father's pretty bad,' she says.

'So? *He's* not got to do the séance.'

Desperation seizes her. Someone needs to sit with Father, to nurse him. Anyone with a heart can see that. She knows she can't make Myrtle cancel the séance. But maybe if she appeals to her sister's vanity, she can get *something* for Father.

'Won't you mesmerise him again?' she pleads. 'It'd help me concentrate, to know you'd looked after him. He's been so much worse since you stopped the treatment, I've really noticed it.'

Myrtle shakes her head. 'He fights against me.'

'He won't. I promise. He's too weak now, and you're so strong . . .'

'Doesn't matter. I'm busy today. Someone's got to fix that front door, ain't they?'

'Please! This will just take a few minutes. I'd be so grateful. You're the best mesmerist there is. Only you can make him well again, Myrtle.'

'Is that so? I thought you knew better than me, these days.' She folds her rag over to find a clean bit. 'Why don't you ask your new *friend* Miss Darken to help you?'

So it's like that: she's still not forgiven.

Flaming with sorrow and outrage, she stomps into the kitchen. On the table is a jar of jam and an empty box of matches. There's no water to cool her forehead – they used it all yesterday cleaning Father's jaw. She can't quench her thirst either, because Myrtle hasn't fetched any ale from the Northgate Brewery. She's sure that's deliberate. Myrtle *wants* Pearl to suffer, and Father too. She still thinks they killed Mother on purpose.

Pearl tries to steady her breathing but fails. She can't take any more of this: closed doors everywhere she turns. If one more person tells her *no*, she will scream.

Father will get better. He *must*.

Myrtle and the doctor think they're so clever, with all their learning, but it's Pearl everyone comes crying to, wanting answers. *Pearl's* the one with the power and she needs to use it. If she can talk for people who are dead, she can surely cure the 'fuzzy jaw'?

Her eyes range the surfaces, fall upon the biggest, sharpest kitchen knife.

And she knows what she has to do.

Chapter 30

Something has happened.

Agnes felt it the minute the crystal ball cracked. She does not know if Pearl has unleashed some dark entity in her distress, or whether this is the presence she has sensed building for so long: the one that follows her through the streets, teasing closer and closer at every séance.

But it is here now.

She sits in her studio, hugging the book of duplicates to her chest. The abbey bells throb, strong as a pulse, through the magpies' chitter and cackle.

One by one, the framed silhouettes drop from the wall to crash beside her feet. Bronzed work, painting on wax, hollowcuts. No visible hand touches them. For years they have hung there, undisturbed, but now they smash onto the floor and hatch as the profiles break free of their glass.

There is a slow malevolence to the destruction; first one frame, then the next, each dislodged without a hurry. Whatever it is, it is working its way towards the centre of the room.

A trio of Etruscan silhouettes painted in vermillion hang directly in front of her chair. The frame to the left of them goes down, then the one to the right. *Thud, crack, thud, crack,* until only the three profiles remain: a man wearing a peruke and two ladies with feathers in their hats.

Agnes stares at them, her agitated brain trying to find meaning. There is no obvious connection between them other than their orange-red colour. She cranes back in her chair as the oval frames start to tremble, but they do not fall. Instead, the one of a man in the centre seems to . . . melt.

Livid drops trickle down the wall, slowly at first, and then they are streaking, gory, splattering onto her desk with the iron scent of blood.

Her work is being exsanguinated.

She surges to her feet, head rushing, and hurries from the room.

Dusk is blooming outside but still the abbey bells toll, on and on, relentless. The shadows of the bannisters waver across the landing like the bars of a cage. A female shadow flits behind; it does not look like her own.

She blunders down the staircase, still clutching the heavy duplicate book in her arms. The profiles hanging on the wall seem to turn and watch her as she goes.

Mamma sits in the darkened parlour with only the fire for company. There are shadows, more shadows, massing around her hunched, shawl-covered frame. Agnes cries out and drops her book onto the wing chair. Picking up the pail of sand that stands beside the poker set, she uses it to douse the flames. The orange tongues hiss, crackle and die, until all that remains is a charred pile of sand and the grey smoke.

'Whatever did you do that for?' Mamma protests. 'It's cold in here.'

Agnes pants and places the empty bucket down. This must be why Pearl keeps it dark – shadows cannot haunt you in the dark.

'I told you, Mamma. No fires.'

'No fires, no papers, no Cedric,' Mamma grumbles, shuffling her swollen feet. 'Very high and mighty with your orders, miss. Who died and left you in charge?'

'Papa did!' she shouts, wheeling round to face her mother. 'Papa entreated me to take care of you all and I have . . .' She softens, ashamed of her outburst. 'I have *tried*. But I have failed. I was not strong enough.'

Mamma looks ancient in the dark; sadder, without the rosy-red hue of her cheeks. She scrunches her wrinkled hands together and glances down at them, contrite.

'Was I a bad mother to you, Agnes?'

This winds her. 'Bad?' She sits down on the sofa beside Mamma and touches her shoulder. 'Why would you think so?'

'Well. I can't help but question it, considering. I never found you a husband. And Constance . . .'

Yes, Constance.

What can Agnes say? This is her mother, she loves her. The last thing she would wish to do is hurt her. Yet what Mamma says is true. Papa never thought of extracting deathbed promises from his wife – he knew instinctively that she would not cope. And perhaps Constance *would* have turned out differently if their mother had not treated her with such open resentment and hostility. It was hardly Constance's fault that she was not born a boy, or that her infant sickness discouraged the usual bond. If Mamma had paid attention, if she had educated the girls herself, maybe Constance would not have developed her obsession with Agnes at all.

'I think,' she says slowly, 'that many mothers would have struggled with a daughter like Constance.'

Something creaks upstairs. Agnes stiffens. The presence must still be there, amongst the broken picture frames. It could not be . . .

It is not Constance herself?

She tries to stifle the panic that wails inside her chest.

A ghost, even Constance's ghost, cannot actually *hurt* her, can it? None of the spirits she has witnessed at séances were physically threatening. Yet Pearl was afraid of them . . . The girl feared to let them use her mouth. To her the spirits were predators, wanting to invade and take control.

Well, Agnes is not a spirit medium. She can only be haunted, not possessed. And thank heavens for that! If it really were Constance . . . She would leap at the chance to control Agnes. Was that not what she always tried to do in life?

Agnes shakes the bitter thoughts away. 'Constance was a woman,' she reminds herself. 'Not a monster. She was a troubled woman . . .'

Mamma sighs. 'That she was. But it was not *you* who failed her, dear. I always wanted to tell you that. The fault was mine. I could never warm to her, like I did to you. Those ways she had! When she used to visit the butcher and just stand there, watching him work. How she would bring a dead cat home if she found it in the street. I took a . . . fear of her. Like she was something sent from above to punish me.'

'You made up for it with Constance's son,' Agnes consoles her mother. 'No one could accuse you of being an unaffectionate grandmother.'

'Hmph. Much good my love did Cedric.' The grey head shakes. 'She was jealous of him too, wasn't she? Jealous that we all adored him. And your father . . .' Agnes goes to speak, but Mamma talks over her. 'The truth is, Agnes, I should have risen to the occasion. It should have been me, not you, reining her in and earning money for this family.'

'You were grieving. And your heart . . .'

Mamma unclenches her hands and takes one of Agnes's. She experiences a twinge of guilt for dousing the fire; Mamma does feel very cold.

'You were always my good girl. You tried. No one can ask more of you than that. Just . . . please don't hold it against me. I already blame myself more than you can know.'

She squeezes her mother's hand and says the only thing a daughter can. 'It was not your fault, Mamma. None of it was your fault.'

There's a thump in the hallway. Agnes jumps.

'Something through the letterbox,' Mamma says.

She is right: it was a soft sound, dulled by a mat; not the harsh crash of the frames upstairs. But it is late for post. Unbidden, that slanted writing comes to mind: Constance's hand.

A coincidence, Simon said.

Cautiously, Agnes rises and goes out to the hallway. An envelope lies in the centre of the doormat. She picks it up and takes it to the kitchen where she keeps her matches. Already she can feel that the envelope is of a good quality and not one of the scraps she so feared to find.

She breaks the wafer and unfolds the paper before striking her match. It hisses. A small bubble of light appears.

The writing it illuminates is Simon's:

Miss Darken,

I was sorry to leave you in distress following our visit to Walcot Street. It is my sincere hope that you have recovered from the disappointment of your unfortunate young friend.

My chief consideration remains your own health, and how it might best be improved. I cannot express half of what I would say upon paper, but I wish for your mind to be at rest as soon as possible. Therefore, I will convey only this: I know where Cedric is. Do not, I entreat you, run to the police upon receiving my communication: the cause of the boy's disappearance is of no concern to them. He was in fact embroiled in an accident, and I cannot bring you to his current location without peril to your health. However, rest assured that I have visited him, he is in a safe position and we are in no danger of losing him.

I will call upon you with further particulars very shortly and, if God is willing, take you to him when the risk of serious illness has diminished.

I am aware that inactivity at this moment will cause you pain, but I must crave your indulgence and ask you to trust me, as you have been so good as to trust me in many other instances. Believe me, madam, I am at all times anxious to prove myself your most humble and faithful servant,
Simon Carfax

'Thank God!' Her breath blows out the match.

Cedric is found. *Found!*

She clasps the letter against her heart. The poor boy must be in a hospital, where Simon will not let her tread for fear of infectious disease. She has half a mind to ignore him and make enquiries at Bellot's, the General and the United immediately. Cedric should not be there amongst the paupers, but treated at home by his family.

Did she not *tell* him that hoop and stick would lead him into an accident? To take more care, to look where he was going? Heaven only knows how he managed to sneak out and play when she had locked the house up tight . . . But it does not signify. Nothing matters, so long as he is safe now. Whatever the injury, she and Simon can nurse him back to health between them. Everything will be different. After such a scare, Simon will no doubt realise how precious Cedric truly is. The rift will be repaired, and together they can watch him grow. It was wrong of her to despair. There will be a future for her, after all.

She must tell Mamma. Prepare her somehow for the prospect of an invalid boy returning home, without frightening the life out of her. She will soften the news. Tell her he has been taken a little unwell.

'Mamma!' she calls, running out into the passageway. 'I have a letter from Simon.'

It is likely that Mamma has nodded off in the brief space of time she has been left alone, but as Agnes pushes the parlour door open, expecting to find her mother dozing, she is struck dumb by what she sees.

The fire is lit again. Not just sparking but blazing, as if it were made up and stirred by a careful hand. The shadows wheel, revelling in their freedom.

She wants to ask Mamma how she accomplished this so quickly; how she bent her arthritic body to relay the kindling and where she got the matches from.

She *would* ask her.

But Mamma is nowhere to be seen.

Chapter 31

There's more blood than Pearl reckoned on.

Some of it's red, some of it's black, there's even a little purple. All of it smells like copper coins.

Shuddering, Pearl steps back from the bed and wipes the tears from her eyes. Now she's got a new pair of spectacles, but these aren't green: everything she sees is streaked with red.

The pillow blooms deep claret. The stain keeps on growing, she can't stop it. All she's managed to slice off is a hunk of corrupted flesh.

She couldn't help him. There was too much badness for her to cut out.

The knife slips from her palm to the floor.

What has she done?

What has she done?

The magic drops kept him asleep, but he's not sleeping now. She knows it, yet she doesn't; the shock still has her in its grip. When he doesn't respond to her whispers and her shaking of his arm, she closes her eyes and tries to hear him inside her head.

Dead or alive, it doesn't matter, so long as she can reach him.

But she can't.

There's nothing.

She stares down at her trembling hands. Blood has soaked into the skin. Frantically, she rubs it off on her skirts, but it leaves a pinkish hue. Finally her white hands have a pigment.

'Help,' she whispers. 'Help.'

Who is she talking to?

She can't hide this. It's not something you can bundle in the wardrobe to make it go away. There's the knife, and the body, and the pillow, and the blood – so much blood.

Now it's on her clothes, as well as smeared onto her skin. She must look like she's walked through hell.

Myrtle's still cleaning in the parlour. She hums 'The Rat-catcher's Daughter.'

What's her sister going to say? What will she *do*? Will she send for the police? Myrtle was angry enough before, about the crystal ball and the broken door, but *this* . . .

Something pops inside Pearl's head. She sees the fishbowl of flowers exploding all over again and she's filled with a feeling more desperate than any she's ever known before: she has to get out.

She has to get out of here, *now*.

She gropes for the doorknob, leaving a gory handprint.

Myrtle keeps humming, brushing up the tea leaves, oblivious to everything but her own plans.

Pearl doesn't linger. Somehow her feet carry her straight into her own chamber. She doesn't even stop to turn her head and check that Myrtle hasn't spotted her.

Mechanically, she goes through the actions she's dreamed of a thousand times: she opens the wardrobe, pulls out the carpet bag and starts to change.

Trousers, shirt, cap. Her bloody dress and petticoats pool on the floor. It looks like the girl who inhabited their folds has melted away.

She takes one last look at the map. Then she creeps behind the curtains and opens the window.

Soft, cool air sweeps in. Her yearning for it fights against the reluctance of a long-caged thing. Does she really dare to leave her home? There will be no turning back.

Myrtle continues her tune in the parlour.

Pearl would pray for courage, but the last time she was courageous, she ended up with a knife in her hand.

There's no point in hesitation, no real choice. All she can do is escape.

It's easy to climb, wearing trousers. She clears the window ledge without difficulty. Only the harsh blast of daylight affects her, but it's not as bad as she thought it would be; maybe the shock's softened that too.

Her feet touch the ground, she straightens up and for the first time in her life, she stands on the pavement outside her house.

What she sees rocks her back on her heels.

There's so *much* of it. More than she could ever glimpse from her station by the door. An omnibus clatters past; she feels the air whoosh with it, and through the window there are people, lots of people, squashed together and gaping out at her.

Light flashes off glass. She winces. It's mid-afternoon; the spiteful winter sun will soon go down and it's already throwing out shadows. Pearl spies her own: monstrous, stretched like a giant. She turns quickly and walks away.

She doesn't know what to do, where to look. How much space should she take up on the pavement? She tries to make herself smaller, but it's not small enough. Men pushing barrows elbow her in the ribs and she can scarcely move her feet without stepping on a lady's hem.

When she walked outside in her dreams, it was beautiful. The reality's quite different. It's scary.

Father, Father. She hears his name, sees his mutilated face with every step. Grief makes her too weak to struggle against the tide of people. She gives up, lets the crowd carry her along.

There's a turn she needs to make, somewhere up ahead. She has no concept of distance; some of the buildings look a bit like Agnes's drawing, but they're so much larger, so *stern*.

Her head pounds fit to split open. The cap only partially screens her tender eyes. At least her face feels cooler now. The wind blows and chills the tracks on her cheeks. She narrows her eyes, shuffles on.

Finally the crowd spews her out and she finds herself standing, small and insignificant before an enormous building that reaches right up into the clouds. It's the loveliest thing she's ever seen. There's shiny coloured glass, prettily carved pointy bits and a statue that looks like an angel, climbing the side.

She lays a palm against the rough stone. Maybe she'll just curl up on the ground here, safe under the gaze of the angels.

Something caws above her. Pearl flinches and peers cautiously up from beneath the peak of her cap.

It's a bird. He's perched on one of the lower roofs: a coal-black thing with a patch of white and one glorious streak of blue down his wing. He cocks his head at her, caws again, then takes flight.

Her watering eyes follow his swoop. Such a graceful, easy motion. Pearl wishes she could move like that.

Reluctant to lose sight of the bird, she starts to totter after him, but her energy's nearly all gone. In another few minutes, she'll faint.

With a last flap, the bird settles himself on a ledge supported by leafy pillars. That must be his home. Half-dazed, Pearl inspects the building, wondering what type of house a bird would choose for its nest. That's when she sees the papercuts in the windows.

Agnes's papercuts.

It's the house from the map.

Relief nearly fells her.

She has no idea what she'll say to Agnes; she doesn't really care so long as there's somewhere to sit down and drink, where it's cool, and the shadow that's following her will go away.

Stumbling towards the door, she risks a glance over her shoulder. It's still there, attached at her ankles.

The door sits right underneath the bird's nest; she can hear him squabbling with his family above her as she raises a hand

and knocks as hard as she can. Only a feeble, hollow sound comes back.

What will she do if Agnes doesn't answer, where will she go? Too late she remembers there's a murderer on the loose in Bath.

An image flashes across her vision: the knife, the jaw. Maybe she doesn't need to be afraid of killers any more; not now she's a killer herself.

The door creaks open a fraction, held back by a chain. Two beady eyes peer out from the darkness within.

Pearl bursts into tears.

'Cedric? Cedric!' The chain rattles off the door and Agnes is out in the street, gripping her by the shoulders, before she realises her mistake. 'Simon said you – Oh! Good God. Pearl, is that you?'

She gasps, choked by sobs.

'Pearl, is this *blood*?'

'Let me in,' she pleads. 'The light, it's too bright.'

Agnes's pointed face shows her astonishment, but she holds open the door and ushers Pearl inside without another word.

Pearl staggers into a narrow hallway with a staircase taking up the left-hand side. There are darker patches on the wall where pictures once hung. For some reason they're lying on the floor now. She sees some dead flowers in a vase upon a little pier table.

She thought Agnes would live in a house much fancier than this.

'What happened?' Agnes urges. 'Come here, into the parlour. Is it your sister? Did she beat you? I can send for Dr Carfax . . .'

She goes wherever Agnes's hands push her. The parlour's blissfully dark, but it smells like the past has been bottled up inside and refuses to leave. Stacks of newspapers crowd the floor. Used plates and teacups litter the surfaces – one with paintbrushes sticking out of the top. She hears the low hum of a fly.

A sofa stretches before the unlit fireplace and Pearl collapses gratefully upon it.

'Dear child! You are worrying me to distraction. Are you ill?'

She's always ill these days, but this is worse, shredding the very inside of her. For the first time she understands why Myrtle's chary of talking about Mother. Grief hurts. It really, really hurts.

'He's dead,' she howls into the sofa. 'My father's dead.'

Chapter 32

The child sleeps deeply. If Agnes stands back from the sofa, she can easily imagine it is Cedric slumbering there. The oversized cap conceals the girl's shock of wintery hair, and her thin, pale limbs are tucked underneath her. Only the rise and fall of the slender chest gives Pearl away; it does not undulate gently, as Cedric's does, but jerks.

Is it safe to let her stay here? Mamma still hasn't returned, and although Agnes tells herself that her mother is her own woman, quite capable of leaving the house if she chooses, she does not truly believe it. In her mind, Mamma's disappearance is connected to the destructive presence that pushed her silhouettes from the wall. There is no evidence of it in the shady parlour at present. Is Pearl holding it at bay? She will keep everything dark. The darkness will protect them, somehow.

Yet ghosts are not the only thing Pearl needs saving from. Now that her father has succumbed to his disease, she will be living alone with Miss West. Could Agnes retain the child at Orange Grove, in secret, and give her a better life? She never told Miss West her address, the horrible woman would not know to come looking for her sister here . . .

But it would only take one mention of 'Miss Darken' to the police and that odious Sergeant Redmayne would be banging on her door. Simon has endeavoured to clear her name of suspicion at the station, and this would undo all his good work. No. As much as Agnes would like the company, and to offer

Pearl a refuge from her cruel sister, she cannot keep the girl hidden here.

As best she can in the scant light, she jots a note to Simon. He will be busy, visiting Cedric and running his usual practice, but she must tell him about Mamma, and she would like him to take a look at Pearl before sending her back home. No one can see the girl and suppose that she is healthy. They may have left it too late to act with poor Mr Meers, but Pearl is young. Perhaps she can still conquer her illness.

The difficulty will be securing her aid without Miss West noticing. The girl has no money of her own, and Agnes's purse is decidedly light. But what about Montague's ring? It must still be on the floor in the upstairs room at Walcot Street, where it fell during the séance. The pawnshop would pay for real gold – enough, she is sure, for Pearl to buy medicine in secret. After a brief internal struggle, Agnes decides. She will tell Pearl where to look for the ring and ask her to keep it as payment for her services. Yes, that is the right course of action. Montague would understand. At least this way his token can deliver *some* of the good it once promised.

Agnes leaves the house quietly and passes the note to her usual carrier: a boy who sits in the churchyard awaiting errands. Mamma is nowhere to be seen, but she is struck by the number of people who are walking abroad at dusk. Everyone seems to have forgotten about the murderer already. Some men even have their wives linked on their arm, as if there is nothing to fear.

Were those lost lives insignificant in the grand scheme of things? She does not like to believe so. But if Simon has found Cedric, and those notes really were just relics of Constance somehow unearthed, it throws doubt on whether Agnes was ever being targeted at all. Maybe it *was* just coincidence that three men and a woman died.

This is Simon's way of thinking. She should have listened to Simon all along. It was folly to consult Pearl and bring the shadows of the past upon her home. What has she learnt, other than that ghosts *do* exist, and they are most of them frightened or in pain? That knowledge offers neither comfort nor earthly use.

She should have left well enough alone.

Now her elderly mother has wandered off, she has a phantom in the studio and a sickly child to nurse.

Gently, she unlocks the door and creeps back inside the house. She need not have taken such care. Pearl is awake and is standing in the doorway to the parlour, rubbing her eyes.

'I had hoped you would sleep a little longer. How do you feel?'

'Terrible,' Pearl whispers.

'Sit down again, dear. I will see if I can fetch you some refreshment—'

Pearl shakes her head vehemently.

'Perhaps my smelling salts?'

'That's not why I'm here.'

There is a mutinous expression on her small face. A streak of blood has dried on her cheek; Agnes wants to wipe it away, but she is worried to bring it to her attention.

'Then . . . what may I do for you, Pearl? Why *are* you here?'

'I never got my séance.'

Agnes shoots a glance at the picture frames on the floor. 'I am not sure it is wise to—'

'You promised! We spoke to your people, now it's my turn.'

'Listen, dear, I have reason to believe there is an . . . unwelcome spirit in this house, and rather than calling things up, it would be better if we tried to send her back—'

But something has snapped within Pearl, she has none of her usual timidity. '*When* I've had my séance,' she cries. 'Or don't you mean to keep any of the promises you made to me?'

This hits home. Agnes hangs her head. 'I do regret that Dr Carfax was not able—'

'He's dead!' – Pearl is almost shrieking – 'You told me I'd be able to cure my father, and now he's dead. Does that sound like you've kept up your end of the deal?'

'No, but—'

'So either you're going to help me talk to him, or you're a bloody liar. Which is it?'

Misgiving wallows within her. What choice does she have? The poor girl is sick and half-mad with grief. Agnes must humour her, keep her occupied until Simon arrives. From the way she is breathing, she is very ill indeed.

'One séance,' Agnes concedes. 'Just one. And then we put the ghosts back, for good.'

Pearl sighs in relief. Then she throws up.

No candles burn this time. It is pitch-black, but Pearl is a faint, indefinite outline in the dark. She is propped up against pillows, determined to proceed no matter how eloquently Agnes entreats her not to.

The house still smells of vomit. If Agnes possessed better eyesight, she would have sworn that the liquid had *glowed*. She scents something acidic, corrosive, like the very reek of death.

'Give me your hands,' Pearl demands.

Agnes obeys. It is like holding a bunch of wet sticks. She closes her eyes and prays for Simon to arrive quickly.

The grandfather clock pings.

Her eyelids snap open. That clock has not made a sound in days. She waits for it to tick, but nothing happens; there is just a taut, expectant hush.

'Father,' Pearl whispers passionately. 'Father, come to me. I'm so sorry. I tried my best.'

A single flame crackles into life in the fireplace.

Agnes attempts to tug her hands back, but Pearl clings to them like a drowning girl.

This is wrong, it is all wrong. The flame is a light, however small, and light creates a doorway for the shadows to come slithering out.

'Father,' Pearl pleads. 'Don't be angry.'

Agnes holds her breath. There *is* anger in the air, palpable but invisible; it seems to pulse and thicken. They should stop, they really should stop.

'Talk to me!' Pearl cries.

The hands of the grandfather clock start to move; faster than any mechanism could push them. The pendulum begins to swing.

'Pearl—'

Sweat stands out on her ivory forehead. The girl is straining with all her might.

Agnes watches, helpless, as the fire climbs in the grate.

Papa once spoke of the French revolutionaries dancing 'La Carmagnole.' The way the shadows caper is like that: savage, with the inherent threat of violence.

A log bursts, spitting sparks.

'Pearl, stop!'

The girl opens her colourless eyes. The flames reflect in her pupils.

Round and round goes the clock; the fire burns higher and higher. Agnes yearns to run from the room, but she is held fast.

Where is Simon? Why hasn't he come?

Pearl's breath catches. Steam issues from between her lips; she is out of control. The entire séance is beyond her command.

Shadows close in around them like hungry wolves. Agnes gasps, tries again to yank her hands out of Pearl's slick hold, but it is impossible; it is as though the girl is focusing every last atom of her strength on this circle.

The grandfather clock chimes. Agnes's eyes flick towards it and she freezes.

There's something there. Unfolding in the corner.

The shadow of a woman rises to her feet. She is tall and slender in profile. Familiar.

Pearl's back is turned to the grandfather clock, she can have no conception of how the shadow raises its hands and stretches long, long fingers towards her.

Agnes tries to make a noise, but nothing comes out.

The hands are like twigs on a tree. The branches reach out, grow larger, longer. One of them touches the tip of Pearl's chin.

'Look!' Pearl exhales and her expression is beatific. 'Agnes! I . . . I *see* her!'

With one final wrench, Agnes tears her hands away.

Pearl seems to come with them. She pitches forward, face first, onto the floor. The fire snaps out, the grandfather clock wheezes its last.

'Pearl? Pearl!'

Shakily, Agnes endeavours to prop her up again, but the girl's head lolls. It cannot be, it *should not* be . . .

She touches a hand to the clammy flesh at her neck. Nothing pulses beneath.

Her translucent eyes are fixed open, staring at the image they so earnestly sought, and poor little Pearl is dead.

Chapter 33

The police call it the Dead Room. Agnes knows, because she has been there before: a space of cold white tiles and metal instruments. It is no place for a child.

Naturally, she is not allowed inside with Simon and the other doctors while they probe and examine. Instead she sits waiting outside on a bench, with a sympathetic clergyman keeping watch over her.

Occasionally Sergeant Redmayne checks up on them and offers cups of tea. All the previous suspicion has fled from his demeanour. Agnes does not think to ask *why*. She cannot think of much at all. She feels trapped inside a bell jar, the air stale and all sound muffled.

The death of a child is not a particularly rare event. Everyone knows that many tiny souls depart from this world before their fifth birthday, especially down in the slums. But it feels as if time should stop, or that at least the city should go about its business with more gentleness and decorum.

Nobody can quantify what has been lost. Pearl might have influenced many lives as she grew into womanhood, and now they will never know. Generations of possible children and grandchildren all perished with her last breath. There is nothing more tragic to Agnes's mind than the future that never was.

And where is Pearl now? Not in there, on a slab. She did not have the faith of a Christian, so Heaven is doubtful too. After the child's sufferings, it would be terrible to think of her wandering the earth, as lost as one of the spirits she so feared.

All Agnes can picture are those dark hands, reaching out.

I see her, Pearl had said. She looked happy. Agnes would like to believe it was the girl's deceased mother, come to claim her and take her home at last. But to her eyes, the figure had resembled someone else. Someone she last saw in the Dead Room.

A shouted curse shatters her torpor. The bell over the street door jangles wildly, and a chair crashes to the floor. Agnes looks up to see three policemen grappling with a young woman. She is all teeth and hair. Although her wrists have been shackled, she has not given up her attempts to escape. She jerks, feints, tries to bite.

'Steady,' one policeman warns the other.

A fourth officer comes forward with a leather truncheon. Clearly he has no compunction about striking a female. He cracks her hard on the shoulder; her head flies back, parting the curtain of her loose hair.

The face beneath belongs to Miss West.

'It weren't my knife,' she spits, 'I never—' But the truncheon swings again, and she is hustled into a side room out of view.

Agnes blinks. Were it not for the clergyman's pursed lips, she would doubt the scene had actually taken place.

What can Miss West stand accused of?

Of course Simon went to the police when he finally arrived and found Agnes with the lifeless body of Pearl. No doubt he told them where to find the child's next of kin. But she did not expect them to fetch Miss West to the station *bound*.

She said something about a knife. Agnes remembers the smear of blood she spotted on Pearl's cheek. She assumed that had rubbed off from her father's jaw as he lay dying, but perhaps not. Just what horrors was the girl fleeing from?

After another half hour of dismal uncertainty, a door opens

at the opposite end of the corridor to the one Miss West was spirited down. The clergyman stands up.

Simon has returned to them.

His shoulders stoop low. He no longer wears a coat, and his shirtsleeves have been rolled back to the elbows. Carbolic soap has scrubbed his hands and arms clean, but Agnes knows exactly what they have been doing.

Her chest turns over.

She keeps her head bent while Simon exchanges a few words with the clergyman and takes a seat by her side. She cannot bear to think of his hands moving over Pearl, or of what substances lay embedded beneath his fingernails.

'Miss Darken,' he says softly.

'Is it done?'

She feels rather than sees him nod.

'And do you know . . . ?'

Simon exhales heavily. 'The coroner found the cause of death I was anticipating. Miss Meers died of phosphorus poisoning.'

It makes little sense – yet what has of late? She is no doctor. For all she knows, being confined in that house with Mr Meers might have caused the infection to leach through into Pearl, like tea leaves colouring water.

'I suppose the miasma . . .' she begins dully.

'No,' Simon replies. He takes a moment, seems to be grappling with some powerful emotion. 'The phosphorus entered the body through the stomach.'

The stomach. Like that suicide weeks ago, the man who ate matches. 'But how—'

'I do not like to tell you this, Miss Darken. It will distress you, but I would rather you hear it from me than another source. You mentioned a glow around the young girl. An – what word do those numbskulls give it? – ectoplasm?'

She swallows. 'Yes.'

'That glow was manufactured. Miss West achieved it, it appears, by crushing match heads and concealing them in jam to mask their unpleasant taste.' He takes a breath. 'She then fed the poisoned jam to her sister. Whole jars of the contaminated substance were found at the property on Walcot Street.'

Agnes sways.

Miss West killed her sister.

Poisoned her.

Can such wickedness exist in the world?

When Agnes thinks back, the clues were all there: Miss West's frustration and aversion to the obligations thrust upon her; her preoccupation with money; Pearl's strange, sickly glow. If she was clever like Simon, she would have realised.

She could have helped.

But as with her own sister, she did not spot the signs until it was too late.

'How could she do it?' she gasps. 'After seeing what phosphorus did to her stepfather ... How could Miss West feed her little sister matches?'

Simon places a hand on her shoulder, holds her steady. 'Miss West proved to be a very bitter young woman indeed.'

Footsteps sound on the tiles. Sergeant Redmayne paces towards them. 'Is she ...'

Simon assesses Agnes and nods to the policeman without saying a word.

'Well, I'll be brief, sir. I mentioned to you the likelihood of a blade being used in the killings. We found one. In Walcot Street. She'd used it to ... ah ...' Agnes has never seen Sergeant Redmayne hesitant like this before. He keeps sliding her wary glances, as if he fears his words might capsize her. 'Miss West had another victim, sir. Her stepfather was discovered cut and ... well. You can imagine.'

Mr Meers, *cut*? Just what happened before Pearl turned up at Orange Grove?

Agnes remembers the girl sobbing *I tried* and *I'm sorry* as she sought to contact her father. She presumed it was an apology for inadequate nursing, but this opens up a new possibility: that Mr Meers did not succumb to his illness at all. That what Pearl had *tried* to prevent was Miss West and her murderous intentions!

It is staggering. Even though she deemed Miss West malicious, she could not have imagined her poisoning a child and stabbing a man in cold blood.

'Is there another body requiring examination?' Simon asks wearily.

'No, there's no call for you to get involved. We don't need your help with—' Sergeant Redmayne breaks off and fiddles with a large brass button on his coat.

She can see him pushing words back. Evidently he did not believe they required Simon's help examining Pearl either, but Simon had still managed to insinuate himself into the postmortem. She is glad he did. If she heard of Miss West's wicked deeds from another mouth, she would not have believed them.

'You had best get the lady home,' Sergeant Redmayne tries instead. 'This has been a shock to her.'

He is not wrong.

She wants to sleep. To lose time, as she sometimes does, while another person takes over the responsibilities.

'Yes,' she pleads. 'Yes, Simon, take me home. I have not spoken to Mamma since . . .' Her memory turns blank. Where *is* Mamma?

'Gently, Miss Darken.'

'I must go,' she moans. 'I have so many chores to perform.'

Like tidying the parlour where Pearl dropped down lifeless. She thinks of the scattered cushions and the tang of vomit. The grandfather clock spinning. What will she do if the terrifying shadow still lingers there?

'I must . . . I will . . .' She attempts to stand, but her legs are fluid.

'Miss Darken!' Simon says from somewhere distant.

She slumps against him. His shirt smells bitter with carbolic and something else.

Dead flesh.

'Simon . . .'

He guides her back to her own feet. She imagines that hand, touching Pearl's corpse, and the last candle in her mind winks out.

Chapter 34

It is a bright, crisp morning in Alfred Street. Not much traffic passes down towards the Assembly Rooms this early in the day, and if Agnes listens carefully, she can hear a robin sing. She swings gently in the rocking chair. Honeyed light dribbles through the window onto her lap, where Morpheus is curled up.

The dog resisted her caresses earlier, but he has a good sense of time and always reconsiders his allegiances around the hour the breakfast tray is due to arrive.

As the carriage clock chimes, Simon's charwoman shuffles in and sets down the food on a table. She tips Agnes a wink. 'Got it for you. Tucked under the egg plate. You make sure to give it back to me when you're done.'

Agnes thanks her. It is difficult not to betray the agitation that she feels, but Morpheus must sense it, for he stirs on her legs.

'That will be my reading for the train journey up to Gloucester,' the charwoman continues. 'Going to visit my brother in a couple of weeks for the holidays. Just as well this nasty business has come to a close before I leave, because I'd be loath to miss anything while I'm away.'

Of course, it is Advent already, and soon Christmas will come. She has lost track of time without attending church each week. Surely Cedric must be out of the hospital by now? She needs to convince Simon she is well enough to see him. Just one glimpse of his face would help her nerves to settle.

'I trust you will have a pleasant stay with your family, Mrs Muckle,' says Agnes, hoping she will soon be with her own. 'However shall we manage without you?'

The charwoman pinks with pride, but she brushes the compliment away. 'You'll get along well enough. Dr Carfax is a capable gent, much more orderly than most of them. Worth hanging on to,' she adds slyly.

Agnes pretends not to hear her.

When the domestic is safely out of the room, she reaches for the plate of coddled eggs and squeezes it onto her lap beside Morpheus. He starts to snaffle the food up at once.

Left behind on the tray is a newspaper, its pages ready-cut. A ring of grease marks the front.

Her heart pumps like a piston.

Simon has said that she requires absolute quiet and detachment from the outside world, and she has tried to be a good patient. But he cannot appreciate how much she frets while she does not know what is occurring in her absence. She has so many unanswered questions niggling inside her. The solutions offered by the press will not be entirely trustworthy, but at least they will give her some idea.

Picking up the paper, she draws in a steadying breath. As she suspected, the story occupies pride of place. She begins to read:

> The regular reader might be forgiven for supposing no further calamity could befall the beleaguered Darken's Silhouette Parlour, Orange Grove, following the twin misfortunes of a client's violent demise and the proprietor's discovery of a murdered body less than a month afterwards. Fate, however, proves capricious, and it is this paper's

solemn duty to report the sad expiration of a female child upon the very premises.

It will be recalled that on the 23rd September this year Miss Darken, native to Bath, was the last known person to see the late Solomon Boyle, of Queen Square, alive. The unfortunate gentleman's remains were found mutilated in the Gravel Walk not one week later.

A further mistreated corpse was discovered buried beneath snow in Royal Victoria Park on 18th October. The body was later identified as belonging to one Edward Lewis of Weston. At the time, Sergeant Redmayne of the Central Police Station, Market Place, advised this paper that a connection between Boyle's and Lewis's killings was probable, given the identical method of execution, which was uncovered despite concerted efforts on the part of the murderer to conceal it. Each gentleman suffered a single, horizontal laceration to the throat.

The latest instalment in this serial of tragedy took place on 3rd December, when police were summoned to Orange Grove and later dispatched from thence to Walcot Street, in order to investigate the sudden death of eleven-year-old Miss Meers.

Miss Meers, a child known to Miss Darken, was a professed 'spirit medium,' living and trading on Walcot Street in the company of her elder half-sister, Miss West. The observant reader will recognise Miss West's name in connection to yet another death: the drowning of Commander Hargreaves in mid-October. Miss West allegedly spotted the Commander's body in the water whilst crossing Dredge's Victoria Bridge and raised the alarm. She was present when the corpse was finally stopped and retrieved at Weston Lock.

However, the attractive appearance and outward virtue of Miss West proved to be a fallacy.

It transpired that on the afternoon of 3rd December, just hours before she was due to perform the mummery of another séance, Miss West assailed her invalid stepfather with a knife. The child Miss Meers, having witnessed this attack, fled from her family home to the misguided refuge of Darken's Silhouette Parlour. Before the night closed, Miss Meers would prove to be Miss West's second victim, falling prey not to the blade, but to the cowardly weapon of poison.

Miss Darken witnessed the collapse of her young guest around dusk and, unable to revive her, called upon the services of Dr Carfax of Alfred Street. As would be expected, the trained medical eye quickly spotted signs of foul play in the untimely death. A post-mortem examination revealed that the child had suffered from chronic phosphorus poisoning through the prolonged ingestion of match heads.

Prompted by motives of wickedness the reader will scarcely be able to credit, Miss West, herself a former match girl, had been crushing and concealing the toxic articles in her sister's victuals over the course of nearly four months. The aim was to produce a phosphorescent glow – or ectoplasm, to the credulous – which could fool the most ardent of ghost-grabbers. The murderess's success was equalled only by her rapacity. This paper can reveal that Miss West's name appears on the register of more than one Burial Club in the local area. Had her plans to kill Mr Meers and his child gone undetected, she would have stood to gain the substantial amount of £30 following their deaths – a sum more than sufficient to cover a simple child's funeral costed at approximately £2.

No further definite information has been obtained at the time of going to print, but this paper takes it upon itself to predict that the fair murderess will stand indicted for a number of additional charges. The deductive mind cannot help but remember that Mr Boyle and Mr Lewis received wounds consistent with a knife attack. Moreover, both gentlemen can be connected to Miss Darken – a lady whom, neighbours in Walcot Street report, Miss West nursed a peculiar antipathy towards and twice threw out of her premises.

Could it be that the bewitching but dangerous Miss West sought to cast suspicion on an enemy through her actions? This paper will offer no further speculation, but awaits with impatience the next official report from our city's esteemed Police Force.

By the time Agnes has finished reading, Morpheus has licked the plate clean.

She tosses the newspaper aside, praying Mamma does not read something similar. Simon has been so vague about how things stand at Orange Grove, simply assuring her that all the expected occupants are now present within the house and he is caring for them in her absence. But where did Mamma go, before? And how much does Agnes's family know about Pearl?

One thing is certain: Agnes's days as a profitable silhouette artist are well and truly over. Unless she means to set herself up as a museum for the ghoulish – and those are the only people who will come now – she must rely on Simon for financial support.

The realisation of this chafes, but not as much as she anticipated it would. She is bone-weary of depending on her own resources. This spell of illness has made her appreciate having someone to care for her; she does not want to struggle alone any more.

There is a knock at the bedchamber door.

'Come in,' she calls.

Simon enters rather gingerly, as has become his custom while she stays in his house. She suspects his embarrassment is not *entirely* caused by her informal attire of a nightdress and a plaid dressing gown: some of it may be attributed to the fact that this was once Constance's room, Constance's rocking chair.

'Good morning, Miss Darken. I trust you slept well.'

Too late, she realises the newspaper is lying splayed on the floor in plain sight.

Simon sees her glance, follows it and offers a wry smile. 'There is no need to attempt concealment. I was already aware. Mrs Muckle is a very able charwoman, but her career as a smuggler requires some development in the area of stealth.'

'Poor woman. Do not blame her, for I am the culprit. Sorry, Simon. Do not be angry with me.'

'No, I am not angry.' He comes further into the room. Morpheus flumps off her lap to the floor, where he dawdles over towards his master. 'Your nervous complaint has shown much improvement. I believe you are ready to hear further particulars . . .'

She leans forward and places the clean plate back on the breakfast tray. 'What is it? What has happened now? Has Cedric taken a turn for the worse?'

'No, no. Cedric is with your mother.' Simon comes over to the window and stands in a pool of light. Bath looks pleasant today. The golden limestone seems to sing. 'A request has arrived. I was inclined to turn it down immediately, but upon reflection I can see the benefits it may bring. It is plain that you need a definite resolution to this . . . sad matter.'

'Whatever can you mean? You are speaking in riddles, Simon.'

'My apologies. I was attempting to introduce the idea gently. The fact is that Miss West has asked to see you at the gaol, before her trial in January.'

'Miss West!' Anger and disgust squirm within her. 'How dare that woman ask anything of me? She is a monster!'

He tilts his head, appraising her. 'A monster? Do you think so? I am wary of judging her as such. From what I can gather, she was deeply unhinged by grief. She lost her parents at a young age and was put under intolerable pressure caring for a newborn. It does not excuse her behaviour, precisely, but I have seen too many cases of imbalance not to feel a modicum of pity.'

Agnes always knew that Simon was a worthier person than her, and this only goes to prove it. She may have sympathised with Miss West on that first visit, long ago, but she certainly does not now. 'Her actions were calculated, Simon. She used the poison deliberately, to deceive and make money. Fools like me really believed . . .'

'I have met at least one woman of a darker disposition,' he says sourly.

She chews her lip and considers. What strikes her is not his veiled reference to Constance, but the thought of the phosphorus. A sharper eye *may* have noticed that the glow surrounding Mr Meers and his daughter was suspiciously similar, but that is not all she founded her faith upon.

'You are right, in one respect, Simon: I do need answers. It does not make sense to me. Pearl was not party to the phosphorus deception, I am sure, yet she said remarkable things . . . She manifested such believable symptoms . . . There must have been *some* truth in her power. I do not think Miss West's abuse can explain Pearl's behaviour at the séances.'

'It can, though,' he says sadly, folding his hands behind his back. 'Miss West is a practitioner of Mesmerism. While that discipline is perfectly useless in curing physical ailments, it can readily supply a range of tricks. I have seen them myself in lectures. The mesmeric trance is a state of altered consciousness, Miss Darken, and it seems that your young friend was particularly susceptible to it. She was completely in her sister's power. All Miss West needed to do was put her in a trance each morning and instil the things she wanted Pearl to see, say and do. She may even have trained the girl's unconscious to respond to certain cues and stimuli. It is impressive, in its way. Beyond the powers of an ordinary match girl. It is a shame Miss West did not put her talents to better use.'

'But . . .' Agnes stops and bites back her words. Simon sounds so certain that it was an elaborate hoax. No doubt parts of it were: Pearl's unearthly lustre, the rocking table, the information about Commander Hargreaves taken from the newspaper and gingered up with the imitation of drowning.

But she remembers how frightened Miss West looked when Ned manifested himself: her expressions were a little too good, even for an accomplished actress. And she was not present at the private séances. Miss West could have no influence upon the sights and sounds that reached Agnes then. She could not have staged the disturbing, incoherent exchange with Montague, or made the picture frames fall down at Orange Grove.

A memory of Pearl flashes through her mind. The child gesturing towards the fireplace upstairs in Walcot Street and saying, *I can't do* that *alone.*

'You are sure,' she asks cautiously, 'that the Mesmerism was the only viable power at play? Pearl's gift was all an utter humbug?'

Simon bends down to scratch behind Morpheus's ear. 'I would stake my honour on it. Pearl's colouration was albino and she suffered acutely from photosensitivity – but that is all. She was no different in any other respect from her peers.'

Agnes frowns. There was definitely *something* in that upstairs room, and in the parlour at Orange Grove.

If Pearl was not channelling the spirits . . . then who was?

'This is the reason I did not reject the message outright,' Simon goes on. 'Speaking to Miss West may be your last chance to obtain the information you seek before she is hanged and takes her secrets with her.'

'You believe she will be found guilty, then?'

'Undoubtedly. And if you visit, you might take the opportunity to urge her towards confession of her other crimes. There can be little dispute that she was responsible for the deaths of your two unfortunate sitters.'

So the paper inferred, but Agnes is not convinced. Miss West could have no agenda against her at the time Mr Boyle and Ned died. She could not have set out to entrap Agnes: the animosity the newspaper wrote about came *afterwards*.

'As a matter of fact,' Simon continues, 'I would like to consult Miss West myself.'

'Oh?'

'I consider it only right to apprise her of an arrangement I have made. I hope you shall approve of it, also. I have paid for Pearl to be simply interred at Walcot Gate. She deserves a dignified resting place. There will be a modest remembrance with her name and the date of her birth, if I can obtain that from her sister.'

He is a good, good man. Her ribcage swells with the consciousness of it. 'Oh Simon, that is exactly what I would wish. I did so worry about what would become of her.'

'I am glad to have your approbation. Of course I shall attend the service myself, but I wonder . . .' He gives her a long assessment. 'I should never ask a lady of your constitution to witness a funeral. But I would welcome your company on a visit to the grave, if you think you would be equal to it. The unfortunate girl will have so few mourners . . .'

The cemetery rises up in her mind's eye, dismal and crowded with row upon row of stone slabs. She always fancied the gravestones looked like teeth in the maw of some hideous beast.

'The thought scares me,' she admits. 'And I am frightened of seeing Miss West too. But I owe Pearl that much. I did not

act well by that child, Simon. I used her for my own purposes.'
Her face flushes with self-consciousness as she adds, 'I worry
that perhaps . . . I have been using people like that my whole
life: taking what I need and discarding them. It is my resolution to do better . . . much better, in the future. I mean to
honour those who have always been so generous with me.'

Simon swallows and turns away to face the wall.

She is embarrassed. She had always assumed . . . But perhaps
that is not the case. Maybe all his boyish passion is long since
spent.

Trying to break the awkwardness, she resumes, 'I have not
been a dutiful daughter these last few months. Mamma is one
of the people I must try harder to please. I know you worry
that seeing her will excite me, but do you think . . . I should so
like to be reunited with my mother and Cedric for Christmas.
Could they not come here, if you think me too ill to travel? I
must see how poor Cedric gets along. Is he quite recovered
from his accident?'

Simon clears his throat. 'I . . . I am hoping to convey you to
them both very soon.'

'Before Christmas, Simon?'

'If you wish it.'

Something has altered. He seems more melancholy than
when their conversation first began.

His gaze is fixed upon a piece of needlework hanging on the
wall: a sampler that Constance worked when she was young.
There are the usual numbers, letters, trees and flowers, but the
verse is idiosyncratic:

> Behold this piece my hands have made
> When I am dead and in my grave

Morpheus whuffs.

'Excuse me, Miss Darken,' Simon says, shaking himself out

of his reverie and moving towards the door. 'I did not remark the time. I have patients I must attend to. Can I have anything else sent up to you?'

'No, thank you. Only remember: my family together at Christmas. I shall hold you to that promise, Simon.'

He gives her one last, pained smile. 'I am unlikely to forget.'

Chapter 35

Agnes still thinks of it as the 'new' gaol, built along the lines of Pentonville Prison. The turnpike road to Bristol is just visible on the horizon; in the other direction, beyond the high walls, steam puffs from engines on the railway tracks. It is cruel positioning. The convicts must watch the world go by without them, continually facing boundaries which they may never cross.

In the early years, there were rumbles about the prison management being too lenient to deter repeat offenders, but Agnes sees nothing of this. The gaol seems as cold and sterile as the interior of the Dead Room; from the morose demeanour of the staff to the harsh clang of metal doors that sets her teeth on edge.

It is fortunate that Simon accompanies her, because without him nothing about this miserable kingdom would feel real. She is painfully aware of her throat, and a blockage within it like a wad of cotton. Every instinct recoils and urges her to run. But this is the last place a person can flee from.

The visiting room is packed with desperation. Coarse, rough-featured women cling to the chaplain and must be prised off; another, more genteel-looking creature sits listening to a lawyer with her head in her hands. There is no prevalent age group. Agnes is surprised by the number of women older than herself. Villainy, it seems, is not something one grows out of.

She thinks of little Pearl, who will never age now, and her empathy for the prisoners withers, replaced by a cool fury. If Agnes were to look in the mirror, she feels sure she would see the flinty expression of Constance staring back.

The warden makes them sit in front of a small desk. The chairs are battered and unsteady; Simon's squeals under his weight. She had hoped they would only be permitted to see the prisoners through bars; in this chamber, there seems so little standing between her and evil.

Boots crunch on the floor beside them. A turnkey with a heavy brow hauls a prisoner to the opposite side of the desk; it takes Agnes a moment to realise that it is Miss West.

Prison has sucked the glamour from her. Her flaxen hair is shorn and concealed beneath a cap; only a hint of her widow's peak shows at the brim. She wears a dingy prison uniform that dulls the lustre of her eyes.

'Strike me blind,' she laughs as she is pushed into a seat. 'You came.'

Agnes cannot speak; contempt almost chokes her. The way the young woman leans back in her chair and crosses her arms is not just insolent, it is heartless. She is still putting on a show: the unrepentant sinner.

'Miss Darken has called upon you, despite her ill-health, as an act of charity,' Simon announces sternly. 'And she hopes to encourage compassion in you likewise. Will you not admit to *all* your atrocities, Miss West? What about Mr Boyle, Mr Lewis and Commander Hargreaves?' He spreads his hands. 'Come, let us bring this awful matter to a conclusion. Give the bereaved families the comfort of knowing that justice has been served.'

Miss West smirks at him. They have not been feeding her well. She looks angular and raw-boned. 'Guess I might as well, eh? In for a penny, in for a pound. Seems better to hang for five bodies instead of two.'

'Confession is not about—' Simon begins.

'I always wanted to be in the papers,' she interrupts. 'If they're going to put me down as a killer, it should be a notorious one with loads of victims. What will they call me, d'you think?' She mimics an aristocratic drawl. '*The Mesmerising Murderess.* I'd like that.'

Finally, Agnes finds her voice. 'They will not credit you with any powers whatsoever. You could not mesmerise the guards into releasing you, could you?'

The pert expression is slapped from Miss West's face.

'Make sure to keep a civil tongue in your mouth,' the turnkey barks to the prisoner. 'I'll be watching you from over there.'

Keys chinking, she moves to a corner of the room. Her unflinching gaze swoops between the criminals, taking everything in. Those beady eyes have the authority here, not Miss West's. The prisoner must sense this, for the air around her sours.

'I wanted to talk to Miss Darken alone,' she gripes.

Simon straightens his posture. 'You are fortunate that Miss Darken condescended to visit you at all. Her health—'

Agnes lays a hand upon his arm. She needs Simon to remain nearby, but perhaps Miss West *would* come to the point sooner with him at a distance. Pearl always stressed how her sister hated medical men; much of this performance may be for his benefit.

'Be so kind as to fetch me a glass of water, Simon. It is very close in here,' she says, pressing his arm and giving him a meaningful look.

The floor shrieks as he pushes his chair back. 'I will ask the turnkey,' he says, eyeing Miss West. 'I will not let either of you out of my sight.'

Miss West gives him a sardonic smile.

As Simon paces out of earshot, Agnes feels her hatred bubbling up. There is no longer a need to appear ladylike and restrained.

She rounds on Miss West. 'How *could* you? What manner of depraved, filthy vermin are you? Pearl was a child. Not a freak or a doll for you to play with. A *child*. Your mother would curse your name.'

The prisoner's chin juts out. 'You don't know what that girl cost me,' she says huskily. 'She . . .' With an effort, she masters herself. 'She wasn't so bleedin' innocent. And she *killed* my mother. Killed her own father with a knife too, before she ran away!'

Agnes rolls her eyes. 'More lies. You have good reason to believe me credulous, but it will not wash now. Come to the point. Why did you wish to see me?'

Miss West does not appear to hear her. Her lips twist and wobble. 'Tell me, was it . . . bad, at the end? Did Pearl suffer an awful lot?'

Agnes remembers the rapt expression on the little face. She will not give Miss West that comfort; she does not deserve it.

'Of what consequence is it to you? You hated the child!'

'I did,' Miss West agrees tearfully. 'I did hate her! I wanted to get rid of her. But now she's gone . . .' She swallows. 'I think maybe part of me loved her too. Just a bit. She was . . . I felt . . . Both. Love and hate. D'you see?'

Reluctantly, Agnes nods. 'Sisterhood can be like that.'

Miss West cocks her head and considers her. Very quietly, she says, 'I know what *your* sister did, Miss Darken.'

Agnes's flesh creeps.

This must be one of Miss West's tricks. Agnes reminds herself that the woman could have found an old newspaper report detailing the Accident, and decided to use it in one last desperate attempt to scare her.

It is all smoke and mirrors.

But it is working.

Miss West leans forward in her chair. Her face is so close that Agnes can smell the fetid confinement of the cells. 'I wish I'd been around when *that* scandal happened. My ma told me all about it. I could have blackmailed you about the boy – you and the quack both.'

Agnes's breath catches. 'Cedric?'

'The little bastard. Would have bled you dry trying to keep his origins secret. But what's the point now?'

She is too astonished to form words. How can Miss West *possibly* know about Cedric's true father? Not one of the family ever breathed a hint in public about the real reason Montague had left. As for Cedric, he was considered a little premature, given the date of his parents' wedding, but all records of birth and baptism clearly show Simon's name.

Yet somehow Miss West has managed to piece it all together. It would be dreadful if she revealed their shame now. Mamma's heart would not take it, Cedric's prospects would be blighted and Simon . . . Poor Simon would have married Constance for nothing.

'Please—' she starts.

'*That's* why you're here, since you asked. I wanted to tell you all about my life, before I hang. I wanted you to know what you've brought me to.' She points a finger. 'Yes, you. You can sit there in your fancy clothes and call me vermin, but I wouldn't have done any of it if it weren't for you and your bloody sister.'

Agnes stares at her, bemused.

'Uncle John might've helped us. My ma wouldn't have married again if her brother were around to help. But he wasn't, was he? He ran off back to sea before I was born, all broken-hearted and never came back. Ma told me he left over a quarrel with some stupid hussy named Darken.'

'Your uncle . . .'

'D'you want to hear the funny thing? Do you?' Hysteria creeps into Miss West's tone. 'After all I did, trying to get that Burial Club money – guess what happened? He's only gone and snuffed it!' Her eyes blur and Agnes realises they are full of tears. 'Left me a legacy. *My beloved niece.* Beloved my eye! He

never saw me in his life! Thought I was still in London and his
lawmen couldn't find me, not until they saw my name in the
papers.' She gasps a terrible laugh. 'It's a bit bloody late now,
ain't it, Uncle John?

'Good God,' Agnes grips the edge of the desk. 'Let me understand you correctly. Do you mean that your uncle was—'

'My uncle's name was John Augustus Montague.'

The visiting room spins.

He *did* mention a sister; only vaguely, the way he spoke of
all his kin. She had married low, against her parents' wishes.
By Montague's account, none of the family were ever close,
which is why Agnes never sought them out.

'But this means that *you* . . .' Agnes searches the wicked
woman's face. There is nothing, no hint of the man she loved.

Then it hits her like a blow to the stomach: Pearl.

Pearl was Montague's niece, Cedric's cousin.

She thinks the knowledge will rip her in two.

Simon was right: Miss West has had a motive all along. That
was why she tried to frame Agnes by murdering her clients.

'You're as useless and pathetic as Uncle John was,' she snarls
as Agnes falters for words. 'You deserved each other. Shame
your sister was such a whore.'

The reappearance of Simon with a glass of water stops her
from responding. Concern furrows his brow.

'You look unwell, Miss Darken. I think perhaps it is time
for us to leave.'

She snatches the water from him and gulps it down. Nothing would please her more than to get far away from this
poorly lit prison and the deplorable souls within. But this is
her last chance. There is so much she needs to know.

'Did you believe any of it?' she bursts out. 'The Spiritualism, the Mesmerism?'

Miss West blinks. 'Well the Mesmerism worked on Pearl,
didn't it? It's a tool. The doctor can tell you – even *they* know
that much.'

Before Simon can retort, Agnes carries on, 'But the ghosts?'

'Pah! I wanted to.' Miss West rubs at her jaw. 'Time was I would've given my right arm to talk to my parents again. I was desperate. So was Pearl's dad.' She shakes her head. 'But it didn't work. So I took that desperation, and I used it. Got to thinking how much other desperate people would pay for a show.' Her glance slides to Simon. 'Because people are stupid, aren't they, Doctor?'

A bell rings. Turnkeys come forward and the lawyers begin to shuffle their papers. Visiting time is over.

'Miss West, I am burying your sister,' Simon declares bluntly. 'I should like to know her date of birth before I leave.'

She remains silent. She looks tired, broken by the concept of a return to her solitary cell. Only when the turnkey comes and seizes her by the arm, ready to frogmarch her back to captivity, does she speak.

'Look up my mother's death in Bow. It's the same date.' She glowers at Agnes. 'I want you to read her name. My mother. Clara Meers, née West, née Montague.'

The last name lingers even through the clamour and the scraping chairs.

For the first time in her life, Miss West has produced a genuine ghost.

But before she can savour its effect she is gone, swallowed back into the dark bowels of the prison.

Chapter 36

Agnes expected Simon would speak to her as they made their way downhill towards the burial ground at Walcot Gate. She would welcome the distraction. It has been many years since she last visited a cemetery and her nerves are strung taught; she cannot decide whether it feels like she is approaching the gallows, or slipping out for an assignation with a lover.

But Simon descends Guinea Lane with solemn determination. There is nothing unkind in his silence: he still shows her the attentions of checking his pace and occupying the side of the pavement nearest to the road, yet he offers no words of reassurance. Occasionally he eyes her, as a horse that might spook.

Following the prison visit, he made Agnes spend more time cocooned inside Constance's room to 'collect herself.' She kept abreast of the news with Mrs Muckle's help. More speculation and dross surfaced around Miss West, and most of it wallowed in lurid detail: accounts of her soldier father's death, although they could not agree whether it was in China or Afghanistan; reports of the debts Mr Meers left behind him in London when the family relocated to Bath; the amount of compensation granted by Livingstone's Match Factory. Many conjectures were formed as to how Miss West could afford the residence on Walcot Street, none of which painted her in a chaste light.

To think that such a detestable woman would have become her niece, had Agnes's marriage to Montague gone ahead!

The weather remains dry, if overcast. Labourers are taking the opportunity to visit the Darby and Joan public house for a dose of the holiday spirit, even though the holidays have not officially begun yet. After her forced seclusion, the men strike Agnes as particularly brash and noisy. Even her nose is sensitive – she can smell sewage on the air.

'Are you well?' Simon asks as she cringes against him.

She nods, trying not to breathe in. He has told her she can see her family at last after they visit Pearl's grave, and she will not give him a reason to go back on that promise.

When they emerge near Somerset Buildings, the spire of St Swithin's church seems to pierce the mutton-coloured clouds. There is the low hum of organ music from within, and women singing carols. It is impossible to hear them and not recall Miss West's voice on the night of the first séance. How sweetly she sang, for a fiend.

They round the church and progress further downhill through London Street. The place heaves and sparkles with the promise of Christmas. Holly, mistletoe and ivy please the eye through glass shopfronts; every man and his wife is trying to sell a turkey or a side of meat. There are wooden toys on display; hothouse oranges stuffed with cloves and the syrupy scents of a confectioner's shop replace the sewer's unpleasant odour.

It feels strange to see the world carrying on in this manner while Pearl lies beneath the soil. Flush-faced servants haggle as if their lives depended upon plum puddings. She wishes she could tell them how trivial it all appears beside the death of a child.

At last they turn left into Walcot Gate, where the air becomes cooler and more peaceful. The burial ground looms before them, its walls interspersed with black iron railings. Bald, ossified trees screen the view of the graves. Agnes tightens her grip upon Simon's arm.

'I have you,' he says.

It feels as though it is an imposter who enters through the gates and passes by the mortuary chapel. Surely Agnes would not be brave enough to countenance the lichen-grazed head-stones that slope towards the river? Yet somehow she does; just as she stood before Mr Meers's terrible face without fainting. Perhaps this whole ordeal will end up changing her for the better.

The burial ground is shady, even though the trees have lost their leaves. There is a hush that feels gentle and kind. Gazing to the horizon, beyond the river that frightens her, she sees the roll of green hills.

There are no mawkish angel statues here. Simon leads her across some grass and down a line of identical markers con-structed of grey stone. She does not read the simple engrav-ings; does not want to know whose bones lie under her feet.

He stops before a headstone that is raw and unmarked by the weather. At its base, bare earth makes a mound four feet long.

Simon removes his hat.

So this is Pearl. Her last home looks pitifully small and nar-row.

Agnes bends down and places the pansies she has brought with her carefully upon the soil. It occurs to her now that they were Constance's favourite flower.

'God rest you, sweet Pearl,' she whispers. 'Sleep tight.'

Her eyes skim the stone.

Pearl Meers
22 June 1843–3 December 1854

Her mind has a momentary blank. She wobbles, disorien-tated. Simon's arm slips around her waist.

'I am well,' she insists, 'I am . . .'

Something troubles her; a general unease she cannot put her finger upon. But why should the dates upset her?

'I thought this was a peaceful spot.' Simon speaks as softly as the wind that moves between the graves. 'At dusk, the shadow of the chapel falls across it and it is most . . . serene.'

A blackbird sings. Agnes glances around. The place is pretty, with the church gazing down over them from above, and the river slipping effortlessly by. She thinks of little Pearl being shut away in the dark for so long, and how pleasant the girl would find this hillside with its shade and its foliage, and the city that she never managed to see spread out before her like a picture.

Her head begins to clear. 'It is perfect, Simon. You chose well.'

They stand for a long time, staring out into the distance. Simon does not remove his arm from her waist. From the corner of her eye, she notices him watching her tenderly. It is comfortable.

They observe a grey-haired couple and their adult daughter tending a grave. They are the only other mourners, which surprises her, given the crowded nature of the cemetery and the season.

Simon inhales deeply beside her. 'I must perform the duty of visiting another while I am here. Do you find yourself able to accompany me?'

It takes her a second to realise who he means. Constance is buried here, her grave woefully neglected.

'I . . . Yes. Yes, I will go with you, Simon.'

She turns to him, and sees that he has tears in his eyes. She never thought to see him weep for his wife.

He coaxes her hand into the crook of his arm. Slowly, they descend the slope, drawing ever closer to the river. A drake plunges his emerald head beneath the water in search of food. She can smell wet dirt and weeds.

'Just a little further,' he urges as she hangs back.

Wind soughs through the naked tree branches. The family of mourners turn and make as if to leave. Agnes wishes they would not. There is a safety in numbers.

Here, the headstones speak of wealth and respectability. They are clean and sturdy, and the engravings are more ornate. Most are white or pale grey in colour, but Simon comes to a halt before a marker made of black marble.

> Constance Edith Carfax
> 18th October 1810–23rd September 1840
> *Respice Finem*

Dark spots cloud her vision. This is worse than seeing Constance's shade appear at the séance. All her sister's complexity has been reduced to a collection of stern, unforgiving words.

When Constance died, Agnes vowed never to give her another thought, yet she has always been there, concealed, like an organ that cannot be removed. She remembers Miss West's description of sisterhood, and it is true: she feels love and hate, blended together. It is impossible to distinguish where one ends and the other begins.

Constance was controlling, and vicious, and grasping, yes. But her sole desire in life was to be with Agnes, always. In the grand scheme of things, in comparison with the abuse Pearl faced, that does not seem so very bad. For all her violent outbursts, Constance never once injured Agnes. Would never have poisoned her with matchsticks. In her own way, she loved her.

Maybe Agnes should have spoken to the shadow when it arose. If she had offered forgiveness then, it might have finally put Constance to rest.

'I should have thought,' she starts, but her voice croaks out. She swallows, tries again. 'I should have . . . brought more pansies.'

Somewhere, a bird calls.

Simon's eyes seem to peel beneath her skin. 'Look, Miss Darken,' he says, and it is a voice she has never heard him use before. 'Look closely. See . . . beside her.'

There are *three* slabs of black marble, she realises. They stand out like the sharps and flats on a piano, but they are in a line, clumped together.

> Cedric Matthew Carfax
> Agatha Darken

Shock holds her immobile.

Simon grips her arm. All she can think is that this is some kind of joke, a monstrous joke, but the names are carved . . . indelible.

'No. No, it cannot be.' Simon does not speak. 'You *promised* me. You told me that you knew where Cedric . . .'

Her legs give way.

Simon kneels with her. She feels his arm encircle her shoulders; inhales the aroma of carbolic soap.

'Who could . . . I don't . . . Was it Miss West? Did she kill them? *How? When?*'

'The dates.' Simon crafts his words with care. 'Please, Miss Darken. Observe the dates.'

Her eyes skate wildly over the shining black marble.

'I cannot . . .'

Simon waves a bottle of salts beneath her nose and then everything comes into terrible focus.

The date of death for all three is the same:

> 23rd September 1840

'They have been dead these fourteen years,' he breathes.

Memories crackle at the corners of her mind. Although the ground is firm beneath her knees, she feels herself being dragged down.

Simon reaches out and strokes her cheek. 'Come, Miss Darken. You *do* recall what happened that day.'

———————

It had been a trip of mortification. Everyone knew about the matrimonial fracas, from the bucks who turned their heads to watch them walk past, to the shop girls who sneered while they smiled. Whispers had followed the sisters like a cloud of flies. Agnes held herself tight and small, praying that no one would call out after them, but Constance had shown no embarrassment. If anything, she seemed to relish the attention.

Returning to the carriage provided no comfort. The day was unseasonably cold, which made the horses skittish. Dozens of parcels jolted against Agnes's legs while she tried her best to sit back from the window and the stares that raked through it.

Of course the horses were Constance's fault too. She had insisted upon high-spirited beasts with an Arabian arch to their necks, delicate mouths and rolling eyes, ignoring the fact that they were unsuited to team a carriage.

The vehicle itself was ill-sprung, creaky and second-hand, yet Constance seemed determined to run it in the manner of a born lady, rather than a separated wife who should be comporting herself with discretion.

She wanted people to see her. Wanted to shame Simon as much as she could.

She was going about it the right way. Today's purchases alone would nearly ruin him. The latest and most extravagant was a swansdown tippet that looped around her throat and fell to the hem of her dusky rose dress. It had cost more than Agnes could earn in a month.

And was Constance satisfied, now? As always, it was impossible to tell. She sat composed with her hands folded on her lap, gazing out of the window as though she had nothing to be ashamed of.

Agnes wanted to pick up the nearest hat box and hurl it at her.

'I shall write to Miss Werrett and cancel that order,' Agnes threatened. 'I have no desire to wear matching gowns. The whole conceit strikes me as terribly affected.'

Constance offered no response. The horses skittered to the left, but she did not lose her balance. Agnes had to reach for the leather strap to brace herself.

'Do you hear me, Constance? I will not wear it.'

'Then I wonder,' Constance observed coolly, 'that you did not say so at the shop.'

'It was humiliating enough, with those gossiping widows peering at us. I did not want to cause a scene.'

Constance continued looking out of the window. 'No. *You* did not.'

How could she be so maddening? One would think her the picture of innocence sitting there in pink and white with a spray of flowers tucked behind her ear.

'I will write,' Agnes repeated.

'Then you must suffer the consequences.'

Anger flared, hot and impotent inside her chest. What would Constance do to punish her refusal to fall in line this time? Slash her other gowns? Take away Cedric's books again? 'Be reasonable,' she pleaded. 'I know you wish to make me a gift of the gown, but I do not need it. How am I to face Simon this afternoon? Do you not consider that he must still pay your debts – even the ones you run up in presents for me?'

'Of course I consider it. I *want* him to pay.'

He could not afford to, Agnes was certain. His patients were numerous and wealthy, but not enough to justify the horses and their livery at Carter's, nor the many gowns, bonnets and necklaces Constance kept frittering away his money upon. Yet he would never refuse to honour a debt. An informal separation was one matter – the idea of *divorce* did not bear thinking about.

The horses spurted forward, eager to canter, while the

coachman attempted to hold them at a trot. Agnes wished he would give them their heads. The sooner they were back at Orange Grove the better; Constance would alight with her infernal boxes and Simon, who was currently visiting Cedric, would take her place in the carriage.

Not that they would enjoy the pleasant afternoon tea she had envisaged. The whole time would be spent warning him of the bills to come. She and Simon never seemed to have anything except difficult conversations, these days. She remembered how they used to laugh together, and play with Cedric as a baby, but now a strain had been put on their friendship.

No doubt that was what Constance wanted.

Constance had taken Montague, she had taken Simon, and she had ruined them both.

'I wish you would leave Simon alone,' Agnes complained. 'He is a good man! He has given you everything: respectability, a name for your child and an income. I know he was always *my* friend, and you never warmed to him, but you are not even forced to endure his company now. What can you possibly hold against him?'

Constance's lips curved in a slow smile.

They were nearing home. Agnes knew her time was running short.

'Answer me, Constance. I will not let you leave this vehicle without you promising to be kinder to your husband.'

Constance breathed a laugh. 'Oh! You dear innocent. You know nothing about marriage!'

'And whose fault is that?'

The carriage jerked ungracefully to a stop. Constance leant forward to open the door; she never waited for the coachman to lower the steps. It was just as well, for he was cursing on the box as he struggled to hold the horses in check.

A cloud of jessamine scent engulfed Agnes as Constance climbed down. With one foot on the street, she fixed Agnes with a last, glacial look.

'Stop thinking about Simon all the time. He is not worth your consideration. No man is. You belong with *me*, sister. Do not forget it.'

Agnes slammed the door on her.

Just as she intended, the hem of Constance's ashy pink gown and one end of her tippet were trapped inside the carriage. They would be marked, ruined.

She heard a faint, strangled cry as Constance tried to walk away and was pulled back.

That would teach her a lesson, she thought.

Then everything happened at once.

There was a rolling, a rushing noise, and she heard Cedric calling her name. 'Auntie Aggie! Look what my father bought me!'

A horse reared, shrieking. The squabs slammed hard into her legs as she was jolted forward without warning, too late to grab the leather strap.

The world turned upside down as the carriage careered out of control. A box hit her in the head, another just beneath the ribs. She fought like a drowning woman reaching for the surface, but she could not tell which direction was up.

Blood filled her mouth.

Suddenly, they hit a bump. Agnes flew up in the air, screaming, and her scream seemed to be echoed outside. There was a sickening crunch as the wheels mounted and crushed whatever lay in their path.

Ribbons and gloves burst from their folds of tissue paper; boxes flew at her head like a flock of birds. She knew she was badly injured but could not tell where. Everything hurt; everything moved.

Clawing for purchase with her torn fingernails, she managed to snag something soft and silken. It was pink. Ashes of roses.

Constance's gown.

Bang.

A heavy weight crashed against the door and she realised Constance was still there, being dragged along with her.

She cried out for her sister, but there was no response except for the banging. She thought of the tippet, pulled taut around Constance's throat like a noose, and she began to choke. It could not be happening. None of this could be real.

Another object smacked her on the temple. Pinpricks danced before her eyes. She could hear screaming, endless screaming, and she yearned for it to stop . . .

All at once, it did.

There was a deafening crack. For a moment she felt weightless, free; and in the next her body smashed against what must have been the door.

She did not hear a splash; only glass fracturing beneath her. Ice-cold, turbid water gushed in around her legs.

'Constance!' she cried. 'Constance, are you still there?'

Then everything turned to black.

Chapter 37

After a long struggle, Agnes has reached a plateau. For the first time since her pneumonia, time does not pass in fits and starts; rather, it has become a paddle steamer that drifts gently, carrying her with it. Or perhaps that is Simon's medicine.

Her world has fallen apart, but it seems to go on perfectly well around her. Simon's charwoman, Mrs Muckle, departs for Gloucester, where she means to stay until Twelfth Night. Miss West is prevailed upon to confess, and she does it with aplomb: admitting not just to the murders of Mr Meers and Pearl, but to those of Mr Boyle, Ned and even Commander Hargreaves, despite the lack of evidence tying her to the crimes. She has the fame, if not the freedom, she always desired.

No one dubs her the Mesmerising Murderess.

The only transgression Miss West is not denounced for is the abduction of Cedric, for Cedric was never there to kidnap; he was trampled beneath the hooves of the horses fourteen years ago. It was the brandishing of his new hoop and stick that caused them to bolt.

Agnes tries to accept this, tries to understand that her recent memories of the boy are entirely false. But sometimes she could swear she hears the *click, click* of his toy rolling down the street at night. Or perhaps it is the sound of a ghostly carriage, wheeling Constance to her doom over and over again.

'Am I quite mad, Simon?' she asks, as he sits up with her by the light of a single candle. 'Have I lost my mind entirely?'

He is always emphatic. 'No. You knew about their deaths and accepted them for over a decade. It was only the pneumonia of '52 that . . . unsteadied you. You were so very ill, Miss Darken. Near to death. I had half-steeled myself to lose you . . .' He breaks off, recovers himself. 'When you were past the danger, you seemed to . . . reset, somehow. You saw them. And you were so weak, I did not dare to retard your progress by breaking your heart all over again.'

She surveys Constance's bedroom. The red and yellow qua-trefoil paper that her sister chose still hangs from the walls. Her four-poster bed remains, without curtains, as was her preference. The mahogany dressing table and mirror stand just as she left them. It seems Agnes is not the only person who has been afraid to confront the past.

But she *does* face it, in stages.

———

Simon pays the subscription for them to drink water from the Hetling Pump. It is still within sight of the abbey, but at least it is a little further away from her house at Orange Grove than the Grand Pump Room. She could not bear to be in such close proximity to the scene of the Accident – not yet.

She sips the tepid, mineral-tasting liquid, trying to make her peace with that element. The memory of the river rushing into the carriage, seeking to engulf her, is now painfully clear. It might not have succeeded in taking her life, but it certainly swept her old self away.

'Tell me, Simon,' she says quietly as they promenade the room arm in arm. 'What happened to Mamma? I do not recall that.'

There are ladies like Mamma here: stout and red in the face with slightly protruding eyes. They gossip, obliviously block-ing the path of the wheelchairs. Old men lean on crutches for their gouty legs; someone complains of feeling bilious.

Simon hangs his head. 'Your mother . . . saw everything. From the window in the parlour. She saw Cedric . . . The shock was too great for her heart.'

Agnes winces. 'I expected as much.' She cannot decide who had it worst: Mamma forced to watch those she loved hurtle towards oblivion or herself; left to imagine the brutal scenes.

And what an imagination she owns. She recalls the conversations, the marks of affection; how she even conjured up Cedric in his torn and trampled clothing. She would not have believed her mind capable of such deceit, but Simon does.

'I have told you before that the brain is a powerful and delicate organ. That was why I wished for you to refrain from activities that might interfere with its natural workings, such as Mesmerism. You must view it from this perspective, Miss Darken: that what happened to you is not so very different from what befell poor Miss Meers. Your subconscious persuaded itself into seeing objects and people that were not there.'

His argument carries the benefit of logic, but Simon does not know what she and Pearl witnessed in their upstairs room at Walcot Street. Ghosts *do* exist.

She would rather believe that Mamma and Cedric were not hallucinations, but visitors. Her love called them up from beyond the grave. Did not Miss West say that the Gift often came after a long illness? It did *feel* like a gift: her short reunion with those she loved best.

But she must never confess her theory to Simon. He would not understand.

An orchestra tunes their instruments, ready to amuse the drinkers.

'Do you think my equilibrium will be restored, Simon?' She looks up at him, unsure of what she wants his answer to be. 'Will I be as I was, before the pneumonia?'

His smile does not waver. 'I am certain of it.'

He is so certain that over the course of the next week, he pays the two shillings for her to use the private baths. The famed healing springs are very different from the cold clutches of the River Avon. She descends into a cloud of fragrant steam, her shift billowing around her ankles, and when she is finally immersed the warm liquid feels like an embrace. She paddles her hands, watching her swollen fingers soften and flex. The mist makes her think of Pearl.

It is all very well for Simon to claim that the girl was being mesmerised. But how did both sitters see the *same* delusions? The shadows; the writing on the floor; the grandfather clock that whirred and the dark figure of a woman, reaching out her hands.

All of these spirits were definitely there.

Someone had the power to raise them. If it was not Pearl . . . could it possibly be Agnes?

She braves a chair back to Alfred Street. The jogging, jolting motion does not disturb her as much as she expects. It is not so very like a carriage after all. Stalwart men carry her along, instead of horses. They seem sturdy and reliable.

Just like Simon.

He has been so good to her. What must it have cost him to care for her these past two years? Few men would have acted with his devotion. He has saved her from death not once, but twice.

She has always reserved the word *hero* for men like Nelson, but it is conceivable that Simon may be one too.

She never thought them suited in temperament; could not imagine them living together. But as the chairmen set the sedan down on the pavement in Alfred Street, she realises that the house behind the black iron railings is already starting to feel like home.

Much of Bath has been a strange welding together. The Royal Crescent is orderly and geometric at the front, yet a jumble of different roof heights and depths at the back.

Perhaps it is the same for her and Simon. Perhaps they can meld, after all.

It may be that, given the right circumstances, two very different people can find a way to become one.

———

After attending the Octagon Chapel on Christmas Day, they set about preparing a feast. Naturally, the holiday will be a muted affair, but what they lack in spirits they make up for in food.

Simon knows how to cook a goose. They have chestnuts besides, butter-coated potatoes, a cranberry pie, ham and oysters which part at the merest touch of the knife.

It is pleasant to spend hours toiling in the kitchen, drinking wine as they work. Agnes finds she does not mind the sweat. While she is busy, she cannot dwell upon the family members she has lost.

It is only when the table is all laid out and she is sat at the end of it, facing Simon across the divide of two lit candlesticks, that she notices the empty spaces.

These gaps should be filled by Simon's siblings and parents. On previous Christmas days, Constance, Mamma and dear little Cedric occupied them. Now there are only two chairs and a dog who noses under the tablecloth, licking her ankles in expectation of dropped food.

Simon raises a crystal glass. He has drunk a touch too much wine and his nose is red. 'Your health, Miss Darken.'

She toasts it.

For a time the only sound is cutlery moving against china. The food is exquisite. Agnes has every reason to be content, yet somehow she is not.

It would be ridiculous to say she is lonely, while she is in the company of her closest friend. But there is something lacking. Perhaps it is the old adage that blood is thicker than water. She certainly felt a sense of fulfilment around her family which Simon cannot supply.

Her happiness should not be contingent upon another person, yet somehow, it has always been. She has clung to the memories of Papa, Montague and Cedric in turn. Lived her life for others, never forming an independent identity outside of her art. Now that the silhouette parlour has gone too there is a flatness; a part of her is missing.

Simon swirls the wine in his glass. He too glances to the sides of the table and the piles of food they will never manage to eat between them. He seems to read Agnes's thoughts.

'We have both of us lost families.' The candlelight shines off the moisture in his eyes. 'The pain of that never fades. I miss them all, my brother Matthew especially. Every day. But if I am honest, Miss Darken . . .' He puts his glass down, hesitates. 'The only companion I ever truly desired . . . was you.'

These words have gone unsaid for many years. Simon must have waited most of his life to say them. But now that they are finally out . . . nothing has really changed.

She knew. She knew before he went off to Scotland; she knew when she accepted Montague's offer; she even knew when he stood at the altar marrying Constance.

But she cannot tell him that. She dabs her mouth with a napkin. 'Your company is always a great pleasure to me, Simon.'

'Then you will . . . stay here?' He touches the stem of his wine glass but cannot look at her.

'I do not know how much longer I am able to. I may be your sister-in-law, but people will start to talk about us.'

'I meant . . .' His throat works. 'Miss Darken. I must ask you, at last. Is there not any way you would consider staying . . . as my wife?'

It is all very restrained; nothing like Montague's ardent declarations and the kisses she showered on him. But Simon is so *good*, so kind, so assiduous for her health. Gratitude has done what affection alone could not.

She wants to accept.

'Could I?' she asks in a small voice. 'I mean to say . . . is it allowed?'

'Not by the laws of England's Church,' he admits. He glances up at last, and his blue eyes are imploring. 'Although Constance and I were never . . . It was not a marriage.'

A log pops on the fire. Somehow her sister still hovers between them.

'What is it you propose, then?'

Simon inhales. Clearly, he has been deliberating this for some time. 'It is a great deal to ask of you. I will understand if you object. But given the circumstances, perhaps it would be better for us both. A new leaf, without memories.'

She cannot think what he means. She blinks at him. The air smells of cooling meat.

'Our marriage would be possible on the Continent. I thought perhaps we could go to Switzerland, or Italy? The climate would be ideal for your lungs. It may even prevent your pneumonia from returning, and you know my work could continue without significant interruption. There are so many English families travelling in those parts that I would never want for patients.' His eyes slide away. 'I knew it was useless to ask while Captain Montague . . . You were always adamant he would come back for you. But now he is truly gone, and I noticed . . . you have stopped wearing your ring.'

'You want us to *leave* Bath?'

'I understand it is not a decision to be made in haste. You will require time to deliberate.'

Trepidation clutches at her. Bath is all she has ever known. Can she really leave?

She always dreamed that she would one day; that she would stop living like one of her silhouettes, forever encased within its oval frame. She thinks of Pearl, who spent her whole life in the dark. It would be awful to end up like that.

'I do not want time, so much as courage, Simon. I have

mastered the hot baths, but facing a sea voyage, after what happened to me . . .'

'I would be there to protect you, as I was fourteen years ago.'

A spot at the centre of her glows. Simon *has* always been there, shielding her. And now he is offering her a version of the future she always wanted. She *will* be on board a ship, cutting across the sea towards new adventures, albeit in the opposite direction to the one Montague intended to take her.

'Would Morpheus be seasick, do you think?' she asks coyly.

She smiles at Simon and it works like a tonic. He has known her long enough to realise this is a tacit acceptance.

He throws his napkin down on the table. He appears handsomer, in his happiness, than she has ever seen him look before. 'Come to the tree, Miss Darken. Dinner can wait – I have a gift for you.'

Agnes obeys, feeling outrageously light and young. Was it really this simple, all along?

The fir tree stands in a pot upon a circular table, adorned with candles, silvered nuts and strings of scarlet berries. Two oranges sit beneath it for their dessert. There is a greasy-looking parcel which she knows is a pig's ear for Morpheus, and a small shagreen box she did not observe before.

Simon takes the box into his palm. 'It was not my intention for this to symbolise . . . I did not believe I would ever have the temerity to ask . . .' He laughs at his own awkwardness. She cannot recall the last time she heard a genuine laugh from him. 'I merely wanted you to have an item of jewellery in place of the one you have resigned.'

He hands her the box and she opens the lid straight away. Nestled inside is a milky opal. It takes the candlelight and splits it into a thousand colours: reds, yellows, purples and greens. These are the hues Montague promised her, and more besides; Simon has provided an entire spectrum.

Reverently, she pulls the gem out and sees it is attached to a solid golden band; a ring of fractured colour and beauty. She slips it onto the third finger of her left hand.

Simon watches, enraptured.

She cannot help thinking of Constance's wedding ring. He did not smile when *that* was put in place. Nor did his bride.

A strange shiver runs through her. No, Constance would certainly not be smiling now.

'Do you like it?'

She glances up, basks in the warmth of his affection. The choice is hers now. Everyone else has gone; she is free.

'I will wear it always,' she says.

Chapter 38

The Feast of Epiphany approaches. They receive a letter from Mrs Muckle's brother, telling them that the charwoman has a putrid sore throat and must delay her return. In all honesty, they are happy to make do without her. There is plenty to eat, and Morpheus gobbles up any leftovers before they turn bad. The laundry can be sent out, so there is only the washing of plates and dishes to deal with for the moment.

Simon is adept at scouring. 'Cleanliness is paramount in medicine,' he tells her. 'A discipline no doctor should neglect.'

The charwoman will have to be given warning, anyhow, if they are to go abroad and wed this year. Simon anticipates being able to sail in late spring when the weather is calm. Any gossip that arises between now and then shall simply have to be borne. England may not accept a man who marries his dead wife's sister, but there are plenty of countries that will.

Agnes decides she will not return to Orange Grove in the interim. It is not just the memories of Mamma and Cedric that keep her away; she does not want to step into the parlour where Pearl died, or see the wreckage of her studio. She thinks of the shattered frames, of the presence hovering upstairs and it makes her shiver even when she is sitting before the fire.

In her dreams she sees the shadow woman rise again. Her black arms open in an embrace, stretching and extending around the walls, until their darkness encircles the room. *Could* it have been Constance, objecting to Agnes's friendship with Pearl? If she managed to call up her other family members, it is conceivable . . .

But it would be safer, Agnes decides, to never find out.

She will send Simon to go and pack the things she needs. He will look after her, always.

On Twelfth Night, Mrs Oswald, the pregnant lady who slipped on the ice back in October, is brought to bed. Simon is obliged to leave Agnes and attend the birth.

'I shall make all possible haste,' he says hurriedly, tucking the summons away and fetching his outdoor things. 'But confinements can be lengthy affairs. I am likely to be absent well into the evening.'

It is a disappointment to be left without company for the holiday, but she hoists a brave smile. 'You must take as long as the lady needs. Do not fear, I shall save some wassail for you.'

He deliberates, slapping his gloves against his wrist. 'And you . . . you will be quite well, on your own?'

'Oh, Simon, I am not alone.'

Morpheus grumbles his agreement. Simon gives the pug a long stare. 'Behave yourself, little beast. I am counting on you.'

At length, he is persuaded to depart. Agnes is strangely charmed to have the house to herself. It is clean and uncluttered, full of gentle sounds like the fire sifting and the dog's snorts. There are no magpies *here*.

'Well,' she says to Morpheus, 'it seems you are King of the Bean and I am Queen of the Pea. We will find a way to have a merry Twelfth Night of our own.'

Morpheus sits down and chews his foot.

Despite her cheerful prognostic, the novelty soon wears thin. She reads, she eats, she sews a little; there is not much else to do. Without Simon's conversation, the day drags. There are only so many times she can throw the ball for the dog.

Her hands itch to make a papercut, but she has given all that up. They have agreed between them that she will paint watercolour landscapes instead, when they go abroad; that will give her a creative outlet free from associations with Miss West and murder. Yet in the meantime . . . Her fingers tug at her skirts. She really does miss the occupation.

But she promised Simon, and besides, she has no scissors. Although perhaps there is a surgical pair kept in the house for emergencies . . . She brushes the thought aside.

As evening bruises the sky, she receives a hasty scribble from Simon, telling her there is a complication with Mrs Oswald and he will certainly not be home tonight. That decides her: she will retire to bed early. Morpheus can sleep by her feet if he likes; she is still not *quite* comfortable with the prospect of facing shadows alone.

She bars the street door, extinguishes the gas lamps and tamps down the fire. Deliberately not lighting a taper, she feels her way upstairs and climbs under the covers fully dressed. It is childish, she knows, but she does not want to give her fancy – or her power, whatever it is – a chance to stretch its legs. Imagine how pleased Simon will be if he comes home tomorrow to find she has managed to pass twenty-four hours with no illusions and no upsets.

Although she drank plenty of the cider-rich wassail, sleep evades her. She is not frightened, exactly; there is simply too much to occupy her mind. She tosses and turns, uncomfortable in her clothing. Morpheus does not share her problem. The dog snores, louder than Mamma ever did.

Somewhere down the street, perhaps in the Assembly Rooms, music is being played. There will be fun and games all over the city tonight, except for at the Oswalds' house, where all is fraught with tension, and at the gaol, where Miss West draws near to her sentence hearing and almost certain death.

She flips over the pillow. It does not feel like a night for ghosts. There is no sense of menace or oppression, nor can she hear Cedric's hoop, clacking over the cobbles.

So why can she not rest?

It is only when a firework explodes, waking Morpheus and prompting him to issue a single bark, that she remembers: Simon left in too much of a hurry to prepare her nightly opiate.

She sits up against the bolster. Morpheus pads around the chamber and she can sense people outside, celebrating. Nothing is eerie or strange. She is quite equal to venturing downstairs and finding a bottle of laudanum.

'Come along, then,' she sighs, throwing the covers back. 'I will not get a wink of sleep without it.'

Morpheus stands behind her legs as she fumbles the door open. There is a pier table on the landing – one that Simon's mother used to decorate with floral arrangements – but tonight it holds a lit beeswax candle, set into a silver holder.

Agnes frowns.

'Simon?' she calls.

Her voice echoes through the empty house.

She certainly did not bring that candle upstairs. Could it be a delusion? It burns like a genuine flame. She picks up the holder, tests its weight in her hands. It *feels* real. The silver is slightly tarnished, engraved with a floral motif that matches the hairbrush on Constance's dressing table.

Morpheus sniffs.

'It comes in handy, anyhow,' she tells him and they set off together down the stairs.

She keeps her eyes trained straight ahead, reluctant to let them wander off and follow shadows. The music from the Assembly Rooms swells outside as she descends. It is sacred, choral, with the deep thrum of an organ beneath.

The consulting room door is unfastened. Agnes slips inside with ease. Her candle flame sparks on glass domes and slides over the gilt tooling on the spines of the books. She lights the lamp upon the desk, illuminating a circle of walnut wood.

Even now, the air is leavened with the scent of carbolic soap.

There are no bottles or medicines in sight. Where in this large room would Simon keep the keys to his cabinets and drawers?

She spies two inkpots standing on the left-hand corner of the desk. Picking each up in turn, she shakes them beside her ear. Metal tinkles in the second one. As she suspected, it is empty and washed out to hide a small brass key: a very simple ruse. Simon has become too used to living alone.

Down the street, the music soars. Morpheus tilts his head comically each time the organ surges into life. She listens, absent-mindedly unlocking the drawers one by one. The single key opens them all. How little Simon must have to hide.

She pulls out the first drawer. It reveals an almanac and newspaper clippings advertising vacancies for medical officers at the workhouse. Simon has scribbled names upon them – no doubt they are people he means to recommend for the positions. She sifts through orders to apothecaries. Under them is a glass vial with *Oil of Vitriol* written on the side.

In the second drawer she finds only a box of matches and some sticks of sealing wax. Where can the laudanum be? She opens another, finds a whole sheaf of letters tied up with string. Most are from other medical men, detailing cases and sharing news; she notices some from Scotland. They must be the doctors Simon studied with.

She gazes over the names. One occurs more frequently than the others: Tobias Dudfield.

The organ in the Assembly Rooms reaches a crescendo. Agnes yawns and a letter slides from the pile, landing directly beneath the light of the glass chimney.

> Dear Carfax,
>
> It gave me great pleasure to see you on Thursday – albeit a pleasure which I would rather have enjoyed under more auspicious circumstances. The difficulties of your situation inspire my deepest sympathy.

I undertook to write you my honest opinion, and so I shall set it out.

To gain an estimation of your wife's character on so short an acquaintance is next to impossible, and she is of the taciturn nature that yields precious little fruit even to the keenest observer. I could detect nothing of incipient insanity other than that she appeared to watch me suspiciously, and served me a peculiarly bony piece of fish.

I have no doubt in the veracity of your claims about her violence, nor in our ability to confine her, should we choose. However, we must question whether it is the best course of action for either you or Mrs Carfax's kin.

Your scruples, I fully comprehend, arise from what became of your patient Mrs B, and do you credit. I doubt there ever was such a regrettable case as hers, although I will maintain that none of the fault can lie at your door. Mrs Carfax does not strike me as similar in the slightest degree; I cannot comprehend her innocence being taken advantage of by unprincipled attendants, nor her refusing sustenance to the point of being force-fed. I could furnish you with details of two or three private establishments I have visited personally and found the inmates to be treated with the utmost respect. However, as you say, one is obliged to surrender a degree of control to another physician, and the fee for doing so is not inconsiderable.

My own inclination would be to agree to the proposed separation in an informal capacity. If Mrs Carfax has family who are willing to receive her and the boy, it is all to the good. Provide her with an ample allowance and wash your hands of the matter. Whatever high terms she proposes, you will

in all likelihood still find yourself in a better position, both financially and with regards to your
good name, than you would should you choose to
commit her to an institution.

Having said thus much, I hope there is no need
to assure you of my full support and assistance,
whatever resolution you should arrive at. I remain,
Carfax, your sincere well-wisher &c,

T Dudfield

A ripple passes over her, like wind moving across a lake. She
puts the letter down.

She knew nothing of this. Simon never told her he had seriously contemplated having Constance *committed*.

Morpheus sighs and flumps down beside her feet.

What could have prompted it? What did Constance finally
do, that was too much? She remembers the dead dogs, Simon's
anguish.

Constance had a talent for cruelty, there was no doubt of that.
But the idea of committing her to an asylum is somehow . . .
revolting. A primal, protective instinct flares inside Agnes's
chest. She was her sister, after all.

Is there anything else? She turns the pile upside down, rum-
mages through the later letters. There is another in the same
hand, although not nearly so neat.

Carfax,

My distress on receiving your last you can well
imagine. Embarrassment to oneself may be endured, but when threats are made to the safety of
those dearest to us, urgent action is required.

The boy's reputation must undoubtedly suffer,
yet better that than what you apprehend. I have fresh
cause to lament you did not follow your heart and
elect to save only the elder sister from the original

scandal – it would leave you both now in a position to quietly adopt and raise the child. But I will not make you bitter with regrets.

Rest assured all shall be set in motion this end. I will send you word when you may expect the two inspecting physicians to assess the lady.

Yours &c
Dudfield

The note is dated about a week before Constance's death.

She drops it as if it has bitten her.

The room falls completely silent. Both the organ and the choir melt away; the concert must be over.

She sits glaring at the letters, shocked, astounded. Finally she separates them from the others and tucks them down the front of her dress. She must keep them. Keep them and present them to Simon, to make sure that they are real, not a chimera.

He has betrayed her, though. It hurts to think he would contemplate something as serious as committal without even consulting her feelings. He has never mentioned it, in all these years. Perhaps he does not want to tell her about the awful thing her sister threatened, that inspired this letter from Dudfield? It is possible. But such a long silence suggests something else: it suggests concealment and guilt.

Constance must have known something of this. It must have been one of the reasons she hated Simon so much. Her determination to punish him, to ruin him financially, starts to make some sense.

Agnes cannot stop thinking about what would have happened, were it not for the Accident.

She will admit there were times in her life when she would have been glad to see Constance sent away. But the *reality* of it . . . Agnes tries to imagine men putting her sister into a strait-waistcoat and hauling her out the door. Mamma would still have died. She would have died from shame instead.

She has a strange sensation of passing outside her body; of watching events unfold from her sister's point of view. What would Mr Dudfield have made of *Agnes*, had she sat at that table for dinner instead? If he had witnessed her delusions in action, watched her talking to the empty chairs that she thought housed Mamma and Cedric?

Two inspecting physicians.

A voice within whispers, 'How long before Simon turns on you?'

He would not. *Could* not; he loves her. He has tended to her in a deluded state for two years. He will have a good explanation for these letters – she will ask him as soon as he comes home.

Shakily, she returns the other correspondence to the drawer. Two silver items glint at the bottom of it. One is another key, tied upon a red ribbon; the other is a pair of surgical scissors.

Agnes takes them both.

Maybe she can calm herself by cutting practice waves in sable paper; rolling out onto that ocean of black . . .

But there is something else that will help her do that much more quickly: laudanum. She came here for laudanum. Everything will look better after she has drunk it, slept, and talked over the troubling letters with Simon.

She glances around the room, but it is still unclear where the medicine is kept. The key on the red ribbon must open something besides the desk; perhaps one of the various cabinets?

Her eyes fall upon a heavy leather trunk beside the window that she has not noticed before. It makes her feel . . . odd. The surface looks worn with much travelling. She imagines it tied to stagecoaches, trundling up the cold roads towards Edinburgh. The people and places it has seen have left their mark, and not just on the leather.

The trunk has an aura, like Miss West spoke of: a tension in the air around it.

Agnes does not want to go near it, but somehow she finds herself kneeling down, trying the key in the lock.

It clicks.

A low growl rumbles from Morpheus's chest.

He watches her intently as she pulls up the lid. The hinges creak like the timbers of a ship.

Inside are two large hooks.

She puts a hand to her forehead, trying to hold things in place. These are the hooks tied to ropes, which Simon used to fish coffins from their graves. Cedric told her about them.

But Cedric was dead.

She *imagined* that conversation. Unless it really was the ghost of her nephew . . .

It feels like she is peering into a coffin now: she has the same sensation of fear and disgust. Her fiancé has robbed the dead, sliced up cadavers . . . She endeavours to remember it was a duty of his employment a long time ago, and he was *forced* to do it.

There are other items in the box. Surgical tools – or perhaps implements for prising open coffins: a crowbar, a mallet, a saw. Her stomach sours.

She does not want to see any more.

It is only as she reaches to close the lid that she catches sight of a familiar face; or not precisely a face, but its outline, empty inside.

The monochrome shape she recognises as her own art.

Pushing rusty nails aside, she closes her fingers around the edge of the shade and pulls it out.

Ice pricks her skin.

The black foolscap has peeled a little at the corners. The white stock card is scuffed and tiny spatters of a dark liquid mark the chin. None of that matters. She would know this piece anywhere, even without her name emblazoned in the corner.

It is the hollow-cut of Ned.

Chapter 39

At dawn, Agnes unlocks the street door and takes down the iron bar. She puts Morpheus in the kitchen, sets out the remains of the ham beside his bowl and shuts him in the room.

Next, she returns to Simon's consulting room and sweeps everything off the desk. It makes a satisfying crash. In place of the lamp, the inkpots, the pens and Simon's various paperwork, she lays out four items: the two letters from Tobias Dudfield, Ned's silhouette and the pair of surgical scissors.

She waits.

There are a thousand conundrums that could be teasing her mind right now, but she finds herself oddly focused. All she thinks about is Pearl.

That little girl was kind of heart, and bright, in her way, but she was kept back; a seed never permitted to rise above the soil. Everything Pearl thought that she knew, her sister had told her, and she believed it. She believed it without question.

The clunk of the street door opening seems to fall right through her. Simon's voice calls out: 'Good news, at last! They are both safe. A healthy girl, named for the Queen.'

Morpheus's paws scrabble in the kitchen, but there is no other reply.

'Miss Darken?' A note of alarm. She hears his footsteps clipping across tiles. 'Agnes, are you there?'

He pounds up the stairs, throws doors open. By the time he

returns to the ground floor and bursts into the consulting room, he looks half-wild.

His face is drained of colour and shiny, like wax. The clothes he has worn since yesterday morning are crumpled, sweat-stained and smell faintly sour. In his arms he clutches an incongruous gift: a set of travelling paintbrushes and water-colours.

Prominent in the tired death mask of his countenance are his blue eyes. They knock from one object on the desk to an-other, settling on Ned's silhouette.

He does not move.

'Miss West did not kill my clients,' Agnes announces.

'No.'

She expected at least *some* denial. 'But you are going to let her hang for it. A crime she did not commit.'

He closes his eyes, takes a breath. 'I would gladly have put myself forward to die for the real culprit.'

And then he starts to cry.

Agnes stares, confused. She cannot recall him weeping like this, even when his family died. But she must not feel pity: this display in itself could be a manipulation.

'*You* did it, to scare me,' she asserts. 'To put me in your power. You wanted me to have no other choice but to marry you.'

He chokes. 'No! Miss Darken, I would never harm another soul—' Dropping the paint set, he starts forward, but stops when he sees her flinch back in the chair. 'I tried so hard to protect you.'

'From *whom*?' She concentrates on Ned's silhouette and the spots of blood that mark it; she cannot trust herself to look at her friend's face. 'I wonder you did not burn this. It is not like you to be sloppy, Simon. But I suppose you had your hands full.'

'You said it was your best work . . .' He breaks off, runs a hand across his sweating forehead. When he recommences, he sounds calmer, resigned. 'No, you are right. I should have burnt it. I should have dissolved the bodies too, rather than hiding them, but I thought their families deserved something to bury. I did not have time to think it through . . . It all started to happen so quickly.'

She should feel frightened of him, but she is strangely numb. 'What did?'

He puts out his hands like he is trying to placate a rabid dog. 'Do not worry, Miss Darken. We will find help. We will stop these spells of disassociation . . . I was wrong to attempt to handle them alone. My emotions got the better of me. I have a friend . . .' He takes a step closer. 'It is not your fault. You were not in control. After the pneumonia . . . there were times you were not *yourself*. You were more like . . .' Another step. 'I thought that if I got you away from Bath, to Switzerland, it might stop.' His face seems to collapse. 'We were so close to being happy. I could have made you well.'

'*Me*?' she disputes. 'Do not try your trickery, Simon; do not try to turn this around on me, you are the one who has lied—'

'It must be in the blood,' he mutters to himself. He is so near now that she can smell the birthing chamber on him. 'A taint. I never thought you and your sister anything alike, but when it comes over you, I see her again . . .'

Agnes scuffs her chair further away. 'Stop there. Right there.' She snatches up the letters and brandishes them at him. 'I am wise to your game. Now I know of your guilt, you will try to send me away, pretend that I am mad.'

'What have you . . .' For the first time he seems to understand what the letters are. His eyes slide across the desk.

Stop on the scissors.

A chill runs over her skin. She remembers how Ned and Mr Boyle died: a single laceration to the throat.

Simon reaches out a hand.

'Stay back,' she snaps.

'Miss Darken, let me take those scissors.'

'I'm warning you, Simon!' Her voice rises, beyond her control.

Simon puts a foot forward. 'You cannot be trusted with them,' he explains. His blue eyes flick between her and the open blades. 'When it has possession of you—'

'You are lying! I could not hurt a fly!' She is screeching. It sounds like her vocal cords are being worked by someone else.

He wets his lips, inches closer. 'You can. You *do*. You lose hours, and I—'

'Stay *back*!'

Simon's pupils lock on hers.

They both lunge for the scissors at the same time.

———

There is a sense of retraction, of snapping back into herself. Her eyes pop open and she is standing alone in Constance's bedchamber, watching the sun set in a riot of pink and Etruscan red.

A pitiful whine comes from downstairs.

Perplexed, hollow, she wanders from the room. The carpet on the stairs is marked with paw prints; Agnes follows them to the kitchen where she finds Morpheus whimpering like a human child. At first, she thinks the dog is hurt, but when she picks up his little black feet to inspect them, they are uncut. His paws seem to be stained with a dark substance that is not his own blood.

'Silly boy,' she says.

He shies under the table.

The house has a comfortable hush. It is empty, yet occupied. She feels free, but not alone.

She finds a newspaper sitting on the doormat and has a quick leaf through the pages. The journalists speak of great wars abroad and plans for 1855; everywhere the old is being effaced and replaced with the new.

Leisurely, she strolls to the consulting room. Her feet kick against glass; empty vials of oil of vitriol lie scattered across the carpet.

'What has happened here?'

The lamp upon the desk is lit. By the light of its chimney, she sees that someone has left her a piece of paper. A painting, in fact – a shade.

The sitter is Simon: there can be no doubt of that. His likeness has been taken as skilfully as if she had done it herself. But this profile has not been brushed with her usual blend of ink and soot; the paint is thicker, rusty in hue. She runs her finger over the bridge of Simon's nose. It feels like a crust.

Words are written beneath in the hand she recognises from the notes: *Now he will never part us.*

She turns her head. A shadow stretches up the wall, created by the failing sun: a slender woman wearing her hair in a chignon.

It is not Agnes, although it is similar.

She has no doubt now. She possesses the Gift.

The shadow holds out a hand.

'Oh, Constance,' she sighs, pressing her palm against the wallpaper. 'Whatever have you done?'

Acknowledgements

The first germs of this story came to me during the 2016 Jane Austen Festival in Bath. My friends and I attended a wonderful talk and workshop with silhouette artist Charles Burns, who was kind enough to let us loose on his own physiognotrace – with hilarious results! Charles Burns's instructive book, *Mastering Silhouettes* (Fil Rouge Press Ltd, 2012) also proved a key resource for me in writing about Agnes's work. I cannot thank him enough!

Pearl's experiences with Spiritualism were largely inspired by the memoirs of Victorian-era spirit medium Elizabeth d'Espérance, quoted at the beginning of this book, but those conversant with the topic will recognise that the name of her 'spirit guide' Florence King is a nod to the famous medium Katie King, who supposedly 'materialised' the spirit of Florence Cook in the 1870s. *Missives from Summerland* is a fictional newspaper, very loosely based on *The Medium and Daybreak*. Similarly, the Bath Society of Spiritual Adventurers is my own invention: I did not wish to associate my fraudulent characters with real people of genuine spiritual belief.

I am indebted to Harriet Martineau's *Letters on Mesmerism* and Wendy Moore's biography *The Mesmerist* for helping me to create Myrtle's world. The Queen of Crime herself, Agatha Christie, must also be thanked for her novel *Dumb Witness*, which sparked the idea for phosphorus at a séance.

Pearl's physical appearance was inspired by Miss Millie

Lamar, 'The White Fairy,' who worked as a mind reader in 1890s America. In the Victorian era, it was sadly common for the unscrupulous to monetarise albinism, as is evidenced by the employment of a number of people with albinism in P. T. Barnum's travelling circus.

My version of Victorian Bath is based on the Cotterell map and Vivian's 'Street Directory' from 1852, plus local information discovered in the British Newspaper Archive. The characters' houses are of course fictional. Any mistakes are my own. The weather of 1854, I purposefully changed for my own devices.

I have borrowed some names from my mother's family for this tale; she had both an Auntie Aggie and a paternal cousin whose surname was Darken. I hope they will not mind me using them in this way – I must stress that the names are the only similarities!

On a personal note I would like to thank my husband, Kevin, to whom the book is dedicated. He came up with the title long before we had heard of the del Toro film! My agent, Juliet Mushens, who somehow still talks to me after reading my early drafts, and the wonderful team at Raven Books. My special thanks always go to Alison Hennessey, Lilidh Kendrick, Philippa Noar, Amy Donegan, Sara Helen Binney and David Mann, but I am sure there are many other silent heroes working behind the scenes who I never meet. My heartfelt gratitude to you all.